The Snow Angel

Lulu Taylor

W F HOWES LTD

This large print edition published in 2015 by
W F Howes Ltd
Unit 4, Rearsby Business Park, Gaddesby Lane,
Rearsby, Leicester LE7 4YH

1 3 5 7 9 10 8 6 4 2

First published in the United Kingdom in 2014
by Pan Books

ISBN 978 1 47128 184 6

Typeset by Palimpsest Book Production Limited,
Falkirk, Stirlingshire
Printed and bound by

www.printondemand-worldwide.com, gh, England

This book is mad naterials

To James Crawford

PART I

CHAPTER 1

Present day

'Are you listening, Emily?'

'Yes, yes . . . of course.' But she wasn't, even though she knew she should be. Will was talking as he drove and she was sitting next to him, thinking about Carrie.

She'll be fine, she thought, trying to quell the uneasiness she felt. *The babysitter seemed very nice and she promised to give her another dose of Calpol if she couldn't sleep. I wish Paula had been free, though. She's so good with Carrie.*

Emily shivered a little and glanced down at her evening dress: a short black sleeveless silk number with a flattering low-cut neckline. It had already seen her through a least half a dozen of Will's work functions, a charity gala and her birthday dinner at the Savoy.

But it's too chilly for this evening. I should have put on a jacket. I'll freeze. Oh dear. Poor Carrie, she did look pale. Perhaps I should have stayed at home.

But Will wouldn't hear of it, and it was too late now. The car was making its stop-start progress towards the motorway, the traffic lights adding their own red, green and amber to the light display. London sparkled, its lamp posts festooned with shimmering lights in red, green, blue and white: bells, stars and angel wings twinkling in the darkness above the slowly snaking traffic pushing its way along the city's arterial roads, slushy with grey-streaked remnants of the snowfall two days ago.

She imagined the evening ahead at Sophie and Alex's party. They always threw lavish dos: cocktails and canapés handed round by waiting staff, a dinner catered for the thirty or so guests, lots of wine liberally poured, some dancing afterwards before taxis came to take them home. It would be fun to let her hair down a little.

I haven't been to a good party in ages. But I'll call the sitter first, to check on Carrie. I won't be able to relax till then.

Life had been dull lately. Evening after evening spent putting the children to bed, waiting for Will to come home from work, then the two of them eating a late supper in front of the television, Will too tired to talk much. He'd been so preoccupied recently, veering between a kind of repressed excitement and a black irritability.

They'd all been tiptoeing more than ever around his moods. The children seemed to know that one spilled glass could set off a fearsome tirade, and they were quiet and wide-eyed around him. Emily knew it was often like this in the run-up to the end of the year but even so, he was touchier than

4

ever. It took all her energy to soothe first him and then the children, trying to absorb as much of his tension as she could. Sometimes she'd wake in the night and sense him wide awake beside her, the whirrings of his mind almost audible. She'd roll over and hug him, hoping that her nearness might calm him. Sometimes it would, but mostly he'd turn over with an irritated sigh and she'd have to leave him to it, blinking in the darkness while she slept.

It'll do us good to have fun, have a drink. She glanced at her husband, who had stopped talking as he negotiated a junction. *I wonder why Will decided to drive tonight. He won't be able to drink much. Perhaps he was afraid we'd have to share a cab back with the Watsons.*

As soon as they were clear of the junction, Will said, 'Please, Emily, this is important.'

'I'm listening,' she promised.

A driver in the lane beside them signalled his intention to push in just ahead and Will muttered a sarcastic comment, his expression thunderous. The way the orange glow from the street lights fell on him gave him unexpectedly cavernous cheeks and hooded eyes, and for a moment he looked almost like a stranger and not like her Will at all. His face had been thinner lately, now she came to think of it. But of course he wasn't the same as when they'd married six years ago, or when they'd got together four years before that.

Ten years, she marvelled. *How can it be so long?*

Where did the time go? She knew where, of course: on producing two children, on moving house twice, on living their lives without noticing that every day changed them just a little more. Will's hair had been a burnished red-gold when she'd met him but now, without her ever seeing the change, it had faded to brown flecked with grey, and he kept it very short to hide its growing sparseness. The lines on his face were deeper and he had a permanent crease between his brows. *But he looks good on it. He still looks young – at least, he does to me.*

She gazed for a moment at her husband's profile with its long, straight nose and firm, round chin. *A strong, decided face.* From the start, Will had always seemed to know where he was going and what he was doing. He always had a plan, an idea of where he would be in a few years' time. She'd let him lead the way, making the decisions about what was best, steering their course unhesitatingly to wherever it was they were going. After all, it was Will's career as the chief financial officer of a hedge fund that paid all their bills, bought the house, and provided the comforts they needed. It was only right that it took priority. Her part of the bargain was raising the family, taking care of the home, running their domestic lives as well as she could, with the idea that she would return to work when the children were older.

'Did you hear what I said, Emily?' Will asked tetchily. She realised he had been talking again and she had not been listening properly. They had made the break at last, the slow dual carriageway opening up into the three lanes of motorway. The lights of the city were behind them as the car accelerated into the relative darkness ahead. Huge street lamps bent over the motorway at intervals, like strange bowing giants, while red tail lights flickered ahead and white headlights glared and spun behind. Emily was glad Will was driving. She always felt bewildered by the flashing, moving beams, and intimidated by the way they approached remorselessly from behind, dazzling in the rear-view mirror. Driving at night seemed to be about understanding the rays and beams, the starbursts of white light that cut through the dark.

'Emily?' Will's voice was low and intense.

'Sorry . . .' *Why am I so distracted? I need to concentrate. What was he saying? Something about work* . . . She remembered an echo of something he'd said before. 'Is Vlady still giving you hell?' She tried to pretend she'd heard. 'What does Helen say?'

There was a strained pause. Will stared straight ahead through the dark windscreen, his gaze hardening. 'Do you ever listen to me, Emily?' he asked in a gritted voice.

'Of course I do!' she said, repentant at once. 'I'm sorry, I've had so much on my mind lately. Christmas is so close, I've still got a million things to do. The school's carol concert's coming up and for some crazy reason I promised to run the mince pie and mulled wine stall.'

'Christmas,' said Will, his voice strangely hollow. 'I'd almost forgotten.'

'Forgotten?' Emily laughed in disbelief. 'How could you? It's everywhere.'

And yet, she realised, it wasn't here. Christmas had suddenly vanished. There were no decorations on the motorway, no strings of lights or dangling baubles. No background of carols or Yuletide pop tunes. No scent of cinnamon and spice. Just the seriousness of the high-speed journey.

'So,' she ventured almost timidly. 'Is it Vlady?'

Vlady was the Russian businessman who owned the hedge fund Will worked for, notoriously temperamental and prone to outbursts of autocratic behaviour. They were grateful to him for giving Will a job and elevating him up that all important step to CFO, but his mercurial nature and refusal to accept that he had to comply with the way things were done led to conflict and exasperation in his team.

'In a way.' Will's knuckles tightened round the steering wheel. The traffic had thinned out and they were speeding along in the fast lane, flying by the slower cars in the middle.

'What's he up to? Arguments with Natalia again?' Emily said, trying to lighten the atmosphere; she and Will had often laughed about the state of his boss's relationship with his wife, which had an operatic intensity, full of rifts, threats and magnificent reconciliations.

'If you'd been listening, you'd know,' Will replied

briefly. His voice was growing flatter, losing its expression. 'I was saying that Vlady hasn't been himself lately. In fact, we haven't seen him for days.'

'Has he gone away for the holidays?' Emily suggested. 'Skiing or something?'

'I don't know. We don't know where he's gone. That's the point. I was telling you that the last time I saw Vlad was when he came in and gave me that rocket over the figures for the Kommer deal. He said I'd made a mistake. But I hadn't. I couldn't convince him.'

'That's odd, isn't it?' Emily looked over at him, worried for Will. He prided himself on handling Vlady's volatility and on always being on top of his brief. 'You can usually talk him round. Show him where he's gone wrong.'

'I know. Not this time.'

'So?' Anxiety curled in the pit of her stomach. *Is he trying to prepare me for something?*

'For Christ's sake, Emily.' He closed his eyes for a moment and she realised that they were flying along the road at over eighty miles an hour.

Oh God, she thought, her anxiety growing. *He's going too fast.* 'Slow down a little, sweetie,' she said, trying to sound calm. *This is why he's been so on edge lately. What's wrong? Has he been sacked?* A whole future flashed through her mind: Will out of work, no money coming in, new jobs hard to find. There would be bills to be paid, arguments over money, the shopping put on credit cards.

9

Perhaps she'd have to go back to work as a primary school teacher while Will looked after the children, workless and hopeless, spending long hours on the internet searching for jobs. *But we could get through that*, she thought, *we'd be fine. It'd be tough but we could do it. At least some of the awful pressure we live with now would be gone.*

In the second that it had taken her to envisage this future, Will opened his eyes and took the speed of the car back down. The needle had been nudging ninety. Now she saw with relief that it was trembling over eighty again.

'So,' he said, his voice calmer, 'we haven't heard from Vlady for four days now. Nothing. No contact. His phone dead. His emails unanswered. No reply from his houses, or his driver, or his pilot, or anyone.'

'Oh.' Emily stared at her husband's profile again, as if she could read some answers in its firm lines. 'Have you tried to reach Natalia?'

'Yes. Of course. But she's vanished as well.'

'Oh.' Emily turned to look at the dark road ahead, the white lines on either side of the lane converging in the far distance as they disappeared into the night. 'So . . . what are you going to do?'

'Today, Helen decided that we had to start investigating. She said that with no contact for so long from the CEO, we had to assume control of what was happening. She said it could be a worst-case scenario and that we can't sit and wait and let the ship go down because the captain had gone overboard. But she's only been on the team six months, she doesn't know Vlady like we do. You and I know that he's a bit of a drama queen. He and Natalia could have had a screaming row followed by a huge make-up session and flown off to some Bali resort and turned off their phones.' Will's jaw tightened. 'That's what I wanted to believe.'

Wanted to believe? Wanted?

'So what did Helen do?' Emily ventured. Her hands, she realised, were clutched tightly together in her lap, hot and tense on the black silk.

'She went into Vlady's office. She called the techy boys and made them open up the system so we could see what's going on. She broke open the whole thing.'

'Did you find out what's happened to Vlady?' The anxiety was back, flickering and hot in her stomach. She was completely focused on Will now.

'We don't need to know now. It's kind of irrelevant, in fact. I'll probably never see him again.'

A nasty coldness spread across her skin. When she spoke, her voice came out almost as a whisper. 'Why?'

For the first time, Will flicked his gaze round to look at her. Those eyes – soft hazel when he was happy, a hard green when he was angry or miserable. She couldn't see them here in the darkness. How many times had he looked at her, and she'd marvelled at how beautiful they were, with their fine almond shape and frame of dark lashes? Now she came to think of it, they'd been green all the time lately.

Will turned back to the road and when he spoke, his voice was heavy and leaden. 'Vlady's been running the fund on empty for a month or two now. He's managed to keep the truth hidden from all of us, even me.' He gave a hollow laugh. 'You can imagine what that does to my credentials as the CFO. What kind of buffoon doesn't realise his fund doesn't exist?' There was a tiny pause, a breath, when, for Emily, the world teetered on a brink – on one side was normality and on the other, something awful waited. She wanted to stop him speaking, as though that would make it all right, but before she could draw the breath or open her mouth, he went on implacably. 'It's over. Everything's gone. The whole damn lot. He's made some spectacular blunders – I mean crazy, rookie stuff, like the trader boys who throw billions away trying to hide a loss of millions. I don't even know how he did it, or what possessed him to throw everything away after the years we've put in building the fund, getting the clients, the investors, and when we were just on the verge of pulling in some really big fish—'

'Wait. I don't understand. So . . .' Emily tried to take it in. It seemed too much to comprehend, too big a leap from her life as it had been ten minutes ago to what it might be now. 'You mean . . . Vlady's done something criminal?'

Will considered this and then said in a bitterly amused voice, 'You know, I've not even thought about that. Yeah. I imagine there'll be grounds for quite a lot of legal action but it will all be pointless. He'll end up in jail – if anyone ever finds him – but they'll never see their money again. No one will.'

The dark road outside flew by in a blur and ahead of them red lights glowed like danger beacons in the distance. Emily knew she ought to feel something but she was numb. Her anxiety had turned to a kind of stillness, as if she wouldn't let herself react until she had a full knowledge of the facts and their implication. There was only a small fluttering sense of horror somewhere just outside herself, waiting to swoop in and take possession.

Fear began to crawl under her skin. 'And you? Can you be made responsible for any of this?'

'I have no idea what Vlad did to cover his tracks. But I do know that I am responsible. For more than you know.'

'Of course you feel responsible, but it's not your fault! How could it be? You had no idea what Vlady was doing.'

'I should have known.'

'He pulled the wool over your eyes. He deceived you. You trusted him. That's not a crime.' She spoke quickly, urgently, desperate to convince him. She knew what Will was like once an idea had taken a firm hold in his mind. Her old uncle used to talk about the painful effort of uprooting the mangels on his land. It was like that, trying to unplant one of Will's notions. 'You can't be to blame for that, Will. Helen knows. Everyone will know. Vlady's to blame. They'll find him and he'll take the consequences. He was always a loose cannon but I had no idea he'd be capable of something like this.' She reached out a hand and put it on his thigh. It was hard and muscled from the hours he spent in the gym. 'We'll be okay. We've got savings. We've got the house. You'll find another job and I can go back to work if that makes sense – if the childcare cost isn't too much.'

'Oh Emily.'

His voice was so freighted with sadness, it frightened her. 'What is it? I know it's awful, but we're still us, we've still got the kids . . .'

'You don't understand. He duped me. He told me everything was great. More than great. He said if I invested now, I'd get a return on my money that I would hardly believe possible. He took me out for dinner, showed me the paperwork, painted great glorious pictures of what was waiting for us both. It seems so stupid to think about it now – sitting in one of those crazily expensive City restaurants, ordering Pol Roger and beluga caviar, toasting how much richer we were going to be.' Will's voice dropped lower and grew more monotonous. 'I believed him. Completely believed him.'

'What did you do?' she asked, fear gradually breaking through the numbness. Her heart began thumping hard in her chest. She sensed that the nub of the matter was close.

'I took it all – everything. I emptied the savings accounts, the ISAs. I cashed in the pension, the shares, everything I could get my hands on. I remortgaged the house as much as they would let me. I got everything together . . . and I gave it all to Vlad.'

The world buzzed and roared all around Emily. Images poured into her mind as she mentally raced through everything they had. All those carefully hoarded bulwarks against the unknown, the funds to provide for the children, a guarantee for their future. All the safety nets – the house (mortgage free), the savings . . . Something occurred to her; she managed to speak. 'My . . . my legacy . . . the money Mum and Dad left me . . .'

'Gone,' he said abruptly. 'I took it. I thought I was making us rich. But I've made us paupers. We've got nothing, Emily. It's all gone, all of it.'

She was dazed and breathless, grasping at her seat, her neck suddenly barely able to support her head. 'What . . . gone? All of it? You mean . . .' She stopped, trying to take it in. An hour ago she'd been sitting at her dressing table, picking her jewellery, spraying scent on her freshly showered skin, finishing her make-up. She'd been listening to the babysitter reading the children one last story before their light was turned off. Even though she'd been worried about Carrie, she'd been happy, though she hadn't known it.

Will went on relentlessly, not trying to soften what he was saying, as though he'd hardened himself to delivering the blows. 'Yes. It's all gone. I don't have a job. There's not enough in the current account

15

to pay more than a couple of months of mortgage payments, before we've bought any food or paid any bills.'

'We'll sell the house,' she said frantically. 'We'll move.'

'The bank will take it and we'll still owe them everything on the slate.'

'No, no, that can't be right. We'll sell it. The market's healthy enough around us. We'll . . .' She squeezed her eyes shut against the chaos exploding inside her head. *Nothing? My money from Mum and Dad is gone?* Outrage boomed in some part of her mind, and a terrible anger was screaming for her attention, but she had no time for it now, not right now. She had to solve a problem first. But what was the problem? *We have no money, Will has no job and he might be criminally responsible for Vlady's actions. He's wiped out everything, everything, everything.* In one part of her mind she was thinking about selling her jewellery, taking all her fancy bits and pieces to market on eBay. In another she was already mourning the loss of what they'd had. And yet . . . that wasn't the problem she had to solve right now. It was something else altogether.

She opened her eyes and turned her head to look at Will. They were speeding again, the needle moving inexorably up from eighty towards eighty-five miles an hour. The car was alone on the stretch of motorway, hugging the central reservation as it sped through the night in the fast lane. Far off in the darkness flickered the red lights of distant traffic on which they were steadily gaining. Slowly, Will turned his head and looked at her, his eyes strange in the blue-black light.

He's been so different lately. Not like my Will at all. How long has he been like this? Not weeks. Months. Even longer . . . She didn't want to admit how long it had been. *Oh Will, what's happened to you? When did you change? Why haven't I let myself see it?* She had the sudden urgent sensation that she had to reassure him that he was loved and needed; she had to pull him back from some awful pit . . . but where were the right words?

'There's no coming back from this,' he said in a tone of such utter bleakness that she felt her blood go icy in her veins. 'We're ruined. It's over.'

'No.' Panic began to speed through her. 'Over? It's not over.'

'Yes. I've failed you. The children. Everyone. I can't face what will happen to us, and you shouldn't have to either.'

She felt the car take another powerful thrust forward. The needle shook up to ninety, and then over. 'Will,' she said, fear gripping her insides. 'Slow down. What are you doing?'

She realised he was still looking at her. How long had it been since he'd glanced at the road? The speedometer moved over ninety-five.

'Slow down! Watch where you're going!' she cried, her voice tinny with panic. *Carrie!* she thought. She saw her daughter tucked up in bed asleep, her forehead a little damp with fever. *Joe!* The little boy was curled up in his cot, thumb in his mouth, eyelashes curling on his soft cheek. 'Will! Stop it!'

The strange hooded eyes didn't take their gaze off her. 'I'm sorry, Emily,' he said in a flat tone. With one swift movement he pulled the steering wheel downwards with his left hand. Emily felt the car career abruptly to her left, the suddenness throwing her to the right, as they hurtled over the middle lane towards pitch black.

She opened her mouth to scream but they were already off the motorway and all around them was an explosion of sound and blackness and vast movement so inexorable that she was unable to do anything but surrender to it.

CHAPTER 2

1962

Oh please, please, don't go!

As she emerged from the side street, Cressie had seen the bus's huge red curved behind and had started to trot, hoping the jostling mass of people waiting to board would keep it at the stop until she got there. But the crowd seemed to melt onto it, and her way was blocked by people stepping in front of her or loitering almost purposefully, it seemed, to prevent her reaching it.

Blast! I must get it. I can't keep Papa waiting. More than my life's worth.

She broke into a run, sidestepping the slower pedestrians who blocked her way, one hand pressing her hat to her head, but she could hear the grating roar of the engine and see the great behind shaking like a huge lumbering animal preparing to pounce on something.

'Please wait!' she cried, hoping a tender-hearted conductor might see her and hold the bus for a moment, but her voice sailed upwards and away

19

unheeded. The bus started to pull away from the pavement.

Oh, bother it! She slowed a little, panting, and then a determination gripped her. *No, I shan't give up. I want that bus!* And she was running again as the bus rumbled away, too big to gather speed at any rapid rate. She was gaining on it now, the platform tantalisingly close, and she was just planning how she would reach out and grab the steel pole to help her leap on-board when it seemed to begin pulling away from her at too great a speed.

I shall have to stop, I've missed it, she thought, her chest burning and her heart pounding. Then she saw a tall shape appear on the platform and a hand extend out towards her.

'Come on!' a voice urged. 'You can do it!'

As if bound to obey, she found a sudden burst of speed, reached out and grasped the hand. It closed on hers, the long fingers wrapping around her wrist, and as she leapt up towards the platform, the stranger pulled and she flew upwards, feeling suddenly quite weightless, as if she'd unexpectedly taken off and begun to fly. The next moment she had landed on the platform, breathless and delighted to find herself on-board the bus as it ground its way up Piccadilly.

'Thank you,' she panted, looking up at the man who had helped her. He released her wrist and she pulled her hand away.

A pair of deep-set grey eyes gazed down at her, a look of amusement making them sparkle with a bluish light. She blinked at him, wondering if she knew this man somehow, he seemed so strangely familiar: the pale complexion, the fine-boned face and the large forehead with a swoop of brown hair falling over it. *But I don't know him. I'm sure of it.*

'You're welcome,' he said in a low, rather musical voice. 'You're obviously in a hurry.'

'Yes . . . yes.' She felt an urge to explain to him exactly why she'd had to catch the bus but then looked away, a little embarrassed. There was no need. Why would he be interested, after all? She went to make her way into the bus but all the seats on the lower deck were taken and a hulking man in a raincoat stood in her way, one hand clutching a leather strap that dangled from the roof.

'No room upstairs either,' her rescuer said conversationally. 'I just came down and saw you pelting along after us. Are you going far?'

'No,' she said, still getting her breath back. Her cheeks felt warm. 'Only to Pall Mall.'

He raised an eyebrow. 'You could have walked that. Or run it, at the pace you were going.' He glanced out at the road through the open gap by the platform where they stood. 'Look, we're stopping at lights again.'

She wanted to explain that, even so, the bus was quicker but she had the faint feeling he was laughing at her somehow, and so said nothing. As he looked out, she took the opportunity to observe him more closely. His face was one of those deceptive types: seemingly rather ordinary, a little too pale perhaps, but otherwise unremarkable until one noticed the structure of it, with the hollows beneath the cheeks emphasising their high bones, and the straight lines of the brow and the nose. It held a hint of nobility and the light in the eyes was intelligent and sensitive. It was only now, standing so close to him, that she could see the shape of his eyes, the flecks of green and gold within the grey of the irises, and the dark lashes.

He's beautiful, she thought, and then, surprised that she should think such a thing, she dragged her gaze away in case he sensed her gawping at him.

The conductor came down the stairs, calling for fares as he joined them on the platform, crowding them even more. Cressie paid her money and he churned out a ticket from the canister hanging from his neck just as the bus pulled up at the next stop. In the jostling of the incomers, she got pushed past the raincoat man and into the depths of the bus. A man stood up to offer her a seat but she refused with a breathless, 'No . . . no, thank you. I'm getting off in a minute.' Her helper was now obscured from her view. She could only catch a glimpse of his mac, a beige gabardine, and his hand on the pole, long slender fingers wrapped around it. The fingers that a few minutes before had been clasped around her wrist. Her skin seemed to burn where he'd touched it.

You're being ridiculous, she scolded herself. *Besides, there's Adam.*

Adam had been paying court to her for a few

weeks now, ever since she'd been placed next to him at the dinner party at the Robertsons'. A pupil in legal chambers at Temple Inn, he had a promising future and Cressie had no doubt that her father would be more than pleased with him as a suitor. He was nice enough and she tried to see the best in him, but she couldn't quite overcome her resistance to his looks. He was plain, that was all there was to it. She didn't find him in the least appealing despite the scoldings she administered to herself for being so shallow and not responding to the person within rather than the outer shell.

Sometimes it occurred to her that while she was telling herself off and suffering waves of guilt for being so superficial, none of the young men at balls and parties ever paid any attention to poor Alicia Bond, who had inherited her father's looks. The fact that she had also inherited her mother's very sweet nature was neither here nor there. There were naked double standards, with the girls judged by their faces and the boys by their intelligence and prospects.

I'm just as bad. Look at me, dazzled by a handsome man without knowing anything about him.

She tried to glimpse him again as she clutched hard at a strap. The bus rumbled on up Piccadilly, making her sway and bump against her fellow passengers as it halted at lights and then surged off again when they changed. She pushed against the drag of the bus as it swung round a sharp bend. Was he still there? she wondered, but she could no longer even see his arm or his hand on the pole. When she got off at the bottom of Haymarket, pushing her way out through the crowded lower deck, he was gone. He'd got off somewhere and she hadn't noticed.

Oh. Her heart fell, though what she'd been hoping for, she had no idea. He was already striding away somewhere, the distance between them increasing every moment. Then she caught a glimpse of the clock hanging over the Theatre Royal. *Only five minutes to meet Papa.* She dashed over the road, dodging cars, vans and buzzing motorbikes, and headed down Pall Mall.

The staff in the club knew her. The man in the gold-buttoned uniform took her coat and hat, and watched sympathetically as she smoothed her hair while she got her breath back. When she'd recovered, she made her way towards the green dining room. Ladies were only allowed in this small part of the club: the stretch of corridor from the marble-floored hall to the dining room and this room itself, green and gilt, lit by crystal chandeliers and hung with huge oil portraits. The rest of the place remained a mystery revealed only to the men who belonged to the club, but she caught a whiff of cigar smoke and the tang of whisky from one room, the musty smell of books and newspapers from another and guessed what lay hidden from view. She was not much interested in it: the snoozing clergy, the portly gentlemen in suits absorbing the day's news while they coughed and drank and nodded at one another. As far as she was concerned, they could have their sleepy old clubs while the world outside changed and grew more interesting. If only they saw what she did when she took the Underground out east.

Standing at the entrance to the green dining room, she spotted her father at once, sitting at his favourite table by the window where he could watch people going up and down the front steps. He must have seen her arrive, but nevertheless he was simultaneously consulting his watch and glancing up at the doorway with a stern expression that barely softened when he saw Cressie standing there. By the time she reached his table, though, he had evidently relented and was almost smiling.

I must be in his good books.

'Only a little late.' He stood up. A waiter hurried up and pulled out a chair for Cressie.

'Two minutes?' she asked, sitting down.

'Yes, two,' her father said gravely, taking his seat again. His mania for punctuality and order ruled all their lives. 'Almost three.'

'I'm sorry, Papa.' The waiter came up, picked up the napkin that lay on her plate, snapped it out and draped it gently on her lap. The rituals of the meal began: the menus in large red leather folders – hers without prices – the choice of the food, the little slip and silver pencil that was brought over so that her father could write out what they wanted. Water glasses were filled, and a decanter of claret was brought over by the white-gloved sommelier and her father's glass filled while hers was left empty.

'What have you been doing with yourself?' he asked, as the ceremonies unfolded around them. 'Soup first. Then beef or lamb?'

'Lamb, please,' Cressie said, although she quailed at the thought of one of the big club lunches which always seemed to sit heavily inside her for hours, so she felt like the wolf in the fairy tale whose belly was filled with stones while he slept. 'I've been in the library, reading up about educational techniques.'

Her father's expression darkened. 'You intend to go through with it then?'

'Of course.' She sipped her water. 'You know I do.'

'I see I won't be able to stop you.' He sighed.

'Why would you want to?' returned Cressie with a touch of tartness, more than she would usually allow herself when talking to her father. *But honestly, why is he being so obstructive? I can't see the problem. I'm not leaving home or anything like that, only spreading my wings a little . . . trying to be useful.*

He hesitated while he handed the menu slip to the waiter. 'I don't think . . . I don't know. If you want education, there are plenty of things you could do – a course or something . . . French, sewing . . .'

She laughed. 'I don't need the educating! I want to educate others, you know that. I want to do what I can to help. If you went out and saw what I've seen, you'd know there's so much to be done . . .' Enthusiasm surged through her and she longed to talk, tell him everything and convince him. If he only knew how things really were just a mile or so from this place with its ludicrous self-importance and all the plush cushioning against reality. Not far away from white-gloved waiters and chandeliers and pudding trolleys, children were going hungry, growing up ignorant and condemned to a life without the kind of comfort or charm her father considered essential to a tolerable existence.

'But really, Cressida, what can *you* do?' he retorted. 'I don't mean it to sound as though you can do nothing, but really . . . If you're bored, why not do a little wholesome charity work – like holding bazaars and so on? Once you're married, which could be very soon, you won't be working. I don't understand why you want to go to such trouble when at most you could be teaching for a year. What good will that do for the downtrodden, eh?'

She stared at him, seeing suddenly how very old he had become lately. She had a picture of him in her brain that must have formed in her childhood: a dark-haired, vigorous man with icy blue eyes and an air of determination. Sometimes it came as a shock to realise that man had gone and the one in his place was stouter, his hair now gunmetal and silver, his cheeks crosshatched with red veins from the club claret, his eyes a little faded. He didn't see the future as she did – a glorious

27

unknown full of adventures yet to be lived – but as a postscript to a vanished time when life was better. He wanted her to embrace his vision of the world as a place of dangers and irritants best avoided, and to see her safely tucked away like a child put to bed at night, where she could slumber her own life through. He disliked the changes in the world and the loud demands of the young for something other than what had gone before.

But I'm young. I want to be a part of it. Life's changing for everyone. For women. For the poor. She looked down at her fingers twisting in her lap, choking silently on her speech, her throat feeling full, as though everything she wanted to say was jammed there, unable to escape.

A waiter came over with a basket of bread rolls and her father took one and broke it open. Then he looked up with a different expression and said, 'That reminds me . . . I was talking to old Few last night. His nephew's only gone and become a painter.'

'Oh?' Cressie was polite but she had no idea who her father was talking about.

'Naturally, it's a blow for the family. Few's the boy's guardian, you see, since the parents died and there's only a sister otherwise. They've all tried to talk him out of it but he's determined, apparently, so Few is trying to take it well.' Her father glanced up with a smile. 'We old men sometimes do, you know.'

She smiled back, wondering if that meant he was telling her he would come to accept her plans. It had been hard enough to talk him round to her taking a diploma in literature at the college. Two years of pleading before he finally agreed had meant she was older than most of the others on the course. She'd been allowed in the end, partly, she suspected, because her mother had done slow but steady work behind the scenes. Perhaps some bargain had been struck, although her father would not usually tolerate bargaining. But in the end he had grudgingly given his permission.

Her father continued: 'He's only just getting started, of course, this boy, but Few tells me that he shows some talent.'

'What sort of things does he paint?'

'Portraits. And not the kind with the noses off kilter and two eyes on the same side either. Quite respectable-looking things, apparently. Few says it's possible that he might become well regarded in time. And there's much less to deplore in a decent man painting portraits of his own class. Take Birley, for example.'

Cressie burst out laughing. 'Honestly, Papa, the way you sound! It's very old-fashioned. Lucky for you that Henry and Gus never wanted to go into art or design or trade.'

Her father looked at her from under his brows. Her brothers were nicely settled in banks in the City and he was more than content with that. 'Indeed. They both know better. But it occurred to me that one should do what one can to help the boy get on. So I told Few that I'd commission him to have your portrait done.'

Cressie blinked in surprise. 'My portrait?'

'Yes. I had the idea as I was talking to Few. I've been thinking of finding someone to paint your picture and it struck me this was an opportunity. His nephew has a studio over in Blackheath so you'll have to go there a few times to sit for him.'

At once irritation sparked through her but she spoke calmly. 'Blackheath? I can't do that, Papa. I'm about to start at the school.'

'You're not going every day, are you?'

'Not at once . . .'

'Well then, we'll arrange it so that the portrait is started right away. It will only take a few hours.'

She opened her mouth to protest but suddenly did not know what to say. There was no real reason why she couldn't have her portrait painted, but she resented her father's bullying, the way he imposed things on her, promising her commitment without asking her first. But it was always the same: he never asked and rarely changed his mind. His dictum was that under his roof, his will held sway. The problem was, there was no way of not being under his roof.

'I do not want to hear objections, Cressida,' her father said, seeing her expression. 'Most young women would like to have themselves painted. An hour or two and it will all be done. You'll be glad of it in the future. You're at the right age to have yourself preserved on canvas.'

'Can't I have my photograph taken?' Cressie

asked, inspired. 'It's more accurate and a great deal quicker.'

Her father ignored her. 'That's settled then. I'll tell Few that you'll be at his nephew's disposal and that we'd like to start immediately.'

'What's his name?' Cressie asked, trying to bite back her exasperation.

'Oh . . . er . . . Few did tell me but I've forgotten. Richard? Robert? Something like that.' Her father lifted his hand to summon the wine waiter for a refill. 'I shall write to him this afternoon and you young people can make the arrangements between you. Now . . . where's our soup?'

Cressie let herself in through the large black front door of their house on a quiet Kensington street. Inside, everything was still. Only the huge grandfather clock by the stairs made a sound, its heavy tock beating time. The place had never changed in her lifetime and she suspected it had always looked the same, with the heavy dark furniture, the potted palms, the fringed velvet curtains that seemed to echo fashions of sixty years before. The rooms were kept dim because of some order given long ago to keep sunlight off the furnishings, and even though Cressie was accustomed to the fusty twilight of the downstairs, she still felt oppressed by it. In her own room, she'd done what she could to bring light and air inside, persuading her mother to let her do away with the heavily floral wallpaper and brocade curtains. She had had the walls painted a fresh green and had put up curtains of plain linen in off-white, and escaped there as often as she could to read or write letters or paint the little watercolour pictures that relaxed her like nothing else.

She took off her coat. The summer was showing signs of finally making way for autumn, but it was still chilly. Ellen, the maid, came into the hall, peering curiously to see who was there, on edge in case it was Mr Fellbridge.

'Hello, Ellen, I'm home.' She smiled as the maid visibly relaxed at the sight of her. 'How's Mama?'

'She's fine, miss. Ruth came down half an hour ago and said she was comfortable and sleeping.'

'That's good.' She had expected nothing else. Her mother had drifted on in her invalid state for so many years that Cressie could no longer imagine her doing anything other than lying propped among pillows so snowy white they made the pallor of her skin more ghastly than ever. Somewhere she had memories of a different mother who was not ill and who laughed and ran up and down stairs. Every year she had taken the young family to their house in Cumbria for the summer, leaving the children's father behind to work in the City. Cressie remembered long train journeys north, their cases and boxes stuffed into the luggage car, the three children bouncing on the seats of their compartment while Mama tried to read despite the huge picnic basket on her lap. At some glorious, long-anticipated point in the journey, she would

open it and they would feast on cold meat sandwiches and cake as the train bore them to that
place of strange wild beauty so far from dirty,
smoky London. The summer would be spent
mostly out of doors, unless the weather was too
bad, and Mama was always there, sitting on a rug
and reading, organising boating on the lake, or
playing cricket with them. She didn't ride the
hardy little ponies they loved so much, but Cressie
remembered her holding the bridle of one, laughing
as the wind whipped her dark hair around, vibrant
with healthy strength. Papa came for a week in
August but usually spent most of it shooting. The
air would be full of the pops and cracks of the
distant guns, and occasionally she saw a drive of
birds rise up in the distance, and small black
shapes flutter and fall to earth. They all went
back when it was time to prepare for the return
to school, and the train ride home had a mournful
air, the picnic basket holding the last sandwiches
of summer, and the sky had always turned grey
by the time they pulled in at Euston.

'Never mind, chickens,' Mama would say,
'summer will be here again before you know it. It
can't always be the holidays. And we'll always have
December House. We'll be back there next year,
never you fear.'

But those days were long gone. Sickness came,
an unspecified condition that was spoken of in
such vague terms, it was hard to know exactly
what was wrong, only that Mama grew weak and

thin, and despite many attempts at a cure – the endless doctors' visits, the huge brown bottles lined up on the chimney piece in her room, the journeys not to the north but to the seaside and the spa towns on the continent – nothing had come of it. They stopped going to December House and Mama had shrunk and diminished to the thin, pale creature in the bed upstairs, coming down only occasionally after great preparations had been made. The presence of a nurse in the house was now quite accepted, and the hush that pervaded it was not only that of a place where the children had grown up and gone, but of one where quiet was enforced for the comfort of the sick. The air had the bitter tang of medicine and disinfectant, the faint sourness of a hospital.

'Would you like tea, miss?'

'Thank you, Ellen. I'll have some in the drawing room while I get on with my reading.'

The maid went off and Cressie walked over to the hall mirror to inspect her reflection in case she'd picked up smudges on her journey home. She smoothed her hair. In the lamplight it glowed burnished brown like the table in the dining room. As she inspected her face, her attention was caught suddenly by another face just behind hers and she jumped slightly before she realised it was something she had seen many times before in this very place: the portrait of her mother that hung on the wall opposite. She turned to look at it. It had been there for as long as she could remember but she had not properly looked at it, or even noticed it, for a long time. Mama had been painted at the age of twenty-five, just four years older than Cressie was now, in the languid style of the early thirties, with an emphasis on her long neck, slender hands and fine-boned face. But, Cressie realised, the face was like hers, the dark eyes set back in the skull with brows arching above, the fuller lower lip, and the mahogany-coloured hair full of glints and lights.

I never realised I look so like her. She put a hand to her own cheek and brushed it over, feeling the contours for herself as though to give reality to what she was seeing, and remembered that her father had commissioned a portrait of her. Here was her mother, still young, still beautiful, wearing a silk blouse that had long vanished and a string of pearls that now sat unworn in her jewellery box, caught forever at a moment in her life that had gone irretrievably. Cressie was struck by a sudden sense that her seemingly immutable youth would vanish and fade just as her mother's had done.

But that's so far away. There are years and years to live first.

She went to wash her hands before tea.

CHAPTER 3

The ventilator moved up and down with quiet determination, hissing lightly as it went about its job of keeping Will alive. The whole place seemed to be nothing but machinery and tubes – the thick white plastic tube taped into his mouth delivering oxygen, the nasal tubes, the lines in his arms and chest and stomach, delivering saline, painkillers, food, removing waste and doing everything his body needed to live while it lay shattered on the bed.

Emily knew it was Will lying there even though his red-brown stubble was not visible under the bandages around his skull and his face was obscured by tape and tubes. It was his eyelids – their pale greeny translucence was something that she remembered from when he was ill at home with the flu. His skin had a papery fineness when he was unwell, quickly taking on the greenish-blue tinge of old copper. Below bandaged wrists where lines into his veins were secured, his hands lay in loose fists on the covers, the skin lightly freckled, the knuckles reddened; their width and strong fingers, one with the red-gold wedding band she knew so well, were unmistakable. The hands and the eyelids were what made the prone man on the bed into Will.

But who is Will anyway? Did I ever know him?

The room was less like a place of sickness and more like a kind of scientific laboratory, with its dozens of power outlets, the hooks and stands, the complex computer screens banked beside the bed where coloured lines waved and undulated across the black background, and where numbers came and went, lights flashed, and mechanical chirrups and beeps sounded at intervals. Even the bed wasn't a bed, but a kind of plastic trolley with sides that could be clipped up or down or taken away entirely. The mattress was filled with air to reduce pressure points on Will's body.

Intensive care was, it seemed, a matter of electrics as much as anything else. Once the electrics were taken away, you were either getting better, or dead.

The question was how long the electrical currents would continue to breathe for Will, feeding him and nurturing him while he slept on, his brain apparently frozen and his spirit locked away somewhere in his depths. Unless, of course, it had already gone somewhere else.

Emily had the sudden thought of a kind of disembodied Will flying about the room, like the Ancient Egyptian concept of the soul after death, with the person's head on the body of a bird that flew off to the afterlife. She pictured a fat-chested pigeon with Will's head, flapping up to the ceiling and roosting on the metal arm of the thing that lifted his tubes away from his face. Perhaps he was there now, head cocked, regarding her with a bright eye, watching as she stood by the door on her crutches and wondering what she was doing there.

Wondering why I'm still alive, maybe. Wondering why it didn't all go according to plan. Her hands tightened around the handles of the crutches. A bitter bolt of fury raged through her. She had a sudden urge to yank out all the tubes and wires and electrical cables and scream, *Die then, you bastard, if you wanted it so bloody much!* and her heart began to pound. She felt dizziness overpower her. *Oh God, am I going to faint?*

The door behind her opened and someone strode in with a cheerful, 'Hello there!'

Emily took a deep breath and turned to see one of the nurses, a smiling black woman in the hospital uniform of loose blue tunic and trousers. On her hands were latex gloves and a badge clipped to her pocket showed her name to be Rita. 'H . . . hello.'

'How are we doing?' Rita went to the machines and began to inspect the screens. The lights and lines and numbers seemed to make sense to her. She checked the plastic pouches of fluid that hung from the hooks – one the colour of dark red wine, one with a sickly straw-coloured middle, and the other clear – and all the other inlets and outlets connected to Will.

'I'm fine,' Emily said. Her heart had stopped racing and her deep breaths had restored some calm to her.

Rita glanced over her shoulder at her. 'How's that leg?'

Emily looked down at the thick plaster encasing her left leg from the ankle to just below the knee. She was getting used to the weight and awkwardness, and to moving with crutches. 'They say it will heal all right. But I'm going to be like this for a while. Then there'll be physio to get it back to health. Months of it, I expect.'

Rita's gaze travelled over Emily's face to the bulky bandage that covered the left side of her head. 'And that?'

'They . . . they won't know for a while. It's been stitched, of course.'

The nurse stared for a moment, frowning, her mouth in a slight grimace that made Emily feel sick, and then seemed to remember her job was to be unfailingly optimistic. Her smile returned. 'It'll be fine. Mr Watkins is the best, you know, the best in the country!'

Emily managed a smile. 'That's good.' Everyone here seemed to be the best in the country or pre-eminent in their field. Maybe it was true and it was simply luck that they had all ended up at this particular hospital. Or perhaps it was just part of something she suspected was the tissue of lies that padded the relationship between patients and doctors. It was like being wrapped in cotton wadding so that the unpleasantness of reality would not cause too much pain. The wadding was only taken away when the sorry truth could no longer be hidden. It was not so much an exercise in deceit, she felt, as one in misplaced kindness and optimism. So many doctors had looked at her injuries and hissed or frowned, and then said brightly how wonderful it all was. Something told her that further down the line they might pronounce quite a different judgement. 'He's going to see me in a few days when the initial healing is complete.'

Rita returned to her work and Emily watched her for a while before venturing. 'How is he?'

'Yeees, he's doing well.' The reply was half distracted, as Rita noted Will's blood pressure on a chart. 'He's doing really very well.'

Emily gazed down at her husband and wondered how he could possibly be described as doing well. He was barely alive. Compared to being actually dead, he was doing well, but in all other comparisons, surely, he was doing very badly. 'Do they think he'll get better? Will he wake up?'

Rita was silent for a moment and then said, 'We'll have to see. He's still in the artificial coma. It all depends on how he responds when they withdraw the drugs keeping him under. We'll just have to wait, I'm afraid. But he's coping well, considering. No infections yet. We're keeping a close eye on the lungs and bladder. I'm just going to massage him now.'

She watched as Rita began work on Will's limbs,

lifting and kneading them to keep the blood flowing and prevent atrophy. Already he looked thinner, his once strong arms more wasted than before. It was so odd to see him weak and floppy, when he'd always been so vital. Those arms had been wrapped tightly around her so often. Now they were useless.

Will he ever come back?

No one had yet given her a straight answer about this, despite the fact that she and Will had been in hospital for over a week. It seemed like an eternity. She was beginning to wonder if there'd ever been a time when she hadn't lived here on a noisy ward, the children brought in by Will's mother to see her, her life shrunk down to a hospital bed cut off from the others on the ward by curtains.

How had her life changed so much? How had she ended up in this place? She remembered being brought in because suddenly, after much darkness, she was dazzled by white lights, orb after orb beaming down on her as she sailed beneath them, people all around her. She was in pain but in such a fundamental way that it became almost more of a mental challenge than a physical one. They took her to strange rooms with more light, where she was pummelled and probed, her dress cut off her (*My dress*, she thought, whenever she remembered. *Where can it be? Discarded in a bin somewhere, cut into shreds*. It seemed as though the dress represented her previous life – expensive frippery, gone forever) and a needle pressed into her skin, the pain negligible compared to the elemental agony she was in elsewhere in her body. She'd sunk into blessed oblivion after that.

When she woke, hours later, the pain was different: sharper, more intense, more localised instead of possessing her whole body. But that was good, wasn't it? It meant she was still alive.

What the hell happened? she thought, dazed. Then it came flashing into her mind. *Will wanted to kill us. He wanted to kill us both.*

She knew it was true and yet it was so utterly incredible that the knowledge left her numb. As she lay in her hospital bed, stunned and immobile, her leg now heavy with plaster, pictures of Will riffled through her mind: he was standing in the kitchen in his old grey T-shirt, turning to laugh as he poured out coffee; he was heading into the sea in Dorset, Carrie clinging on to his hand as she raced along beside him; he was jiggling Joe on his lap and singing a song to him, making him chortle; he was kissing the children just before they went to sleep. She knew he hadn't been that Will for quite a while, but even so, how could he possibly want to orphan them, abandon them? How could he imagine leaving them? How could he take her away too? Hot tears leaked from the outer corners of her eyes to be absorbed by the thick white bandages that encased her head.

But I'm still here, she thought. All she knew was that she had to survive.

★   ★   ★

At first she didn't even wonder what had happened to Will. No one told her anything. She assumed that he was dead – they'd obviously been in a traumatic crash of enormous impact; he must surely have been killed. She didn't care, she realised. She hoped he *was* dead, so that she would never have to face him, look him in the eye, say something to him. Dead or alive, though, he stalked her dreams, trying to get her attention, shout at her, while she ran away as fast as she could, only to come face to face with him around some corner. Sometimes he was trying to get to the children to kill them, and her dream would take her on a desperate, dreadful journey to stop him.

She'd wake, tearful, breathless and panting, and find herself in the relative silence of the night-time ward, trying to recover from the panic. Nausea swirled around her stomach and she almost longed for the release of vomiting. Everything in her was revolted by Will now.

On the first morning, she'd woken to find her brother sitting at her bedside, hunched over with his hands clasped tightly together, his eyes reddened.

'Em? Em?' he'd said huskily, his voice shaking a little. 'Em, are you okay?'

She'd groaned. Speech hadn't come. Her tongue had been too thickened, her jaw restricted by the bandage wound tightly round her skull. Besides, every tiny movement hurt, and as her brain was moving sluggishly, she couldn't seem to get her thoughts from her mind to her mouth.

'Oh God, I can't believe this.' Tom blinked hard, his lips tightening. 'Christ, Em, what happened? You were both nearly killed. Was Will driving too fast? That bloody car of his, I knew it was a deathtrap.'

She'd wanted to shout, *He did it on purpose, he tried to kill me!* But only another groan came out.

'You're all right,' he said, reaching out and taking her hand. He squeezed it gently. 'You've been amazingly lucky. You've broken your leg just above the ankle, and you're a mass of cuts and bruises, and . . .' His eyes flickered up over her face and she knew he was looking at the bandages swaddling her head. He looked away from them quickly and smiled at her. 'And a few other gashes here and there, but you're going to be fine.'

Fine? Fine seemed an unimaginable condition that might be achieved in some future so remote it was hardly worth considering. All she could do right now was exist from moment to moment, considering in turn the bits of her that hurt or ached or tingled or itched, and wondering how she could endure it.

God, I'm thirsty, she realised. She had been continually thirsty since she had arrived in this place. The little cups of water they gave her to wash down pills were tormentingly small. Despite the dryness of her mouth, there was one word that she managed to force out through her swollen lips. It came out thick and husky.

'Children,' she whispered. '*Children.*'

Tom's grasp tightened around her fingers. 'Don't worry, they're okay. They're completely fine. They went to Polly's last night. She can keep them for a bit. I'll move in and look after them if you need me to.'

In a distant part of her brain, a voice was piping up with problems. Polly couldn't be expected to look after the children for long; she had three of her own, one of them a small baby. Tom could move in, but how would he know the children's routine? He was a single man with no real experience of small children. How could it possibly work? But her brain refused to let her care. It knew her limitations, it seemed. It told her that there was nothing she could do but lie here and attempt to recover her strength. As a kind of recompense, it offered another word.

'*Diana,*' she whispered. Will's mother would know how to look after the children. She had taken them for weekend stays and knew what they needed.

Tom nodded. 'She's here. She's with Will at the moment. I'll talk to her as well. I'm sure we can sort out the children between us. You mustn't worry, Em, we'll take care of everything.'

She wished it could be so easily solved, this terrible mess she'd woken and found herself in. But between Polly, Diana and Tom, she had to trust that the children would be looked after.

'Shall I bring them in to see you?' Tom asked earnestly.

She shook her head as well as she could, a

movement that turned out to be tiny, barely more than a shift. She longed for them but she didn't want them to see her like this, it would frighten them.

'Maybe another day soon,' Tom said, understanding. 'You have to rest. You must sleep and concentrate on healing.'

She sighed. A moment later she slipped into sleep and when she woke again from another racing nightmare, she was alone. It was then that she remembered Tom's words – *You were both nearly killed . . . Diana is with Will* – and realised with horror what they meant.

She began to shake and a violent sickness swept through her.

Oh Christ. Will's alive.

Now here she was standing in front of him, watching his chest rise and fall, obedient to the commands of the machine keeping him in existence, as he occupied the strange half-world between life and death.

Rita carried on her checks, recording the results on Will's notes. Emily stared hard at the face just visible beneath the tubing, the mask and the bandages.

All I hope is that I never have to see you again in my life.

'Mrs Conway?'

The consultant smiled down at her. His little flock

of medical students hovered behind him, peering over his shoulder with earnest expressions.

She turned to look at him. She'd been in hospital for a lifetime, or so it felt. *How long is it? A month?* It was something like that. Or perhaps it was just a few weeks.

'We are going to discharge you today. You can go home.' He smiled at her with jollity, as though this meant she was completely restored to health, the same Emily as the one before she had arrived here.

'That's good,' she said blankly. Home? She wanted to go home, of course, but here at least she was safe. No one had tried to make her do anything impossible, or tell her things she was too frightened to hear. At home, she would have to start facing life again. It would be her job to piece together the fragments of the existence that had been shattered by Will. She was afraid.

The consultant nodded. 'You'll be seen as an outpatient for your leg . . .' *Eight weeks in plaster at least, they said, then physio to rebuild its strength.* 'And as for the facial wounds, they're healing very nicely.' He nodded with satisfaction. 'Very nicely indeed. You're lucky that Mr Watkins is such a competent plastic surgeon.'

She already knew that something awful lay underneath the bandages down the left side of her face. The thick swaddling had gradually reduced to bulky bandages and was now a dressing taped from the side of her skull down past her ear to the curve of her jaw. It had been lifted and inspected only by medical staff. By the time she was standing in front of the mirror in the loos, it had been covered again, the clean snowy white outer covering making whatever was underneath look benign, almost innocent. When her friends had come in, they'd studiously avoided talking too much about the injury to her face, accepting it when she said, 'Oh, a bit of a cut, apparently. It'll be fine.' She didn't mention the plastic surgeon's work, or the intricate cleaning and checking that went on when the nurses uncovered it, or the antibiotics she was on.

'You're so lucky!' they said almost admiringly. 'It could have been so much worse. Fancy getting out of a crash like that with some minor cuts and a broken leg!'

Then they remembered Will and clutched her hand, offering all their help and support and anything, anything they could do.

She said they were very kind and of course she would ask.

But what can they do?

Besides, it was her dirty secret that if she had her way, Will wouldn't be lying upstairs being kept alive in a peaceful painless sleep. He'd be dead.

When they'd asked what happened that night, she said she couldn't remember. The police had come to interview her about the accident, and the insurers had sent an assessor to talk to her as well, and she'd said the same thing: that she had a complete memory blank. They all seemed to understand and accept this, and no one pushed her on it. She didn't know why she couldn't tell anyone the truth, except that she felt ashamed of it – perhaps for not being able to stop him, perhaps because only a monster would do such a thing, and how had she not known that's what he was?

Maybe when she got home, discovered whatever was waiting for her – letters, phone messages – she might be able to start admitting the awful, shaming, stupid, cruel thing that had happened to them, not by accident but by terrible and malicious design. But at the moment it was such a sickeningly awful reflection on Will and by extension on her, that she couldn't bring herself to imagine telling anyone. It would make her look at all sorts of other things she had hidden from herself.

'When do I go?' she asked at last.

'We'll start discharge right away,' the doctor said, 'and I'll pass you on to the very competent care of the outpatients' department. You should be able to leave this afternoon.'

This afternoon? She longed to be in her own space again, with her own bed and bathroom, to have the ability to make a cup of decent tea when she wanted one. She'd craved the presence of the children, their sweet scent and the comfort of their cosy room. *But* . . . The fear gripped her again. *I'm afraid.*

'I'm sure you'll be pleased to go home,' said the consultant. 'You'll need to arrange for someone to collect you, though. Will that be a problem?'

'I don't think so.'

'Good. Then goodbye, Mrs Conway, and all the best for your continued recovery.' He turned to go, his brood of students following obediently.

'Doctor . . .'

He swung back, peering at her over his glasses. 'Yes?'

'I . . . I . . .' She swallowed. 'My . . . husband. How is he?'

The smiled faded, his expression became grave. 'Much the same, I believe. But you'll need to talk to the staff in intensive care about that.'

Tom came to get her at four o'clock, driving his small white van. Emily limped on her crutches through the wide hospital corridors with their signs to the many departments every few paces. Some of the nurses stopped to say goodbye and good luck, but on the whole, she left unnoticed, feeling as though her trauma was just one small story in this vast house of human sorrow.

The van made slow progress on the way back to the house. Christmas had come and gone in her absence, and the decorations had been taken down. She was grateful to Tom for not talking too much as she absorbed the strange sensation of being out in the world again. She felt unanchored, cut loose, afraid that if she wasn't careful, she could spiral up and out of the car and away over the London sky. It was such a curious feeling – knowing that she was going home after leaving weeks before, thinking she was going to a party.

'Diana's going to bring the children back later,' Tom said conversationally. 'And I'm going to stay with you for a while. No arguments.'

'Okay,' Emily agreed, relieved. She didn't want any kind of argument. She could only take kindness at the moment.

'Polly's going to look in too. Apparently your freezer is full to bursting with stews and lasagnes. The girls have all been busy.'

'That's nice,' she said. The thought of the fridge packed with homely, comforting food was a balance to the fear she felt of whatever was lying on the mat.

Tom slid his gaze across to her as he drove. 'You okay?'

She nodded. Of course she wasn't okay. But she was alive and she was going home to the children. That was all that mattered right now.

Tom parked in front of the house. From the outside it looked just the same, perhaps a little abandoned, with no sign of life behind the windows. The burglar alarm was off. No one could have set it since they'd left that night. She felt a sudden feverish hope that there had been a break-in and everything inside had been taken, so that she could consider the past utterly wiped out and she would be free to start again with the children. Then she felt just as severe a panic that it might have been, and she'd be left stripped bare of her entire life.

Oh God, I have no idea what I want. Why has

everything become so terrible? Why the hell did this have to happen?

The picture of Will on his bed rose before her eyes again and she felt the same murderous rage, the desire to yank out the tubes and then pick something up and begin to pound it down on his head and . . .

She gasped for breath under the onslaught of her rage, trying to damp it down and hide the dread cramping her chest as Tom got her keys from the plastic bag that contained all her possessions. The evening purse she'd had on the night of the crash had vanished along with her dress and shoes. Polly had brought in the clothes she was wearing. Tom came round to her side and helped her get out of the car. She moved slowly, manoeuvring her plastered leg and taking the crutches from Tom. She watched apprehensively as he went ahead down the path and unlocked the house. The front door swung open but the mat was clear of post, just littered with a few circulars. As she limped inside behind him, her gaze flew to the hall table and there it was: a neat pile of unopened envelopes. The coloured ones were probably get-well and sympathy cards, but there were enough manila and white window-fronted ones to make her feel sick and shaky.

Ignore them for now. They'll wait a bit longer.

The house had a musty chill from being unoccupied. Tom went about switching on lights and the heating, and getting the kettle on so that they could make some coffee while Emily was mute, overwhelmed by the force of the emotions racing through her as she looked at all the familiar things in their places, all blamelessly normal and somehow touchingly unaware that everything had changed.

When they had their coffee and were sitting at the kitchen table, Emily's crutches propped against a chair, Tom tried to keep the atmosphere as jolly as possible but eventually he paused and said gently, 'Do you want to talk about it?'

She gazed at him. He was her junior by four years but they'd always been close. They looked alike, people said, though she couldn't see it. Tom was good-looking, with bright blue eyes, regular features in a well-shaped face and a slightly pointed chin. His sandy hair was short and untidy, and he wore dark stubble speckled with sandy patches. She felt that they'd been closer since their parents had died, now that it was just the two of them left, but of course it had been hard lately to see him often when she had the children and the busyness of daily life to negotiate. She felt a rush of gratitude that he was here for her now. 'You mean talk about the accident?' she asked.

'Yes.' An expression of worry crossed his face. 'You've hardly spoken about it . . . about what happened. You've hardly mentioned the fact that Will is . . . so ill.'

She stared back at him. Inside her head, a flurry of words began, a breathless explanation that felt as though it would never stop. But she couldn't begin to get the torrent to her lips. *I can't tell him.*

I can't tell anyone. I've already lost enough. I can't have them all knowing the truth.

Tom looked down into his mug. 'I'm sorry. I shouldn't press you. You're probably still in shock. It's such a huge thing to happen to you. But I'm worried. I won't lie about that.' He looked back up at her, sorrow in his eyes. 'It's brought back such awful memories, Em . . . of when Mum and Dad died. Their accident. I thought I'd lost you too.'

'I know. I'm so sorry to put you through that.' She bit her lip. She'd guessed how awful it must have been for him, to think his sister might die in the same senseless way their parents had been killed. 'But I'm still here.'

'You're not yourself, though I suppose that's hardly surprising. I thought it might help to talk a bit, that's all. You haven't said a word about how you feel.'

Emily wrapped her chilly fingers around the hot mug, relishing the sting of heat. That was another thing. She'd been constantly cold since the accident. She was thinner, perhaps that was why. But this tingling chill in her hands and feet was frequently there, banished only when she finally managed to sleep. She longed for a hot bath to soothe and comfort her, but with this plaster on her leg, it was impossible.

She knew she had to speak. She wanted to tell Tom what was wrong but she felt an impassable barrier between the words in her head and her mouth. She couldn't tell him, or anyone, the truth about the crash. There was a darkness around it that she couldn't bear to look into herself, let alone speak about. She opened her mouth and let her thoughts emerge as they wanted. 'Diana came to see me yesterday,' she said.

Tom glanced up, glad that she had initiated something. 'Yes? What did she say?'

'It wasn't the first time she came. She visited me just after the accident. She didn't say much then – just held my hand and said, "I'm sorry".'

'We're all sorry,' Tom replied earnestly. 'More than you can know.'

'No, not like that. She wasn't saying that she sympathised. She was apologising.'

'Apologising?' Tom frowned. 'For what?'

'The accident.'

'Why should she apologise for it? She wasn't to blame.'

'But Will was. He was driving. Perhaps she felt she ought to apologise on his behalf.'

Tom snorted. 'I'm surprised she'd ever blame Will for anything. If she hadn't worshipped him quite so devotedly his whole life, perhaps he might be less of a shit sometimes.' He flicked his gaze up to her. Usually when he said something like this, she rebuked him immediately, made excuses for Will. But she said nothing. 'Sorry,' he said, as though he was prepared to go through the usual routine even if she didn't play her part. 'I know I shouldn't – not when Will is lying in hospital in a coma.' He closed his eyes, and screwed up his face, then opened them again. 'Christ, I can't believe I really just said those words. This is a totally terrible thing, Em. I want you to know that I'm behind you every step. I might not have been Will's biggest fan, but I wouldn't wish what's happened to him on anybody. He's going to get better, I know it. You're going to get your life back on track.'

She stared at him. *But I don't want him to get better. And my life will never be on track again.*

'So what did she say?' Tom asked.

'What?' She was confused. Her brain still felt as though it was on a two-way system, her involvement with the outside world moving sluggishly while her interior mind raced and talked almost incessantly.

'Diana. When she came to see you yesterday. What did she say?'

Emily remembered. Diana, elegant in a blue skirt, white blouse and grey cardigan, her white hair as carefully styled as ever, had sat by the bed, her hands, veined and liver-spotted, folded in her lap. Her hazel-green eyes, just like Will's, were anxious, full of strain and sadness.

'Oh Emily,' she had said in her soft patrician tones. 'Oh my dear girl. You mustn't worry. He's going to get better. I have absolute faith. We'll get through this together.'

They had never been very close but now the gulf between them felt so vast, they might as well live on different planets. Emily could sense her mother-in-law's deep need for her son to return to her but she understood it only in the vaguest way. She was completely untouched by it.

'Well?' Tom pressed.

'She said we're to go in for a talk from the doctors about Will's condition. They've been doing all their tests – the scans, the imaging, MRI. They're going to give us the long-term prediction.'

Tom reached out and took her hand again. She could see his sympathy for her all over his face. 'Em, I'm so sorry. This is so hard for you. But Will's young and strong. If anyone can recover from this, it's him. But . . . brain injury.' He seemed to wince at the thought. 'God, what a nightmare.'

'I have to think about what will happen if he doesn't come back,' she said. She sipped the hot coffee, letting it burn her tongue before she swallowed it. *Will can't do this*, she thought with a tiny pang of triumph that she was able to lift a cup to her mouth, savour the taste of the coffee, feel it track its hot path down her throat.

Tom nodded seriously.

'There's so much to sort out,' she said, and the surge of sickness returned to her stomach. *How long will I have this house? How long will money come out of the bank machine? What about the bills?*

'Don't think about that now,' Tom said stoutly. He squeezed her hand and let it go. 'Let's just concentrate on getting you all better.'

She nodded, vaguely comforted. If Tom was happy to postpone the moment of truth, then she would be docile and let him protect her from it. But it seemed as if a small wailing siren of panic, one that only she could hear, was sounding from the hall, where the pile of letters waited on the console table.

All I want is the children home. Once they're back, I'll get the strength to look.

CHAPTER 4

'So, Miss Fellbridge, I hope you're not feeling too disappointed.'

Cressie stared at the headmaster, a man who seemed older than her father. In fact, all the staff seemed extremely old. 'Well, I—'

'Lady Atwell said you were rather keener on the primary school.'

'Yes, I had thought . . .' She'd envisaged herself at the huge old Victorian school down the road, surrounded by the shining faces of very young children as she taught them their alphabet and multiplication tables. 'That's what I thought,' she finished lamely.

The headmaster smiled at her. He had white wisps of hair around a shiny bald head and there was something that repelled her about the pink and grey tint to his complexion. But he seemed kindly enough. 'Of course. I know that women are drawn more naturally to the care of the younger ones. And the teaching is not as rigorous as we require in a school like this. Do you know much about us?'

'Nothing,' she said blankly. She had arrived at

St Mary's primary school in Forest Gate that morning, taking an Underground train from Liverpool Street out to Upton Park, a part of London so far from home it was hard to believe it really was still part of the city. She'd enjoyed her tour around the school, the headmistress pointing out the classrooms full of children hard at their books, and she'd watched them racing and squealing in the playground. She'd seen the dear little things lining up for their milk break and noticed how many of them were in patched or too-tight clothes, some with an air of skinny grubbiness, and she'd longed to rush in and make it all better.

But at the end of the tour, the headmistress had suggested that if there was time, she might like to see Fleming Technical College just a short walk away, and had told her that the headmaster, Mr Granville, would be glad to see her. In fact, she'd been bold enough to tell him to expect her. There was no call for extra staff, even volunteers, at the primary school but the college would be glad of additional help, particularly in their English department, and wasn't reading and writing where Miss Fellbridge wanted to offer her services? Wasn't her diploma in literature?

Cressie had been bewildered by the turn of events but could think of no reason why she shouldn't go, and a child from the oldest year had been commandeered to take her there.

'Thank you so much for coming to see us,' the

headmistress had said, shaking her hand. 'I only wish there were more people like you, willing to give up their time to help us in our work.' But the headmistress's smile made Cressie suspicious that she was actually glad to have shaken her off so easily. 'Billy will take you to Fleming. Billy, come straight back, do you hear?'

Billy had marched ahead of her, hands in the pockets of his frayed shorts, and muttered commands when they reached the road – 'Watch yerself, miss, there's the gutter' and 'Mind the bus, miss' – then walked her around a corner and up to the front gate of a large, red-brick building with a boxy regularity that lacked the charm of the primary school but was nevertheless impressive with its three storeys and rows of many-paned windows.

Billy had scampered off before she could thank him and now, after a quick walk around the school with a teacher, she was here with the head in his study.

Mr Granville looked at her over the top of his spectacles. 'We were founded in 1921 as the Fleming Day Continuation Institute, and occupied the congregational hall down the road.' He smiled. 'We've grown a little since then. These premises were built in the thirties, and luckily for us escaped the bombs. Now we've assimilated another school and have become a technical college. Do you know what that means?'

She shook her head. Her own experience of school

seemed vastly simple. She'd arrived at her girls' day school in Kensington at the age of four, smart in shiny Mary Janes, a blue blazer and a miniature straw boater, and had left it fourteen years later, educated. Her brothers had gone away at seven and made their smooth journeys from prep to public school and then to university. But she knew there was a whole other world beyond her experience where things were not so straightforward.

'The pupils here have passed the Eleven Plus, but not with such distinction that they're considered grammar school material. Those who failed entirely, of course, are at the secondary modern. The children we have here are smart and show potential, but they'll never be top academic material. We hope to cater for them by paving the way to rewarding careers that require brains and skill – engineering, design, technologies and so forth. We don't look to the humanities as much here as you would expect in a grammar school.' The headmaster smiled at her again, this time with a conspiratorial air. 'I'm sure you understand me.'

'Yes,' Cressie said. Her spirits swooped downwards. She pictured a mass of eleven-year-olds, still such young children, herded off onto their inexorable paths towards a life in trade, or in skilled work, or else towards university and a profession. Who had the right to decide all this for them? What about their choice, or their potential to grow and develop? Was any child fully formed at eleven? She imagined a child who somehow, unexpectedly, managed to pass the exam and became condemned to the misery of failing expectations, and another who didn't pass despite a clever brain and afterwards was never allowed to use his talents. It didn't seem right somehow that such a big decision was made so early and was then unchangeable.

Mr Granville fixed her with a piercing look. 'This must be very different from what you're used to.'

'Yes . . . I suppose it is.' She felt ashamed somehow, as though she was displaying her pampered upbringing in every expression that crossed her face. *Do I look horrified? I don't mean to.*

'The boys and girls here are from a variety of backgrounds but mostly modest. You mustn't feel too sorry for them. They don't expect or want more than this, I can assure you of that. Many of them resent school, and don't particularly want to be here. Their parents have little understanding of the value of education, and most want their children to leave and begin work as soon as possible. My job – the job of all of us here – is to give those children a solid knowledge of the things they will need to support themselves decently in the future. They must be made to be responsible members of society, men and women who can raise and support families. They need us to help them with firmness and insistence on work and standards. Do you understand that?'

'Of course.' She didn't like the way his voice was taking on a hectoring edge and was filled with a disdain for him because he implied such superiority over the children in his care. Why was he so adamant that their aspirations were so limited? She suddenly saw that his suit was saggy at the seams and his waistcoat had a button dangling by a thread. She noticed hairs in his ears and wondered what he had eaten for lunch and whether he cleaned his shoes himself in the evening. Then she caught herself up, mortified. *But I'm as bad. Sizing him up. Judging him. Wondering if he's a gentleman or not. We're all trapped by wherever we've come from. I hate these boxes. Why can't we get out of them?*

The headmaster said, 'Then if you would like to offer your services here, we'd be very glad of them. We can't pay you, unfortunately, but if you have expenses – bus fares and so on – you can submit them and we shall reimburse you. You may have a lunch here at the school if you require it. We only ask for a commitment of the hours we need for at least a term.' He smiled at her, his eyes bright again, his authority mysteriously restored to him. 'How does that sound?'

She stared at him, flummoxed. She'd intended to work with small children and here she was in a world of adolescence, where education was no longer about the simple certainties of ABC and 1 + 1, but a more serious opening of minds to the complexities of life, the wonders of learning, and the adult world that awaited them just beyond the school gates. Self-doubt fluttered around her. Was she really up to this task? What did she know of the world that most of these boys and girls would grow into, with her life in the tall house in Kensington, looked after by maids and cooks, her allowance paid no matter what. *But,* she said to herself, *that doesn't mean I'm forbidden to offer whatever I can.*

'Of course,' she said firmly. 'I should like to very much.'

Mr Granville's smile broadened. 'Excellent. Then let's go at once to the office and make the arrangements. You can start as soon as you like.'

Cressie left the school feeling oddly invigorated, as though someone had just told her that without any training and barely any equipment she would have to climb a mountain, and she felt a kind of fearful excitement at attempting something so difficult.

She walked back to Upton Park Underground station. Along Queen's Road, there were newly built houses, smart and square, squatter than the old Victorian terraces that flanked them. Opposite was a large stretch of allotments. The bombs had probably flattened a great many of the houses around here, and gradually the old sites were being cleared and developed. She was glad to see it: a new London for the new generation. Something would be done about the lot of the poor. Things would be better when the crumbling old slums harbouring mould and diseases had been ripped down and clean, modern housing with good drains and electrics were put in their place. A new start.

That horrid old man, she thought, remembering Granville, the headmaster. *Writing off all those children just because they're working class. As though they haven't got dreams and aspirations like everyone else. As though they're not capable of living like civilised people because they're not going to the grammar school.*

She wanted fervently to change things and make a difference. She saw herself opening the eyes of the wondering youngsters of Forest Gate to the beauties of poetry and Shakespeare, to books and history. They would step out into the world finer and nobler because of it.

Could I? Is it possible?

Her face flushed with pleasure at the thought that she might achieve something, change lives. Her father thought she was dallying with teaching, just marking time until she married Adam, or someone like him. He was so powerful, so determined, that it was hard to resist his vision of her future. But perhaps she would find the strength to forge her own path. She wouldn't marry at all. She'd devote her life to teaching, create wonderful new methods of imparting knowledge to children, alter hundreds, even thousands, of lives. Perhaps she'd end up as the head of a famous school or college, a distinguished elderly lady, the kind whose portrait hung in the entrance halls of their institution . . .

Cressie drew up short with a gasp. 'Oh bother it! Oh crumbs . . .' She looked at her watch. 'It's impossible, I can't do it.' Cursing her stupidity, she tucked her handbag under her arm and ran as fast she could towards the station.

She emerged red-faced and hot in the late afternoon sun, the station steps leading out into a different world from the one she had descended from in Upton Park, the Georgian elegance contrasting with the wreckage and poverty of East London. She didn't have time to consider it, but instead peered at the letter she was holding, rereading the spidery copperplate hand and deciphering the scrawled map. The black arrows directed her away from the station and the busy main road lined with shops, up the gentle hill and around to the right. Within moments, she was in a quiet leafy neighbourhood of large Regency houses in various states of repair, some spruce and well kept, others fading and bedraggled. The little map pointed her towards a church, the golden spire of which rose high against the blue sky and into a road that skirted the churchyard and led into a near silent street, where only birdsong ruffled the air. The houses were large and white-painted, with tall arched windows. Cressie consulted the letter again. The house she was looking for was number 16, and she found it easily, set back from the road and obscured by a large tree. She peered towards it curiously, looking out

67

for signs of life behind the window. There were none. Pushing open the black wrought-iron gate, she went cautiously up the garden path.

This is horribly embarrassing. She looked at her watch. It was well after four o'clock and she'd been expected at half past two. She considered turning around and going home. She could send an apologetic note saying she'd been unavoidably detained somewhere. After all, what did she owe anyone? This whole thing had not been her idea. In reality, she didn't want to do it at all. It was nothing more than a bore, a stupid distraction from things that really mattered.

As she stood on the path, she saw a flicker of movement behind the glass of the window and realised that now she'd been seen she couldn't leave. Taking a deep breath, she walked along the grass-edged path, up the stone steps to the front door and pressed the bell marked 'Few'.

There was no noise from within and her mood switched from humble apology to irritation.

Well? Where is he? Has he just gone out? Or is he pretending not to be there?

She could hardly blame him if he had gone out, but really, after the long journey back into town and out again, all the way to Blackheath, when she could now be at home having tea and getting ready for the exhibition she was supposed to be attending tonight, if he was playing silly games because he was cross that she was late . . . *Well, honestly . . .*

Then from within came the sound of a door opening and strong determined footsteps crossing a hard surface, and the front door opened. There he was, one hand on the door frame, the other on the handle, in a strangely relaxed attitude. He wore a white shirt under a plain black jumper that was flecked with paint, and black trousers. His brown shoes were spattered with dots of colour: white, scarlet, blue and green. He stared down at her, a smile flickering over his lips.

'Hello,' he said.

Cressie stared up; she stood lower than him on the front step so that he towered above her. He was tall anyway but he seemed to loom over her. She felt the world around her disappear. Everything narrowed down to only him. 'Oh!' she gasped.

He raised his eyebrows. 'Do you have the right place? Or are you selling something? Because I shan't be buying, I'm afraid, unless you are particularly charming. But I'm notoriously hard to please.'

'It's you!' she said, her voice breathless with astonishment.

'Of course it is,' he returned. 'And you are you too.' He smiled again as though they were playing some kind of mysterious game

'But . . .' She stopped, bewildered, looking down at the step as she doubted herself, then she turned her gaze back to his face and felt the same instant jolt of recognition. 'You were on the bus.'

He smiled again, but a frown creased the space

between his brows and he peered more closely at her. 'What?'

'The bus . . .' She felt distinctly odd; not ill but giddy and wrong-footed, as though she'd jumped off a spinning roundabout onto the still ground. 'Piccadilly. You helped me on. I was chasing the bus.'

His eyes narrowed – grey, flecked with green and gold, deep-set beneath straight brows; she felt as though she knew them intimately but she'd only seen them once before in her life – and a look of recognition filled them. His smile grew broader, his lips lifting at one corner more than the other as they revealed the straight white teeth beneath. 'Of course. I thought I'd seen you before. You're the runner girl. Did you manage to make your appointment?'

She nodded. It was like meeting a friend again even though he was a stranger.

'Glad to hear it. And what are you doing here?' He lifted his hand from the door frame and brushed away the lick of hair that fell over his forehead, pushing it back out of his eyes. It fell forward again almost immediately.

'I . . . I'm late.'

He looked enquiringly at her. 'Late? For what?'

'For you!'

'Me!' Surprise filled his eyes.

He's so beautiful. It was the same thought she'd had the first time she'd seen him on the bus. She'd been half looking for him ever since that day last week, but with only the vaguest hope of ever seeing him again. Now here he was, right in front her.

He's the artist.

She said, 'Yes. If you're Ralph Few.' The strange giddy feeling washed over her again. It was like some kind of pleasant sickness – the sort of excitement that meant it was Christmas Day or that some wonderful news was expected. 'I'm Cressida Fellbridge. I'm here for the sitting. At least, I'm late for it. It was at two thirty. Aren't you expecting me?'

He was evidently astonished to hear it, his eyes widening as he looked her up and down. '*You're* Cressida Fellbridge?' Then he burst out laughing, and slapped his hand against the door frame. 'Well, you'd better come in then.'

'Weren't you waiting for me?' she asked, taking a step towards him, half hurt to see him laughing so much at the mention of her name.

'In a way. If I'm honest, I'd completely forgotten you were coming. I've been painting and it tends to wipe things like that from my mind. But you see, Catherine and I were wondering what you'd be like and . . . well, we had someone quite different in mind.' He turned and led the way into the hallway. 'Come this way.'

She went through the front door after him. There was a marble-floored communal hall and a staircase that led up to the first floor and down to the basement. Ahead of them was a glossy black door, half ajar.

'Catherine usually keeps me on track,' he said over his shoulder, pushing the door open further and stepping inside the ground-floor flat. 'But she's not here today. I've been left to my own devices. Look.' He pointed at a large square of black paint on the plain wall of the hallway. On it in white chalk was written a message in a firm, clear hand:

R

   Cressida Fellbridge is coming at half past two. Don't forget! Please offer her tea. I'll be home at five.

   C

Beneath it was more writing which Cressie couldn't understand. It read: *Med: 11, 3.*

It looks like a Bible reading, she thought. *The Book of Med, chapter 11, verse 3.*

'There, you see? What did I say?' Ralph said cheerfully. 'She tries her best, but I'm a tricky customer.' He read the message again and said conversationally, 'Can I offer you a cup of tea?'

'Who's Catherine?' she asked.

'Catherine?' He stood still, his hand going up to his hair again. He pushed the forelock out of his eyes. 'Why . . . she's my wife.'

'Oh.' She felt deflated, as though a sharp pin had pierced her skin and let out the giddy excitement she'd been feeling. *How stupid. As if it matters that he has a wife. Why should it affect me?* 'I don't want any tea, thank you.'

'All right. There's some good stuff, Fortnum's Royal Blend. My current favourite. If you change your mind. Come through to the studio. Catherine was hoping to meet you,' he said, leading the way, 'so she'll be glad of the change of time.'

'I don't think I can stay long,' she said lamely. 'I'm sorry, I've made rather a mess of today.'

'Oh, don't worry at all,' Ralph replied with a shrug. He opened the door to the studio. It was, she realised, the sitting room of the small flat, a well-proportioned room with a high ceiling, a marble fireplace and a huge arched window that stretched almost from floor to ceiling and nearly the width of the wall. It gave out onto a lush green garden and a splendid view of the church she had passed, its spire reaching up into the clear blue sky, the gold hands of the clock on the tower glinting in the afternoon sun. The window framed the picture perfectly. Inside the room was furnished in shabby good taste: a battered old carved wooden sofa, a round mahogany table with mismatched chairs of various ages and stages of decline, a pocked and speckled mirror in an ornate Empire frame propped over the fireplace. On the floor by the hearth was a large marble bust of some hollow-cheeked, Roman-nosed statesman. The wooden floorboards were bare and covered with paint, except where rugs were placed as if to claim a little space for living away from the room's main function as a studio. The walls were hung with pictures – some portraits and some abstract creations in bright jewel colours – and a number of canvases were stacked against them. Near the window stood a large easel with a canvas in progress upon it, and beside it a side table held jars of brushes, old palettes, bottles of oils and spirits, boxes of paints and a pile of stained rags.

'Well, I do think it's strange.' Ralph looked at her gravely, then smiled. It seemed to be his way to stare earnestly, and then to unleash a smile that transformed his solemn handsomeness into delightful boyish charm. The effect on Cressie was powerful: the smile seemed to create a miniature tornado inside her.

'Strange?' she echoed, still gathering her impressions of the room. She wanted to study the paintings and see what they revealed about Ralph.

'That you should be who you are, of course.' He was so tall, almost a foot taller than her. His height gave his boyishness a strength and presence he might otherwise lack. It made something in her respond to him.

She stared at him, unsure what he meant.

'You're the girl I helped on the bus. Very odd that we've already met like that, isn't it? I held your hand long before I knew your name.'

His gaze was strong, direct, and she felt herself almost overcome with giddiness again. Her hands tingled with the memory of his grasp. 'Yes,' she said weakly. 'It's very odd.' She felt as though that first link had pulled them together across time and distance. *But that's so silly – Papa had already started this whole thing. It had nothing to do with the bus.*

Ralph eyed her with a touch of concern. 'Are you sure you won't have that tea? You look a little tired.'

'I . . . perhaps I will, thank you,' she said, glad of a moment to recover herself.

'Good. You won't regret it. Now, you make yourself at home, I won't be a moment.' He headed out of the studio and a few seconds later she heard him turning on a tap. The flat, she realised, was very small: the ground floor of one of those Regency houses that made up in height what it lacked in depth.

She turned to look at the paintings that had been almost vibrating in the corner of her vision as though desperate for her attention. She went to examine them, moving slowly past the hanging unframed canvases, taking them in at a first pass. There were around a dozen, most unfinished, and the portraits seemed to her to be masterly: vivid, intense and lifelike to a point that was almost photographic, and yet with a painterly style that made them the creation of an artist. The colours had a translucent strength as though they were lit from behind, and a particular shade of bright blue appeared again and again: in the colour of a hat, a dress, a tie, a flower in a vase. Many of the subjects were middle-aged men, some in uniform and most in formal suits, but a few were women. One caught her eye: a young woman sitting against a stormy sky, caught in a three-quarters profile.

She had short dark curly hair and intense eyes almost as grey as the sky behind her, and wore a man's overcoat that was too big for her and hung off her shoulders, a shapeless green tunic beneath it. Tucked in her hair was a flower, star-shaped and in that particular shade of rich bright blue. The subject stared out of the picture, her gaze direct and her slight smile unable to conceal the stubbornness of her mouth. One hand was on her hip in an attitude almost of challenge.

'Here we are. Tea for two.' Ralph had returned with a tray bearing a china teapot and two cups and saucers. Nothing matched but everything had a certain loveliness to it. It was good china, she could tell, even though it had the air of something scavenged.

Ralph put the tray on the table and poured out the tea. 'Have you been having a look?'

She nodded. 'What amazing pictures. You're very talented.'

Ralph shrugged. 'Nice of you to say. I'm quite pleased with some of them. Others I can't stand the sight of. But often that has to do with the people I paint. I can't always be choosy.' He flashed her another smile. 'We starving artists have to eat, you know. I take commissions where I can, and most often they're the portrait of some businessman for the boardroom, or a colonel for the mess, or a headmaster for the school hall. Nothing lovely or inspiring about them, just so much puffery and self-importance. But they pay.'

She looked back at the portraits. 'They look brilliant to me.'

'You're very kind. I'm just starting out. I've got to fight for commissions. I'm up against all the members of this or that royal society, the hoary old knights of the art world and the aristocratic lady painters who do the children of dukes. All of them. I'm unknown. And besides, I don't love it.' He gestured with the tea strainer to one of the abstract canvases, spraying drops of tea over the tabletop and the floor. 'That's what I really want to do. But no one wants them. They don't pay the bills. Every time I paint one, Catherine gets furious with me. But I can't help it.'

Cressie stared at the abstract painting. It meant nothing to her except that the colours, like those in the portraits, hummed and vibrated with extraordinary vividness. It was entrancing and seemed to promise revelations if only she could look long enough.

'Here's your tea.' He came towards her, holding out the china cup. She noticed his long, slender fingers. As he came closer, she felt the buzz of his presence and everything about him – the pale fineness of his skin, the thickness of his dark hair – became intense.

'Thank you.' She took it, clutching it in both hands, wondering at the sudden weakness in her arms.

'There's no sugar. Catherine won't allow it.'

'I don't need sugar.' She stared down at the

milky surface of the tea, and then looked back up into his grey-gold eyes.

'So.' He stared down at her. The half-smile played at the corner of his mouth. 'What are we going to do with you?'

He seemed to be looking at her in a way that she'd never been looked at before, really seeing her in intense, microscopic detail – noticing everything about her face and hair but also reading her whole character from the way she held herself and how she returned his gaze.

Why does he make me feel this way? She had to drop her eyes. She couldn't take the power of his stare, the way he seemed to be able to look right into her soul. When she managed to raise her eyes again, he was frowning, thoughtful.

'Yes. I think it's going to be interesting. I think . . .' His voice trailed off. He looked around as if he was trying to find something. 'I wonder how . . . perhaps in profile . . . what you wear will matter . . .' He seemed suddenly irritated. 'Oh, where is Catherine? She should be here.'

Cressie's gaze went to the clock on the mantel. It showed that it was nearly five o'clock. She remembered with a nasty plunge in her stomach that she was supposed to meet her father at half past six. She hastily put her tea down on the table. 'I have to go.'

Ralph looked surprised. 'But Catherine will be here soon. We can discuss what you want, how you'll sit. I can make a preliminary sketch.'

'No, I can't stay. I'm sorry. We'll have to make another appointment.'

'But your tea . . .'

'I'm sure it's delicious but I have to go. I'm sorry, it's my fault – I was so late today. I shouldn't have come at all but I felt I must.' She looked about, agitated. She felt sure that if Catherine returned, she would be kept here another half an hour at least, and that mustn't happen. 'Please forgive me.'

'Of course.' He looked startled but not annoyed. 'You're the sitter. We must do whatever suits you. I'm usually here.'

'Do you have a telephone?'

'There's a communal one in the hall that receives calls. Usually we get to it first as we're on the ground floor. I put the number on the letter.'

'Then I'll telephone.' She felt as though she'd woken from an afternoon nap: groggy and shaking off dreams. 'Goodbye.'

'I'll see you out,' he said, leading her back down the narrow hall to the front door. He watched her as she hurried down the steps and towards the gate.

'Thank you!' she called over her shoulder as she went.

He waved after her but said nothing.

CHAPTER 5

Diana brought Carrie and Joe home the same day Emily returned from the hospital and the moment they pelted back into the house, yelling with excitement at seeing her again, life and light seemed to return to it. They dashed into her arms, not even noticing the plaster on her leg or the bandage on her face, overwhelmed with delight at being with her, and covered her with wet kisses. Everything about them – their bright faces, the touch of their soft skin, the sweet scent of their hair – filled her with a pleasure that made her feel alive again for the first time since the accident. They were with her, at home. Her two reasons for being were back and she could begin to face the work that had to be done to protect them.

Tom made a cup of tea for Diana while the children played at Emily's feet, rushing off to get toys from the playroom and then settling back close to their mother as though loath to be far from her. Emily reached out to touch their hair or their arms as they played, wanting continual reassurance of their presence. Each touch seemed to dispel the emptiness she'd been feeling, the longing she'd had for them. Strength began to creep back into her body.

'How are you going to cope, Emily?' Diana asked, her expression worried. 'I'm exhausted even though I've had plenty of help with the temporary nanny, and I'm not recovering from a serious accident.'

'I'll be fine,' Emily said firmly. 'Besides, I'll have plenty of help and the leg will be mended before too long.'

Diana looked down at the plaster with scepticism. 'Really? But you're some weeks off that, aren't you? I don't like to think of you here all on your own like this. Perhaps you should come and stay with me. It'll be a bit of a squeeze but we'll manage. That way I won't have to worry about you as well as Will.'

Emily stared at her with dismay. The thought of being taken from home, after the huge struggle she'd been through to get back here, was horrible. She didn't want to live by someone else's rules in a place that wasn't her own. Diana's house was comfortable enough – warm, orderly, tasteful and always spotlessly clean – but she would be a guest and no matter how kindly Diana's intentions might be, Emily could foresee that most of her time would be spent keeping Carrie from playing with precious ornaments and Joe from spilling food on the cream carpets. 'Oh, no . . . really . . .'

Tom spoke from the sink where he was rinsing

out mugs. 'There's no need, Diana. I'm going to be here.'

'You?' Diana looked over at him as though she'd seen him for the first time. She was well aware of Tom's existence but he counted for little in her assessment of the world and the worth of the people in it. Here was a man in his thirties with no apparent career – freelance graphic design didn't really count for much – no property, no family of his own. To her, he had slipped through the net, one of those children for whose parents one felt sympathy because their offspring had failed to amount to anything.

Emily stared at her brother. She'd expected him to be around but even though he'd offered to move in, she'd imagined there would be too many practical difficulties. Was he serious?

He gazed back at Diana with a frank, open look. 'That's right.' He put a rinsed cup on the draining board. 'I'm happy to. I'm perfectly able to help Emily when she needs me.'

Perhaps he's right, Emily thought. *The children adore him. Why not?* She felt relieved that she would not be entirely alone, and looked over at Diana, who was absorbing this.

'Well,' her mother-in-law said, 'if it's been decided—'

'It has,' Tom said firmly.

'All right then.' She looked to Emily. 'I'm glad you'll have help, dear. I can't pretend I haven't had some sleepless hours thinking about it all.'

She sighed and looked suddenly older, her eyes tired, the skin beneath them dark and puffy. 'This has all been so terrible.' She shook her head, then mustered a smile. 'But we can't be beaten by this. We have to stay strong. For Will.' She leaned over and took Emily's hand, her eyes anxious. 'You're coming to the hospital on Thursday, aren't you? For the progress report?'

Emily nodded.

'Good.' She tightened her grasp around Emily's hand. 'Together we can bring him back. I'm certain of it.'

Emily stared at her, wondering if she could ever tell Diana the truth. Will was her adored only son, unable to do wrong in her eyes. *She just wouldn't believe me, that's all there is to it. And besides, she's all Will has now.*

But there was still the matter of whatever lay in those envelopes in the hall.

Two days later, they were still unopened. Tom had put them all by her plate at breakfast, and she'd opened the cards – around two dozen of them, some from people she'd not thought of in years – and put them up around the kitchen, even though she had no interest in looking at them. She even opened all the junk mail almost as reverently as the cards, reading all the offers of credit cards and broadband deals, leafing slowly through the catalogues as though she really were considering buying a heritage-style kilt, fake flowers or the latest cashmere collections. The rest – the official-looking ones – stayed unopened on the table. They moved to the windowsill and sat there ignored, each postal delivery bringing a few more to add to the pile.

When Polly came round, her eagle eyes spotted them at once. 'That's a lot of post,' she said, holding her struggling toddler on her lap and trying to wrestle a biscuit off her. 'No, darling, you've had enough, you really have. Give it to me.'

Ruby squealed and screwed up her eyes with the effort of holding on to her prize. Joe was heavy on Emily's lap, lying back against her, his head on her arm and his feet resting on her cast. He wanted to be close to her all the time, was constantly climbing on her or begging to be held. Then he would nuzzle in to her the way he had when he was a newborn, and stay still, as though he was drawing something vital from her closeness. Polly's baby lay asleep in the pram in the hall.

'Yes, it is a lot,' Emily said, stroking a hand over Joe's soft head. She longed to tell Polly what had happened but she was afraid to. As soon as she voiced the truth, things would start to happen in earnest. She'd be made to face the situation. Someone would make her find out what was going on and then her world – the one she felt she was sustaining by the force of her imagination alone – would start to implode. As it was, she knew she was living on borrowed time. She'd had to order a supermarket shop online and as she'd pressed

'Pay now', she'd felt almost like vomiting with fear at the thought that her payment card might be rejected. But after a couple of sickening seconds, the message had flashed up that her order had been confirmed. The relief had been almost overwhelming.

Polly eyed the envelopes again. 'I suppose it's been building up the whole time you've been in hospital.'

Emily nodded. 'Weeks' worth. I've got to start working through it. I'm not sure I can face it.'

Ruby yelled again, and Polly gave up her struggle for the biscuit. 'All right, have it then. You'll only wake Bert if you scream like that. Off you go.' She released her writhing child onto the floor and leaned in towards Emily. 'Is everything okay, Em? I mean, with Will in hospital and not working. What about his job? What's happening?'

'They've been very understanding,' Emily lied. She felt like a lowlife. *How can I lie to her? She's been nothing but a friend to me.* They'd been close ever since they'd met in the local antenatal classes when they'd been pregnant with their first babies. *Polly cares, I know that. She'd only want to help me.* And yet the truth stubbornly refused to come out. It would show everyone what a sham it had all been. They would know things Emily could hardly bear to acknowledge to herself, even now. 'They've said they'll keep his job for him until we know more.'

'That's good.' Polly smiled but she still looked

concerned. 'But his wage . . . I mean, are they paying him?'

'The first three months,' Emily said, wondering how the lies came so smoothly. 'But after that, I'm not sure. I think Will has some kind of insurance in case he gets ill. I'll have to look it out. But there's no need to worry.'

Polly looked reassured. 'Will strikes me as the kind of guy who's been very careful. He's probably saved a lot too.'

Emily nodded. It was easy to talk about this Will – the Will everybody else knew. The decent family man. The prudent investor. The perfect husband. 'Oh yes. He's a cautious type. We're going to be perfectly all right.'

'And there's the money your parents left you,' Polly reminded her. 'You've kept that, haven't you?'

'I was going to use it for school fees,' Emily said vaguely, remembering that once, in a different life, she'd had hopes and expectations that had now utterly vanished. 'If Will couldn't cover it. I suppose I might need the money for something else now.'

'Well, it's terrific that it's there for you,' Polly said comfortingly. 'We never know what life is going to throw at us, do we? Thank goodness your parents were able to leave something.'

Emily stared at the floor, noticing how the lines between the floorboards were melting and bending in her vision. She felt very calm, as though everything she'd said to Polly was true, and her legacy was still sitting there in the bank, a little pile of security.

'If you needed help, you would tell me, wouldn't you?' Polly asked earnestly.

'Of course. But we're going to be fine.' She smiled. 'More coffee?'

But on the windowsill, the pile of letters seemed to emit a hum of malevolence: *Open us, open us, open us . . .*

She woke, almost choking, from another nightmare. They plagued her sleep, not letting her get more than a few undisturbed hours at a time. Now that she was home, they seemed worse than ever. Perhaps it was not helped by her fear of returning to the hospital tomorrow and whatever news was waiting for her there.

In this dream, she'd been in the intensive care room where Will was lying comatose, with only the hiss of the ventilator and the beeps of the machines making any sound. She'd gone over to his bed, feeling herself pulled towards him despite her revulsion. Standing next to him, she'd stared down at his inert body and his closed eyes, wondering what was going on inside his head and whether he could hear or sense her, when suddenly his eyes had flicked open and his hand had reached up lightning fast to grasp her round the throat and start to choke her. She'd fought desperately to make him release his grip but it was like an iron vice, squeezing her breath out, killing her, separating her forever from the children . . .

'Oh Christ,' she said out loud, panting and

recovering herself. It never got easier, no matter that she was beginning to realise inside her dream that she was dreaming. It didn't make the experience less vivid. She turned over to get back to sleep and realised that she could hear a noise coming from downstairs. After listening for a moment, she manoeuvred herself out of bed, grabbing her crutches, and went down the stairs as quietly as she could, the carpet muffling her steps. In the hall, she wondered if Tom was watching television, then realised that the sound was coming from the kitchen. She went cautiously down the corridor, her stomach fluttering with nerves but nothing like the desperate terror she felt in her dreams.

Perhaps, in a strange way, I'm getting braver.

She went to where the kitchen door stood ajar, and looked through. Tom was at the kitchen table with his back to her, sitting in front of his open laptop in the darkness, the room lit only by the glow from the screen. He was watching some kind of film – for a moment she wondered if it might be pornography but the images were not of people – with the volume turned down low. In a saucer to the side sat a burning roll-up cigarette, the smoke curling prettily in the light from the computer. There was a strong aroma of cannabis.

'Tom?'

He jumped violently and turned round. 'Oh! Em, hi. Sorry, I thought you were asleep.' He turned back hurriedly to his screen and froze the images, then picked up the roll-up and squashed it out on the plate. He looked back, sheepish. 'Sorry. I know I shouldn't smoke inside. I was going to go out into the garden but it's raining. I thought the smell would be gone by morning.'

She went in, limping over the wooden floor, and sat down in the chair nearest to him. 'What is it?'

He shrugged. 'Just a joint.'

'I didn't know you still smoked this stuff.' She looked at the bent dead roll-up in the saucer. Tom had been a big cannabis smoker in his twenties but he'd become clean-living since then, turning vegetarian and hardly touching alcohol. She'd imagined that smoking joints had gone the same way, but clearly not.

'Occasionally,' he said. He stared at the ceiling and blinked hard. 'When I'm stressed, I guess.'

'Are you stressed now?'

'Of course. Your accident. All of this. I'm worried about you. This helps me calm down.'

She looked at him, feeling suddenly selfish. She hadn't really thought of much beyond her own world for so long now, she'd almost forgotten that life went on as normal for other people. She'd taken everything Tom had to offer without really thinking about him. 'How are you? How's work?'

He smiled at her. 'Stressful. When isn't it?'

'Deadlines?'

'Of course. I've got to finish a commission for that company in Shoreditch, and I'm trying to win a pitch for the autumn. I need to get the preliminary designs sent over so that they can decide if they want to invite me to apply for the final stages.'

'You shouldn't be here looking after us,' she said, worried. She remembered that Tom had been working for a small company too, using their space for his own work as well as theirs. 'You should be working in the studio. Doesn't Shelley mind that you're not there?'

Tom picked up the dead joint and started shredding it into the saucer, releasing more of its pungent aroma. 'I'll get it done, don't worry. When I'm sure you're all right, I'll be able to get to the studio and get some work under my belt. Shelley knows what's happened, she doesn't mind a bit of a delay. And I also need to relax' – he indicated the scattered weed in the saucer – 'and this helps.'

'Does it?' She looked at it suspiciously. She'd always felt that the relaxing nature of drugs was mythical. Those claims were deceptive: they were stimulants or depressants masquerading as something else and rarely designed to create states of true calm.

'Yes.' Tom sounded defensive. 'It helps me. Look, I won't smoke here, okay? I shouldn't have done, it was stupid.'

Emily bit her lip. Maybe he was right, and he did find smoking calming. *I don't want to act like some kind of sanctimonious older sister.* 'Okay. You can smoke outside, I suppose . . .'

'No, don't worry. I won't.'

She looked over to the frozen image on the screen,

seeing buildings and fuzzy objects in the sky above them. As Tom noticed where she was gazing, he closed the page with a quick movement.

'What were you watching?' she asked, interested.

'Just YouTube. A documentary.'

'What about?'

'Oh . . .' He looked vague. 'About what's really going on in the world. You know.'

'No.' She frowned. 'What do you mean?'

He paused as though wondering what to reveal, blinking fast in the way he did when considering things. 'Well . . .' He laughed lightly. 'Just stuff. The kind of things you'll laugh at. You won't believe it, that's all.'

'Believe what?' She smiled, glad to hear him laugh. 'Try me. Go on.'

He fixed her with his blue stare. 'That the world is under attack.'

She laughed uncertainly. 'Under attack?'

'Yeah. From within.'

'What do you mean?'

'I mean . . . there are powerful and dangerous forces at work in the world, ones that want to control us all and prevent us from having access to the great knowledge there is out there, the knowledge that will transform mankind and save us.'

She stared back at him, wondering if he was joking or playing a part, pretending to be paranoid. 'What are you talking about? What kind of forces?'

He shrugged. 'The people at the top of governments.

Cabals of the industrialists, arms dealers, oil tycoons, media barons – everyone with a vested interested in keeping us all in a state of unknowing stupidity, addicting us to material things and stupid gossip to keep us all in our place. While they destroy the planet in the pursuit of power and money.'

She was startled at the strength of his tone. She'd never heard him express ideas like this before. Perhaps it was the cannabis talking. How much of it had he smoked?

'Oh. Right.' She sounded uncertain, she could hear it in her voice. 'You mean . . . like . . . the American government?'

'The entire capitalist right-wing world power,' he retorted, then seemed to catch himself up. He sighed. 'Sorry. I shouldn't have said anything.' He sat back in his chair. 'I've been really worried about you, Em. For a long time. From the time you married Will, if I'm completely honest.' He looked over at her with sudden intensity. 'This accident has brought it all to the surface, hasn't it? Now your life has changed course so radically.'

'Don't worry about me,' Emily said. She didn't want to talk about the accident. 'You're my little brother. I should be worried about *you*.'

Tom smiled wryly. 'We worry about each other, right? After all, right now, we're all we've got. We'd better stick together.'

Emily nodded, glad that his smile seemed to restore him to the Tom she knew and loved, the straightforward one with his design work, his devotion to martial arts and his love of country music. She wasn't sure if she could cope with anything more complicated at the moment.

But it isn't that simple. It never is.

Limping through the sliding glass doors into the hospital, Emily felt instantly sick and panicked. Every step she took inside this place brought her closer to Will, and that knowledge conjured up the powerful feelings she had been experiencing in her nightmares: panic, fear and dread.

Once I loved him. The thought floated into her mind, bringing with it the same mild surprise that came when she remembered a band she'd once revered, or a fashion she'd yearned to wear. The woman who'd loved Will, longed to hear him walk through the door in the evening, pressed up against his warm body at night, leaned in for kisses and desired him to make love to her, was gone – that Emily was another creature from a different life. Now whenever she thought of him, she was possessed by the instincts of an animal in danger: alert, with adrenalin surging through her, teeth bared, ready to fight.

He's my deadly enemy now.

Diana was waiting for her just inside, sitting on one of the orange plastic chairs in the lobby, looking as though she was on her way to a smart luncheon party in a silk pleated skirt, navy jacket, strings of pearls, and patent court shoes. A neat handbag in navy crocodile leather hung over one arm.

93

This will be part of her way of coping, Emily thought. *Keeping up her appearances, as though she's the kind of person that nasty things like this simply don't happen to.*

Diana got up when she saw Emily and waved to attract her attention, as though she wasn't immediately noticeable among the tracksuits and dressing gowns around her. 'Hello! Emily! Over here!'

'Hi, Diana.' When she got close enough, she leaned in to kiss her mother-in-law's cheek, inhaling the powdery rose scent of her skin. 'Have you been here long?'

'I just arrived. Shall we go straight up? It's nearly time for the meeting.'

The lift, broad and long enough to contain hospital beds, took them up to the sixth floor and the Gerratt wing. 'I'm going to sit with him for a while afterwards,' Diana said as the lift ascended. 'Will you join me?'

Emily imagined sitting by Will's bed, sick and shaking, prepared to strike if he moved a muscle, while his mother sat placidly beside her, not noticing anything was wrong, her attention focused on the one person who was entirely oblivious of her. 'No, I need to get back home. The children hated me coming out as it is.'

Diana fixed her with an earnest look. 'Have you thought about bringing the children here? Don't you think they ought to see their father?'

Emily pulled in a sharp breath, filled with horror

at the thought of bringing Carrie and Joe anywhere near this place or the man lying upstairs, who'd been happy to orphan them. 'No,' she said sharply.

Diana blinked in mild surprise at the strength of her retort. 'But it might help him. It might help bring Will back if he can hear their voices.'

'We don't know what he can hear,' Emily replied, trying to sound calmer. 'And I think it would be terrible for the children to see their father in that state. They'll never believe he can get better – it would be traumatic to see him unable to wake up or speak.'

Diana sighed. 'Perhaps you're right,' she said sadly. 'But wouldn't it be worth it, if it brings him back?'

Emily was prevented from having to answer by the lift doors opening and the two of them having to squeeze out past the people on their way to other floors. Diana led the way, knowing the route to the unit very well, and they reported to the reception desk. After a short spell in the busy waiting area, where televisions were showing a daytime home improvement show, they were called to the consultant's rooms.

Mr Theodoropulous was sitting behind his desk, casual in rolled shirtsleeves and open collar. He got up as the women came in and emerged to shake their hands, before returning to his seat and picking up a black fountain pen. He began to doodle on a pad, looking up at them only occasionally, as though he was shy of meeting their gaze. Emily wondered if this was a habit he had when delivering bad news, or if he did it all the time.

He gave them a fast preamble, recapping what they already knew: Will's severe traumatic brain injury; the miracle that he was alive at all; the preliminary scans and imaging that were determining the extent of the damage he'd suffered.

'The brain, you see,' Mr Theodoropulous said, 'is extremely fragile, which is why it's encased in the very hard structure of our skull. We can injure it in a variety of ways: the most common is non-traumatic, usually through infection, stroke or chemical overdose. Most comas are brought on by drug overdose of some sort. But the other way we can hurt it is by trauma – a violent blow to the head. And that's of course what Will suffered in the car accident. He took a big impact that's caused a lot of injury through bruising and internal haemorrhage. As you know, we had to operate at once to release the pressure on his brain and drain off the fluid, and we made the decision to keep him in an artificial coma while we assessed what the damage is. Often the secondary injury, which takes place after the actual impact, can cause more damage than the first. So the impact might not be terrible, but the fluid released into the brain, for example, can start the real problems. We still don't understand exactly how or why this happens – it's a complex process of biochemical cascades that can cause ischaemia, cerebral hypoxia, cerebral oedema or intracranial pressure . . .' He had begun to talk more rapidly, as if finding a kind of retreat in the medical terms falling from his lips.

For God's sake, thought Emily, feeling frantic. *Just tell me if he's going to wake up or not!*

'Have there been any developments?' Diana asked, interrupting. 'When is Will going to regain consciousness?'

Emily was briefly grateful for Diana's obstinate persistence. At least she refused to be brushed off.

Mr Theodoropulous looked up briefly then returned to his geometric doodling. 'Our tests have established that Will's brainstem is functioning. But we've had to keep him in a coma for over three weeks, and we have reason to think that even without the drugs keeping him under, he's likely to remain in a comatose state. Generally, the longer the patient remains that way, the more dangerous it is for his long-term outlook. We would like to begin the process of withdrawing the coma-inducing drugs and see what happens.'

'But he'll wake up, won't he?' Diana demanded quickly. 'Once you take your drugs away. I told you weeks ago you should do that. People wake up from comas all the time. Will's only been unconscious a few weeks, and I've read about people waking up after months or even years.'

The consultant blinked down at his drawing. 'It's possible. Waking after a very long period is not common, though. But we can't tell. No two comas are the same. The drugs will start to leave his system and the first thing to assess is whether he can breathe unassisted and if he begins to establish a sleep/wake pattern. Then we'll see what happens. That's all we can do. There's no way of knowing in advance whether he'll wake up or not. The brain is a very complex thing. I've seen cases we've written off come back to function as well as ever. And I've seen some patients never recover.'

'But . . .' Diana's knuckles whitened as she clutched the handle of her crocodile-skin bag even tighter. 'Will has a good chance, hasn't he?'

Mr Theodoropulous looked reluctant to answer.

'Hasn't he?' she persisted. 'He's young and healthy. He can get better, can't he?'

The consultant paused, drawing furiously and colouring in the little squares he was creating. 'Mrs Conway, I can't make any promises. We can only take one step at a time. You must prepare yourself for the eventuality that he won't wake up. He's also very vulnerable to infections that could potentially be fatal in his situation. If he does emerge from the coma, we may find that he moves into a state of unresponsiveness, where he is able to breathe unassisted and perhaps open his eyes or make noise, but he's actually unconscious. Or to a state of minimal consciousness, where he wakes occasionally and can obey some simple commands and communicate a little, but no more than that. I must warn you that if he does regain full consciousness, he will in all likelihood not be the man you remember. The kind of injuries he's sustained mean that it's entirely possible he'll be severely disabled – he may not be able to speak or walk. If he should regain consciousness, I foresee many years of rehabilitation. In the meantime, we can put you in touch with charities and support groups who can help you during this very difficult time.'

A feeling almost like relief washed over Emily as she received this news. Wasn't he saying that Will wasn't going to wake up? She glanced over at her mother-in-law to see how she was taking this news. Diana looked as though she simply had not heard what the consultant had said.

'So,' she said, in an almost triumphant voice, 'I was right. I knew he could recover. We're all praying for it. I knew that anything is possible. If anyone can come back from this, it's my son.'

Tom was grilling fish fingers and heating up a tin of beans for the children's supper as she came in.

'How was it?' he asked as she swung into the kitchen on her crutches. She could hear the television blaring in the playroom.

'Okay,' she said, and lowered herself into a chair. 'It was the best we can expect.'

Tom wiped his hands on a towel as he came over to sit with her. 'What's the prognosis?' he asked quietly. 'Is he going to recover?'

She looked away. 'They can't say. He's been kept in an artificial coma while his brain has a chance to recover from the trauma and the effects of the operation they did to release the pressure on his brain. They plan to remove the drugs and see what happens, see whether he can breathe on his own. But there's also the risk that an infection could get him at any time.'

'Oh God.' Tom put his hand on her arm, his expression full of pained sympathy. 'Em, I'm so sorry. He doesn't deserve this. You don't deserve it. The kids don't deserve it. What a fucking nightmare. Let's just hope a miracle happens and he manages to come back. Look, I'm here for as long as you need me, okay? You don't have to worry about a thing.'

She glanced over at the pile of letters on the windowsill, another couple of envelopes flung on the top by Tom. They must have arrived that day.

She took a deep breath. There was no longer any way she could put it off. 'Thanks, Tom. Would you mind giving the children their supper without me?' She hoisted herself to her feet, fingers tightly clutched around the crutches. 'I've got something I have to do.'

CHAPTER 6

Cressie could sense the atmosphere, cold and resentful, as she walked through the staffroom of Fleming Technical College. No one wanted to meet her eye or speak to her. Backs turned as she passed.

One female teacher murmured sharply, 'Lady Bountiful!' as she went by.

Cressie pretended she hadn't heard and went to the tea table to fill her cup from the urn. She guessed what they all thought: that she was a privileged debutante, able to dip in and out of their world as she wished, protected by the wealth and status of her family.

They're right in a way, she thought. *But isn't it better to try to help, rather than ignore what needs doing and simply please myself? I don't have to do this. But I want to do my bit.*

She knew that no one else would see it that way. They would dislike the fact that she was doing something for free that someone else should be paid for. What would happen to them if more people like her offered to work for nothing?

But what if I can't do it? What if I've made a mistake?

Her first day had passed in a blur of faces and names she would never remember, while she tried to learn her way around the school and get used to the noise, smells, bad food and yet more noise. Her second was much the same. By the time she got to the end of the third day, she was exhausted and sure that whatever she was doing was absolutely futile. She couldn't keep order in her classes; no one would listen to her. They seemed to know instinctively that she had no experience and no ability to hold the attention of the class or manage them.

She was too embarrassed to tell anybody that she had a problem, and nobody had asked how she was getting on. The moment the class sat down, she could feel their attention wandering, and before long the chat would start, a murmur at first, which would soon grow as she pleaded ineffectually for quiet. Sometimes she tried to ignore the noise, talk to those who were listening, but eventually she'd feel that she had to do something, and would start to raise her voice against the babble. In some classes, where the leading personalities were particularly audacious, she would spot things being thrown, notes being passed, and knew that she was failing the test badly.

As she found an empty chair in the staffroom, her teacup in one hand, and faced the silent hostility of the room, she wondered if she should simply give up.

No. I can't. I must be brave. I have to press on, show

them I can make a success of this. I'll teach someone if I die trying.

'How is your little job?' her father asked when she joined him at dinner at the end of her first week. 'Ready to throw in the towel?'

'It's going very well, thank you, Papa.' Her heart sank. She could tell by his cutting tone that he was in one of his bad, bullying moods. He'd never scrupled over taking out his irritations and frustrations on the family. Not so much on Harry and Gus – they had a different, grander kind of pressure from Papa, and had both slipped out and away from him as soon as they could – but on her, and on Mama. He seemed to like sharpening the vicious edge of his tongue on them, releasing all the bile and pettiness he never showed the outside world.

'Really?' He raised his eyebrows at her. 'Are you going to tell me about it?'

I can't tell him the truth. I don't want him to tell me he was right all along and I'm hopeless. She began to describe the school, tentatively at first, but the look of scepticism in her father's eyes encouraged her to start spinning a story of success. She was an effective teacher, controlling her classes with ease, inspiring the perfectly behaved children of the East End to previously undreamed-of heights.

'Well, I must say I'm surprised,' her father remarked acidly. 'Perhaps this country isn't going to the dogs quite as quickly as I'd imagined.'

Cressie looked down at her plate. *I will do it*, she told herself firmly, feeling invigorated by her own storytelling. *I'll make it come true. I'll be a splendid teacher yet.*

He listened, then sat back, put his cutlery down and fixed her with a beady stare. 'I hope you understand that this little jaunt will only last for a year at the most. It's all I'll permit.'

'But . . .' Cressie's heart began to pound and she felt the familiar panic seize her. As soon as they were in a position of confrontation, a sick powerlessness possessed her. No matter how much she longed to take him on and win, the fear was too much. She knew he was too ruthless an opponent, prepared to win at any price. *I've got to try*, she thought desperately. *I can't be afraid of him all my life.* 'You know I'm thinking about a career in teaching.'

'No daughter of mine needs to slum it in a poor school. And anyway . . .' He picked up his fork and stabbed a carrot. 'Teachers are miserable spinsters, everyone knows that. Bluestockings or ugly. You're neither, I'm glad to say.'

The blood rushed to her face. 'Papa, that's ridiculous. It's nonsense. I don't want to just get married and be respectable. I want to achieve something with my life.'

'Have some children,' he returned. 'There's no higher calling for a woman than that.'

She could hardly speak through her indignation but managed to splutter, 'You know that's not true!

Think of all the great women, the scientists, the doctors, the writers . . . Things are changing! I want more . . . more than—'

'They're not changing here,' her father retorted. 'Not in this house. As long as you're under my roof, Cressida, there will be no careers.'

She stared at him, red-faced and agonised. That was just the problem. She was under his roof, and there was no way out that she could see.

After dinner, she crept miserably up the stairs to her room. On the way, she saw the door to her mother's room standing ajar. Lately it had seemed as if her mother was kept as a prisoner under guard; there was always some nurse at the door, pressing a finger to her lips, urging Cressie away. 'She's sleeping!' or 'She's tired and must rest'. As far as she could see, there was no one at the door now, no uniformed figure drifting about the room keeping watch.

She went and looked through the gap. Her mother was lying in bed, propped against the pillows, a book resting on the sheet which she kept open with one slender hand while her eyes moved slowly across the page. She looked the epitome of frailty, barely able to combat the weight of the paper.

'Mama?' Cressie whispered.

Her mother looked up and her eyes brightened. 'Darling! There you are. Come in.'

'Where's Ruth?' Cressie advanced quickly and quietly.

'She's gone down to the kitchen for an early supper. I'm on my own.' Her mother patted the covers. 'Sit down and tell me all about what you've been doing. I feel as though I haven't seen you for ages.'

Cressie sat carefully on the white counterpane, and took hold of her mother's hand. It was slender and bony, with a bluish-white tinge to it. 'How are you, Mama?'

Her mother smiled as gaily as she could. 'I'm doing very well! There's a new doctor coming – isn't it exciting? Perhaps he'll make me better and everything will be all right again.'

Cressie smiled back, nodding, even though she had long since ceased to be excited by the advent of a new expert or to hope that her mother would ever recover. She was wasting away, anyone could see that. Perhaps if her father permitted her to be taken away to a hospital, they might discover what was wrong with her, but he wouldn't allow it. He thought that home was the best place for a patient, even while she faded in front of his eyes.

'How are you, my darling?' Mama asked. She scanned her daughter's face. 'You look a little sad. Is something wrong?'

Cressie looked back at her worn face and felt bound again by the conspiracy of silence that they were all part of. No one dared say that they were trampled down by her father's huge and domineering personality. The boys had escaped through the doors that were open to them – university, careers, their own homes – and the fact that they were accorded the respect due to men. Cressie, it seemed, could only escape by marriage. *Or running away. But I could never leave Mama when she needs me so much.* After all, her mother was a life prisoner, with death her only way out. 'No,' she said, 'nothing's wrong.'

Her mother gazed at her keenly. 'How is Papa today?'

Cressie said in a tight voice, 'A little tired perhaps.'

Her mother understood the code. 'You mustn't let him upset you,' she said gently.

'But he does upset me!' blurted out Cressie. Her emotions were still churned up from the encounter at dinner and she couldn't hold it in. 'You know what he's like, what he does . . . He doesn't care anything for what I want in life. All he wants is to control me. I'm not allowed a thought or an action of my own!' She was panting, her cheeks flushed, looking pleadingly at her mother for support.

Mama's face creased with concern. She was so loyal despite her hopeless situation and the misery she'd endured over the years. What was bad had been made ten times worse by the attitude of her husband, but still she found it hard to breathe a word against him. She gazed earnestly at Cressie and said, 'It is not easy, I know. But you won't change him, there's no point in hoping for that. And he'll need you in the future – when I'm not here.'

A flash of fear went through her. Was her mother asking her to stay here, take her place and devote her whole life to caring for the old tyrant? The idea was too terrible. 'I . . . what am I supposed to do?' she asked, almost fearfully.

'I know what you put up with, darling. You're an angel to him, though he doesn't see it. I know you squash your own spirit to keep him happy.' Her mother leaned forward, her expression suddenly intense. 'But I don't want you to be defeated. He'll try to stop you, but if you see an escape – one that's worth anything – you must take it, no matter what. I'm too selfish to set you free right now, I still need you so much myself. But even if it means I lose you, you must walk through the door when it opens.'

Cressie stared at her, astonished. She had never heard her mother talk in such a way before. She wanted to ask her to say more, but just then there was a knock on the door and Ellen put her head round to say there was a telephone call for Miss Cressie.

'Come and see me soon,' her mother said. 'Come tomorrow afternoon and tell me everything. I long to hear about what you are doing.'

'I will,' Cressie promised, dropping a kiss on her thin cheek. Then she went downstairs.

A tingle of excitement ran through her as she went down to the hall where the telephone sat, huge, black and stately on the table under the mirror. The receiver was placed carefully beside it on the shiny surface, looking almost menacing with its thick black cord curling away. *Could it be him?*

108

She picked it up and said, 'Hello?'

'Cressida?'

Her whole body vibrated at the sound of Ralph's voice, and she shut her eyes, clutching at the side of the hall table. She'd put him out of her mind, not wanting to think about the way he had affected her, and the unavoidable, unchangeable fact of his wife. It was wrong to feel the way she did about someone who was married. She'd almost decided not to telephone him, to let the whole thing float away and disappear. It was as though she could see trouble ahead and had made the decision to avoid it if she possibly could. But here he was. He wasn't going to slip out of her life so easily after all.

His voice came down the line again. 'Hello? Are you there?'

'Yes,' she answered.

'You haven't called. Are you coming back?'

'I . . . I don't know.' She had thought she might not see the studio again, but now she pictured it vividly – the way it was so different from the constraints of her own home. Ralph and Catherine were free, able to please themselves. They were not rich, but they had their liberty and evidently lived in the way they chose. She envied it suddenly with all her heart, and longed to be in the large light studio, looking out over the golden church, with Ralph.

'Oh,' he said in a low voice.

'I'm sorry, I'm so busy,' she said wretchedly. She must sound so rude.

'I must have offended you,' he said, his tone mournful. 'Did I say something stupid? I often do.'

'No, it isn't you, it's my job. I'm working very hard.'

'You didn't like the pictures.'

'Of course I did!'

'Then you don't want your portrait done.' His voice took on a tone of intensity. 'You should do it, Cressida. I mean it. As soon as I saw you, I wanted to paint you. I think you could be my best portrait ever. There's something about you that I long to capture on the canvas. Please, will you think again?'

'Well . . .' She looked up and saw her own face staring back at her in the mirror. She was pink-cheeked, her eyes wide. 'I'm so busy . . . there's so little time—'

'It won't take as long as you think. Come back and see me, one more time. Let me convince you. I'll start to sketch you. It'll be rough at first but I know exactly how I want you to look, how I want it to be. It'll be amazing.' His voice dropped to a whisper, becoming more intimate, and it buzzed in her ear. 'You'll look incredible.'

She began to tremble at what he seemed to promise her: a connection between them that would be unique, creative, intimate. Could she really allow that to happen, knowing how she responded to Ralph's presence? Would she make a fool of herself?

'Please, Cressida. Come tomorrow? It's Saturday, isn't it? Come and have lunch with me and

Catherine. Give this whole thing another chance, please. If you don't want to be painted, then fine. But let's at least be friends.'

She didn't know how she could refuse him. 'All right. Thank you.'

'Come at twelve. We'll expect you then.'

It was a fine autumn day, and Blackheath seemed almost like a country village, with its quiet streets lined with sleepy houses, and the air filled with the sound of birdsong. Cressida felt too warm in her coat and small brown hat. Outside the station, she stopped to buy a bunch of roses from a flower seller's stall and she held them carefully so that she could admire the velvety furls of dark red petals as she walked. She didn't hurry – there was no need to rush towards whatever she felt, obscurely, was coming for her. Just as the clock tower rang with the chimes of midday, she turned into Ralph's street, scattered with the first fall of leaves, and made her way to his front door.

At her ring, the door was flung open almost immediately, and a woman stood there beaming at her. She had curly dark hair cut short in a bob that stood out springily from her head, and well-shaped grey eyes with a dark blue rim around the iris. Despite their cool colour, they were dancing merrily at her as she spoke through her smile. 'You're here! Oh, I'm so glad! I'm so happy you came back!' She reached out and grabbed Cressida's hand, and for a moment, Cressie thought she was going to lean over and kiss her, or even lift her hand and kiss that, but instead she grasped it tightly and shook it.

Cressie proffered the bunch of roses she was holding in her other hand. 'These are for you.'

The other woman gasped. 'Oh! They're too beautiful! You're so kind, thank you.' She took the bunch and pressed her nose into the blooms. 'Divine.' She looked up with sparkling eyes. 'I might have known you'd do something like this. Ralph told me all about you. I guessed you would have delicious impulses and perfect taste. Please, come in. Let me take your coat.'

She turned to lead the way into the hall. Cressie followed, slipping her coat from her shoulders, noticing the other woman's plain dark skirt and white smocked blouse, and the thick woollen stockings and sensible shoes. She felt suddenly awkward and overdressed in her brown wool frock, the gold snakeskin belt from Hermes that had been her Christmas present, and her high heels. Feeling that she ought to make an effort for her portrait, she'd set her hair so that the ends curled and it was heavy with lacquer, the little hat firmly pinned to its crunchy surface. She'd carefully made up her face and put on lipstick and now she felt full of artifice next to the other woman's naturalness.

'I'm Catherine, by the way,' she said as she led Cressie into the flat. 'I'll put your coat here. Now . . . I thought we'd eat in the garden. It's too delightful out there in this balmy autumn weather

– the colours are magnificent, like being in a scarlet, green and gold drawing room. Ralph's already out there. I'll show you the way.'

Cressie followed her down the corridor past the studio to where a pair of doors opened onto the back garden she'd glimpsed during her last visit.

Catherine threw them open and raised her arms with a flourish. 'There!'

The garden did look beautiful, in a romantic, shaggy way, the grass long and the trees tall, their leaves turning yellow and golden brown. There were late summer blooms bright in the undergrowth, and pots of lavender still had plump bees hovering around them. Nothing was neat or kempt, but everything had charm and beauty. The view was made complete by the great golden church rising high just beyond the wall of shrubbery at the back of the garden, but all Cressie could see was Ralph, sitting in a wrought-iron chair by an iron table, his long limbs stretched out before him, a hat tipped low over his face so that he could block out the sun and concentrate on whatever he was sketching on the pad he had propped up against the table's edge.

'We're here, Ralph!' Catherine called down, and he looked up, acknowledging them with a lift of his pencil.

Cressie swallowed, realising her mouth was dry and her hands were tingling lightly. *Good. He doesn't care I'm here. Perhaps it's going to be all right.* She'd been restless the night before, replaying their telephone call and wondering what it meant when he had whispered to her how much he wanted to paint her and how incredible he could make her. It had been a kind of delicious agony to wonder if he felt anything of the same intensity and magnetic attraction that she did towards him. Seeing him react so casually to her presence ought to be a relief, and yet . . . a gloom settled inside her. *Of course it's all a dream. And that's how it ought to be. That's all it* can *be.*

Catherine turned to her confidingly. 'I hope Ralph didn't put you off horribly when you came here last. He's got such strange manners sometimes; you know how it is with artists, they live by different rules to the rest of us. He meant to be charming and friendly but often when he tries hardest, he gets it most wrong. Do forgive him if he offended you.'

'No, really, he didn't,' Cressie said, not wanting Ralph to be blamed for her avoiding them. 'He was very charming, really.'

'Oh good.' Catherine put her hand on Cressie's arm and fixed her with an earnest look. 'He was utterly bowled over by you, you know. Enraptured! He's talked of nothing else since but how much he'd love to paint you. Believe me, he doesn't say that about many people.'

Cressie blinked at her, surprised and somehow embarrassed that Catherine should admit so freely that her husband was charmed by another woman. She must mean that he was enchanted by the possibilities of her as a sitter, surely. Perhaps it was normal to express it like this in painterly circles.

I wonder why she looks so familiar. Cressie felt sure she'd seen Catherine before – the thick short hair and firm gaze, the high cheekbones and the slight cleft in the chin – and then she remembered. *Of course. She's one of the portraits in the studio. The girl in the overcoat against the stormy sky.*

'Would you like a drink? I think we should have champagne, to celebrate your visit,' Catherine said. 'I'll go and get it. You sit down with Ralph. Ralph!' she called. 'Put the drawing down! It's time to entertain our guest.' She turned back to Cressie. 'I'll be right back.'

She disappeared back into the flat and Cressie went carefully down the lichen-stained steps in her high heels. At the bottom, she had to tiptoe across the grass so as not to sink down into the lawn. It was still damp with the morning dew where the sun had not yet reached.

Ralph seemed to ignore her, his pencil still moving in rapid back-and-forth movements over the paper. When she reached the table, she stood by another of the iron chairs, seeing that it was still wet. At last he looked up, his hat tipping back so that she could see his eyes.

It was almost too much. She reached out and grasped the cold iron of the chair to steady herself against the giddiness that seized her when their eyes met. What was it about him that affected her so strongly? It was as though his gaze was too powerful for her, stripping away everything she kept close to protect her tender soul from the world.

That's it. I feel naked in front of him. That thought made her head whirl. She hadn't been naked with any man, but every cell in her body seemed to want to offer itself to Ralph. She tried to get control, gripping the chair hard and letting its iron chill eat into the palm of her hand, as though that would help her steady herself.

'Hello again,' he said softly and smiled, his lips curling slowly upwards, more at one side than the other. The sight of his mouth made her stomach twist and drop with pleasurable agony.

'Hello,' she replied, hoping she sounded normal. 'Isn't it a lovely day?'

'Isn't it just? How are you?'

'Very well, thank you.'

'So now you've met Catherine. Did you like her?'

'Yes, yes.' She nodded, feeling a little awkward as she stood on tiptoe on the wet grass. 'She seemed very nice, very welcoming.'

'She couldn't wait to meet you. She's afraid I scared you off. But I didn't, did I?'

She hesitated for a moment. 'No . . . you didn't.'

Ralph looked back down at his sketch. 'I knew you'd come back eventually. You had your reasons not to ring at once, I'm sure.'

'Yes, I've been very busy. I'm teaching at a school in the East End.'

'Really? How fascinating.' He looked back up at her, frowning. 'Why on earth don't you sit down? Are you going to stand there all day?'

'The chair is wet.'

He glanced at it. 'So it is.' He pulled a large white handkerchief from his pocket, leaned over and mopped the drops of water off the chair. 'There. Now you can sit.'

She obeyed, glad to take the weight off her toes. Ralph watched her and then there was silence, his eyes fixed on her and hers on the patterns of the wrought-iron table as she concentrated on keeping herself from trembling under his gaze.

'I meant it, you know,' he said softly.

'Meant what?' she said, following the loops and turns of the iron as it laced in and out.

'What I said on the telephone. That I want to paint you more than anything. I've honestly thought about nothing else since we met. I don't know why you've captured my imagination but you have. I don't think I could be happy again if you don't let me.'

His words made a sharp heat flash through her. She bowed her head slightly so he couldn't see the way her eyelids fluttered and closed. 'Really?' she whispered.

'Yes. You're like a muse. You seem to hold the promise of my art inside you. I don't know why that should be or why it has happened . . .' His voice was low and musical, the way she'd first heard it on the bus in Piccadilly. 'But it has happened, and I can't resist its siren call. Promise me you won't run away again. Promise me you'll let me paint you.'

She swallowed again and pulled in a breath, feeling faint. She looked up at last, and somehow managed to return his stare. 'I promise. You can paint me.' It felt as though she was offering him her deepest self. The look in his eyes, of deep satisfaction and calm after a fight or struggle, seemed to confirm it.

'Good,' he said in a heartfelt voice. 'Thank you. I'm more grateful than I can say.'

'Champagne has arrived!' called Catherine, stepping out of the house and bearing a tray with a bottle and glasses. 'Ralph, you must open this quickly while it's cold!'

She came across the grass, confident in her sensible shoes, smiling broadly again. She put the tray on the table. 'There. Open it, boy, do . . .'

He lifted the bottle and pulled off the gold paper, letting it fall on the grass where it glinted and flashed like forgotten treasure. Then he put the bottle between his knees and his thumbs against the cork, wiggling it out until suddenly it popped with a satisfying noise and a gush of white spume.

'Oh, well done!' cried Catherine, clapping. She looked at Cressie. 'Isn't it wonderful? Champagne in the garden! And we'll eat here too. Lunch is almost ready.'

'Catherine's a wonderful cook,' Ralph said, pouring out the champagne. 'She's really a marvel. You won't believe she's made it all herself, but she has.'

'Flattery,' she reprimanded him, but in a mild tone.

'There's more to celebrate, Cat,' he said, looking up at Catherine, squinting against the sky in a way that made him seem almost more adorable to

Cressie. He looked over at her. 'Cressida has agreed to sit for me. The portrait is back on.'

Cressie glanced over at Catherine and saw an expression of great relief pass over her face.

'Has she? Well, that's marvellous, it really is! I'm so glad. Ralph's so talented – he can't say that himself, but he is – and you'll be very happy with the result, I promise you.' Catherine sat down on another of the iron chairs, ignoring the wetness. She raised a glass. 'Let's drink to it. To the portrait!'

They all lifted their glasses. Cressie sipped her drink, the bubbles prickling over her tongue. She felt as though she was simultaneously part of a secret plan, and its object. Who was in charge? she wondered. Who was manipulating things to their own end? *Perhaps we all are.*

'I'll get my diary after lunch and we'll map out the sittings,' Catherine said. 'We'll need at least eight sessions, won't we, Ralph? There's the under-drawing, then the grisaille, then the tones to add, hot and cool; sometimes the paint will need to be dry and sometimes wet . . . well, we can explain all of this as we go along. The main thing is that we can make a start!' Catherine smiled at her again. 'I'm so happy. I really am.'

'So am I,' said Cressie, smiling back. She sipped the drink again. *This place feels enchanted. The whole thing seems a little unreal. But it's strange – I am happy. I really am.*

CHAPTER 7

'The big day.' The nurse smiled at Emily as she scrubbed her hands in the sink. 'I expect you've been looking forward to this.'

'In a way.' Emily took a deep breath as she sat down on the bed, settling herself as well as she could with her feet dangling off the floor. 'And in another way, not.'

'That's understandable. Right. Let's get this off.' The nurse approached her, her expression now serious as she examined the dressing at the side of Emily's head that had been left on after her last appointment at the hospital. 'So you've had some plastic surgery on the wound, haven't you? The notes say it was healing well the last time they examined it. Let's see.'

She came and stood close, her chest almost pressed against the side of Emily's head as she began carefully to undo the bandages. Not so long ago, Emily would have felt uncomfortable with someone so close, but her experience of being nursed over the last few weeks had made her accustomed to it. In a way, she felt comforted by the warm nearness of the nurses. She had no mother to hug her, stroke her hair and hold her hand, and give her physical reassurance. There were Tom and the children, of course, but the tender touches of the doctors and nurses as they looked after her healing were the nearest thing she had to that type of maternal care.

No husband now either, she thought. That was something nobody had yet wanted to talk to her about. Was she still a wife when her husband was in a coma? He was technically alive but it was no more use than being married to a table or a gatepost. Was she supposed to muddle through, giving all she could to a man in a permanent sleep while she faced a lifetime of loneliness and physical abstinence?

But I'd rather that than him being awake. She felt obscurely as though it might be some kind of cosmic bargain: she taking a nun-like vow of chastity in return for Will's permanent state of sleep. *And that's fine with me. As long as he stays that way.*

The idea of sex and love seemed ludicrously inappropriate in her circumstances. She'd been more on edge than ever as the doctors had removed the coma-inducing drugs that had been keeping Will in oblivion. They'd said that the drugs should leave his system within a few days and, as the time passed, her nightmares grew more intense until she'd woken screaming, sure that Will was scrabbling at her upstairs window, trying to get in and kill her. Tom had rushed in to her, panicked by the noise, and helped her sob her way back to calm. The hospital reported that Will's breathing had gone through some dangerous times – when he breathed too much or too little and disrupted the oxygen flow to his brain – but that it had subsided to a fairly regular pattern. Other than that, there was still no sign that he was emerging from his coma. Scans had shown great areas of damage in the frontal lobes.

'The nurse who was on today said he'll never wake up,' Diana said in one of her nightly telephone calls. 'I told her not to be so ridiculous. Of course he will. We don't need that negativity.'

'No,' Emily replied mechanically. Diana's certainty did not seem to require much more than that.

'I don't know why you can't be at the hospital more,' she said snappily. 'You're never there. I asked the nurses; they say they haven't seen you. It's not very supportive, Emily. I know you've had your own problems, but Will needs you if he's going to get through this.'

'It's not easy,' Emily said, trying to sound reasonable. 'I've got the children at home. My plaster doesn't come off for another three weeks so I can't drive. And to be brutally honest, Will's in a coma. What's the point in sitting by his side day and night when I've got Carrie and Joe who need me? Especially with their father gone.'

'Most patients in intensive care have someone with them constantly.' Disapproval soaked Diana's voice. 'Poor Will looks quite abandoned.'

'He's got you,' Emily said. 'If he knows anything, he'll know you're there for him.'

But she could sense that Diana's disapproval had not softened.

Emily closed her eyes now as the nurse peeled back layer after layer of dressing. *Once this is all gone, I'll be able to wash my hair properly again.* Dry shampoo had only been able to do so much. What she really wanted was for the plaster to come off her leg so that she could lie in a hot bath and soak away the accident. She felt as though she hadn't been able to get properly clean since it had happened. The grubby tawdriness of the whole thing clung to her. No wonder it was still oppressing her.

The nurse's chest rose and fell gently against her cheek. She smelt of soap and antiseptic. 'So,' she said softly, 'you must have been in quite an accident.'

'I was,' Emily murmured sleepily, lulled by the gentle touch against her face.

'You hit a windscreen?'

Emily nodded, then remembered she oughtn't to move her head. 'Yes.'

'You must have lost a fair amount of blood through this cut.'

'I did.' They'd given her a transfusion, she remembered. Big squashy packets of purple fluid, like the bags inside a wine box, pumped into her. She'd barely been conscious for that, though.

'It's healed very nicely. You must have been badly lacerated. It looks like the surgeon has done a good job. One of the results of this kind of cut is that it can heal with livid puckering and you end up with a raised scar with the skin kind of pleated around it. It's unsightly and upsetting, particularly on the face. But he's done very well with you. I think you'll be pleased.' The nurse stood back, discarding a wad of bandages and padding into the waste bin. 'Do you want to see it?' She gestured to the flat mirror screwed to the wall on the opposite side of the room.

As Emily stood up carefully, grabbing a crutch to support her, she realised that she had barely looked in a mirror since the accident. She'd stood in front of them, yes – to brush her teeth, or comb out her hair, or to scrabble for her keys in the hall in front of the glass there – but she hadn't looked, not really. She hadn't wanted to see the draggle-haired woman with the tight lips and sad eyes and the great bandage round the side of her face. It was bad enough going out and seeing the way people eyed her with mild curiosity, wondering how she'd got herself so battered, without looking herself full in the face.

Now she approached the mirror tentatively, keeping herself purposefully out of focus. Then, when she was close, she looked up and slowly turned her head so that she could see the scar. There it was. She took a deep breath and put her hand to the side of her head.

'There,' said the nurse, smiling. 'Isn't that good? I knew you'd be pleased.'

★   ★   ★

The children didn't seem to notice anything different about her. They didn't appear even to spot that the bandage had gone from her face. Tom, though, saw at once. He came to meet her as she stood in the hall taking off her coat, and his eyes flew to the scar. He winced and bit his lip, sucking in air over his teeth. Instantly his expression changed to apologetic sympathy.

'Oh God, sorry, darling. Sorry. It's just . . . Oh, your beautiful face.'

Her eyes began to sting and her chest felt shaky with potential tears but she tried to stay brave. She suddenly became aware that she'd hardly cried since the accident. *That's strange. I hadn't realised that before.*

'I don't think it was all that beautiful to start with,' she said as airily as she could manage. 'But I suppose it was better than this.' She turned to the mirror in the hall, tilting her face round so that she could see the scar. It ran down the side of her face from the top of her temple almost to her jaw, not in a neat curve but in an uneven, jagged line. 'The nurse said it could have been worse. I could have had one of those great red ridges with creased skin round it. The surgeon has done a marvellous job, apparently.' It was true that the scar was a fine one, with no raised edges or puckers, but it cut through her skin in a dark red line, as though someone had taken a red marker pen and scrawled hard down her face in rough zigzags. 'She said it will fade a lot in time. I can use various creams and potions on it to help the healing. And after a year or so, we can think about laser treatments and so on. But the skin needs to restore itself first.'

'Oh Em.' Tom came up and hugged her. 'You're right, it could have been so much worse. You could have lost an eye or had your whole face sliced off. You've been bloody lucky.'

'I know.' She buried her face in his chest as he held her close. 'I know. I just wish it felt like it, that's all. That's all I wish. Because I don't feel lucky.'

The secret knowledge of what had been inside those letters lay heavy and nasty inside her. It felt as though the whole world had turned against her, was baying for her blood and the children's. It turned out that her entire existence had simply been borrowed; none of it had really been hers at all, and now the world wanted it back and intended to rip it from her if she wouldn't surrender it. *Take it!* she wanted to scream. *Just let us get out alive, that's all I ask.*

'But you're strong. You'll get through this.' His voice rumbled through the wool of his jumper and buzzed around her face. 'I know you will.'

If only you knew how strong I'll have to be, she thought. No one knew yet. But she wouldn't be able to keep it a secret much longer. She felt that she'd been staying silent in order to keep her old life for as long as she could. But now that was no longer possible. She turned her head and glimpsed the hall floor, the children's coats and shoes left by the door, the mat, the bump on the skirting board from the buggy. She knew it all so well. It felt so permanent and yet it wasn't at all.

Because all of this has to go.

'Mrs Conway?'

'Yes.'

The young man on the path outside the front door put out his hand. 'I'm Ollie from Loxley's. Hi. Great to see you.' He shook her hand as she gave it to him and cocked his head at the girl standing behind him on the path. 'This is Tanya. She'll be helping me out today. May we come in?'

'Of course.' Emily stood back to let him come into the hall.

Ollie, smart in a suit, a clipboard and pen in his hand, stepped inside, looking about appreciatively as he did so. 'Oh wow. This is nice. Isn't this lovely, Tanya?'

'Yeah,' agreed Tanya. She was also neat and professional in a black trouser suit and red lipstick.

'How shall we do it?' asked Emily. 'Shall I show you around first?'

'I think that's best,' Ollie said cheerily. 'Let's have a nice look around and then I can talk you through our service. Oh goodness!' He looked down at her leg in concern. 'You've been in the wars! How did you do that?'

'Oh . . . just a silly accident,' Emily replied.

'Are you all right to show us around?' His brow was creased with worry for her.

127

'Yes, I'm fine. I'm used to limping about with it now. They're taking it off next week.'

'That's good to hear.' His equanimity was restored and he looked cheerful again. 'Right then. Let's take a look.'

Emily showed the agents around the entire house, unable to take any pleasure from their gushing admiration. They loved her kitchen and the extension she and Will had put on at the back of the house when Carrie was born, so that they had a playroom with doors to the garden. ('Never a-bloody-gain,' Will had declared when at last the builders had departed. 'That was the worst experience of my life! No more building work. Next time we need more space, we move house.') They adored the period features, the original tiles in the hall, the fireplaces, the airy rooms, and the en-suite and dressing room off the master bedroom.

Back in the sitting room, Ollie was full of enthusiasm. 'You're going to have no problem selling to a family,' he said happily. 'There's loads of demand for good properties like this, especially in this area, and you're bound to get lots of people through the door immediately. In fact, I'd suggest that we keep it off the market for a bit to show to our registered clients first, then perhaps sort out an open day—'

'How much?' interrupted Emily.

'Oh.' Ollie blinked at her. Tanya looked thoughtfully at the ceiling. 'Of course you'll want to realise the absolute best price you can and the good news is that the market is very healthy at the—'

'I need a quick sale. A really quick sale. If possible, a cash buyer without a chain.'

Ollie stared at her again, absorbing this. 'Okay. Well, that might cut down your options. Most buyers of a property like this will be families moving up the property ladder, with something to sell to fund the move, but you might be lucky—'

'All right, give me the best- and worst-case scenarios. I want to know how much the house is worth, and what you think I can get for it if I have to sell in, say, six weeks.'

'We'll find you a buyer in six weeks, no worries,' Ollie said, looking relieved.

'No.' She tried not to sound impatient. 'I mean sell. Complete the sale.'

'Complete? In six weeks? From now?' He blinked at her, his mouth in a little round O, and he exchanged glances with Tanya before recollecting himself. 'Well, that's a tall order but . . .' His tone became confident again. 'If that's what you want, then Loxley's can deliver. You might have to be prepared to take a bit of a hit on the price but then again, you may be lucky.'

Emily sat back in her armchair, her plastered leg sticking out stiffly in front of her. 'I want all I can get in the fastest possible time. It's as simple as that.'

★　★　★

'Emily!' Polly came in, hauling Ruby with one hand and pushing the buggy holding a sleeping baby with the other. Stanley had already run in to find Carrie and Joe in the playroom. 'There's a For Sale sign outside your house!'

'I know,' Emily said, hopping up the step from the kitchen, steadying herself against the wall.

'Well, is it a mistake? Ruby, let me take your coat off, for goodness' sake! And don't scream, you'll wake Bert.' Polly looked up from her struggling toddler and noticed the change in Emily at once. 'Oh, your bandage has gone!' She lowered Ruby to the floor and strode down the hall towards Emily, looking anxiously at the side of her head. When she saw the scar, she gasped. 'Oh shit!' She put out a hand and pressed it over the scar. 'Oh God, honey. What happened to you?' Her eyes filled with tears and her lower lip trembled suddenly.

'Hey,' Emily said, touched. She took her friend's wrist and gently lifted her hand away from the scar. 'I was in a car crash, remember? Quite a while ago now. What's wrong?'

Polly sobbed, two tears overflowing and running down her face. 'I'm sorry. I've just realised . . . it's just hit home what happened to you. How you nearly died. The scar . . . it makes me understand how terrible the accident was.'

'I don't seem able to forget it,' Emily said wryly. She brushed her hair away from the scar, catching a glimpse of its jagged red line in the hall mirror. 'I can't now, even if I want to.'

'Oh darling, don't worry about that. It'll get better. And you can get utterly marvellous camouflage make-up too. I've got a friend with a birthmark right over her face and she's learned how to cover it completely whenever she wants to hide it. You'd never know it was there.' Ruby trotted past, on her way to join the others in the playroom. Polly looked bewildered. 'But what about the For Sale sign?'

'Come with me.' Emily turned back to the kitchen, where the long refectory table was covered in piles of letters. She pointed at it. 'That's what it's all about.'

Polly stared at the piles and frowned. Her eyes were still damp from her tears and she wiped them with the back of her palm. 'What is it?'

Emily took a deep breath. It had to happen. People had to know. Tom had gone off to work but he'd know too, when he got back and saw the sign that had gone up outside the house today. There was no hiding it any more. In a way, it would be a relief to let the dirty secret out. Now her bandage was off, with her plaster soon to follow, she was feeling stripped away and left naked and new. That process was only just beginning. There would be a great deal more to lose before it was over.

As they stood by the kitchen table, Emily took a deep breath. 'Will made a big mistake just before the accident,' she said. 'He's lost all our money. All of it. His job has gone, the hedge fund has imploded. There's no salary, no insurance, nothing. Even his critical illness cover had run out and he hadn't renewed it. He was looking for a new provider. He emptied our savings, cashed in pensions and shares, and all the rest of it. If I can sell the house within six weeks and get the mortgage paid back to the bank, I'll be able to keep what's left – such as it is after I've paid the agents – and that will be all the money I have.'

Polly listened open-mouthed, evidently shocked. She moved to a chair and sank down onto it. 'What? I . . . I can't believe it. Are you sure?'

Emily gave a hollow laugh as she sat too. 'I'm afraid so. Last week I saw the bank manager and our financial adviser. And a lawyer. Two of them, actually. And they might not be the last, either.'

'Oh Em. Oh God.' A look of horror crossed Polly's face and she seemed to blanch. She whispered, 'Shit. How did you find out?'

Emily leaned back in her chair, remembering the long night she'd spent in Will's study. She'd opened the stack of post, reading all the letters and taking in what they all meant. After a while, she'd had to stumble to the loo and retch down the bowl, the fear making her vomit. Will had been telling the truth: he'd cleaned out all they owned and remortgaged the house for as much as they would let him. The repayments were emptying what was left in their current account at a frightening rate. There were letters from his stockbroker advising Will not to cash in his shares at the current price. There was even a letter to her confirming the instructions to empty her personal ISA and to access her e-savings, where the legacy from her parents had been held. Will had not scrupled over hiding her post then. He must have been very, very sure that the gamble was a good one. But he had guessed she would never have allowed him to risk everything they had on it.

Sitting on the floor of the study, her plastered leg sticking out awkwardly, she'd turned her face upwards and addressed his absent spirit in a shaking voice. 'What did you want, Will? What the hell did you want? We had everything! We had enough money, a lovely house, a family. We didn't need more . . .'

But she knew that Will had been dissatisfied. Their house was not big and impressive enough. He wanted a private education for the children and had calculated that it would cost them the best part of a million to put them both through good London schools. He hankered after a really special car, something Italian and low-slung that could reach ridiculous speeds. Their holidays had to be hot and frequent, and there was talk of a boat if Will took up sailing as he'd always wanted to. He'd been thinking about throwing a really splendid party to celebrate his fortieth – a castle, fireworks, a famous band . . .

Bitterness and disbelief had swamped her, along with a kind of cold pity for his stupidity and shallowness. *He threw away everything for a load of glossy magazine dreams. In the end, he even preferred to die than face losing his status.*

She'd sat there weeping until the day broke.

Now Emily looked Polly in the eye. 'There was no way I couldn't find out. I'm not that far off penniless.' She laughed lightly. The fear had become something she could handle by pushing it away, keeping herself apart from it all. She'd already begun to detach from all her possessions. All that mattered now was the children. 'It seems crazy, doesn't it? Here we are, in this big house in London, with all the stuff we've accumulated. I've got designer clothes upstairs. Jewellery. Art on the walls. Gadgets galore. And I'm almost broke.'

Polly shook her head, appalled. 'But what does it mean?'

'The house has to go. I have to sell as much as I can.'

'But what will happen to you?'

'Honestly? I have no idea.'

'Where will you go? Where will you live?' Polly's face contorted as she began to absorb the extent of it. 'Will you be able to buy a house?'

'Not without a job,' Emily said grimly.

'Can Will's mother help?'

'She doesn't know.'

Polly looked shocked. 'You must tell her – tell her what Will's done. She'll have to do whatever she can to make it up to you. She's got money, hasn't she? And a decent-sized house?'

'We're not going to live with her,' Emily said decisively. 'I do know that. I couldn't bear it. The way she is – her utter stupid faith that her beloved boy is going to wake up, like some miracle in the Bible. I can't stand it.'

Polly stared at her. A realisation began to dawn in her eyes. She whispered, 'You don't want him to get better.'

Emily returned her gaze. It was, at last, a relief to admit it.

'No,' she said. 'I don't.'

CHAPTER 8

Cressie stood in front of the blackboard, scrawling white chalk on the shiny surface. The blackboard was a bad one. It seemed to reject the chalk so that only dotted, unstable lines were left behind.

'I'm going to talk to you about Keats,' she said as she wrote the name out. 'John Keats. He's one of the most famous English poets. Now.' She turned to face the class. Outside the windows the day bloomed blue and gold, almost as hot as summer. No wonder the pupils were restless. The old radiators were blasting out heat as though it was mid-winter and the room was stifling. Faces were turned away from her – to the window, to desks, to each other. Girls were huddled and whispering, exchanging notes and secrets. Boys fidgeted, slinging small objects at each other or swinging on their chairs, hands in pockets. Only one face, near the front, was fixed on hers, that of a boy she had noticed before. He had a thin, pointed face and round glasses with bright blue eyes behind them. He was neatly turned out, his tie always properly tied, his shoes clean. *What was his name?* She racked her memory but it delivered nothing.

She said loudly, 'Keats's ode "To Autumn" is one of his most famous poems and I thought we would look at it today as it's appropriate to the season, isn't it?'

One of the more obedient girls near the front sang out, 'Yes, miss' but Cressie knew it was just a reflex response to the questioning tone in her voice.

She scanned the classroom and saw one of the boys, a big fellow with a meaty face and huge hands – she'd never known that boys of twelve could be so large – staring out of the window. His name came into her head.

'Fowler, can you please open your book to page ninety-one and read the poem out to us?'

Fowler turned at the sound of his name, his mouth dropping open. 'What, miss? Me, miss?'

'Yes, please,' she said, trying to sound patient but wishing that she'd chosen one of the girls. She'd have to stick with it now, though. 'Open your book.'

He stared stupidly at his desk where the book lay unopened. He was being aggravating, she was sure of it.

'Come along, Fowler. Please do as you're told.'

The boy reached out and slowly opened his book. The other children began to turn their attention to him, some giggling lightly, as though they were anticipating an enjoyable display from Fowler. She waited, her expression as stony as she could make it, while Fowler took his time flicking through the poetry book to find the ode. At last he found it and began to read.

'Season of mists an' mellow fruitfulness,' he droned slowly. His accent seemed to mangle the words she knew so well but it was the way he plodded meaninglessly through them that was destroying it.

Anger rose in her, and she felt her cheeks redden. *He's spoiling it on purpose. He's going to ruin it. How can I teach it if this is what they hear?*

'Close . . .' Fowler paused and grinned, then said loudly, 'Close . . . *bosom* . . . friend . . .'

The room erupted in laughter.

'Stop!' called Cressie. 'Stop reading, Fowler.'

But he said it again, stressing 'bosom' in a strange, squeaky voice that convulsed the boys.

'Stop it, Fowler, do you hear me? Someone else can read, someone who's going to take this more seriously. It's very silly . . .' Her voice climbed higher, losing whatever authority it had as it did so. 'Quiet, please, everybody!'

But she had lost control. No one was paying attention. Some of the girls, shocked by the word, began rebuking Fowler while others returned to their private discussions, and the boys took up the squeaky refrain of 'bosom', laughing and jostling each other. Only the face of the boy with the round glasses remained fixed on hers.

'You,' she said, pointing at him. 'You read it out.'

The boy obediently turned to the right page and began to read in a clear voice. No one paid any attention. If anything, the noise in the class grew louder.

'Be quiet, please, and listen!' she called. Just then she felt something hit her square in the chest. She looked down, startled, and saw a dark blot staining the white front of her blouse. Someone had flicked a piece of ink-soaked paper at her. It had landed plumb and then tumbled down, leaving a trail of spattered ink down her blouse and light skirt. 'Who did that?' she demanded, furious. 'Come on, who?'

The room was descending into uproar. The boy with the glasses looked meaningfully at another who still held a ruler in his hand, and was guffawing loudly with his neighbour.

Just then the door to the classroom swung open, and another of the teachers stood there, a man she'd seen in the staffroom, in a tweed suit and burgundy waistcoat, his hair stuck down in a military style, and with a neat moustache. His face was thunderous, his fists clenched.

'What on earth is going on here?' he roared. The room was instantly silent. He looked around with icy eyes, taking in the chaos and the stain on Cressida's blouse. 'Miss Fellbridge, who is responsible for that mark?'

'I . . . I don't know,' she stammered.

The teacher scanned the room and spotted the boy with his ruler, the bottle of ink perched precariously on his desktop. 'Thornton, come here.'

Thornton, pale now, got up and went to the teacher, who grabbed the boy by his ear, twisting him round and making him cry out in pain.

'You vile little boy. Go directly to Mr Granville and tell him that you're to have a good thrashing for this.' The teacher shoved the boy out of the classroom, kicking his behind as he went. Then he turned back to the room of now quiet children. 'Anyone else?' he demanded.

There was silence, eyes fixed on desks or books.

'All right. Now, if I hear a squeak out of this classroom for the rest of the lesson, I will punish each and every one of you. Do you all understand?'

'Yes, sir,' they murmured.

He glanced back at Cressie. 'Carry on, Miss Fellbridge.'

'Yes. Thank you,' she said coolly. The teacher went out, closing the door behind him. 'Now, you . . .' She looked at the boy in glasses.

'Baxter, miss,' he said helpfully.

'Baxter. Please read the poem out from the beginning.'

His clear voice began to fill the room. The others were quiet, listening obediently. For the first time she had the complete attention of the class. But Cressie could find no joy in it.

In the staffroom later that day, the teacher in the tweed suit came up to her.

'Getting it rough, aren't you?' he said sympathetically, stirring the cup of tea he was holding.

'I'm afraid they can be tough on the new teachers. You need to get a few of them well caned. Show you mean business.'

'Thank you for helping me today,' she said politely. 'But I don't want to use those kinds of methods if I can help it.'

He laughed. 'You're wasting your time trying anything else. Fear is the only thing those little blighters understand. They don't want to sit there listening to you. Forcing them is the only way.'

'Surely there are other ways to reach them,' Cressie said helplessly.

'No. You have to be tough with boys like those; the girls not so much, perhaps, but their insubordination is more insidious. Boys don't dissemble. You can see when they're misbehaving and the thing to do then is beat them. It's all that works. The girls . . .' He shrugged. 'I'm a bachelor. Women are a mystery to me. But I do know that the girls need their little covens broken up. They're all obsessed with each other – who likes who, who says what. If you want to get through to them, rewards are things that the girls like. Pretty pencils, badges and so on. But if you think it's love of poetry that's going to get them all going, you're very much mistaken. You have to force the knowledge into them and then leave 'em to it. As it is, they all want to be driving trains or having babies. I don't know why we bother sometimes.' He looked at her almost sympathetically. 'You've had no training for this, have you?'

'No,' she admitted. 'I thought I could do it on instinct.'

'Pah! Listen, come to me if you have any more problems. I'm an old hand. I'll sort 'em out. I had worse than this in the army.'

'Thank you.'

'You're most welcome. The name's Crofts, by the way. And you should try gin on that ink stain.' He turned away with his cup of tea and walked away.

She watched him go, her spirits sinking even further, wondering if she would rather give up than turn to Crofts and his ear-twisting ways.

Cressie walked towards the school gate, heading for the station. As she went to step through, a small figure appeared and blocked her path.

'Miss?'

She looked down, startled. There was the boy from her Keats class. *What was his name? Oh yes, Baxter* . . . 'Hello, Baxter. What is it?'

'I just wanted to say, miss, that I'm sorry you got the ink thrown at you today.'

She looked down at the stain on her shirt, grown to a large blossom with blurry edges. It was like a branding, a permanent marker of her shame. 'Thank you. That's kind of you.' She was touched but also embarrassed. She shouldn't be in a position of accepting sympathy from a pupil like this. It was almost worse than Crofts rescuing her.

'And . . .' The boy looked up at her, eyes wide

behind the lenses of his round spectacles. 'I wanted to say how much I liked that poem, miss.'

She blinked at him. 'You did?'

'Yes, miss. I thought it were very good.' He frowned and recited in a sing-song voice, 'Season of mists an' mellow fruitfulness, close bosom friend of the maturin' sun, conspirin' with 'im how to load an' bless with fruit the vines-that-round-the-thatched-eves-run.' He ran the last bit into one long word and stopped proudly. 'I spent all me lunch hour learnin' it. An' I'm gonna learn the rest too.'

She smiled, filled with pleasure. 'That's wonderful, Baxter! Well done. Did you really like the poem?'

'Oh, I did, miss,' he replied solemnly.

'Would you like to learn more about poetry?'

'Yes, miss.' Baxter nodded eagerly. 'I love books. An' comics. I read my comics all the time – me mum buys 'em for me. She works, you see, so I go 'ome and she lets me get comics for when I get back and let meself in. But we don't 'ave so much in the way of books. I get 'em from the library.'

'What do you like?' she asked, picturing Baxter on a narrow bed in a tiny box room, reading away in a silent house, waiting for his parents to get home from work.

'Adventures,' he replied briskly. '*Treasure Island*'s a good one. *Last of the Mohicans* is a corker. I like mysteries too. But my favourite is Jack London.'

'Those all sound marvellous.' She looked at him

tentatively, her heart lifting. 'Perhaps, if you like, I could teach you a little more about books and poetry. In the lunch hour or something like that.'

The boy grinned. 'I'd like that ever s'much, miss.'

'That's wonderful. I'll see what I can do.'

'All right then. See ya, miss.' Baxter pushed his satchel back and darted off as swiftly as he'd appeared.

At home a letter was waiting, addressed in the hand she knew from Ralph's first letter. She thrilled to see it on the front of the envelope and held the letter close to her chest as she ran up the stairs to the privacy of her bedroom.

In her room, sitting on the bed, she opened it carefully and pulled out two sheets of paper, one writing paper and the other finer. She unfolded the finer one and saw it was a sketch: it was her, unmistakably, as she had looked in the garden at lunch the other day. He'd caught her in just a few lines and scribbles. She looked ethereal, her eyes holding a note of something mysterious and vulnerable, and yet there was a strength about her too.

She stared at it for a few long minutes, wondering if this was truly how Ralph saw her, or if he was flattering her with the freshness and beauty in the lines of her lips, the curve of her cheekbones and the depth of her eyes.

The letter read:

Cressida

You're possessing my imagination at the moment. I want to draw you over and over. I already have you in my mind and soul.

Until I see you again,

Ralph

She read it, trembling. How should she interpret this? Did all artists express themselves in this romantic way? Were they allowed to write in ways that would seem to mean something serious if they were from anyone else? After all, this read deliciously and dangerously like a love letter. But how could it be? He and Catherine appeared so united, so at ease with each other. What did it all mean?

She threw herself back on the bed, the letter pressed to her chest, and stared up at the ceiling, wondering. She couldn't help hoping, almost fearfully, that she really had possessed him somehow, that he felt something for her in the way that she did for him.

Another thought occurred to her.

Or . . . perhaps Catherine told him to write this.

She remembered the look of relief that had passed over the other woman's face when she had heard that Cressida would sit for her portrait. How much would Papa pay them for a portrait? It must be a good sum. The little flat was charming but while it showed evidence of good taste and refinement, it was quite clear that they were poor.

Suddenly she pictured them at the table in the

145

studio, cups of tea cooling in front of them as Catherine gave Ralph his instructions. 'Woo her,' she was saying. 'Flatter her. We need more commissions and Cressida Fellbridge will have dozens of society friends who will want their portraits painted.'

'Portraits.' Ralph turned his eyes up to the ceiling. 'I don't want to do these bloody portraits. You know what I want to paint.'

'We need *money*, Ralph, don't you understand? You spend what we have on things like that marble bust, but we need to pay the rent too – and buy food and clothes and all the other necessities. Your uncle won't help us with money, and his introduction to the Fellbridges is the only good thing he's ever done for us. We need to make it work, capitalise on it. Turn it into a real income. Wouldn't you rather paint society misses than fat, old, red-faced colonels?'

'Oh, all right.' Ralph pushed out his lower lip mulishly. 'If you think it's best.'

'I know it is,' Catherine replied determinedly. 'Get this girl, and we'll get more. We'll be able to pay the rent a year in advance. If we stockpile some money, then . . .' she said, looking crafty for a moment, 'we can take some time off so you can do the painting you want to do.'

'Really?' He looked at her, frowning. 'Do you promise?'

'Yes. As soon as we've earned enough, you can take three months to yourself to paint whatever you please.'

'All right. It's a bargain.'

'Good.' Catherine pushed the sketch pad towards her husband. 'Now, sketch her. Make her look divine. And we'll write something to her about how she's captured your imagination too. We have to make sure she's in the bag.'

Ralph took up his pencil and began to sketch.

The picture in Cressie's mind faded and she was looking up at the ceiling again, the feeling of delicious excitement ebbing away.

Is that how it was? she wondered gloomily. *How will I ever know the truth?* She picked up the sketch and examined it again. It looked suddenly silly and meaningless, a scribble of someone who didn't really exist, a figment of Ralph's imagination, designed to flatter her.

She let it fall onto the bed and sighed.

It's better if it is like that. The other way can only lead to trouble.

CHAPTER 9

The doctor buzzed his little saw against the cast, cutting it away from Emily's leg. She had anticipated pain but there was only a faint tickle as the saw made its way from her knee to her ankle.

The limb that was revealed looked different from when she had last seen it: it was smaller somehow, with a wasted look. The skin was flaky, dry and speckled with scaly patches, and covered with a fuzz of dark hair. A pungent smell of unwashed skin filled the room.

Emily stared at it with horror. It looked awful. She'd imagined she'd see her normal leg the way it had been, and that she'd be able to get up and walk away.

'Don't worry,' the doctor said, seeing her expression. 'You'll be perfectly fine but you'll need to look after it carefully for a while. Don't shave that hair off for at least three days, do you hear? I know you'll be dying to. You need to treat the skin very gently at first. We don't want any infections starting there. Soak it in warm water for twenty minutes every day, dry very carefully and apply an unscented lotion to the skin – you need to pamper it for a bit. You might get some pain and swelling – that's completely normal. Use some gentle massage and hot packs if that happens. Meanwhile we'll get you started on a course of physio to rebuild the muscle. And you'll need a stick for walking until your muscles have a bit more strength.' He smiled at her. 'But I'm very pleased. You've healed very well.'

'That's good,' she said. 'One less thing to worry about.'

'Just take it slowly.'

She smiled up at him. 'I'll try.'

But it's just not that simple, she thought as she went home on the bus, her leg feeling curiously light now that it was out of the cast. It was frustrating that in one part of her life she was being forced to move fast – getting the house sold, working out how to pack up their lives and where they should go – and in another she was being told to slow down, look after herself and take things easy. *How can I, when there's only me to do things?*

She and Tom were sharing the childcare but that meant that when she was at home, he headed off to work. Of course she was grateful to him for moving in – *What on earth would I have done without him? I couldn't have coped at all* – but there was a limit to what he could do. It was her responsibility to take on the dismantling of her life.

The revelation of her situation had affected Tom oddly. He had listened quietly, clearly shocked, and asked questions, but he had quickly accepted

149

it. He did not question what Will had done with the money. In fact, though appalled, he did not seem at all surprised.

'He had the potential for it,' he said thoughtfully. 'I always knew that.'

'Did you?' Emily was startled. She knew that Tom had never felt close to Will – they were too different for that. Tom was sensitive and creative, and not ambitious for material things, while Will was hungry to prove himself in the world, judging himself and others by what they had. The two of them had been superficially friendly, but neither bothered attempting anything more. Emily and the children were the only things that bound them together.

Tom looked at her meaningfully. 'I sensed things about Will,' he said.

'Really?' She was alert, wondering if Tom had guessed how things were even before the accident, if he'd seen below the glossy surface to the truth about how things were. She half hoped he had, and was half afraid. She'd tried so hard to make sure no one knew that she'd scarcely admitted it to herself. Things were not good. They hadn't been for ages. She asked carefully, 'What did you sense?'

He shrugged. 'Things. Destructive elements. It's no surprise to me that he was attempting to scale higher than he was supposed to, and in doing that, he brought his edifice toppling down.' He thought for a moment and then said, 'It wouldn't surprise me if the car crash were not entirely an accident.'

Emily froze, a nasty shiver shooting down her spine. 'What do you mean?'

'I mean that karmically perhaps it needed to happen. To release you all from the path he was taking you down.'

'Oh.' She was relieved that Tom was so far from the truth. It felt more important than ever that no one knew what Will had done. What was the point now? He was more dead than alive. But more than that, once people knew that he was prepared to kill her and abandon the children . . . well, then they would ask other questions and she couldn't bear to face the answers. 'Do you mean it was all for a purpose?'

Tom nodded. 'Maybe. The universe has ways of working things out.'

She looked at him, wondering. He'd always been attracted to the esoteric side of life but he hadn't ever spelt out what it was he believed. She remembered the odd outburst of a while ago, when he'd talked about the world powers and their desire to crush humankind, and realised suddenly that despite her closeness to her brother, she really had no idea of how he viewed the world.

'So if the house is being sold, where are you going to go?' Tom looked worried. 'I wish I could ask you to live with me but it's just not possible . . .'

'Of course not. We need our own place. Once the house is sold I'll know more about what my options are.' Emily smiled at him. 'I'll work it out somehow. Don't you worry.'

'I'll pray for you,' Tom said earnestly.

She looked away, her skin prickling suddenly. She'd never heard him say anything like that before.

As she hobbled back from the bus stop, getting used to the walking stick, she thought longingly of a cup of tea in the quiet house. Polly had the children for the afternoon, and it would give her a chance to tidy up a little bit for the open day on Saturday. Loxley's had told her that there were seventeen appointments lined up already. They were full of enthusiasm and had bolstered her hopes that she might be able to sell in time.

As she neared the house, she frowned. A familiar-looking blue car was parked just outside, and as she watched, the car door opened. Diana got out, slammed the door shut behind her and stalked towards her, her face full of an anger that Emily had never seen before.

'What is the meaning of this?' she shouted. She gestured towards the For Sale board outside the house. 'What's going on? You've got some explaining to do, young lady!'

Emily stopped and sighed. 'You'd better come in, Diana.'

Her mother-in-law came close, her hands shaking with rage. As usual she looked immaculate, in dark trousers, a pale pink jumper and puffy blue gilet over the top. Her white hair was set in tidy curls. It was odd to see someone so neat looking so furious. 'Don't you . . . don't you give me any lies! What's going on, why is the house for sale?'

'Come in,' Emily repeated. 'I'll explain inside. I don't want a shouting match on the street.'

Diana followed her into the house, breathing heavily. She and Emily had always had a good relationship, with apparent mutual affection, civil if not exactly intimate. Emily knew that she could never have measured up to whatever ideal Diana had wanted for Will, and she appreciated that Diana did her best to hide this and to be kind and welcoming. There were always thoughtful gifts and gestures, little notes and flowers sent, a keen interest taken in Emily's life. The arrival of Carrie and Joe had marked a new closeness between them; Diana took huge pleasure in her grandchildren and admired Emily's capabilities as a mother. Besides, everything was proceeding very nicely: her son and his wife settled with two beautiful children, a girl and a boy, with Will providing a comfortable life while Emily ran the home. There was nothing to unsettle the waters. But Emily had sensed that this was a phoney peace, and that if Diana ever had to choose sides, she would not hesitate to turn on her mercilessly.

In the hall, Diana threw her keys onto the table and said, 'Explain at once.'

'Would you like a cup of tea?' Emily said. *So much for noticing that my plaster is gone and that I'm using a stick. She hasn't even seen that my bandage is off. She really doesn't give a shit.*

'No, I wouldn't! What I want is an explanation for why you are pulling Will's life down around his ears, when he's not here to stop you!' Diana's eyes glittered with rage. They reminded Emily of the way that Will's grew hard and bright when he was angry. She could see that this had been building and now Diana was relishing the excuse to release some of her resentment. 'Some wife you've been to him! He's lying in the hospital, desperately trying to get better, and you won't so much as visit him. Don't think I haven't noticed – you *never* go to him. You've never taken his children to see him – the children he worships! Their voices, their touch . . . he must be longing for them, and they might have the power to help him recover. But oh no. No! You won't hear of it! You'd rather that crazy brother of yours looks after them than take them to see their own father. Goodness knows what the poor little mites are making of all this. I don't doubt you're traumatising them for life by denying them access to their father. You might have told them he's dead for all I know!'

Diana stood there, panting, as she reached the end of her outburst.

Emily stared at her, her heart pounding hard. It was exactly what she'd expected but that didn't make it any easier to hear. The injustice of it wounded her even while part of her dismissed it as the ravings of a woman who was utterly unable to accept the truth about her supposedly perfect son. She'd raised him practically alone; he was her world and her purpose. No doubt she was in deep grief for the loss of the one human being she truly adored. But even before the accident, she'd always refused to accept that Will was in any way flawed. If there were problems, it was Emily's fault. Will was always excused.

Emily longed to tell her the truth, to rip through her illusions and bring them crashing down. She wanted to tell her that Will was no better than a conman and murderer, to lay out in clear, excruciating detail how he had tried to kill them both.

But what's the point? She will never believe me. She couldn't. It would probably kill her. Then her death would lie at Will's door too.

She closed her eyes so that she could let Diana's anger simply wash over her and drift away. She didn't want it to affect her. She knew what her role was now: to get the children somewhere safe so they could all start their lives anew. She wasn't going to let her mother-in-law's hysteria stand in her way.

Seeing Emily close her eyes spurred Diana's anger back to life. 'Don't you ignore me, young lady! What have you got to say for yourself? Well? I demand you answer me!'

Emily opened her eyes. She felt curiously powerful. The knowledge of Will's true character seemed to give her a strength and a mastery over Diana that helped her stay calm in the face of all this rage. She looked down at the hall table and saw the day's post had come. On the top was a white envelope franked with the name of a firm of solicitors. *Oh God. What now?* She picked it up, then looked at Diana. 'Let's not get carried away. If you don't want any tea, we'll go and sit down and I'll explain.'

'Thank you. Because if you think I'm going to let you desert Will, you've got another think coming.'

Emily led the way to the sitting room and sat in the chair opposite the sofa. She lay the solicitors' letter on the arm of the chair, wondering what nasty surprises it contained. Her secret fear was that Will had done something illegal, or was somehow implicated in Vlady's schemes, and that, by extension, she was as well. She was dreading the knock on the door and the appearance of policemen asking her to accompany them to the station, or whatever it was they said. She touched the surface of the letter while Diana went to the sofa and perched herself on the edge of it, as though ready to fly up at an instant's notice.

'Well?' her mother-in-law demanded.

Emily took a deep breath. 'This isn't going to be easy for you to hear, Diana.'

'You want to desert Will,' Diana said shrilly. 'You want to divorce him now he's no good to you. He needs your help and he can't supply the living you want any more, so you're leaving.'

Emily held up her hand. 'You're going to have to let me talk without interrupting me. Of course I don't intend to divorce Will' – *yet*, said a voice in her head – 'but I have to sell the house. Luckily I'm able to do that without his consent. Will and I granted each other power of attorney, at his request. I thought it was in case we found ourselves in exactly this type of situation; in fact, it was for another reason entirely.'

'Oh? What?' snapped Diana.

'He needed power of attorney so that he could empty our bank accounts and access my savings without my written consent.'

There was a pause. Diana frowned. 'Why would he do that?'

'Like I said, this won't be easy, but you need to know that Will has virtually bankrupted us. He risked everything we had – without telling me – on a punt recommended by his boss. I'm afraid it didn't come off. The hedge fund itself has lost everything and so have we. That's why I have to sell the house. If I don't, it will be repossessed within two months and Will and I will most certainly be declared bankrupt.'

Diana stared at her, taking this in. She seemed to gulp several times, like a fish out of water. 'It can't be true . . . you're making it up!'

'I wish I were. I've got all the paperwork that I can show you if you don't believe me. I don't have a choice, I have to sell. As it is, I have no idea how the children and I are going to cope.'

She watched Diana's reaction with a mixture of pity and interest. So many emotions flitted across her face as she absorbed Emily's words. When she spoke again, her voice was stammering and softer. 'I . . . I don't understand how . . . how he could do this . . .' She stared at the gnarled hands clenched in her lap and then looked up again, her eyes moist. 'He really did that? Took it all? . . . Lost it?'

'Yes. I'm afraid so.'

She frowned with the pain of accepting it, her soft skin creasing into dozens of lines like crumpled tissue paper. 'Oh my goodness. Oh Will.'

'I'm sorry, Diana. I didn't want to have to break it to you, but you had to know.'

'My poor, poor boy. What he must have suffered,' she said in a low voice. 'He must have been tormented by it. If only he'd come to me. He could have talked to me, I would have listened.'

Emily felt her heart harden. *All she cares about is Will. She's got no thought for me and the children, for what we're going through.*

Just then, Diana looked up at her, her eyes flinty again. 'If you intend to ask me for money, I have to tell you that there's very little. I have the house and I have my pension but that's all. I have nothing else to spare.'

You selfish, horrible old woman, Emily thought, scorn swelling inside her. *It's because you're like this that Will has turned out to be such a disaster. You never criticised him, never told him that he was being an arrogant bastard. All you've ever cared about is you and him.* 'I don't want your money, thank you. I had my own, the money my parents left me, but unfortunately Will stole that and threw it away. I'll take what's left from the house and consider it mine to do what I want with, to provide for the children.'

'I shall consult a lawyer in Will's interests,' Diana shot back.

'My God.' Emily shook her head in amazement. 'You really are the limit. You can't take it in, can you? Will has destroyed everything. I'm trying to get what I can from the wreckage in order to provide for your grandchildren, don't you understand that? And incidentally, it was while Will was telling me this that the car went off the road.' She fixed Diana with a stare, as if to challenge her to take what she wanted from that.

There was a pause, and then Diana rose to her feet, looking majestically enraged. 'So it was you,' she said heavily.

'Me?'

'You caused the crash. I can see it now. You must have become hysterical. He must have lost control because of you. It's because of you that he's lying there half dead. That's why you can't face him, isn't it? You're too afraid to look at what you've done. And now you're going to try and blame Will for all of it. Well, I won't have it, do you hear? You'll have me to contend with. I always thought you had problems, and now I know for sure.'

Emily stared at her, stunned, as Diana made her way towards the door. Her mother-in-law turned to look at her with a haughty stare.

159

'I shall give instructions that you're not to be allowed to see Will again.'

Emily drew in a breath at her audacity and laughed hollowly. 'I'm his next of kin actually, Diana, so you might have a problem with that.'

'Your malicious laughter is exactly what I would expect,' Diana said loftily. 'I shall protect him. My precious boy has only me now.'

'And that's just the way you like it!' Emily called, as Diana made her way out to the hall. 'I hope you'll both be very happy!'

The front door slammed. There was a moment of silence and then Emily began to laugh. Soon she was giggling so hard, tears were rolling down her cheeks. The image of Diana, with her ridiculous maternal pride, standing guard over her comatose son was too much. They deserved each other.

As the laughter died away, she caught her breath and noticed the letter on the armchair. She picked it up, slipped her finger under the flap and opened it. The letter inside was typed on thick headed paper. She unfolded it and began to read.

Dear Mrs Conway

We have been instructed to deal with the estate of the late Mrs Catherine Few, who passed away last month. She has included a bequest to you in her will and we would like to arrange an appointment to discuss matters pertaining to this.

We would be most grateful if you could contact us at your earliest convenience and look forward to seeing you soon.

Yours sincerely . . .

She dropped the letter onto her lap and stared unseeingly out into the sitting room.

'Oh my,' she said to the empty room. 'What now?'

CHAPTER 10

When Cressie returned to the flat in Blackheath for the first sitting, Catherine greeted her like an old friend, kissing her warmly on both cheeks.

'We're excited!' she said as she led Cressie down to the studio. 'We can't wait to get started. Did you bring some clothes we can look at?'

'Right here.' Cressie held up the leather travelling bag. She'd come dressed more simply this time, in a mustard wool skirt and cream jumper. Catherine had told her not to wear make-up – 'Ralph needs to see your face as it is, and anyway, you don't need it,' she had said. Cressie added, 'I put a selection of things in so you can help me choose.'

'What fun!' Catherine clapped her hands. 'Let's unpack and take a look. Take it into the studio. I'll be there in a moment.'

Cressie went down the corridor, surprised to feel so at home. But this was her third visit and the little flat was now familiar. Catherine's friendly welcome comforted her in a way she'd not known she needed, and her suspicions of the Fews' motives now seemed mean-spirited. They appeared to like her and she felt suddenly hungry for their affection. *It's silly, really. I've got plenty of friends. I don't need more.* But the truth was, she was something of a loner. For so long, she'd been living in the atmosphere of an invalid's convalescent home, keeping company with her mother and supporting her through the difficult periods of her illness. The house was a place where quiet must be kept and where there was the constant anticipation of a crisis for her mother, or an outburst of temper by her father. Everybody's nerves were always strained. Her brothers had long since moved out and only returned for occasional visits, when their voices, loud in the quiet house, and looming presences had seemed jarring and disturbing. Cressida had become accustomed to being either with her mother or in the sanctuary of her room. Perhaps it was her recent experiences at the school that had made her so hungry for the friendship Catherine seemed to be offering her. She'd never experienced outright hostility before, such as she now did from her fellow teachers. The warmth she felt from Catherine was a counterbalance to it, reassuring her that she was likeable.

She went into the studio. Ralph was there, dressed in his dark trousers and paint-stained shoes and jumper. He was staring at the blank canvas he'd placed on the easel, but turned as she came in and pushed the dark forelock out of his eyes with the now familiar gesture.

He smiled. 'Hello. It's delightful to see you.' In two strides he was next to her, his hands on her arms as he dropped a kiss on her cheek and said in a quiet voice, 'Did you get my letter?'

Her breathing quickened despite herself. 'Yes,' she whispered.

'I meant it. I hope you know that.' Then he turned to indicate the corner of the room by the window where a chair had been positioned, angled so that it faced out of the studio and over the garden. A piece of light blue cloth had been pinned up on the wall behind it. 'I thought you might like a view to look at while you're being painted. You won't have much else to do.'

'Thank you. I'll enjoy that. I love looking at the church.'

'It's a beauty, isn't it?'

Catherine came into the studio. 'I've put the kettle on, and in your honour I made some scones so I hope you're hungry. Now, where's that bag? I'm dying to see what's inside.' Cressie handed it to her and she took it with an admiring cry. 'Oh, it's beautiful! What a gorgeous bag. And it's monogrammed too.' She glanced up at Cressie with an amused look in her grey eyes. 'Well, well. We have the same initials. Look.' She pointed at the gold letters stamped into the dark leather. 'CEF. What's your middle name?'

'Elizabeth,' Cressie replied.

Catherine laughed. 'Mine too. How funny. Now.' She knelt on the floor of the studio and unzipped the bag. 'Let's have a look.' She began to pull out the clothes inside and lay them reverently on the floor. Cressie had put in a stiff cream jacquard evening dress with a square neckline that she'd worn to one of her very smartest deb parties, a black cocktail dress, a plain twinset in navy lambswool with a dark skirt, and a bright, patterned silk shirt.

'I wasn't sure what you'd think was best, or how much of me will be on show,' Cressie said. 'So I tried to put in formal and informal.'

'They're all beautiful,' Catherine declared. 'Such magnificent quality. I guessed you'd bring wonderfully stylish clothes, it's exactly what I expected.' She looked over at Ralph, who was watching proceedings. 'What do you think?'

He pointed at the evening dress. 'Not that.'

'No,' agreed Catherine. 'Not that.' She smiled up at Cressie. 'We don't want this to look like it's your state portrait.'

'Whatever you think is best,' she said. She looked at Ralph. He was frowning at the clothes on the floor.

'I don't think black,' Catherine said to Ralph. 'Unless you think . . . I mean, we want the potential for altering the background, don't we? If she's in black, we'll be restricted.'

'No . . . I like the black but . . .' He glanced at Cressie. 'With the colouring, her brown hair . . . I want it to glow.'

Catherine touched the patterned shirt. 'This?'

165

Ralph shook his head. 'No.' He turned to Cressie and grinned. 'I'm sure it's the height of fashion but I can tell you now that the pattern would add an extra session or two to the painting time. Besides, it would be the focus of the painting. We want that to be you.'

Catherine put her hand into the bag and pulled out a blue velvet case. 'What's this?' She opened it to reveal a strand of pearls curled inside the satin interior. 'Oh, aren't they divine?' She looked up at Cressie. 'Do you want to wear these?'

'If I can – they're my mother's. She wore them in her own portrait. I'd like to have them in mine too, if you think that would be all right.' It was ridiculous to feel so tentative about saying what she wanted when her father was paying for the portrait. But it seemed important to have the approval of the artist. *And Catherine's approval too?* she wondered. It was surprising but it seemed that Ralph's wife had just as much influence over the portrait as he did.

'Of course you must wear them,' Catherine exclaimed. 'They'll look wonderful against your skin – so luminous. Don't you think, Ralph?'

'Yes,' he said. Then after a moment he said, 'Catherine, get that shirt of yours. The white one.'

Catherine stared at him then jumped up. 'Of course. You're absolutely right.' She disappeared through the door of the studio.

Ralph smiled at Cressie. 'You'll see in a moment. The vision is coming to me. I'm beginning to understand how it will come together.'

Catherine returned a moment later holding a shirt. 'Here.' She handed it to Cressie. 'I think it will fit you. We're about the same size, I think. Go next door and you can put it on.'

'Next door?' Cressie echoed, taking the shirt.

'Yes. It's our bedroom. There isn't anywhere else you can change, except the bathroom and it's full of plants today.'

'All right.' Cressie took the shirt and went out of the studio and into the next room. It seemed almost impertinent to go into the bedroom of a married couple but she couldn't help being curious. The room was dominated by a huge mahogany bed that she only glanced at, too shy to look at the place where the two of them slept. A large armoire stood against one wall. There were paintings hanging on the walls and one, she guessed, was Catherine, though it was little more than an oil sketch, the features of the sitter blurry. There was a dressing table, an armchair and a chest of drawers, all the furniture similar to that in the other room: good quality, but battered and well used. She took off her jumper and put on the white shirt. Catherine was right: they were the same size. It was a mannish, tailored shirt in thick, expensive cotton, with neat buttons and a blunt collar. She tucked it into her skirt top, examining her reflection in the mirror set in the armoire door. It was a style she never would have picked for herself, but it did look good, she had to admit that.

'Oh yes!' exclaimed Catherine, clapping her

hands as Cressie came into the studio. 'That's just right. But wait . . .' She came over and began to adjust the shirt, pulling it tighter, undoing another button at the chest and opening the collar wide. She rolled up the sleeves into thick neat cuffs that ended just below the elbow. 'Now for the necklace,' she said, and fastened the pearls around Cressie's neck. They sat over her collarbone, a touch of femininity against the masculine quality of the shirt.

Catherine stood back to admire her efforts. 'I think that's it. This shirt is one of my extravagances. I had it made by a tailor on Savile Row. I had to try a few before they'd consider making something for a woman, but one little man in a basement room took on the challenge. I think it looks rather dashing. I always feel like a pirate or a highwayman when I'm wearing it. Do you like it?'

'Yes,' Cressie said, catching a glimpse of herself in the pocked mirror over the fireplace. 'I love it, actually.'

'It looks marvellous,' Ralph said appreciatively. 'Cat, can you do something with her hair? Brush out that stiffness.'

Cressie coloured at the dismissive tone; she'd thought her hair looked nice. But she said nothing as Catherine played about with it, brushing it lightly and cleverly arranging it so that it looked fashionable and yet natural and timeless. Her hands were tender, almost loving, as she lifted strands into place.

'I shall have to do this for you every time,' Catherine murmured. 'As though I'm your personal lady's maid, your own coiffeuse.'

'Oh,' Cressie said awkwardly, not wanting there to be a hint of her social superiority over the other woman, but Catherine didn't appear to feel it. She smiled almost conspiratorially.

'That's very good,' Ralph said. 'It shows off the neckline of the shirt. Good. That's it. Now let's begin.'

She took her place in the chair and they settled on a pose that would be comfortable to hold and would look natural in the painting.

'There won't be much to see at first,' Ralph warned her as he took up tubes of oil paint and squeezed them out onto a palette, little fat blobs of black, brown and tan. 'Just relax, look out of the window and I'll start the underdrawing. It won't look like you but it's a necessary part of the process.'

'All right,' she said, settling in to her pose.

Catherine fluttered around her for a few minutes, adjusting the backcloth, putting a rug over her legs so that she wouldn't get cold sitting still for so long, and tweaking the shirt collar. She and Ralph kept up a broken conversation that was difficult for Cressie to follow; they seemed to understand one another using only half the words that normal communication needed. Ralph loaded a thick brush with paint and went to the easel. Frowning first at her and then at the canvas, he began to

169

put down broad strokes. She could see nothing of what he was painting, only his movements as he paced back and forth in front of the easel, regarding her and then taking his brush to the canvas, occasionally loading it with fresh paint. Catherine settled down on the sofa opposite, watching Cressie as she sat staring out of the window and observing the progress of the underdrawing.

'We've been looking forward to seeing you. Ralph's talked of nothing else,' she said cosily. 'He thinks you're going to be his masterpiece.'

'That would be . . . nice.' Cressie stared out of the window, her gaze fixed on the spire of the church opposite.

'It would be fun to show the portrait when it's finished, wouldn't it? I mean . . .' Catherine laughed. 'I know it's barely started but I have complete faith in Ralph. You'll love the picture. Perhaps an unveiling would be something to think about. A party.' She shrugged, adding quickly, 'It's a long way off, of course. But you should think about it.'

'I will,' Cressie said. She wondered when Catherine was going to leave. Surely at this point the main relationship was between the painter and the sitter. Ralph said nothing, a frown of concentration on his face as he scrutinised Cressie, his head tilted to one side, and then returned to the canvas. Cressie had been anticipating silence in the studio; she'd even rather looked forward to it. But Catherine showed no sign of being about to depart. Instead, she kept up a steady stream of questions and chatter. She wanted to know all about the house in Kensington and about Cressie's family. What did her father do? What a shame to hear that her mother was ill – they wished her all the very best for a speedy recovery. And her brothers – what were their names? What did they do? How often did she see them?

She answered as well as she could while keeping the pose, flattered by Catherine's curiosity. Nothing seemed too small to interest her. As the hour passed, she became stiff and cold, anxious that she was moving her head and losing the pose, but Ralph said nothing. Catherine talked on, idle inconsequential chatter interposed with piercing little questions about Cressie's life. She answered honestly but without expanding her answers beyond what was asked. She wasn't sure how much of herself she wanted to reveal, and it was strange, knowing that Ralph was listening all the time as well, saying nothing.

At last he stood back from the painting. 'Cat?' he asked.

'An excellent start,' she said. 'The pose is right.' She smiled over at Cressie. 'The shirt is chic, unusual. It works very well, I think you'll agree.'

Cressie stood up, stiff and chilled from her long stint. Catherine came over with concern and took her hand. 'Are you all right?' Her grey eyes were anxious. 'You're cold, aren't you? I'm sorry, I've been very remiss. I'll make sure I sort that for next time. This old place is so draughty, especially by the window.'

Catherine's own hand was hot, almost too hot on Cressie's cold skin, and she pulled hers away lightly. 'I'm fine. Really.' She moved around the easel to look at the painting. Ralph stood back, regarding her as she took her first glimpse of it.

He was right, there wasn't much to see. There was little more than a sepia blob on the canvas, a crude outline of her shape, with straight lines across the top of her head, along her back and around the edge of her fingers to mark the extent of her body. Her hair was little more than an empty helmet and there were no features on the blank face.

'You have to trust me,' Ralph said quietly. 'Little steps. A portrait is built up, layer by layer. We work from darkness to light. You'll see.'

'I'm sure it's going to be wonderful,' she said. Her glance travelled to the portrait of Catherine hanging on the wall. It seemed a long journey from the bare bones on the canvas to that astonishing likeness, and the masterful portrayal of the stormy sky.

'You must get dressed,' Catherine urged. 'And Ralph, you must rest too. You know how this exhausts you.'

Ralph sighed, and pushed his dark hair out of his eyes with the back of his wrist. 'Yes,' he said. 'I know.' He looked at Cressida and smiled. 'But I could go on all day.'

'Nonsense,' Catherine said briskly. 'I wouldn't hear of such a thing. Now, you must change and rest. I'll walk Cressida to the station.'

'There's no need, really,' Cressie said, her circulation coming back into her stiff limbs. 'I can manage perfectly well on my own.'

'Don't be silly. I'll go with you. Ralph, you sit down and I'll prepare everything when I'm back.' Catherine picked up a shawl and wrapped it around her shoulders. She looked more Edwardian than a modern young woman, with her thick hair pinned up, and wearing her plain, almost shapeless wool dress and the same thick stockings and sensible shoes as before.

Cressida changed and gathered her things. On the walk to the station, Catherine was as merry as ever, full of enthusiasm for the portrait and what it meant to Ralph.

'You can probably tell he's a real artist, hardly a businessman at all,' she said confidingly as they walked the broad pavements to the station. Piles of coppery leaves had gathered in the gutters but the weather was still warm. 'I have to do all that for him.'

'How did you meet?' Cressida asked, curious.

'Oh! Oh . . . it's very dull. We grew up in the same place. Our parents were friends. We were always close, very close. And of course, from the first I saw and admired his talent. Ralph's quite different from anyone else – you've probably sensed that yourself. There was no question that I would ever leave him, and I never have.' Catherine smiled, the small cleft in her chin dimpling as she did, and wrapped her shawl closer to her. 'We work together. He relies on me utterly. I intend to make sure he is the most successful painter of his generation.'

Cressie was startled by the iron strength in her voice. She felt sure that if sheer will could achieve such a thing, then Catherine would do it. *He has the talent. She has the drive. What an extraordinary partnership they must be.*

And she realised then, feeling shame at her own secret dreams, just how stupid it had been to think that she might ever come between them.

CHAPTER 11

'Catherine who?' asked Tom, frowning.

'Catherine Few.' Emily pulled up the search results on her computer. They were in the kitchen, which was looking very tidy after the estate agent's open day the previous afternoon. There was a period of quiet today while everyone went off to consider. Ollie had told her that he expected the first offers for the house in on Monday. At least it meant she could forget about it and enjoy a calm Sunday.

'Few? That's an odd name. It's like breathing out, not a proper word at all. Let's have a look. Who is she?' He bent down over her shoulder to peer at the screen.

'An artist, by the looks of her, but there's hardly anything I can find out about her as a person. Just her dates. Look . . . it says she was born in London not long before the war started. And that she died in Cumbria this year. There's a tiny Wikipedia entry, just saying she was a painter and listing some of her works and where they're held. There are a few images of her paintings – landscapes.'

'Oh,' said Tom, a touch of dismissal in his voice.

'She's just one of those lady artists, the kind you find in fishing villages, with a little gallery in their front room displaying their watercolours.'

'Maybe.' Emily scanned the painting she'd pulled up: a wild wintery scene of a harsh but beautiful landscape blanketed in snow, the spiky skeletons of trees against the horizon and a vast white sky. It had a depth and magnificence that spoke to her more than a gentle little sea view in watery blues.

'But,' Tom said in a puzzled tone, 'why on earth has she included you in her will?'

'I've no idea. I've never heard of her. Never met her, as far as I know.'

Tom sat down, his eyes bright suddenly. 'Maybe she's left you a fortune!'

'I think if she were that rich, we might have heard of her,' Emily said wryly.

'She might have been one of those wealthy society dames, painting for fun because they have nothing else to do.' He sighed. 'Lucky things.'

'Perhaps. But I can't get too excited about it. It's probably a mistake, don't you think? I mean, how many people get left things by complete strangers? They said I should bring in my passport, birth certificate and marriage certificate, so they'll probably work out in double-quick time that I'm the wrong Emily Conway. There are at least six others on Facebook.'

'Whereabouts in Cumbria is she from?'

Emily clicked on another link. 'A little village about twenty miles from Carlisle.'

'Is it near the Lake District? That's jolly nice, I've been there.'

'Not that far, but on the other side of Carlisle. North. Heading towards Northumberland and Scotland.'

Tom shivered. 'Bloody cold up there.'

'Not all the time. I expect they have summer the same way we do.'

'No wonder her paintings look full of bloody snow.' Tom laughed. 'Well, well. It's a nice little mystery, isn't it? I wonder what she's left you.'

'A painting, probably,' Emily said with a laugh. 'Maybe she picked strangers at random to leave her masterpieces to.'

Tom laughed again. 'Let's hope it's better than that.'

'Well, I can't think why a complete stranger should leave me anything.'

'Maybe she was some kind of friend of Mum and Dad's. Someone we never knew about. When's your appointment with the solicitors?'

'Tuesday morning, first thing. Can you take the children?'

Tom made a face. 'Er . . . not so easy, actually. I'm really up against my deadline. Sorry.'

'Don't worry, I'll take them with me,' Emily said. 'It'll be nice to have an outing now that I'm not on crutches. And it's only in Richmond, so not too far away at all.'

'And all will be revealed . . .' Tom said, lifting his eyebrows. 'Can't wait to find out.'

* * *

177

It was harder than she'd expected to manage the children on her own. It had been so long since she'd had to cope and she'd grown rusty. Her old, competent self had vanished and she lacked the energy and strength she'd once taken for granted. It seemed to take forever to get both children into her car, with Joe screaming and Carrie moaning. She had to settle each of them into their car seats with packets of raisins and stow the bag of everything she might need in the boot, along with the buggy, before she could think of setting off. When she did, driving seemed unfamiliar and unexpectedly difficult. Luckily the car was an automatic so she didn't need to use her weak leg much. But as she ventured out into the heavy London traffic, she remembered that they were due an insurance payment for Will's car, which had been utterly destroyed. They were still investigating the accident. She ought to find out what was happening.

They'll never be able to guess it was deliberate, will they? she wondered as she pulled out to skirt the common. The children were quiet now. Joe was already drifting off to sleep, his fat fist clutching his raisin packet. He looked so like Will. He was going to have the same dark copper hair, though it was wispy and golden red right now, and he'd inherited the Conway green eyes. His mouth hung open in a cherubic pout as he slept.

He's been fine, she thought, stealing glances at him as she drove. *He's barely noticed that Will isn't around. Perhaps because he didn't see him all that much during the week anyway.*

But Carrie was showing signs of upset. Her sleeping, usually so good, had become ragged and broken. She was complaining of bad dreams and throwing more tantrums, simultaneously demanding Emily's attention and pushing her away. 'I don't want you,' she would howl. 'I want D-D-Daddy!'

'Darling, Daddy can't be at home right now. The doctors are making him better,' she would soothe. 'It won't be long, I promise.' She felt cruel making such a promise, but it was the only thing she could say. What was the alternative? Daddy is in a coma and will never wake, and if he does, he probably won't know you. That was even harder, surely. Better to give her hope for now. As Carrie sobbed and beat her fists on Emily's chest and begged for her daddy, Emily wished, despite everything, that Will would wake up.

No, no . . . she thought miserably. *I just wish this had never happened. I wish we could go back and I could stop all this, take us to before it turned so rotten.*

She looked now at her daughter, her heart full of love for her. The little girl was gazing out of the window, her head back against her car seat, and her lips were moving as she sang to herself. The purity and innocence of her face were heart-breaking: her wide blue eyes, her button nose, and her soft brown hair with a hint of Will's red in it.

She was like Emily's side of the family, though, with her dark colouring.

There's no doubt about it. She's definitely a Fellbridge.

The solicitor was a young woman, with neatly pulled-back black hair and striking dark eyes.

'How do you do. I'm Mischal Diwani,' she said, shaking Emily's hand. 'Thank you for coming.'

'I'm sorry I've had to bring the children,' Emily said, pushing Joe's buggy into the small office.

'Don't worry at all,' the solicitor said kindly, then watched as Emily began to settle the children, lifting Joe out of his buggy and giving them both books, toys and snacks to keep them quiet. Without the buggy to lean on, she needed her stick, which she pulled out from the buggy's undercarriage and used to limp across the room. 'Can I get you something? Tea or coffee?' Mischal asked, when Emily was at last sitting in front of her.

'No thanks, I'm fine. We'd better get on, I'm sure they won't stay quiet for long,' Emily said cheerfully.

'All right. Fine. Now. You'll have understood from our letter that Mrs Catherine Few has left you a bequest in her will. Did you know Mrs Few at all?'

'I didn't. I'd never heard of her.' Emily laughed shyly. 'If I'm honest, I think you're probably going to find out that this is all a mistake.'

'I don't think so, Mrs Conway,' the solicitor said solemnly. 'We do our homework pretty thoroughly before we start alerting beneficiaries. As you can imagine, it could cause a lot of trouble if we started passing bequests to the wrong people.'

'Yes, yes.' Emily hoped it didn't sound as though she was impugning the company's professionalism.

Mischal shuffled some papers on her desk. 'I've got a coda here, written by Mrs Few in order to explain why she has left you her bequest.'

'May I . . .' She halted, not wanting to sound greedy. 'May I just ask . . . what has she left me?'

'Oh!' the solicitor looked embarrassed. 'Of course. I do apologise. Mrs Few has left you her house.'

Emily gasped, astonishment coursing through her. Had she just heard correctly? 'Her house?'

'That's right. I've got the details here . . .' She started reshuffling her papers and then produced one. 'Ah. Here we are. December House. Howelland, Cumbria.' She passed it over to Emily. 'This is it.'

Emily took it, still bewildered, and found herself looking at a blurry photograph of an old, white-painted house set in a green landscape, long and low, with attic windows visible in the tiled roof.

'It's not a recent picture, I'm afraid. I don't know when it was taken. It's all we've got but it will give you an idea.'

Emily looked up, still trying to take it in. *This house? It's going to be mine?* 'But . . . why me? Didn't she have any children, any family?'

'Apparently not. She was married but her

husband predeceased her by some years. His name was Ralph Few; he was a painter as well. There were no children. As I said, she's left a coda to tell you why she's left you this legacy. Here it is. I'll read it out.' The solicitor cleared her throat and then read aloud in a clear, unemotional voice. 'I hereby leave December House to Miss Emily Fellbridge, the only female relative of my bene-factor, Miss Cressida Fellbridge. It was Miss Fellbridge's generosity in giving December House to my husband and me that enabled us to live in pursuit of our art free from financial worries for the rest of our lives. It is my wish that, without descendants of my own, I am able to repay that generosity by returning December House to the Fellbridge family, in particular to a female member. Furthermore, I instruct that my estate, if able, should pay for any inheritance taxes or other duties liable on this gift. I desire that, if possible, the house should not be sold but, if Miss Fellbridge does not wish to possess it, that it be passed on to other members of the Fellbridge family, with female members to take priority in the bequest.' Mischal Diwani put the paper down. 'There will be some legal issues to sort out in order to transfer ownership, and the estate must pass through probate.'

'Who are her executors?' Emily asked.

'A Mr and Mrs Pendleton, also of Howelland, Cumbria. No relations, of course. She doesn't seem to have had any family.'

182

Emily stared at her, still trying to take in this momentous news. 'But . . . I don't understand why it's only for me. I'm not the only relative of my Aunt Cressida. There's my brother Tom too.'

'It seems that Mrs Few particularly wanted it to go to a female.'

'I wonder why,' Emily said, intrigued.

The solicitor shrugged. 'I'm afraid there's no way of knowing.' Then she smiled. 'She certainly was very grateful to your aunt.'

Emily stared down at the photograph again. She had no idea that there had been a family home in Cumbria. As far as she knew, she had never been there. Her father had certainly never mentioned it. But then, he was not exactly forthcoming: he had rarely mentioned his sister Cressida either. Emily had grown up knowing she had an aunt who lived in Australia but she'd had the distinct impression that there had been some kind of rift. There was certainly no bond anyway. No letters, cards or calls.

But then, that was all before email and Skype, Emily thought to herself, *when it must have been much harder to stay in touch.* However, that didn't really explain the complete lack of contact between her father and his sister. Her jolly uncle Harry had never married, had no children and had retired to Spain, where he had a beautiful villa and sunshine most of the year round.

The solicitor's voice broke into her thoughts. 'As you'll see, Mrs Few was against the idea of your selling the house. I'm not sure if her wishes carry legal weight in this context, as she hasn't forbidden it, but—'

'That makes no difference,' Emily said suddenly and firmly. Behind her, Carrie started to beg for a biscuit and Joe began to crawl over to the bookshelves to see what he could find to play with. 'I'm not going to sell it.'

'You'll keep it? For family holidays?'

'Oh no.' She got to her feet. 'I intend to live there. As soon as the will is passed by probate and I can take possession.'

The solicitor looked surprise. 'Well, that is a quick decision. You haven't even seen it yet.'

'I don't need to,' Emily said. 'It's a gift that's come exactly when I need it. And I intend to make the most of it.'

CHAPTER 12

'You're doing very well, Terence.' Cressie smiled down at Baxter and he grinned back at her happily.

'Thanks, miss,' he said, swinging his thin legs under the desk. He seemed to enjoy their lunchtime meetings in whatever empty classroom they could find.

'And you liked the book?'

'Oh, I loved it, miss. I really did. That Sherlock Holmes is a marvel.' He gazed up at her through the glinting lenses of his glasses.

'Yes. There are lots of other stories about him to read as well.'

'Cor.' Baxter's bloom of happiness faded a little.

'Are you all right?' she asked, noticing.

'Yes, miss. It's just . . .'

'Yes?'

'I like yer stories and everything, but I don't know how long I'll be able to borrow the books for, that's all.'

'You can borrow them as much as you like, and for as long as you need them.'

'But miss, I mayn't be 'ere.'

She blinked at him in surprise. 'Not be here? What do you mean?'

'Me mum 'n' dad. They say we're to move abroad. Australia, they said. It's not settled yet but they're talkin' 'bout it. I heard 'em when I was supposed to be in bed, but I was readin' on the stairs and I heard it all. They're gonna give up our house and take a ticket on a ship, all the way to the other side of the world, and that's where we'll live.'

'Oh. I see.' She felt a sudden burst of disappointment that her one success, the only person who made being at Fleming worthwhile, was going to leave. But she suppressed that at once. It was, after all, very selfish. What would this mean for Terence Baxter? Would it be good for him to leave London and all its troubles and difficulties, and start a new life where there were plenty of opportunities for a boy like him? After all, did Australia have the same schooling system as England, separating them all off at eleven? Or were there chances for everyone? *I hope there are.* She gave Baxter an encouraging smile. 'That sounds like a great adventure, Terence. I'm sure you'll love it over there, if your parents decide to go.' She knew that plenty of families were taking advantage of the chance of a fresh start. All they had to find was the money for the passage and a bit to get them going at the other end, where land was cheap and there was work to be done. She could see how much more appealing it must be than crowded, dirty London with its almost uncrossable barrier between the slums of the east and the grace and wealth of the west.

'But I'll miss you,' Baxter said in a small voice. 'No one's ever given me books before. Me mum doesn't like me readin'. She says it's a waste of time.'

'What does your father do?'

'He's a fish delivery man. He's even delivered fish to Buckingham Palace,' Baxter said proudly. 'And me mum's a seamstress in a factory.'

'What do they want you to do?'

'Anything with a wage,' Baxter said. He shrugged. 'I don't exactly mind what I do. But I don't think I'd be much good as a builder's boy. I'm not as strong as me dad.'

She put out a hand and rubbed his hair lightly. 'You'll do very well, I'm sure. You'll find something you want to do as long as you work hard and try your best. And until then there's plenty of time to read lots more books. Shall we look out another Sherlock Holmes for you?'

Baxter and his fate on the other side of the world filled her thoughts as she made her way to Blackheath for her latest sitting, but he disappeared from her mind as soon as she saw the spire rising above the trees behind the flat. It felt like something of hers now, she knew it so well. The sittings, now twice a week, were more of a solace in her life than she could have imagined.

She'd arrive to Catherine's warm welcome and the fuss around her welfare: would Cressie like tea? A hot water bottle for her feet? Something to eat? There was always something delicious waiting in the tiny kitchen: little tarts made with apples from the garden and sprinkled with sugar and cinnamon, or buttery biscuits with shards of almond set in the top. Then she would sit in her position while Ralph anointed his palette with blobs of paint and then started work at the easel. Catherine would curl up in her position on the sofa, sometimes ripping old shirts or curtains into rags for wiping Ralph's paintbrushes, and begin her light, amusing chatter while Cressie fixed her eyes on the spire opposite and relaxed. It was strange to be the centre of attention, but rather pleasant, especially as nothing was ever asked of her. With Catherine there, she felt that she could ignore her attraction for Ralph. He barely talked to her as he painted, only occasionally gruffly asking her to move her head back to the correct position, or even more occasionally, interjecting into one of Catherine's stories in a way that showed he was listening all the time, even when he appeared to be oblivious.

The painting grew from a sepia blob with patches of white to show where the light fell, to a skeleton of grey and white – 'the grisaille,' explained Catherine – and her features began to appear, rough and rather spiky but unmistakable.

As it proceeded, Catherine gently directed Ralph's

efforts. 'Ralph, darling, the brow is more arched than you have it,' she said one day, very casually as if she were only half interested.

Ralph frowned, staring at the painting and then back at Cressie's brow. 'Really?'

'Yes, yes,' Catherine replied idly as though it hardly mattered. 'More arched. Just a little.' She pointed. 'There. There. You need a lift, a point, and you have a curve.'

After a long pause, Ralph altered it with a few strokes.

'Yes, yes. Better,' Catherine said, then immediately changed the subject, as though it was bad manners to dwell on her role in the portrait, and so that Ralph could forget that at first he'd created a curved brow rather than an arched one.

Then, suddenly, when Cressie looked at the portrait at the end of a sitting, she saw that it had come to life and gained depth. There was her face, still in tones of black, grey and brown but with a delicacy appearing on it, white paint lifting her face from the flat canvas, giving her depth and reality. Now she had shadow beneath her cheek, a tiny flash of light at the end of her nose, an eye that sat deep in its socket, and there she was, rough but unmistakable. Around her, blue clouds had begun to appear, darkening around the curve of her cheek and the outline of her hair. Her body was still unshaped, her hands just streaks of paint and bare canvas, her chair a crude outline, but above it her face was gaining refinement.

'How amazing,' she said, delighted.

He smiled at her. 'It's coming along.'

'Ralph's going extra slowly,' Catherine said, from her place on the couch. 'He wants the sittings to last as long as possible so we can have you here as much as we want.'

Cressie glanced at him, but he kept his eyes firmly on the canvas, his expression unreadable.

Today he was going to add the cool tones, he'd said.

When she rang on the door, Ralph answered it, smiling broadly at her. 'Hello,' he said. 'Come in.'

She went in, sensing something different in the flat.

'Catherine's not here,' he said. 'She's had to go out.'

At once the atmosphere was loaded. A strange excitement rippled through her. 'Oh. Well, I'm sure we'll manage without her.'

'Of course,' he said. He looked towards the bedroom door. 'Why don't you get changed? I'll make some tea for you.'

In the bedroom, as she unbuttoned her cardigan and pulled her jumper off over her head, her skin goosebumped. It was cold, certainly; the autumn weather had darkened and chilled lately. But the shivers across her arms were not to do with that. She felt the potency of undressing in Ralph's bedroom while they were alone together in the flat. Now she was brave enough to steal glances at the bed, which she noticed had a headboard with a double swoop, and bedposts with finials halfway along the foot of it. She stared closer and realised it was actually two beds, pushed close together. At once she saw them in her mind's eye, Ralph reaching for Catherine across the tiny gap between them. Then she put herself in Catherine's place, and her attraction to him, which she had convinced herself she had managed to damp down, came flaring up again.

It frightened her that as soon as Catherine, whom she'd begun to consider a friend, was absent, all the wicked possibilities that haunted her secret imaginations returned more strongly than ever. They even seemed plausible. With Catherine present to keep check on unruly emotions and desires, both she and Ralph had let their connection loosen. But now . . . Her breathing was coming fast and her heart was pounding.

She could see her reflection in the mirror opposite as she buttoned up Catherine's shirt. *I mustn't let all this show. I'll only make a fool of myself. If there's one thing I've learned, it's that they are very happy together. I've got a schoolgirl crush, that's all. My imagination's running away with me.*

Taking a deep breath, she left the bedroom. Ralph was in the studio, today with a paint-encrusted black smock over his clothes. He looked sweet to her, like a boy in a costume that was too big for him. He was squeezing dark and light blues and lots of white onto his scraped palette.

191

'There you are,' he said. 'I made some progress while you weren't here. Have a look.'

She walked over to inspect the canvas, aware of his nearness again. Now she could see that the shirt had begun to emerge from the flat canvas into a real garment with folds and shadows, the buttons proud of the cotton, the swell of her bust evident under the cloth.

'It's marvellous,' she breathed. 'Did you do it from memory?'

'No. Catherine put on the shirt and your pearls. She sat for me. I made her do it. I really couldn't think of anything but painting your picture and as you weren't here . . .' He smiled at her, something ambivalent in the way his lips curled upwards.

She looked back. The portrait changed slightly under her eyes. She felt strange knowing it was now a hybrid of her and Catherine.

'I'll retouch some of the details now, once you're sitting,' Ralph said, as if reading her mind. 'It's easy enough to change anything that isn't exactly as I want it.'

The way you want it . . . she thought. Did it matter how things actually were? As long as they looked the way that Ralph wanted them to look. Perhaps he needed to shape life to his brush and his vision. Could she trust that the painting was really her, as she looked in life, or was it what Ralph wanted her to be? His vision was the one growing to life on the canvas, after all. But then, what of Catherine's role and her quiet directing of the painting? Cressie had noticed moments when Ralph had stopped painting and sat there waiting, until Catherine had looked up, observed the portrait with a swift glance and a nod, and then he continued.

She sat down in her chair, which was carefully placed on the taped marks on the floor. Settling back, she took up her pose. How long had she sat like this? It must be hours now.

Ralph went over to a gramophone in the corner. 'Do you mind if we have music?'

'No, not at all.' She was relieved. Music meant they would not talk and if they didn't talk, then perhaps nothing frightening or dangerous would be said.

He put a record on the turntable, and lowered the stylus. There was a harsh burst of sound and then silence. A moment later, the strains of a piano floated out, lyrical and fluid, into the air.

'My painting music. Do you know it?'

She shook her head and listened to the elegant, romantic fall of notes. 'Is it Chopin?'

'Good guess. No. It's an Englishman called John Field. Have you heard of him? He was a very talented pianist and composer. It was he who actually invented the nocturne, which Chopin then took and developed. Isn't it lovely?'

She listened. 'Yes. Beautiful.'

'He never realised his potential, despite his genius. He moved to Russia for his career, but died quite young there. Sad.'

'Very sad,' she agreed. The music flooded out and filled the room. Ralph began to hum along as he descended into his painting trance. He paced back and forth in front of the easel, staring at her hard and then at the portrait, and then touching his brush to the canvas, frowning, biting his lips or pursing them. Sometimes he would stand, his head to one side, staring at her, seeing her with an intensity no one ever had before. She felt utterly real and completely whole, as though her soul and body were merged at that moment. Her face was a window, and every angle of her body told something about her; the turn of her head, the fall of her hand, the set of her mouth all expressed her character.

This is terrifying, she thought. *I feel completely exposed, as though he can see everything about me.* All her defences fell away under Ralph's steady grey gaze.

He stared at her and then approached her. Her breathing quickened as he reached out towards her. He turned his brush and gently, almost tenderly, with the pointed end of its handle, he lifted a lock of her hair out of her face and carried it over to one side.

'There,' he said softly. 'It wasn't quite right.'

She felt her chest rising and falling rapidly as he stood by her. The music seemed to fill the room with more intensity than ever. Her consciousness became heightened and she was aware of everything: the vase of roses on the table by his brushes jar; the blue tit hopping on the bird table outside; a leaf fluttering through the air and a swirl of grey cloud behind the church spire. She noticed his long, slender fingers, the way the palette sat in one hand, the brush held elegantly in the other. He wasn't wearing a wedding ring, she noticed. But nothing so very strange in that. 'You're very beautiful,' he said in the same soft tone. 'I don't know if I shall ever be able to do you justice, not if I painted you a hundred times.'

She moved her head and looked up at him, wondering if her eyes showed the mix of fear and hope she felt. She was terribly afraid of anything happening between them and yet couldn't help longing for it. She'd fantasised in secret about the touch of his lips on hers, yearned for the feel of his skin. She imagined being in bed with him, wondered what it would be like if he made love to her, until the pictures she conjured up were too powerful to bear and she'd writhed under her own sheets, not knowing how to cope with the desires flowing through her own body.

His expression had become deadly serious as he gazed down at her, the brush still in his hand. For a moment she wondered if he'd forgotten she was the real Cressie and had begun to think she was his portrait, and whether he would lean forward and begin to paint over her skin, turning her into his work of art. Perhaps he would give her the beauty that he could see and that she couldn't.

Her mouth fell open, a sigh coming hard between

her lips. Ralph's eyes seemed to burn with an intensity she hadn't seen before.

'Cressida,' he said in a low voice.

There was the sound of the front door opening and sturdy footsteps entering.

'Hello!' It was Catherine's voice, loud as she came down the corridor.

They both froze, each looking guiltily at the other. Then, without haste, Ralph turned away from her, dipping his brush into the palette, his face grave.

Catherine came into the room, her glance flying between the two of them. Despite the outward normality she seemed to sense at once that something was not quite as usual.

'Is everything all right?' she asked, looking at Ralph, a frown creasing her brow.

'Yes,' he said brusquely.

She turned to Cressie, who was trying to regulate her breathing and hide the pounding of her heart, which she was sure was visible beneath the cotton shirt. 'Is he being a good host, Cressida? I hope he's looked after you.'

'Yes, he has,' she said as brightly as she could. 'Very well.'

'Good. It turned out Mrs Bathurst didn't need me as long as she thought she would. We've been sorting things out for the Christmas fair. It's going to be quite lovely. We'll be making wreaths this weekend . . .' Catherine's cosy chatter fell easily from her lips. Calm seemed to be restored.

She took up her place on the sofa to watch proceedings.

It's as though my guard is back, Cressie thought. She'd been left unattended but she was certain that Catherine would be unwilling to let that happen again.

She glanced over and saw Catherine's eyes staring at her. The other woman had pulled her legs up, resting her chin on her knees, her arms crossed over her calves. The afternoon light glinted off the ring on her wedding finger.

A bolt of shame struck Cressie's heart.

I'm wicked. Evil. He's another woman's husband. I can't think of him the way I do – I can't. No matter how he makes me feel.

PART II

CHAPTER 13

The van followed Emily's car as they bumped along the country roads. She could only just glimpse it in the rear-view mirror over the piles obscuring the back window. As the road twisted and wound, its white nose would disappear for a while and then appear again round a bend, following determinedly on.

These roads are incredibly narrow. I hope the van doesn't get stuck. And they're making us take forever. When on earth will we get there?

The little arrow on the satnav just directed her on and on, along the twisting lanes. The last thing the electronic voice had instructed her to do was follow the road for eight miles. It hadn't spoken for ages.

They had set off from London early that morning, vigorous with the adventure of their undertaking. The car had been unaccustomedly heavy with all the paraphernalia that she'd loaded into it – and that was just the immediate necessities for an unknown house.

'You're mad,' Polly had said to her, when she'd heard the plan. 'Moving into a house that you've never seen!'

Emily had shrugged. 'Beggars can't be choosers. I'm not exactly going to turn it down, even if I don't like it. As far as I'm concerned, this house is a gift at the time I most need it. I think it's going to be perfect, don't ask me why. And anyway, there isn't time to go all the way up there and back.'

There had been far too much to do to contemplate taking the time to visit December House. The solicitor had been in touch with the executors, who had sent a sketchy floor plan of the house and a few pictures in an email, but they had been taken on a dark day without a flash, as far as Emily could see. They were shady and hard to make out – just gloomy rooms with fireplaces and deep-set windows. There was no explanation as to which room was which either – was she looking at the sitting room or a bedroom? Did the kitchen lead out from the dining room or were they not connected at all? She spent hours squinting at the floor plan – which didn't have all its rooms labelled in any case – and the dark photographs, trying to make sense of them.

But who cares anyway? she had said to herself. *All will be revealed in time.*

She was clinging on to a secret hope that the house would be exquisite, and she imagined inglenook fireplaces and slate floors, even though she had a feeling that what she should be concerned with were the boring things like electrics, plumbing and heating. Goodness only knew what state the old place would be in if there had been just one old lady occupant for years on end.

That day, the one when she'd learned about the bequest, had been a lucky one. On her phone there had been four messages from Loxley's, each one more excited than the next. Ollie was delighted to tell her that there was a bidding war for the house.

'That's good,' she said to him when she called him from the car. 'But the main thing is how quickly they can move. It's no good if they're not able to complete within a few weeks.'

'Two of the buyers are chain free!' said Ollie happily. 'They both have funding in place. It's a shame we can't take just a little more time,' he wheedled, 'because we could get another ten or fifteen if we could—'

'It's tempting, of course, but the hard fact is that I have to pay the bank back within their deadline or none of us gets anything. So let's get the best offer we can from the person who's a cast-iron certainty in terms of moving quickly.'

'Understood,' Ollie said wistfully, and she had accepted the offer from a cash buyer, taking less money for a guaranteed sale. But it was still a good deal, and she would be left with a decent bulwark of cash that would keep them going for a while. She had sold all her most expensive clothes on auction sites, shedding bags and shoes and hardly worn designer purchases. She took her jewellery, bar a few sentimental pieces, into a little shop in Hatton Garden and sold the lot. Her engagement ring, with its flashy rock and platinum band, had brought her in almost ten thousand alone. Any furniture or art that she thought had value went to an auction house, and it all sold. Will had chosen most of the art, and she had to credit him with a good eye: quite a lot of it had gone up in value. It replaced just a little of what he had taken of her parents' legacy.

We'll be all right until I can get a job. Exactly how she was going to do that in the wilds of Cumbria, while looking after two small children on her own, she wasn't sure. But there would be something.

She had called Diana to tell her the news. Her mother-in-law had taken it all very frostily but there was, at least, no more talk of calling in lawyers to protect Will's interests, and the threat to bar Emily from the hospital was not repeated. Perhaps the news that Will had taken her parents' legacy had managed to penetrate Diana's maternal armour. Perhaps she realised that it was only fair, now that Will was incapacitated indefinitely, that Emily should be allowed to do whatever she could to protect the family. But there was no mistaking her anguish at the children moving so far away.

'But Emily,' she said plaintively, 'how will they ever see their father?'

Emily had stayed silent. As far as she was concerned, their father was incapable of being a part of their lives in his current state, and the sight of him would only terrify them. Besides which, the thought of the children going near him made her insides curdle with revulsion. He wasn't the man she'd thought he was, and perhaps he never had been. She'd known he was stubborn, selfish and materialistic, but he'd also been clever, funny, often kind, and a loving father who had delighted in his children. Even when things started to turn bad, she'd been prepared to put up with it. What had turned her implacably against him was his desire to hurt them by robbing them of both their parents.

How could he even have thought it? No matter how bad things got, they couldn't have been so bad as to merit orphaning the children.

She had felt that familiar horror and hatred twist and burn inside her. Her teeth clenched, her lips curled back and her breath hissed over her tongue just thinking about Will.

Once I loved and trusted him. I gave myself to him. I did all I could to protect him. He destroyed it all. Wrote it all off the same way he smashed the car into smithereens. And now it can never be mended.

'Emily? Are you there?'

She said at last, 'If Will's condition changes, I will bring the children to him.'

She had expected an outburst from Diana but the other woman said nothing. Perhaps she had guessed the way Emily's feelings towards Will had changed, and realised that if what Emily said was true, there was a real prospect of Emily divorcing her son and even keeping the children at a distance from him and Diana forever.

'All right,' Diana said wanly. 'I can't stop you. As soon as Will opens his eyes, I'll let you know. Emily . . . is . . . is there anything you need? I know I said there was very little money, but if you're short—'

'We're fine,' Emily replied crisply. She was still smarting from the way Diana had treated her at their last meeting. 'The house sale is going through and we'll have enough for a good while.'

'Very well. Please keep in touch. Don't forget, whatever Will's done, he still needs you. And he still needs Carrie and Joe. They're his children too.'

She paused and then said curtly, 'Goodbye, Diana.' As she put the phone down, she realised her hands were shaking with the effort of not screaming out the truth to her mother-in-law. But she could never tell. Despite all he had done, she still wanted to protect Will from people knowing that, and protect herself from others knowing that she had somehow allowed it to happen. *I can't stand anyone knowing the truth. I can't bear what they would think. If only I know, then maybe it didn't really happen . . .*

Emily had been afraid of leaving London and all she knew, and of losing herself in the obscurity of the remote countryside, but as the car travelled the final few miles towards Howelland, she found her heart growing ever lighter. The countryside was spectacular and the burst of spring seemed to have touched everything: white hawthorn blossomed snowily in hedges and against hills and woodland. Banks of bright yellow daffodils nodded on road-sides and the trees with ivy-covered trunks were dotted with the juicy green of fresh leaves emerging from twigs and branches. White clouds scudded over a watery blue sky and the sun shone.

'Look, children, isn't it lovely?' she cried, feeling brighter than she had for a long while. *Since the accident, in fact.* The snowy darkness of that awful night felt a long time ago; it seemed to be some other Emily screaming in the whirling roar of chaos and pain as the car flew them towards the dreadful impact. She glanced for a moment in the rear-view mirror at the side of her face, and the dark red scrawl that tracked its way down it. She was glad she couldn't remember the actual moment, or what it had been like to have the windscreen tear its way through her skin, or feel the crack and crunch as her leg broke under her.

She pushed those dark thoughts out of her mind and concentrated on taking the next tight bend as carefully as possible. *What must these roads be like in winter?*

They passed a lake, a large glassy smear of blue beyond the hedges, the shadows of the clouds blotted on it. In the fields, lambs just past their wobbly newborn stage gambolled and jumped on hillocks. Carrie exclaimed when she saw ponies grazing, their small bodies hardy and strong.

'Maybe we can go riding,' Emily suggested, smiling at her in the rear-view mirror.

'Oh yes, I want to ride a pony!' exclaimed Carrie, clapping her hands.

'Pony!' echoed Joe, but he seemed to be looking at a hedge.

Suddenly the voice of the satnav spoke up. 'You have arrived at your destination,' it announced with finality.

'What?' Emily peered out of the window. 'What do you mean, we've arrived? We're still on the road!' Just then, on the rise of the hill off to the right, she saw a large dark red sandstone house, tall and austere with rows of narrow windows gazing down over the hillside like a stern guardian keeping watch on everything below it. That was not her house, was it? She recalled the picture she had seen: the long low white house, its windows with light blue painted surrounds, and a steepled porch at the front. No. That chilly-looking house on the hill might seem as if December House was a good name for it, but it was certainly not the place.

Just as she thought this, her gaze was caught by the very words she was thinking, and she realised she was looking at an old sign pointing to the right, inscribed with old, curling lettering that read 'Private road – December House only'.

She gasped and signalled a quick right, just in time to take the turn into the lane, which seemed even narrower and windier than the road she had just left. It went on for about a quarter of a mile before suddenly, after rounding a thickly hedgerowed bend, she saw it, just as in the picture, but more beautiful. She drew her breath in at the sight of the house, melded so perfectly into its landscape, as comfortable as a cat nestling in a nook. Its white-painted render was soft and faded, the slate-tiled roof mossed and speckled. Chimneys topped the gables at each end and three large windows spanned the upper floor, with two on either side of the front door on the ground floor. Attic dormers sat neatly in the roof. It was larger than she'd expected, and she felt a sudden pang of fear that she'd taken on too much. But then she had to concentrate on pulling round into the area at the front, and coming to stop outside a large stone outbuilding, leaving enough room for the van to pull up next to the dry stone wall that ran directly in front of the house. She stopped the car engine and relaxed, her healed leg feeling weak and shaky after the strain of driving for so long, her head still buzzing with movement.

'Are we here, Mummy?' Carrie piped up from the back.

'Yes, darling. This is our new house.'

There was a pause while the children gazed out of the window, taking in their surroundings, Joe with his head resting against the side of his seat, tired from so long in the car.

Carrie said, 'But where are the other people?'

A town child, no doubt about that. 'Good question,' Emily said. 'Somewhere about, I'm sure. We'll make some new friends, don't worry. But it is going to be a little bit different.' *No dashing to the corner shop when I've run out of milk or fancy a bar of chocolate. No shipping us all off to the pub when I can't be bothered to cook.* She thought about winter in a place like this. *I'll have to have a stockpile. I'm going to need a freezer.* She shook her head, biting her lip, suddenly anxious. *I hope I've done the right thing. Could it actually be dangerous up here?* She imagined a news reporter on the television staring into the camera earnestly and saying, 'No one quite understands why Emily Conway thought she could cope in a place like this on her own, with two children. It was a tragedy waiting to happen.'

Idiot, she scoffed at herself. *As if we haven't already been through enough, no need to imagine disaster as well. We'll be fine. It's not like we've moved to the Antarctic.*

'Let's get out,' she said, and opened her door. As her feet hit the ground, she felt a kind of psychic shock, as though she'd literally stepped from her old life and into a new one. She'd left the ground in London and now here she was, landing in north-east Cumbria. The van crunched to a halt beside the car, sending up a wake of dust. Two of the movers jumped out.

'Bloody hell,' said one feelingly. 'That was one hell of a journey.' He looked about disbelievingly. 'This is it?'

'Yes!' Emily said, trying to sound cheerful and strong as though she had everything perfectly under control and was not arriving at a place she'd

210

never seen before. She went to unbuckle the children and let them out of the car.

'Brave,' muttered the other, lighting a cigarette. 'It's pretty, all right but . . . well, remote in't the word.'

The driver climbed down from the cab, stretching theatrically. 'I thought we were going to drop off the edge of Britain.'

'I'll get some tea on,' Emily said brightly, 'and then we can get started. The sooner we unpack, the sooner you can get to the pub.'

She'd booked them rooms at the nearest place, which was four miles further on, in Howelland itself.

The children, released from the car, tried out their legs unsteadily and then began to run about, their attention instantly caught by the hundreds of interesting things demanding it: dirt, stones, puddles, marshy places, and squelchy areas where creatures might be found. Emily got out the arrival box, which had been packed in the footwell of the passenger seat. She'd stored her immediate necessities in there: the kettle, teabags, coffee, milk, sugar and mugs, along with a packet of biscuits. There was a tub of a supper prepared for the children and some beers for her to give the movers when they'd finished. One saucepan, a wooden spoon, cutlery, a knife and a pair of scissors, some plates and bowls and cups. Everything else was in a box in the van marked 'Kitchen' along with a cool box of more food. Hauling out the arrival box, she

211

headed for the house, pushing open the gate with her hip and walking up the path to the front door, painted the same soft blue as the porch around it. Putting down the box, she lifted up a large flower pot and there were the keys, a modern Chubb and an old-fashioned black one for the original lock below the handle. She picked them up, suddenly breathless.

This is it. We're here. Now I find out the reality.

She'd conjured up the house in her mind so many times, in the long hours when she couldn't sleep with worry over the sale of the London house, or to steady herself in the shaking breathless aftermath of a nightmare. She'd paced its rooms, designing and dressing them in her imagination. But now she would face the way things actually were, and all the dreams would disappear forever.

She put the iron key in first and twisted it. The bolt inside the door moved slowly but surely, falling into place with a clunk. She took the small gold key and slipped it into the little shiny round lock above the handle. Its jagged teeth caught the tines of the lock and she moved it to the right, pushing on the door at the same time. The door stuck at first, but a few jolts of her hip sent it scraping open, revealing a grey flagstone floor and shadowy darkness beyond. A musty smell came out to meet her, heavy with dust and the bitterness of emptiness.

Behind her, the children had followed her onto

the path, but were occupied with picking up the shiny pebbles dotted among the dun-coloured gravel at the edge of the flower beds that lined the path. She could hear the movers talking and calling to each other as they unfurled the back of the van and began handing down crates and furniture, loading up the grassy mound in front of the stone wall with what was left from the London house.

She looked back to check that Carrie and Joe were all right, then stepped forward into the hall. Her eyes grew accustomed to the gloom inside and she released a breath she'd not known she was holding. She was in a main room, with a fireplace at one end, a staircase in the middle that disappeared into blackness, and two doors at the other end, one leading to the left and the other towards the back of the house. Sweeping the wall with her palm, she found a light switch and flicked it on. A bare bulb hanging down from a flex in the middle of the room glowed dimly and revealed an old table with piles of circulars on it.

Oh my goodness. She sniffed. At least the air was dry, despite the mustiness. Going to a window, she unfastened the shutters and folded them back into the recess at the side of the window. Below it was a deep window seat. The walls were three feet thick at least. As the shutters opened golden light fell into the room, brightening it and revealing the dust that coated everything. There were ashes in the huge fireplace, and cobwebs were strung along the beams.

Well, it's better with a little light in here. And at least I know the electricity is on.

It had occurred to her on the way up that she hadn't thought to ask the solicitors if the utilities were still connected, but if there was electricity, there was bound to be water as well. *And gas?* she thought hopefully.

The door to the right led to a smaller room, this one with windows at the front and side, and a fireplace in the far wall. There were shelves built along one wall. A study, perhaps, or a small sitting room. She opened the door that led to the back of the house and found herself in a long corridor with three wooden iron-latched doors leading off it, one on each side and one straight ahead. The door on her right opened into a pitch-black cupboard under the stairs, which smelt strongly of turpentine; she hastily shut the door again. The one opposite opened into a chilly storeroom lined with shelves, with a window covered in wire netting and whitewashed stone walls. This was probably a larder, designed to keep food cold. She closed it and advanced to the door in front and opened it.

'The kitchen,' she announced to herself. 'Good. I can get some tea on.'

The room was not at all like the country kitchen of her dreams. There were beams, yes, and tucked into the fireplace on the left was a range cooker, but not the shiny red Aga she'd fantasised about. This was a boxy old cream enamel thing with square lids to the hotplates, and it was chipped and grubby. She went over and touched it.

Cold. Of course. She looked around. *But it could be worse.*

At least no one had tried to install a modern kitchen circa 1985 in here. She could just imagine how bad it would look if there were a riot of chipboard and Formica, tan-coloured tiles and decorative edgings. As it was, it was a battered old collection of oddments: scrubbed pine counter-tops, with mismatched cupboards underneath. One storage area had no doors but a red gingham curtain strung on a piece of wire. The sink and draining board were stainless steel, scratched and well used, tucked beneath the window that looked out over the back garden. There were, she noticed, no high-level cupboards.

Where did she keep everything? And, she thought with sudden panic, *where on earth can I put the fridge? And the washing machine?*

She put her box down on the counter, spotted a door to the right of the old range and went to it. Pushing it open, she saw that beyond lay a scullery which was now a cold utility room, with pipes that must be intended for a washing machine.

I suppose it's a blessing I had to leave the dishwasher behind. No space for one here, anyway. At least the fridge can go in here.

Another door beyond that led to an even colder, tiny lavatory, with the cistern high on the wall, a long chain hanging down from it.

The height of luxury, she thought wryly, noting the grey cobwebs gathered thickly in the corners of the ceiling.

She returned to the kitchen and tried the other door, which led into a morning room where there had no doubt once been a table and chairs.

So this is where we eat. Her eye was caught by the huge old dresser running the length of the wall opposite the windows. *And that's where she stored her crockery.*

She realised she'd been infected by the need for one of the ubiquitous huge eat-in kitchens that she and her friends had in London. The idea that the larder was in one place, the crockery in another and the fridge out in the scullery all seemed bizarre, old-fashioned and inefficient. But, she reasoned, people didn't think of eating in their kitchens once upon a time. Probably the ones doing the eating weren't the ones doing the cooking: there'd have been maids, cooks . . . She saw another door leading out of the morning room to the far side of the house.

What's through there? But she remembered that she'd left the children alone outside for too long. The movers wouldn't necessarily keep watch over them.

What am I thinking? I must have been at least ten minutes in here. They could have wandered off, got lost somewhere, gone into one of those old buildings and found an axe or a saw or tripped over something . . .

Panic raced through her, and she turned, stumbling blindly for the door, thinking only that she had to find the children as quickly as possible. She felt choked with a sudden black fear, the kind she knew from her nightmares, and she gasped as she hurried back through the morning room door, into the kitchen and out into the passage that led towards the front of the house.

Just then, she heard a sound that filled her with sick terror: Joe's voice, rising in a wail, screaming out for her. 'Muuuu-uuummy!' he shouted on the crescendo of a sob.

Emily pushed through the door and ran into the great hall at the front of the house. A shape was silhouetted in the open doorway, a huge, towering man with Joe, screaming and crying, in his arms.

She stood paralysed with fright. *Will's here! Christ, he's here.* The thought burned through her mind like a red-hot knife. *He's come for us, he's found us. I didn't run far enough.*

'Now, little lad,' said a deep voice from the hulking shape. 'Here's your mummy, here she is, don't worry.'

'Put him down!' she yelled in a tremulous voice. 'Put him down right now!' *It's not Will*, her brain told her – the voice wasn't his – but her emotions were having trouble catching up. Adrenalin was still racing through her, making her heart pound fiercely.

'All right,' said the voice calmly. 'I think he wants you anyway.' The shape bent and released Joe, who staggered over towards her, his eyes scrunched shut and his mouth open as he howled. She scooped him up and hushed him, stroking his head, feeling him all over as though checking for broken bones.

'Where's Carrie?' she snapped, blinking as the figure moved towards her, resolving from a silhouette into a proper flesh-and-blood person whose features she still could not make out.

'The little girl's outside. She just showed me her first pet. It's a woodlouse. I think she could do better.' There was a laugh hidden in his voice. 'You must be Mrs Conway.'

'Yes.' Her panic was subsiding. She frowned as the man in front of her at last came into focus. He looked as though he was in his early forties, tall, and dressed in the kind of classic country clothes that she thought no one really wore outside magazine shoots: dark cord trousers, a checked shirt of worn soft cotton, a fuzzy wool jumper in mossy green under a tweed jacket in autumnal colours. His face was open and friendly, battered and lined as though he'd spent many hours outside in the teeth of a strong wind. His hair, short and brown, stood straight up on top, as if just fluffed by a breeze.

'I'm James Pendleton,' he said, holding out his hand to her. She took it and let him shake hers vigorously. 'I've been keeping a lookout for you. Welcome to December House.'

'Thank you. You must be one of the executors.'

'That's right.' He smiled. 'Good to meet you at last. You obviously found the key all right.'

'Yes. Thank you for leaving it out.' Joe had stopped crying and was nestling in her arms, eying the newcomer suspiciously.

James looked out through the open door to where the movers could be seen stacking up the boxes and furniture outside. 'They're going like the clappers, aren't they? You should have everything inside in no time. Have you managed to have a look around? You'll need to know where to direct them soon.'

'Only the ground floor,' Emily said.

He rubbed his hands together. 'Well, shall I show you the rest?'

She instantly felt that she didn't want him to rob the house of its mystery by striding through it, revealing it all to her in his bluff, friendly way. She wanted to discover it for herself. 'I tell you what, you could show me how to get the oven turned on. I'm going to need to cook something before too long.'

'Good point. You will need it. The range provides all the hot water and the heating too. Come on, I'll show you how it works.'

In the kitchen, James knelt down in front of the range. 'Yes. It could do with a clean.' He looked up at her sheepishly. 'Sorry. I didn't think of it. Let's get it started, anyway.'

'Where's the switch?' Emily said, looking along the walls for it. She put Joe down and he settled on the floor, interested in whatever lay behind the gingham curtain that hid the cupboard space.

'No switch. Solid fuel.'

'Solid fuel?' She was confused. What was he talking about? 'Like . . . hard oil?' she said stupidly.

He laughed. 'No. Solid fuel! Wood, in this case. Your supply's outside in the store. I had a look a while back and there were plenty of good seasoned logs, but you'll need to top up a few times a year.'

She was still taking in the fact that she would be keeping her cooker alight with logs as James led her out of the back door in the scullery and out into the garden. The log store was tucked away at the side of the house, beside the jutting wing of the old lavatory. She could see now that it had once been an outside one, but the old door had been blocked up and a new one knocked through from the scullery.

'There,' James said, indicating rows of logs, well dried and cracked, smelling strongly of bark. 'A good store there. It'll keep you going for a while. You grab as much as you can and we'll soon have the range going.'

She followed him back into the kitchen with an armful of scratchy logs that she suspected were full of beetles and spiders.

Is this what life will be like? Full of tiny, scuttling things? And – she wrinkled her nose against the powerful, woody smell of the logs – *it's going to be a lot smellier than I imagined.* Her nose was full of the aroma of dust, mould, cold stone and now wood. This was going to take more adjustment than she'd anticipated. The country idyll she'd dreamed of was clean and orderly and scented by home-baked cakes.

As James knelt down to get the range going, Emily unpacked the kettle, filled it from the stiff tap over the sink, and plugged it in. Leaving James to keep an eye on Joe who was comfortably ensconced in the cupboard, she headed back out again to find Carrie, who was building a home out of gravel for the woodlouse she'd adopted.

'He's called Roberto,' Carrie said gravely as Emily bent down to look. 'He's in his bedroom.'

'He's lovely, sweetheart. And his home is splendid, I'm sure he'll love it.'

One of the movers called across to her. 'We'll be moving furniture in soon. Van's nearly empty. You'd better decide where you want us to put it.'

'Okay. There'll be tea in a few minutes.' She stood up and held out a hand to Carrie. 'Do you want to come and choose your bedroom?'

Carrie nodded. 'Will Roberto be safe?'

'I'm sure he will. You can come back out again soon.'

The upstairs of the house lifted her spirits: it was cosy but light, with four bedrooms, each with a view over either the front or the back garden.

'I want this one,' Carrie said as they went into a tiny box room with a sloping ceiling just big enough for a single bed, a chest of drawers and, perhaps, a small bookcase. It was papered in a pattern of tiny pink sprigged roses.

'Don't you want to share with Joe?' Emily asked, holding her hand.

Carrie shook her head. 'This is just for me.'

'All right. This is your room.'

The largest bedroom had a cast-iron fireplace with a white-painted surround and was also papered in a country floral. It had honey-coloured wooden floorboards and a built-in cupboard.

This is more like it, Emily thought, cheered by the comfortable feel of the rooms. They needed a good clean but there were curtains at the windows and beautiful views of the gardens and the fields beyond.

Next door was another small bedroom where Joe could sleep, and a bathroom with an old enamel bath and loo. *No shower. I suppose it can't have everything.* She went to the last door, fastened by a latch like all the others and opened it. *This will be the spare, I guess.*

Inside, the room was wonderfully light and not papered like the others but painted white. It felt different to the other rooms somehow and she noticed that the floor was speckled with paint in a rainbow of different shades, in tiny specks or larger blobs, some smeared as though they'd been stepped on when wet. Propped against the wall was a large easel, closed, also smeared with stripes of paint. Apart from the dresser downstairs, it was the only piece of furniture she'd seen.

It must have been a studio, she thought, intrigued. *Of course. Catherine Few was an artist. This must have been where she painted.*

She rubbed her foot along the floor, wondering if she could sand the boards to get the paint off. Carrie tugged at her hand.

'Mummy, let's go down.'

'Yes. Let's. I promised the movers some tea.'

James had the range alight. 'There,' he said happily, sitting back on his haunches. He showed her how to use the vent to alter the strength of the fire. 'You want to turn it down to burn slow during the night. Then turn it up again if you want to bring the ovens up to a high temperature quickly. You'll soon get the hang of it.'

She examined it, still mystified. 'How will I know what temperature the oven is?'

'This is the hot one – and look, there's a dial on the front.'

'It's in Fahrenheit,' she said faintly.

'Of course. The bottom oven is a warming one. Just do a bit of experimenting. You'll be fine.' He smiled at her and climbed to his feet. He towered over her. 'Now then. You've got plenty to be getting on with, so I'll leave you to it. But call me if you want anything or have any questions. I'm only over the way.'

'Where do you live?' she asked, getting out mugs for the tea.

'In the house on the hill. We're your nearest

neighbours. The telephone is in the study and I think it's still connected.'

'I have a mobile.'

'I'd be surprised if you get much in the way of reception.' He grinned apologetically. 'I'm afraid it's patchy up here. Best to rely on the old-fashioned kind. Have you got our number?'

'I think the solicitors gave it to me.' A thought occurred to her. 'What about the internet?'

James laughed again, his eyes crinkling up. 'I don't think Mrs Few ever used it. The telephone people will hook you up, I expect. Now, call any time but I'll drop by in a day or so and see how you're getting on. It's a busy time, you see – there's still some late lambing.' He rubbed his large dusty hands on his trousers. 'Right, I'd better get off. Bye for now.'

Emily watched him as he headed off down the passage to the front. He seemed a good sort, a kind man. It was comforting to know that there was someone nearby. *But now I live in a world where the nearest neighbour is at least a mile away. And there's no internet. That's a shocker. I'd better call up about that right away.*

Turning back to the kettle, she started to make the tea.

CHAPTER 14

The portrait progressed and changed, as Ralph finished the cold tones and moved on to the warm. Now his palette was brightened with blobs of yellow, pink and red. Cressie hadn't thought it could be improved but at the end of each sitting, the woman in the portrait seemed more alive, more vivid, as her skin flushed, her lips reddened and her eyes appeared lit from within.

Occasionally, Ralph would lift the canvas from the easel and hurry out of the room with it.

'He's checking it against the mirror,' Catherine remarked from the sofa, seeing Cressie turn her head to watch him go. 'Seeing the portrait reflected back helps him to understand it. It's rather strange but it works.'

'Oh,' Cressie said, intrigued.

'Do you like it?' Catherine asked suddenly.

'Very much.'

'It's his best, there's no doubt about it.' Catherine's gaze went to the portrait of herself that hung on the wall, and then she looked back at Cressie. 'He's caught you exactly.'

'Oh, I think he's flattered me,' Cressie said with an embarrassed laugh. She was well aware the version of herself in the painting was a romantic one. Her complexion was not so perfect in real life, she knew that.

'No, he hasn't,' Catherine insisted. 'But it's not simply physical – there is an essence of you in the portrait. It's quite remarkable.'

Nonetheless, Catherine continued her quiet direction of Ralph's creation. Cressie was sitting for what Catherine told her would be one of the last sessions when Catherine coughed lightly to draw Ralph's attention.

'The hair. It's not right.'

'Not right?' Ralph tilted his head to one side and examined the painting. Cressie stayed still. She could not see what was on the canvas in any case. 'What's wrong with it? It's fine.'

'No. It's orange. You've used orange there.'

'I haven't,' Ralph replied shortly.

'Yes.' Catherine uncurled herself from her place on the sofa and went over to the portrait. She pointed at it. 'Here. Streaks of orange. What did you use?'

'I mixed the same as before. It's the same – look. Burnt umber. Sienna.'

'No. You must have used something different.'

'I tell you, I didn't,' Ralph said crossly.

Catherine bent down close to his ear and murmured something Cressie could not make out.

'It's not orange,' declared Ralph, his eyes fierce now. 'It can't be.'

Catherine turned to Cressie with a smile. 'Would you excuse us, please?'

Ralph stood up and took the portrait down from the easel. The two of them left the room together and Cressie heard their voices coming from the bedroom beyond. She sat alone in the studio, wondering what they were saying.

It's so strange that Catherine has so much influence over him. He's the artist. Surely he knows what to do. Why does he listen to her? She felt vaguely defensive of Ralph. Why couldn't they be left alone occasionally, so that Ralph could paint without Catherine's gimlet eye always focused on what he was doing? But ever since that day when they'd been together just the two of them, Catherine had not left them alone for an instant.

The door to the studio flew open and Ralph burst in with the portrait, his eyes burning a flinty grey-gold and his lips tight. He put the painting back on the easel and sat down in front of it on the stool he sometimes used when he wasn't pacing about. He looked hard from the painting to Cressie and back.

'Is everything all right?' she asked timidly. He was evidently in a state of emotion.

'Yes. Yes. Fine,' he said tersely. 'I'm a bloody idiot sometimes. Every now and then Catherine has to give me a good talking-to and then I see sense. She's right, of course. The hair is orange.' He got to his feet. 'I'll need to find that new box of paints. Excuse me.' He strode out of the studio.

A moment later, Catherine came in, still very calm and unruffled by Ralph's temper, a smile on her lips. She was shaking two tablets from a bottle into her hand, and she put them down on the stool by the easel.

'Is Ralph all right?' Cressie asked, worried.

'Yes, don't worry.'

'But those pills . . .'

'Yes. He needs them for his heart condition.'

'What?' She tried to keep the shock from her voice. *He's ill . . . oh God, no, not Ralph.* A tremor passed over her skin. She hoped Catherine had not noticed. *But she's so sharp.* Cressie dropped her own gaze to the floor in case she was giving anything away. 'That's terrible, I'm so sorry. What's wrong with his heart?'

Catherine blinked slowly. 'Oh . . . occasionally, when he gets excited, he suffers from arrhythmia. Those tablets help him. I make them myself. I've researched the condition thoroughly and discovered many ways we can combat it through herbs and so on. Magnesium helps too. I prefer to look after him, rather than trust him to doctors. My mother died after the quacks got their hands on her. Since then, I've only trusted remedies I believe have a provenance from the past.'

'I'm so sorry to hear that,' Cressie said, trying to keep her voice steady. She thought of her own mother, confined to her bed, so weak and sickly, with the many doctors who trooped in and out of the bedroom always leaving another bottle of medicine or more pills to be administered. It was awful to think of Ralph, so young and vital, in the grip of the kind of illness that was seeping the life from her mother. 'Is his condition dangerous?'

Catherine smiled comfortingly as she sat down. 'You mustn't be concerned. It's something he was born with. They don't think it will kill him, don't be afraid of that. But it isn't pleasant for him when the arrhythmia starts; it feels quite nasty. I usually send him to bed with a very dull book and strict instructions to be as bored as possible. No painting is allowed when it happens. It's too intense for him.'

Cressie stared at her. Catherine, she thought, was very mysterious: this calm presence, capable and nurturing and yet steely too. She seemed in complete control of Ralph, and of his art. 'So there won't be any more painting today?'

'No. I've told him that we must stop the session.'

'Oh.' Cressie was bewildered. When had Catherine been intending to tell her that the session was over? She started to get up. 'I'd better go . . . My clothes are in your bedroom . . .'

'I'll get them for you in a moment,' Catherine said. She held up a hand. 'Please, don't go immediately. I want to talk to you.'

Guilt washed over Cressie and blood rushed to her face; she knew her cheeks were stained scarlet. *She's going to confront me. She knows how I feel about him.* She stiffened, desperately uncomfortable, but she looked to Catherine. To her surprise, there was a kind of amusement in the other woman's eyes.

'Don't look so frightened. You don't need to be. I just wanted to explain that little scene about the colour of your hair.'

Cressie blinked at her, unable to read Catherine's attitude to her. 'There's no need,' she said in a stumbling voice. 'Really . . .'

'No, you should understand what's happening, how Ralph and I work together. Because although it might not always look like it, that's what we're doing. He's the genius, of course, but he needs me.'

'I can see that,' Cressie said quietly.

'No – he *really* needs me. I'm his eyes, you see.'

'His eyes?' She was puzzled.

'Yes.' There was a pause, then Catherine smiled her secretive smile again. 'You see, Ralph is almost completely colour-blind. He sees in tones and he gets a few colours quite clearly – orange is one – but the rest are a murky mystery to him.'

Cressie stared at her, astonished. 'Colour-blind? But . . .' She tried to absorb this idea. A colour-blind artist? How on earth was that possible?

'Yes,' Catherine said firmly. 'So now you understand. I'm his eyes, I see his colours. That's why I'm always here, watching over his creations. And the blue he puts into all his portraits? That's my blue. My special colour. I mix it for him and he puts it into every painting.' She gave Cressie a keen look. 'He hasn't put it into your portrait

230

yet. But don't worry. He will.' The faint light of a challenge entered her eyes. 'I'll make sure of it.'

Lying in bed that night, Cressie found she could think of nothing but Ralph and Catherine. They had become more intriguing, more fascinating than ever. They were so closely, intensely entwined, like two halves of the same person. She had never seen a relationship like it. They didn't seem to be out of each other's company for longer than a few hours at a time, and they lived and worked entirely together.

But I know there's something in his eyes when he looks at me.

She felt a shiver of delight as she remembered him staring down at her with that intense gaze of his, telling her she was beautiful. She could feel him reaching out to her, a yearning for her that matched hers for him.

But I must be imagining it. There's no other way it can be. Unless . . . She didn't want to think of it, but she couldn't help it. *Unless he's a cad.* The kind of man who pretended to fall in love with girls even though he was married. Or perhaps just the sort who had room in his heart for more than one love at a time.

She saw in her mind's eye a different kind of Ralph, one who enjoyed flirtations with his models and exerted his power over them. And Catherine, his devoted wife, who let him. Perhaps she was even complicit.

231

'Do you think this one will let me seduce her?' Ralph was saying idly to Catherine. Her imagination put Catherine in the white shirt, and placed her in the chair by the window. Catherine was sitting in Cressie's position, occasionally touching the string of pearls around her neck – Cressie's pearls.

'I should think so,' Catherine remarked. 'She's clearly enamoured of you and trying to hide it. I've seen her looking at you. Cow eyes. Rather sweet.'

'Mmm, I've noticed it too.' Ralph held his brush still, glanced over at his wife and smiled with satisfaction, then he dipped the end of his brush into the fat blob of white paint on his palette. 'She's an open book, this one, isn't she?'

'Delightfully so,' agreed Catherine.

'Do you think she's a virgin?'

'I would say it's a certainty.'

Ralph breathed deeply. 'I would certainly relish unburdening her of that.'

'After the portrait is done. After we've secured more commissions. We have to keep her sweet until then.'

'And you don't think my seduction of her would make her even sweeter?' He raised his eyebrows at her. 'You don't think much of my prowess.'

'Quite the opposite, my love – I'm sure she'd adore you more than ever afterwards. It's the fact that you'd have to cast her off that would make her bitter. And a broken heart might give that little kitten some claws.'

Ralph smirked. 'How can you be so sure I would cast her off?'

Catherine turned her head to look at him. 'Because I know you, my darling. The thrill of the chase is what you enjoy.'

'And the thrill of the chaste.' Ralph looked pleased with his own witticism.

'Precisely. Once you'd had her, you'd grow tired of her. It would be the next fresh little miss who enraptured you. And anyway, you've got something more important that I know you'd never risk losing.'

'Really?'

'Yes. Me.'

'Of course.' Ralph put down his brush and palette and went over to Catherine. He took her hand and stroked it gently, brushing her hair tenderly with the other. 'My eyes,' he said softly. 'I could never live without you. You know that.'

He bent down and pressed his mouth to hers, as she reached up to pull him closer and they sank into each other's kiss.

Cressie moaned as the scene faded from her mind. It made sense, a terrible shaming sense. She was an open book, a virgin tormented by her desire for a man she couldn't have. She'd been kissed a few times, by young men at dances, some she had wanted to kiss and others she hadn't, but only Adam had touched her in the ways she knew men wanted to touch women. She had allowed it because she was curious and because his sudden panting desire had possessed him, turning his face dark red and his eyes glassy in a way that it seemed almost rude to interrupt. He'd fumbled under her jumper, pressing his fingers under the cup of her bra and rubbing them over her nipples, pinching them lightly, as his tongue had rolled and flickered in her mouth. His breath whistled through his nose as he clutched at her. She'd wondered if it was normal to feel nothing at all. Now she imagined Ralph's mouth on hers, his tongue venturing between her lips and a great shudder of longing went through her. It was too much to imagine what the touch of his fingers on her breasts might be like, but at the thought, her insides clenched hard, burning with what she knew was desire.

So that's what it's like, she thought miserably. *I'm a desperate little virgin, fired up for someone else's husband. It's . . . it's humiliating.*

She screwed her eyes shut against the pictures in her mind.

But I won't believe it. He's not that philanderer, I'm sure of it. Not Ralph.

She called him to mind as he had been in the studio: handsome, intense, his eyes burning fiercely as he concentrated. She remembered with a pang that he was ill, with his heart condition. And those beautiful gold-speckled grey eyes were blind to nearly all the colours in the world. Knowing his frailty made her yearn for him even more, if that was possible.

But he doesn't need me. Why can't I get it through my stupid head? He has a wife to be his companion, to nurse him and be his eyes. Perhaps it's best if I don't see him again. I won't go back. The portrait is as good as done anyway. They can finish it without me.

Her mood was low for days afterwards. When she couldn't sleep, she would tiptoe into her mother's room and hold her hand as she slept, not quite sure who was comforting who. She wanted to confide in her about Ralph, and about how miserable her desires were making her. She wanted to explain that she hated herself for how she felt about another woman's husband, and ask her mother what she should do to kill her desires and be good again. But in the dimness of the bedroom, her mother's skin paper-white against the pillows, she stayed silent, afraid that she might draw too much on the last reserves of her mother's strength.

I must solve this on my own. I have to be strong. I know what's right.

A sitting was due but she sent a letter explaining that she was ill and couldn't come.

At the end, she wrote:

> Are you able to finish the portrait without me? Catherine said it needed only some final touches. You should press on just in case this wretched cold lingers.

She dropped the letter in the postbox at the end of the road on her way to school.

★　　★　　★

The headmaster requested that Cressida go to see him in his office after lunch and she made her way there, still very low in spirits. Perhaps it was the way the weather had changed quite abruptly from autumn to winter. The afternoons were so dark and her hands and feet felt continually chilled. Night seemed to be pressing in, trying to gobble up the hours that didn't belong to it. The wind was up, blowing icy gusts that stung the eyes and whipped hats from heads and dirt up from the gutters to spatter the face, and it brought squalls of rain with it.

It was raining now, she noticed, as she passed a window and saw drops pelting hard against the glass. She hadn't brought her mac and her umbrella was worse than useless in the howling wind. She'd be soaked on the walk back to the station.

'Ah, Miss Fellbridge, how are you?' Mr Granville rose to his feet as she came in and gestured to the seat in front of his desk. 'Do sit down.'

She sat obediently.

'Now then, how have you been getting on?' He pressed his fingertips together and inclined his head towards her, as if eager to catch every word.

'Fine . . . I think. I've tried my best.'

'Hmm. Reports have reached me that you've had a little trouble with aspects of the classroom. Control, for instance.' He looked at her over the top of his spectacles.

'Yes,' she said hesitantly. It was no surprise that the headmaster had heard of her problems holding the classes' attention. No doubt Crofts had reported everything back as soon as he could. She'd been expecting some sort of reprimand for her weakness but when it had not come immediately, she had put it out of her mind. Her classes had soon become just as unruly as before.

'We're nearly at the end of term,' Mr Granville reminded her. 'I wonder if Fleming is really the right place for you, Miss Fellbridge. It takes a certain sternness of character to teach children like the ones here. London children, working-class ones at least, are tough little creatures and you need to be just as tough to tame them. I wonder if you might not be happier in a private school, perhaps somewhere a little less . . . testing than here.'

She stared at him, her heart sinking. 'I see,' she said stiffly.

'Now, that's not to say we haven't valued your contribution, because we have. But your talents could be better used in another environment. That's all I'm saying.'

'But,' she said, feeling her temper rise, 'I have made a difference. I may not have been able to reach all the children, that's true, but I have affected some of them. And look at Terence Baxter – I've been giving him private lessons and he's been a dream. He's reading so many wonderful books and writing splendid little essays too. His vocabulary is extraordinary and he's got such a bright, questioning mind—'

'Ah, yes. Baxter.' Mr Granville frowned and tapped his fingertips against each other. 'I was going to mention him myself. You see, Mrs Baxter has been in to see me. She's not very happy about the extra attention her son has been getting.'

'What?' Cressida said, disbelieving.

'That's right. She doesn't like the ideas Terence has been absorbing. Apparently you've talked to him of university.'

'Yes, I have. He's bright enough—'

'It's not a question of brightness,' interrupted Mr Granville in a condescending tone. 'It's the fact that university is not what Terence's family want for him.'

'And what about what he wants? He was very excited about the idea,' retorted Cressie hotly, unable to credit that someone might not want their son to improve his lot.

'Miss Fellbridge, do you think that Terence wants to be educated out of his class and away from his family? You will turn him into a different creature from his own parents. He may not thank you for that in the end.'

'Or he may bless me for it!'

'Well, that's as may be . . .' Mr Granville shrugged. 'It makes no odds, really, as Mrs Baxter tells me that the family is leaving for Australia after Christmas. Baxter will be going to a new school wherever they end up living. So you might as well give up on trying to turn him into a working-class genius or whatever it is you're attempting.'

Cressie stared at him, desperate to throw back a perfect retort but unable to summon one.

'And I think,' he continued, 'that we should agree that you'll not return here for next term either. Your contribution has been valuable and we wish you well.' He stood up. 'I'm sure I'll see you before the end of term, Miss Fellbridge. Good day.'

She stood up wordlessly, turned on her heel and left, filled with fury.

Baxter shall have a box of classics to take with him. He'll have six weeks on a boat to do nothing but read. I'll see to it that he damn well arrives in Australia as educated as I can make him, no matter what his blasted mother thinks.

CHAPTER 15

At first, it seemed to Emily like being on holiday. There was no internet until the telephone company arrived to install it and her mobile was without signal here in the dip between the hills. The television, once it was plugged into the cable that snaked into the study from a spiky aerial on the roof, delivered only terrestrial channels and not even those very well, so it stayed off most of the time. She and the children were free of all distractions.

Of course, there's less housework on holiday, she thought, as she worked her way around the house with a bucket of cleaning things and a broom.

But it was therapeutic somehow. As she tackled each room, starting with the bedrooms, washing, dusting and polishing, rehanging freshly washed curtains that had dried in the clean Cumbrian air, before arranging the furniture just as she wanted it, she felt lighter and happier, as though this whole thing symbolised a thoroughly new start, the old life washed away in buckets of grimy water. The house smelt cleaner too, as though the musty smell had ebbed away, buffeted out by the gusts of fresh air coming in through the open windows. Life was leaner now. There was less of everything.

Owning less made her more serene somehow. She'd had so much stuff, and, it had turned out, she'd really needed very little of it. They could get by without the Gaggia Baby coffee machine and the tap that delivered boiling water. She didn't need a huge double-doored fridge with an ice maker, which was lucky as there was no room for it here. She'd bought a smaller, cheaper one before they'd left, but even so, it had been a struggle to get it and the washing machine into the scullery; when the plumber had arrived to install the machine, he'd been clever with pipes and sorted it out for her.

The children came with her around the house, as though they wanted to stake out the new territory with her, watching as their familiar things took up a new residence. In Carrie's room, her little white bed looked snug against the wall. Once the drawers were in, her doll's cradle filled most of the remaining space. She loved it, and went there several times a day just to look proudly at it and admire her very own bedroom.

Emily's room made her happiest of all. There was nothing in here to remind her of Will. Everything in their bedroom in London – from the huge hand-made emperor-sized bed to the dressing table – had gone, all of it sold. She had spent some of the money on furniture: a second-hand French double bed with a cane headboard, a small pink armchair, an old chest of drawers with holes in the back but the lovely patina of good waxed wood. It all fitted well in this much smaller room. Even the linen was new, a splurge at an expensive shop in Marylebone that she thought was justified; every sheet, pillowcase and duvet cover was now untainted by Will. She didn't have to remember him, or making love to him. It was strange to think about how in love they'd been once, and how she'd craved his body. By the end, she'd begun to dread his hand reaching out to her at night, the sound of his heavy breathing and the insistent need he'd had. He'd made love to her roughly, with something like repressed fury, as though he was barely aware of her presence and only needed the release of his climax to find a moment's calm.

I can't bear to think of it.

It made the guilt come back too strongly, and her horror at everything that had happened and her own part in it sickened her.

But I don't need to think of it here. It's all behind me, and I hope that's the end of the nightmares too.

So far, they hadn't come back. She was free of him, she felt. Surely up here, in this beautiful, lonely place, she was liberated.

On the third morning, she woke to the sunshine already streaming in through her curtains, and the sound of Joe talking to himself in his cot next door. She went in to him, yawning, and lifted him out.

'Ready for some breakfast, little man?' she said. 'Come on, let's get Carrie and go downstairs.'

The kitchen was always warm thanks to the

range; she was already learning its ways and beginning to treasure the comfort its heat provided. There was something very satisfying, almost primitive, about opening the door of its furnace and tossing logs into the glowing depths, seeing the flames leap up to devour them. She liked to turn the vent down at night, knowing that the fire would glow, sleepy but intense, till morning. As she went about the morning routine of making the children's porridge on the hotplate while the kettle boiled for her coffee, she realised she could hear a noise from outside the cottage: a rhythmic banging that echoed through the air.

Curious, she went to the window and strained to see through the orchard at the bottom of the lawn. The garden was in a state, but she hadn't had time to look at it properly yet. Through the blossom-covered branches, she could make out a shape at the bottom of the garden and the noise came again: tap, tap, tap.

She put the children's porridge bowls in front of them. 'Eat up now. I'm just going outside for a moment.'

In the scullery, she swapped her slippers for boots and let herself out through the back door. The wind was blustering around the garden and it rushed under her nightie and chilled her legs. She shivered, pulling her cardigan more closely around her as she strode through the orchard. She could see someone now, at the bottom of the garden, driving a post into the ground.

'Hello!' she called as she ducked to miss the low-hanging branches of the apple trees. 'Who's there?'

The banging stopped and the man at the bottom of the garden straightened up, wiping his brow with the back of his arm. The hammer showed up starkly against the green hills beyond.

'Ahoy there!' he called. 'Hope I didn't wake you.'

She saw that it was James Pendleton, a little more casual than last time in a lumberjack's shirt with the sleeves rolled up and a pair of tatty jeans. He looked much younger out of his tweed jacket. 'James, what are you doing here?' she said, coming up to him, digging her cold hands into her cardy pockets.

'I thought about how you've got the two little ones and I remembered that this fence and gate needed mending.' He gestured with the hammer to the field beyond the garden. 'There's a cattle trough in the field – it's a deep one. You don't want the little boy wandering out without you knowing and falling in. Or the little girl, come to that, even though she looks a sensible little thing. So I came down to fix it.'

'That's very kind of you,' she said with a smile. 'Thank you.'

'You're welcome.' He smiled back. 'I'm just about finished.'

'You're up very early,' she said.

'I've been up since about three a.m., if you must know. In the lambing shed for most of it. I wanted to get this done while I thought about it.'

'Come in for coffee,' she offered. 'I'm just making some.'

'Sounds very tempting. Thanks. I will.'

They walked back together through the orchard towards the house. *Amazing*, Emily thought as they approached. *It feels like mine already. I've only been here three days.*

James sat down at the table in the morning room while she made the coffee, chatting easily to the children. She could hear his deep voice interspersed by Carrie's high-pitched chat and the banging of Joe's plastic spoon on the table of the high chair. It was strange to have a man with them again, one who wasn't Tom at least. She took the coffee through to the table and sat down to pour it out.

'You seem to have settled in,' James remarked as she passed him his mug. 'Thanks very much.' He looked around appreciatively. 'It looks cosy.'

'I was worried our London furniture wouldn't fit but actually it looks all right. And luckily the dresser was left here.'

He poured milk from the jug into his mug. 'We couldn't get it out without breaking it up. God only knows how they got it in here. So we had to leave it. Everything else was sold according to the terms of Mrs Few's will.'

'Of course, you know all about it,' she said, curious. James had such a pleasant, friendly air about him. She felt completely comfortable around him even though she was wearing her nightie and a pair of sheepskin bootie slippers.

'That's right, as an executor. The old lady didn't have any other friends and no relatives, as far as we could tell. That's why she appointed us, I suppose.' He lifted his mug to sip the coffee. She noticed that his hair stood up even more straight and fluffy today.

Emily remembered the solicitor telling her that the executors were Mr and Mrs Pendleton. 'You and your wife,' she said.

'Not the wife,' James said bluffly. 'Nope. The Mrs Pendleton you're thinking of is my mother. She knew the old lady quite well – as well as anyone.' He gave her a curious look. 'But you must know all about her yourself. I've been looking forward to finding out a bit more about her. She was such a mysterious, lonely old thing. Mum remembered her husband but he was dead by the time I knew her. Once he went, she hardly ever left this place and as far as I know, she saw nobody but the chap who delivered her shopping and did her odd jobs – and us. But not even us very often.' He took another sip. 'So you can probably enlighten me quite a lot.'

'I'm afraid not,' Emily said, disappointed. 'I thought you'd be able to tell me something. I know even less than you – I never even met her.'

His brown eyes met hers over the top of his mug. 'Well, I did wonder,' he said as he put it down. 'I wondered how she'd found anyone to leave this place to. I thought you must be a distant relative we'd never heard of.'

Emily shook her head, and leaned over to spoon some porridge into Joe's mouth while it was open. 'No, I'm no relative at all. The explanation was that she left me the house because she was grateful to my aunt Cressida for selling her this place years ago. Apparently it was in our family at one time, though I'd never heard of it before.'

'What was your family name? Conway?'

'No. That's my married name. It was Fellbridge.'

'Fellbridge,' he repeated thoughtfully. 'Nope. I've never heard it. I'll have to ask Mum. She knows more about the characters who lived here ages ago – she grew up round here.' James paused, and she noticed how his cheeks were pink on the apples. 'So . . . you're married then?' he asked cautiously, looking around as though he expected a husband to jump out of the dresser.

She felt her own face redden. She'd been expecting this question at some point but she hadn't decided exactly what she would say, only that she would dodge the issue cleverly. But all her cleverness seemed to have deserted her right now. 'Yes, but . . . my husband isn't with us.'

James nodded. 'Working in the City or something? Is he going to commute at weekends?'

'No.' Her cheeks grew hotter. She pushed her hair out of her face and tucked it behind her ears. She saw his gaze go to her scar, linger for a second and then look away. She shook her hair back. 'He's . . . not with us.'

Somewhere at the back of her mind, she had

247

planned to tell people that Will had died. But she couldn't tell a lie like that, and certainly not in front of the children. And anyway, she had reckoned without Carrie being there, who licked her spoon and said conversationally, 'My daddy is very ill. He's in a hospital and he won't wake up, even if they shout really loudly in his ears and bang a drum.'

'Oh.' James took this in, growing pinker. 'Oh dear. I'm very sorry to hear that.'

Emily bit her lip and looked at the table. 'Yes. I'm afraid my husband's in a coma following a serious accident.'

'Well, that's awful.' James looked upset. 'I'm sorry for blundering in like that. I simply didn't realise.'

'There's no reason why you should,' she said, pained by his embarrassment. 'I know it sounds awful but we've all had some time to come to terms with it. Please don't feel bad.'

There was a pause. James took a gulp of his coffee and consulted his watch. 'Goodness, I need to get on.'

'Please don't go,' she said as he got up. 'I was hoping you could tell me more about Mrs Few.'

'I really must, I'm afraid,' he said, 'if I'm going to finish that fence and get back to the farm. I've got plenty on – this is the busiest time of year.' He stopped and stood very still for a moment, then fixed Emily with his open brown gaze. 'I hadn't realised how on your own you are.'

'You don't have to feel sorry for us. We're fine. Honestly.' She smiled back at him.

'I'm not sorry for you – well, I'm sympathetic about your husband, obviously – but a lonely place like this must be a shock for you after London. None of your cinemas or theatres or coffee shops. I don't suppose you know anyone up here either.' A thought seemed to occur to him. 'Why don't you come up to the house sometime? If you feel like it. My mother would be happy to tell you all about Mrs Few, as much as she knows anyway. You could ask her about the Fellbridge connection. She loves to talk about the past. We ought to invite you up anyway. I'll arrange it, get some neighbours over too so you can make some friends.'

'Well, that would be very nice,' Emily said, her heart sinking. She wasn't sure she wanted to be paraded to the neighbourhood quite yet. She was enjoying this quiet healing time with just her and the children. Visits and invitations . . . *I'm not ready for all that yet.*

'And if you need me' – his face was grave – 'any time of the day or night, you can ring me. Here's my card.' He fished a crumpled piece of cardboard out of his back pocket. 'I get reception if I'm up on the hills or at the top of the house. Otherwise, call the landline. They can always get a message to me.'

'That's very kind,' she said, taking it. 'But I'm sure we'll be fine.'

'Just in case.' He smiled, his open, pleasant demeanour returning. 'I'd feel happier knowing that you've got me to call on. Now, I'd better get back to mending that fence.'

The engineers arrived to put in her internet service. They fixed a satellite dish to the side of the barn in a discreet out-of-the-way place, and ran the wires into the house through the hole that had been drilled for the old aerial cable.

Emily stood watching as they set it up. *I swore I'd never have a dish on my house. But I'd be waiting about fifty years for them to lay cable all the way up here. So a dish it has to be.*

It meant that she could have all the things she was used to in London: catch-up on the television, dozens of channels, most of them rubbish, and a decent internet service. As soon as the engineers left, the children spent two hours in front of cartoons in the study, while she set up her computer on the morning room table and went through her crammed inbox. Even though it was lovely to reconnect, she was a little wistful for the calm and peace of those few days when she'd been separated from all of that. With nothing much to watch on the telly, she'd been going to bed early with a book. The children had been playing with toys they'd ignored for years, and listening to story tapes rather than sitting dazed in front of the rapid over-bright images on the children's channels.

Polly had sent several emails begging for news, the last one threatening to arrive on the doorstep with all three children if Emily didn't get in touch soon to let her know how things were going. Emily typed a rapid apologetic response, explaining why she hadn't been able to answer. She downloaded some of the pictures she'd taken of the house on her phone, and posted them on her Facebook page so that she wouldn't have to send them out dozens of times. Almost at once, the replies started, exclaiming over the beauty of the place and the house, and telling her how much she and the children were missed. She enjoyed reading them, even though it felt as though she was being deceptive. How could those pretty pictures of the house all tidy and cosy tell the real story of their arrival here, and everything she'd gone through? How could it explain the feeling of isolation, or the majesty of the hills and the scenery and how it both refreshed and unburdened her, making her problems seem small and fleeting in comparison to their age and grandeur?

Just then her computer chirruped and a chat box opened. It was Tom.

There you are. Hello, stranger. Was beginning to get worried. How are the kids?

She typed back rapidly.

Sorry. I've been offline and no phone reception either. I should have called to let you know we're all right but we are. Settled in. Kids v happy.

251

Great. How is it?

Gorgeous. You should come and see it.

I'd like that. In fact, was thinking of coming this weekend. I'm handing in the finals of my designs for that pitch tomorrow, so thought I'd catch the train up to Carlisle first thing on Saturday. Would that suit you?

She paused. A visitor already. It felt far too soon. But it was Tom – family. She typed:

Yes, of course. Please come. Bring wine, though – I don't have any yet. Must find a supermarket. Let me know your train time and we'll collect you from the station.

Great. I want to talk to you about something. See you on Saturday.

The next moment his name showed that he'd gone offline. Emily stared at it, feeling a little strange. The phrase about wanting to talk to her about something sounded ominous, as though he was planning to discuss something that wasn't altogether pleasant. She thought back to the evening when she'd told him about her inheritance. He'd been eager to hear all about it and when

252

she'd explained that the lady artist had actually left her her house, and that she intended to live there, he'd been as astonished as she had been in the solicitor's office.

'But . . . why?' he'd said bewildered. 'Why you? Are you sure you didn't know her?'

'No. It was because of Aunt Cressida. Catherine Few left me the house because I'm her relative. It once belonged to Cressida apparently.'

There was a pause as Tom absorbed this. Then he said, 'But I'm her relative too.'

'I know.' Emily looked at him and said hesitantly, 'I did say that in the lawyer's office. But Mrs Few specified a female relative. She was very clear about it. Even if I hadn't wanted it, another female relative would have taken priority.' She knew she wasn't being entirely honest; Mischal Diwani had said that there was nothing really binding in the specifying of a female relative being next in line. Emily was free to leave it to whomever she liked.

Tom was frowning, tracing his fingertip around the pattern of dots on the table's oil cloth. 'It's just a bit weird, isn't it? It sounds sort of sexist. And I mean, why not give the house back to Aunt Cressida?'

Emily shrugged. 'She must have assumed she's dead.'

'Perhaps she is.' Tom made a face. 'No one's heard of her for years, have they?'

Emily shook her head. 'Not as far as I know.

Perhaps Uncle Harry would know but I'm sure we'd have some idea if he'd ever been in contact with her. Dad barely mentioned her; I'm sure they weren't in touch. I wonder why on earth they were so disconnected. Perhaps she did something awful and they couldn't forgive her for it.'

'Maybe she ran away with someone unsuitable,' Tom suggested with a small smile. 'Gave her daddy a heart attack or something.'

They were both silent. They'd never known much about their grandparents on their father's side, both dead before they were born. Their mother's parents had been the only grandparents they'd really had.

'Well, I expect she's long gone,' Emily said finally. 'And the house is back in the family, like Catherine Few wanted.'

'Back in *your* family,' Tom had said, a sharp edge in his voice.

'*Our* family,' Emily said. 'We're all we've got now, remember?' She smiled at him, wanting to make peace. 'You must be a part of it too. I can't help thinking about what you said about the universe sorting things out. I feel like I sent up a big cosmic prayer in my hour of absolute need and, like some kind of miracle, back came this. A house. Just right for me and the kids, far away from all the bad things that have happened.'

Tom softened and he smiled properly. 'You're right,' he said sincerely. 'You deserve a break after all the shit you've been through. I'm glad this house has come to you.' He put his hand over hers and squeezed it. 'Maybe you're right. The universe has answered your prayer.'

After that, things had moved so swiftly she hadn't had time to think again about how Tom had taken the news. There had been so much to do – the legal issues to sort out, emptying out the London house and selling all her extraneous goods. The probate had taken longer than the completion of the house sale, and everything had gone into storage while Emily and the children had squeezed in with Polly, her husband Frank and the children for a chaotic few weeks. Then, somehow, all the hundreds of tiny things that needed doing had been done, and the jigsaw pieces fell into place – the bank was paid back and her bank account safely held the profit from the sale; the probate was passed, the taxes settled and the bills paid; and the deeds of the house were transferred to her name. Then came the day that the moving van arrived to load up all their things and off they set on the road.

But the night before they left, as Emily slept in Polly's spare bedroom, she dreamed again that, as so often, she was in Will's room at the hospital, standing at the end of his bed looking down on his supine body. He wasn't as withered and thin as he had been when she had last visited. Now he looked healthy, his arms muscled and vital as they had been before the accident.

She looked at him and was filled with a magnificent triumph. 'I've done it!' she said, power coursing through her, igniting her blood with strength. 'I've saved us. I'm taking the children and we're leaving. We're going far away where you'll never find us! So get used to being alone here in this coffin of a hospital bed. It's what you wanted and it's what you've got!'

He lay unresponsive for a moment as she relished her triumph over him, feeling free of him and all the evil he'd brought on them. But at the moment that she felt most victorious, she saw his arm quiver, then move. It went to his face and began to pull out the tubes from his nose and mouth and rip away the tapes. His eyes flicked open, hard and furious, then his mouth opened too and the most terrifying sound she had ever heard issued forth from it: a harsh satanic roar, like a demon's voice. As he roared, the room filling with the awful sound, he sat up, swung his legs over the side of the bed and stood up.

Trying to scream, she backed away to the door as he began to walk stiffly towards her, his eyes demonic and that ghastly bestial roar issuing from his open mouth. The door wouldn't open until his fingers were almost at her throat, and then she stumbled out into the corridor and began to run and run and run as fast as she could, knowing that Will was following her, determined to catch her . . .

She woke shuddering and shaking, a scream

still in her throat, and had to rush to the little bathroom next door and throw up violently.

That had been the last nightmare. Surely there were no more.

CHAPTER 16

The school was in a fizz of excitement as the holidays approached. Every classroom was decked in something Christmassy – cut-out snowflakes, strings of paper chains, handmade Christmas cards. Attention on the lessons waned and instead thoughts of Christmas fairs, the carol concerts and end-of-term celebrations were on everyone's minds.

Cressie felt detached from it all. She couldn't get excited about the end of term because she already felt as though she were not really a part of it. She would not be coming back next year. She had failed at her great project.

Her father had been delighted to hear that she would not be returning to Fleming in the New Year. 'You gave it a good stab,' he said condescendingly. 'But if you really want to work in a school for a few more months, I could have a word with the head of that girls' prep down the road. That would do nicely until you get married and have a family yourself.'

She felt deflated by this rescaling of her ambitions to something neat and manageable, nothing to cause any stir. She had meant to leave her own comfortable world, not embed herself ever more firmly in it.

'Perhaps,' she'd said wearily. 'I don't know. I think I need a rest from it all for a while.'

'Absolutely, you must rest. I'm sure you're tired out,' her father said. 'And what about this portrait of yours? Is it finished? You seem to have been sitting for months now.'

'It's finished, yes. Almost. Just the varnishing to do, and the frame if we want them to frame it for us.'

'What's it like? Is he any good, this Few boy?'

She thought of Ralph, sitting so intense in front of the painting, of the hours he'd devoted to it and the luminous beauty he'd given her. 'Yes,' she said wretchedly. 'He's very talented. The picture's wonderful. I think you're going to love it.'

'That's good,' said her father, taking up his paper again. 'Because his wife wrote to me asking for another instalment on the money owing. I was rather surprised as I've not seen it. But if you think it's decent, then I'll send her a cheque tomorrow.'

The next day, on her way out of the house, Cressie picked up a letter addressed to her that she must have missed the previous evening. On the train east, she opened it and read the elegant, sloping hand.

Dearest Cressida

Where have you gone? We love you and you've abandoned us! Your portrait is so

259

nearly finished it's trembling on the brink of completion, but we want you back so that we can pronounce it done. There is champagne waiting, of course, for the great moment. We can't open it without you, our angel of art. You were ill and we are praying that you've recovered and are ready for the very last session.

Please write or telephone and we'll arrange our next rendezvous.

With love and anticipation,
Catherine and Ralph

She felt the sickness of guilt as she read it over twice. She could imagine Catherine curling up to write it, sitting on the sofa, a book on her lap as a table. The light from the arched window fell on her pale complexion and touched the glints in her dark hair. Nearby Ralph was saying, 'Perhaps we should leave it, Cat. She doesn't want to return, that much is certain. Let's send the picture to her dad, get the last of the money and forget all about it.'

'No, no,' Catherine insisted as she wrote. 'We can salvage this. She's scared about something but we can calm her down and win her back. Perhaps I told her too much when I mentioned your heart. Perhaps our little argument over the colours distressed her. She's evidently very sensitive. Don't worry. I know how to reach her.' She waved the letter to dry the ink. 'This will do the job.'

Cressida folded the letter and tucked it back into the envelope. She would send a pleasant letter in return, saying how sorry she was that she couldn't come back to Blackheath for the foreseeable future. They must finish it without her. It was already marvellous; there was no need for her to be there.

At the school, as she made her way to the first class, she was startled to be stopped in the hall by a small, slight figure standing in her way.

'Oh, hello, it's you, Baxter.' She smiled down at him. He was the only person who could cheer her up at the moment.

'I wanted to thank you, miss,' Baxter said in his high voice. 'The postman brought a terrific parcel around last night an' I opened it. So many beautiful books. You're an angel, miss, you really are. An' I got your card too. I will read 'em all, I promise, an' I'll do my very best in Australia.'

Cressie's smile grew. She wished she could have witnessed Baxter's pleasure when he opened the box she'd ordered to be sent to his house. 'I'm so glad you like them,' she said happily. 'There are some wonderful books in there, some you might not like at once but you will one day, I'm sure of it. What did your mother think?'

'Well . . .' Baxter's glance slid away with a touch of embarrassment and then he said, 'Well, she did say that she wished you could of sent something useful, like the money all them books cost. But she was dead impressed that you thought enough of me to send 'em all. And she's said I can keep some of 'em with me for the trip. The rest'll go in our boxes that follow along afterwards.'

'That's excellent news.' Cressida laughed as she reached out and ruffled Baxter's hair. 'I'm going to miss you, Terence. I hope you have a marvellous life in Australia.'

'But . . .' He looked up at her hopefully. 'Miss, will you let me write to you? I'd be ever so honoured if you would.'

'Write to me? Goodness . . . why not? All right. You write to me if you like. I would like to have a friend in Australia. You'd be my first.'

'Thank you, miss. Where shall I write to?'

She thought for a moment. Where would Baxter always be able to find her? Not at her father's house. Surely, before very much longer, she would move out and start to stand on her own two feet. She was beginning to feel that living in that great house in Kensington was stifling her. To where would she always be connected? On impulse, she ripped a page out of the notebook she was carrying and pressed it against the wall so she could write the address. 'Here. You can always reach me here, at December House. It might take a while to get a reply from me, but eventually you will.'

Terence took the scrap of paper reverently, looking at it with wide eyes before he folded it up and slid it into his pocket. 'I'll never forget you, miss,' he said in a whisper.

Her eyes stung suddenly with unexpected tears. 'I'll never forget you either, Terence.' She put out her hand. 'Pals for life?' she asked.

He took it eagerly and shook it. 'Yep. Pals for life, miss.'

When Cressie arrived home, the doctor was just leaving. He nodded to her in the hall as he put on his hat, but didn't stop to talk to her.

'Is everything all right, Ellen?' she asked anxiously when the maid had shut the door behind him.

Ellen looked at her gravely. 'The nurse has been worried today but I'm sure it's nothing serious. The doctor's left another tonic and apparently your mother's sleeping now and she's a little better.'

'That's good.' Relief coursed through her. She knew it would come eventually, but she'd never wanted to peer too hard into the darkness of life after her mother died. 'I'll look in on her later, once she's awake.'

Ellen bustled past her on the way to the kitchen. 'Can I get you anything, miss?'

'Oh no, thank you. I don't need anything till supper.' As she spoke, there was a knock on the door. Ellen turned to answer it but Cressie held up her hand. 'Don't worry, I'll answer it. Look, the doctor's left his gloves. He's probably just noticed and he's back to collect them.' She scooped up the gloves. 'I'll give them to him.'

'Thank you, miss.' Ellen disappeared into the passage.

Cressie went to the front door and opened it. Ralph stood on the doorstep, muffled by a huge black coat and a grey scarf at his neck. His complexion was almost as pallid as the scarf and he looked cold and unwell.

She gasped. 'Ralph! What are you doing here?'

'I'm sorry, I hope you don't mind. I know you haven't wanted to return to us but I felt I had to see you if I possibly could . . .' His eyes were pleading, almost desperate. 'May I come in and talk to you? Just for a few minutes?'

'I . . . I . . .' She gaped at him. There had to be many reasons why he could not come in and why she shouldn't talk to him, but at this minute, she couldn't think of any. 'Of course. Come in.'

She dropped the gloves on the hall table as she passed, and led the way into the drawing room, indicating one of the large, stiff sofas for him to sit on, but he ignored her and went to the fireplace, resting one hand on the marble surround as though he needed support.

'Can I send for some tea?' she asked, still coming to terms with the fact that Ralph was right here, in her house. And without Catherine. 'Or whatever you'd like?'

He turned around to face her, and the emotion in his eyes almost made her gasp. 'No. No! I don't want anything. Only to speak to you.'

'Of course,' she said. 'How . . . how are you?'

'I'm in torment,' he said bluntly. 'It's making me ill. It's almost more than I can stand.'

'What is it? What's wrong?' Her heart went out to him. He was still the same Ralph, tall, elegantly shabby, the lick of dark hair falling into his eyes; but she could tell that he was in a state of desperation.

'You know what's wrong.' He looked at her, fixing her with his burning gaze. 'Why have you left us? You never came back after that day when Catherine told you about my . . . about the colours. Why not?'

She gaped at him, answers cascading through her mind. How could she begin to tell him that she was afraid of her own feelings and of the way she was sure that Catherine knew exactly what they were? And if Catherine knew, then what did Ralph know? How much were they complicit in their strange seduction of her, and what did they want from her exactly? She didn't know how to tell him that she was afraid they had created a trap for her between them, and that what scared her most was the idea that, in her deepest self, she longed to fall into it, to let the pair of them seduce her, use her, do what they wanted with her. When she was with them, she felt alive. The experience of being looked at so intensely by them both – after years of solitariness in her bedroom upstairs, when she'd felt utterly invisible – was intoxicating, giddying and addictive. But she feared what lay along that path because it involved things she knew were wrong: loving another woman's husband, even if – perhaps – that woman gave her permission for it; indulging her physical longings that must, surely, be sinful.

So she had pushed it away and tried to be resolute, calling on all her strength to pull herself out of their honeyed web while she still could.

When she didn't answer, Ralph bowed his head. 'I've done something to make you hate me.'

She stepped closer to him. 'No, you haven't . . . and it isn't the portrait either. That's beautiful. But I can't go back to the studio.'

'Why not?' He moved towards her. She caught a glimpse of them both in the mirror over the mantel behind Ralph. Her cheeks were pink and her eyes wide, while the dark hulk of Ralph's over-coat blocked out the rest of the picture. The sight of the two of them together, contained within the mirror's frame, excited her. It gave them a together-ness she had longed for, as though they were united inside their own picture.

She stared at him, revelling in being able, at last, to look without fear at his beautiful face, with its fine structure and fair skin and those incredible intense grey eyes. She'd had to steal glances at him for all these months, aware that Catherine's gaze was continually on her. 'I daren't,' she said in a low voice.

His face changed as he absorbed her words, his expression losing some of its desperation. 'Why? What are you afraid of?'

Cressie looked away, unable to say it. She stared at the slippery silk damask on the sofa, following its patterns with her eyes even though she wasn't really seeing it. The room, full of dark, heavy

266

furniture, crammed with ornaments, stifled by the great fringed velvet curtains, was oppressive, and she felt breathless.

Ralph took another step towards her. 'Is it the same thing I'm afraid of?' he asked. He reached out and took her hand in his. His skin was cool and smooth, and where it touched her, she felt a tingling sensation as her flesh responded to his. His closeness was making her heart race and her head spin.

'I don't know,' she whispered. She couldn't look at him at all now, only thinking of her hand in his, the shrinking distance between them, the way her body was beginning to tremble.

'I've fallen in love with you, Cressida. You know it, don't you?'

'Yes.' She sounded almost wretched, even though she'd longed to hear it. *We're done for now. It can't be unsaid. I'm afraid of it. But we can't keep denying it.* She realised that she had known almost from the first moment they met that they were destined to love one another. The feelings that had grown between them in the studio were beyond their control. Her attempts to keep her distance and repress what she felt had been pointless, she saw that now. Besides, she was only one half of this mysterious, unlooked-for union; what could she do about Ralph and the power of his feelings? *You know what you can do,* her inner voice told her. *You can refuse him. Send him away. Make him go back to where he belongs.*

'Cressida, do you . . . can you . . .' Ralph's voice

was full of yearning. He paused and then laughed wryly. 'I'm an idiot. How could you? Look at you – a beautiful girl, with all of this. And me – a poor artist with uncertain prospects. I'm nowhere near good enough for you. I'm an arrogant fool to think you might love me too.'

She gasped and looked up at him, her heart pierced by love for him as she saw the vulnerability in his eyes, that mixture of hope and fear she knew so well. 'But it isn't that!' she cried out. 'It would never be that!'

'Then what is it?' he asked breathlessly.

She stared at him, bewildered. How could he ask? She said it in one word. 'Catherine.'

A kind of shock passed over his face and his brow wrinkled as if in confusion.

'Your wife,' she reminded him.

He put his hand to his head, screwing his eyes shut as if a great pain had seized. 'Oh God,' he said in a desperate voice. 'Oh God.'

'I know. It's wrong of us,' Cressie said, clutching his hand now. 'That's why I couldn't come back to the studio. You and she . . . you are everything to each other, I can see that. I couldn't bear to come between you, I knew what I felt was wrong. I was afraid that I'd spoil everything.'

'No,' Ralph said, still unable to look at her, his head bowed. 'You don't have to be afraid of that.'

'But you love her and she loves you. You need her, your art needs her. She's your eyes,' Cressida said wretchedly.

Ralph took a deep breath and looked at her at last, his eyes desperately sad. 'It's not like that,' he said in a hollow voice. 'Our love isn't like that at all.'

'Like what?'

He paused then said, 'Married love.'

She was confused. 'But . . . what do you mean? You live together, you share a bed . . .'

'That bed . . . Didn't you notice when you were in our bedroom?'

She dropped her gaze, embarrassed, and nodded. 'They're two single beds. I thought . . . I don't know . . . I suppose I thought you just liked that style. They're close together, after all.'

'That's right. Close – but separate.' He bit his lip, an expression of agony crossing his face. 'You must believe me, Cressida. My relationship with Catherine is very complicated, perhaps even dangerous, but it isn't anything like what I feel for you.'

She stared at him, a kind of wild joy growing in her chest as his words sank in. She knew as soon as he said it that it was true. What she'd seen between them had lacked some vital spark. It was missing the element that fired passion. 'Please, believe me,' he said again, yearning in his voice.

'I do believe you,' she said almost wonderingly. His heart wasn't Catherine's at all, but only hers. *But* – the joy faltered a little – *that doesn't change the fact that he's married, even if he doesn't love his wife.*

Before she could think anything more, Ralph pulled her into his arms, enveloping her in the great black coat, wrapping her close to him. 'Cressida,' he said in a voice full of love and longing. 'You are my guiding star, my light. I love you. I can't help myself.' His fingers were under her chin, tilting her face up to his, and then his lips were on hers. The sensation was so giddyingly sublime, as though she was falling down a sweet dark tunnel lined with stars. Everything about him intoxicated her and as he coaxed her mouth open to kiss her properly, she wondered how she could ever leave his arms, or surrender this moment to the past.

Too soon, he pulled away to gaze down into her face. 'My Cressida,' he said tenderly. 'What have you done to me?'

She smiled back, knowing that the kiss had left her eyes shining with joy, and wanting to taste his lips again and again and again. 'What happens now?' she asked. She felt a reckless boldness growing in her. *We've done it now. How can we ever go back? This is just what I was afraid of . . .*

Ralph looked at his watch. 'My darling, I have to go. I told Catherine I was buying brushes. She'll be waiting for me at the Underground station.' He smiled at her, and kissed her lightly again. 'You don't know how happy you've made me. You will see me again, won't you? I can live if I know that.'

'Of course,' she said, 'but how?'

He pulled away from her reluctantly, lifting her

hand to his mouth for another kiss. 'I'll think of something.'

'I can't go back to the studio,' she said. 'Don't ask that.'

'Of course not. That would be madness.' He released her hand and walked to the door. 'I'll write to you. We'll find a way.' He smiled at her again, the old enchanting Ralph, the pain gone from his face. 'I love you. Never forget it.'

'Goodbye,' she whispered, hating to lose sight of him. A moment later, she heard the heavy front door close and he was gone.

CHAPTER 17

Emily woke to a strange scratching sound, almost like the patter of light rain. Bright moonlight came through the chink in the curtains. She knew it wasn't raining but she didn't feel afraid as she lay in her bed, coming to wakefulness, wondering about the noise she could hear. It was coming from directly above her, in the attic. She knew that there were attics, no doubt where the servants used to sleep, but she hadn't yet been up there. A small door next to Joe's room had a narrow staircase behind it that led up there, but she hadn't climbed it.

Getting out of bed, she put on her slippers and picked up the torch she kept by her bedside in case of a power cut. She went to the door to the attic and opened it, shining her torch up the dusty bare staircase. Would there be electricity up there? She looked for a switch but couldn't see one, so she climbed up anyway. It seemed to be fairly light at the top and as she got there, she saw that the moonlight was streaming in through the little dormer windows. There were three of them, one here on the central landing, and one for each of the attic's rooms that led off on either side.

She opened the door to one of them. It was illuminated by the moonlight that reflected off the whitewashed walls and shone on the dusty boards. It was a simple room, the sloping ceilings giving barely enough space to stand upright, and there was a tiny fireplace at the far end. A maid or the cook must have slept here once.

Shutting the door, she went to the other one and pushed it open too, expecting to see the same thing, but this room was different. The floor was covered by small round shapes glistening in the chilly light spilling through the little window.

What are they? she wondered. Then she realised. The moonlight had leached them of colour. *Apples. Dozens of them. They must have been stored up here where it's dry.*

She stared at them for a moment, and then heard a scratch and a scuttle and saw a tiny black shape whisk under the wainscot, a slender tail flicking after it.

Mice. Of course. This bounty must provide them with a good source of food all winter. I wonder why no one took them away when they were emptying the house. She noticed a crate in the corner. *There's something else they left behind. Maybe they forgot to check this attic.* She advanced into the room, treading carefully to avoid the apples. The crate was pushed against the far wall and she had to bend under the sloping eaves to reach it, but when she got there she found the top was nailed down and she couldn't lift it.

Mysterious, she thought. She wondered briefly if she ought to tell James about the crate, and give it to him without opening it. *I'm too curious. There are so few clues here about the past. I can't resist it. I'll come back with my hammer and open it.*

She went nimbly back through the field of apples and left them to the mice.

James called in the following morning with a delivery of milk, eggs and freshly baked bread. 'With my mother's compliments,' he said. 'We thought you might be getting a bit low. Do you know where the village shop is?'

'Not yet,' Emily said. 'Thank you so much for this.' She took the basket of food gratefully. 'I've just got to the end of my stores and was wondering where's best to go for supplies.'

'Your biggest supermarkets are in Carlisle but you shouldn't need to go all that way. There're plenty of shops over in the next village and you can arrange deliveries if you want them. We'll sell you eggs.' James smiled at her. 'You'll get the hang of it. There's plenty to find out. You probably don't even know the extent of your property yet.'

'No, I don't.' There had been a plan from the solicitors to show the boundaries, but they hadn't meant much to Emily without being able to see the place. She had the vague idea that there was more beyond just the garden but she wasn't sure how much.

James pointed towards the hills beyond the house. 'You've got the garden, orchard and the paddock beyond in that direction.' He moved his arm round towards the road. 'The fields over that side and . . . see that patch of woodland? Keeper's Cottage is there. That's yours, up to the road. The rest is bordered in by hedges along the roadside, and the stone wall.'

'Keeper's Cottage?' Emily echoed. She had seen something on the plans, now she thought of it, but had assumed it was an outbuilding of some sort. 'Another house?'

'House might be stretching it,' James said with a smile. 'It's just about habitable. Two rooms downstairs, two up, and an outside lavvy. But it's got electricity and water. I can't think when someone last lived there. I'll take you over there sometime if you like.'

'Is there a key?'

'It'll be under the flower pot by the door, I expect, if it's not in your house. Check the dresser drawer.' James climbed back into the muddy Land Rover. 'Right, I'm off. I've got lambs to attend to.'

The Land Rover roared off and Emily headed back to the house with her spoils.

The children were fizzing with excitement to see Tom again. As he got off the train, his old backpack slung over one shoulder, they both shrieked and ran along the platform to greet him. Emily was glad to see him too.

Perhaps I've become a bit too hermit-like for my own good, she thought, smiling broadly as she went to meet him. The two children were in his arms, smothering him in kisses. *It'll do me good to see Tom. And anyway, I want to show him the house.*

'How was the journey?' she asked as they drove back through Carlisle. The boot was full of supplies now from the big supermarket shop she'd done before meeting the train.

'Rather amazing. The scenery is spectacular, isn't it? I don't know this part of the world. Looking out of the window was breathtaking.'

'I know,' Emily said proudly, as though she'd discovered it herself and no one else had ever known it was here. 'And it's just an hour to the Lake District. The children and I will explore that at some point; I've always wanted to.'

He looked over at her keenly, his sharp blue eyes missing nothing about her. 'You look better,' he pronounced. 'More like your old self.'

She smiled, looking over at him and then back at the road. From the stereo, a Winnie-the-Pooh story played, the children listening, absorbed. 'I know. I feel like I'm beginning to get better here.'

'I don't mean like Emily before the accident. I mean Emily from a long time back. From before Will.'

She negotiated a big roundabout and then said brightly, 'I suppose that's a good thing.'

'Yes,' Tom replied. 'A very good thing.'

* * *

The children wanted to show their uncle around the new house so he was led by the hand at a snail's pace while they showed him everything they'd discovered about the new place. Emily was quite astonished to see how many hidey holes they'd found, and what they already knew about the house.

'This is Samuel Whisker's secret staircase,' Carrie announced solemnly, pointing out what was undoubtedly a mouse hole by the stairs.

'Oh dear, it is, I think,' Emily said, laughing. 'We've definitely got mice. I heard them in the roof and then saw one in the attic.'

'No reason why you can't all exist together, if they're not doing any harm,' Tom said with a shrug.

She wrinkled her nose. 'But not in the kitchen.'

'Maybe not there. But don't put out those horrible traps that squash them, will you? Do something kind.' He fixed her with his penetrating blue gaze again. 'I think we all need a bit more kindness in the world.'

'You're right. Besides, I don't want to the children to find poor little mashed mice in the mornings. Shall we go upstairs? I'll show you your room.'

'My room first!' cried Carrie, as she dragged him up after her.

Afterwards, when the children had been fed their supper, bathed in the old enamel bath, the water gurgling noisily through creaking pipes, read several stories by Uncle Tom, who had a very good line in funny voices, and finally settled to sleep,

Emily and Tom ate their own dinner in the morning room, candles on the table, a bottle of wine open, while they talked. Emily told him about the things she'd done to the house, how dirty it had been, and what a shock the range had been, though she loved it now she'd got the hang of it. 'It's like a pet – I have to feed it in the morning and again in the afternoon and last thing at night. In return, it purrs away happily and keeps us toasty warm.'

Tom laughed. 'A cooker with a personality. Excellent.'

She told him about finding the apples in the attic and how they must have been stored there but somehow forgotten when the house was cleared.

'Or someone couldn't be bothered to clear away dozens of apples,' Tom remarked. 'Apple crumble from now till Christmas, is it?'

'That's an idea. I should start using them if they're still in a decent state.' She sipped her red wine. She hadn't had a drink for ages and she was enjoying the muzzy, comfortable feeling. 'There was an old crate up there too. It's the only thing that might give me a clue about whoever lived here before – apart from the easel in your room, which I think was the old studio, but it makes quite a comfortable bedroom now the bed's up, if you ignore the paint on the floor.'

'You didn't open it then?' enquired Tom.

'No. I meant to but haven't got back up there. Shall we take a look tomorrow?'

'Yes, let's. I'd be interested.'

'I've met a neighbour too. He's called James Pendleton. He lives up in the farmhouse that looks down over the valley. Did you notice it as we came up to the house? He's been very kind. I asked him about Catherine Few, but he didn't know much about her. He'd never heard our name before either.'

'Oh?' Tom raised his eyebrows.

'He said I should speak to his mother – she knew Mrs Few apparently. She grew up here, so she might be quite a useful source of information.'

'Hmm.' Tom sat back in his chair, frowning. He sipped his wine thoughtfully.

Here it comes, Emily thought. *The thing he wanted to say to me.* She had a feeling she might know what it was – roughly, at least.

'The house is lovely,' Tom said, looking about. He gazed out of the morning room windows. The sun had almost entirely vanished now but there was still a little dark lavender light to show the shape of the orchard at the bottom of the garden and the massy hills almost black against the sky beyond. 'Really lovely. It's a haven.' He smiled at Emily. 'For some reason, it speaks to me. I feel at peace here, the same way I think you do. It's a safe place, isn't it? There's a natural goodness all around us – in the house and out of it.'

'Yes.' Emily nodded her head slowly. 'You're right. That's just how I feel.'

Tom hesitated, then said, 'But . . .'

'I knew there was a but,' she said wryly.

He gazed over at her, his expression serious. 'Yes.

But. I've been thinking about it, and I can't help thinking that it's very unfair that you've been left this house. If it was because you knew Catherine Few . . . well, that would be one thing. But it's because you're Aunt Cressida's relative. And that's both of us.'

Emily gazed at him helplessly. 'She wanted it to go to a female.'

Tom gave a scornful laugh. 'I can't believe you would support sexism in any form, Emily! It's wrong to distinguish on grounds of sex and I'd have thought it's just the kind of thing you'd want to take a stand against.'

'What do you want me to do? I know it's lucky for me, but you understand that this came at just about the worst moment in my life, don't you? To be left a house where I could live with the children when we were on the verge of being homeless?'

'I think that's rather overstating it,' Tom said curtly, tapping the table with his fingertips. 'I saw what you sold the London house for. I don't think you were down to your last twenty grand, were you?'

'The house was mortgaged by Will, for as much as he could get. Most of the sale money – and yes, it was a lot – went right back to the bank. The amount I did get . . . well, it's all I've got to live on for the foreseeable. I can't work right now, not with Joe so young. And that's even if I could find a job up here.' She looked at him pleadingly. 'Besides, Will stole all the money Mum and Dad left me. You've still got yours. In a way, this is a kind of replacement for that.'

'Oh,' Tom said airily. 'Mine's gone now.'

She looked at him, astonished. 'What, all of it?'

'Just about.'

'But you'd saved it so carefully for ages! What did you spend it on?' She frowned, trying to take it in. Tom had talked of using his inheritance as the down payment on a flat so he could move out of the rented place he shared with a friend. He'd had ideas about starting up his own business or investing it in various different ways. 'Where's it all gone?'

'It's not *all* gone,' he said defensively. 'There is *some* left. But I spent a lot last year. When I went travelling.'

Emily thought back to Tom's long, extended trip the previous year. Like a gap-year student, he'd packed his backpack and set off to see where the fancy took him. She'd rather lost track of him over the weeks he was gone, but then she'd been taken up with the children and the pace of everyday life. She'd got occasional emails, some from Peru, some from America. He'd been to India, where he'd Skyped her, brown and with sun-kissed hair, from a wooden hut in the hills. He'd emailed her a photograph of himself standing in front of the Great Pyramid in Egypt.

'I suppose that must have cost a lot,' she said uncertainly.

He nodded. 'Flights, accommodation, and all that.

281

And I wasn't earning during that time, so I had to pay rent and so on while I was away. And . . .'

'And?'

He leaned in towards her, his eyes suddenly intense. 'I had some pretty incredible experiences, particularly in Peru. Have you heard of something called ayahuasca?'

She shook her head.

'It's a very powerful tea brewed in the Peruvian jungle from the ayahuasca vine and a shrub called the chacruna, and it's been used for millennia for spiritual enlightenment and healing.' His voice became fervent and fast. 'There are retreats you can go on, where the shamans hold ceremonies in which you drink this tea, and then experience something . . .' He shook his head and blew out a stream of air between his pursed lips. 'Something amazing.'

'So you did this?'

Tom nodded. 'Yeah. Several times. I went on a fantastic retreat in the mountains of Peru, stayed there a whole fortnight.' He looked grave. 'I took part in rituals designed to help me identify pain in my spirit, and to find the cures I need. And to unlock my spiritual potential too. I needed to see some deeper realities.' His expression took on a beatific look. 'I've been in pain since Mum and Dad died. I'd never really confronted the accident or what it did to me. You know how guilty I felt about that row Dad and I had just before it happened. I was left with some bad guilt about the way he was taken before we'd resolved our conflict. I've also been battling some very dark forces.' He looked over at Emily meaningfully. 'Some of them to do with you.'

'Me?'

He nodded mysteriously. 'That's right. I've had to do battle on your behalf.'

She was confused. All this seemed a long way from her inheritance. 'So, what was it like, this aya . . . aya . . .'

'Ayahuasca. Well, it's quite an event. You have to purify yourself before you do it. Then the ceremony starts at night. We sit in a circle, each with a bucket. The shaman comes and administers the tea. It tastes pretty vile, I have to admit that, and a lot of people purge not long after taking it.'

'Purge?' she asked. 'You mean . . . be sick? Into the buckets?'

'Yes,' Tom said, almost defiantly.

'Well, that sounds revolting.'

'I suppose so, but that's not the point of it. You don't feel disgusted when it happens; it almost feels right, as though things you don't need are being expelled from your body – negative forces even. After that the visions begin.' He looked dreamy at the memory. 'The most incredible visions. Some are frightening, it's true, but I never had a bad trip. I experienced great bliss, a sense that I was seeing into the heart of the universe, and a realisation that I know some of the secrets of existence.' He stared into her eyes, his own intense. 'I mean it, Emily. I met Mum and Dad again, and we talked through

283

so much stuff. I wish you could have been there with me, it was incredibly moving. We all forgave each other for any hurt that remained unsettled while they were alive. Dad and I fixed everything between us and it gave me real peace. They told me that they're happy now, they really are, and they watch over us all the time. They adore your children, Emily. They really love them.' His face brightened and he laughed. 'I mean, they've seen everything! They honestly have!'

Emily's eyes stung with tears. As he talked, for a moment she had seen her parents again, talking to Tom, and believed for a second that they were watching over her and the children and the thought made her chest tighten with hope, love and longing. *But it's not possible . . . is it?*

'But,' she ventured, 'you said trip. That makes it sound like a drug, like LSD or something. You know, psychedelic.'

He looked pained at the very idea. 'Ayahuasca is, of course, a drug, just like this wine we're drinking is a drug, but it's not like LSD. It's been administered for thousands of years, and it's completely non-addictive. It's virtually impossible to overdose and only qualified shamans are allowed to use it. But it is the most powerful tool we have for spiritual knowledge.'

'It sounds like you've used it more than once.'

Tom nodded. 'Yes. I've done fourteen ceremonies.'

'Fourteen! That sounds like a lot.'

'It is. I'm quite experienced in the whole thing now.'

Emily looked over at him, disconcerted. She and Tom had always been close but she'd not known about this side of him. She remembered the night when she'd found him smoking cannabis in her kitchen, and the strange things he'd said then. It seemed that was only the start of it all. He was on a journey that she had only the vaguest idea about. She loved him dearly and had always trusted his view of the world, but going with him into this new place was a step beyond what she was comfortable with. Her parents visiting and talking to him? It was a fantasy, surely . . . Or was it? 'Well,' she said diplomatically, 'it sounds amazing.'

'It's led me to think about what this legacy you've got really means.'

'Oh?' They were back at the legacy again.

'I think Mum and Dad would want you to share it with me.'

'Well . . .' She blinked at him. 'I'm happy to share it – more than happy. I want you to feel at home here. You can come anytime you like.'

'I mean financially,' Tom said bluntly. 'I'm broke, basically. You could get a mortgage on this and give the money to me.'

She stared at him, astonished. She hadn't expected this. 'Tom, I don't even think I'd be allowed a mortgage with no job. But if you need something to tide you over, you know I'm always happy to help out . . .' An idea suddenly occurred to her. 'You know what? Apparently the house has a cottage attached to it. It's called Keeper's Cottage. James told me about it this morning but I've never seen it. It's supposed to be a sweet little place, with electricity and water. Why don't we think about that for you?'

Tom looked interested. 'That sounds intriguing.'

'We'll take a look at it tomorrow,' Emily said, 'and you can tell me what you think.'

There was a pause while he thought about this. 'All right,' he said at last. 'Maybe that's a solution.' He looked over at her almost beseechingly. 'I only want what's fair, Em.'

'I know,' she said. 'I want that too. I know I've been very lucky and if I can share that with you, I'd be very happy.'

'Me too,' he said, lifting his glass and draining it. 'Me too.'

CHAPTER 18

Cressida's mood fluctuated from a state of unbelievable joy to terrible despair. She could think about little else but Ralph, the things they had said to one another and the glorious moment of their kiss. It had been so intoxicating, so instantly addictive, that the idea she might pass the rest of her existence without another kiss from him was unbearable.

She moved in a dream, half in the real world, half with Ralph. The last day of the school term passed in a blur and only her farewell with Baxter managed to draw her from her dream for more than a moment.

'Don't forget, miss,' the boy said, as he shook her hand for the last time, 'I'm going to write to you.'

'I won't, Terence,' she said fondly, smiling at him. 'Enjoy your journey and your new life. I want to hear all about it, so write as soon as you can.'

The farewells from other staff members were perfunctory, most doing little more than wishing her a merry Christmas, but she didn't care a bit for any of them. Leaving the school no longer stung. Her future was a mysterious place, alternately exciting and full of bliss, and miserable and lonely. Her imagination spun incredible scenarios in which, somehow, she and Ralph were able to be together without hurting Catherine, and with the approval of their families. After that, a gilded life awaited them, with Ralph ascending the summit of artistic greatness – a fellow of the Royal Academy, knighted perhaps – with her at his side, becoming his eyes as Catherine had been, tending to him and helping him as she had, but with the difference of the great love they shared.

Those dreams were pleasant and seductive, but when she wasn't lost in them, she was counting the minutes until Ralph contacted her again and wondering when and how they might see one another. It was agony, but a different kind from the shame she'd felt before, twisting under the sheets of her bed in self-loathing at her desires. Now she veered between hope and despair in another way: beneath it all the great knowledge that she was loved by the man she adored, a knowledge that could provoke a gleeful, girlish excitement that fizzed almost unbearably through her body, or a deep delightful calm in which she felt that all the vicissitudes of the world could not now touch her. She had Ralph and he had her, and that would make everything all right.

Except that we don't have one another – not yet.

The joy of being loved by him was shot through with the agony of their being separated, and the fact of her inability to see him and speak to him when she needed him. There was the torture of knowing he was with another woman, even if there was nothing between them. It was almost too much to bear at times.

She was sure, though, deep inside herself, that somehow it would all work out.

But when will I hear from him?

Christmas was almost upon them, and Cressida found herself in a whirl of parties. The cards she'd left on the hall table, ripped open with excitement and then abandoned impatiently when the contents weren't from Ralph, had all been accepted on her behalf and her father insisted she went.

The girl staring back at her in the hall mirror as she went to leave of an evening looked like the Cressida from another life: she wore stiff cocktail dresses, spike-heeled shoes and little fur jackets, and her dark hair had been set and styled by Raymondo of Queen's Gate with a lift at the crown and a sharp curl at the edge. Her eyelids were heavy with false lashes and her lips moist with pale pink lipstick. She drank champagne at parties in rooms with sparkling chandeliers, ate supper with thirty others at long shiny tables shimmering with candlelight, danced in a late-night club to music by a band from America. She knew the people at these parties; the girls who came up to chatter to her and tell her excitedly about engagements and weddings and yet more parties were her friends. And yet she felt as though she were with strangers, going through motions, left untouched by what was happening around her. Only her dream life, with Ralph, felt real.

'Cressida, hello. How are you? It's been ages.' The voice was nervous beneath the bluster.

She was standing on the upstairs landing of a grand house, watching the many guests coming in through the huge front door below, moving on the chequered marble like dressed-up chess pieces. Startled by the voice, she looked around to see Adam beside her. It had been so long since she'd seen him that she almost didn't recognise him for a moment. He wore a dinner suit, his black bow tie neatly tied, the jacket sleeves just a little long over his wrists. He had a sheen of sweat over his nose and he shifted awkwardly from leg to leg. She wondered how she'd ever been able to endure him touching her.

'Hello, Adam, how are you?' she said politely.

'I'm very well. You look jolly nice.' He gazed at her appreciatively.

'Thank you.' She looked down at the black shift dress she was wearing, belted in around her waist with a strip of shiny patent leather that sported a big round buckle. Long white evening gloves went up to her elbow.

'I haven't seen you for a little while,' he ventured. 'I've missed you. Did you get my messages? I telephoned a few times and sent you a letter.'

Her brow wrinkled. Had he? She had a vague

memory of Ellen leaving her a note by the telephone with a list of calls she'd missed, and perhaps a letter. She felt irritated by him. Didn't he realise it was a waste of time? There was nothing between them, surely he could tell that?

She leaned in towards him suddenly, her glass of champagne pressed to her chest. 'Adam,' she said, 'have you ever been in love?'

He was immediately more awkward than ever, his gaze sliding away from hers and then back again. He gave a forced laugh. 'Well, what kind of question is that to ask a chap? Bit of a tricky one, isn't it? Hard to say the right thing.'

'Well, have you?' she asked firmly.

He swallowed and said, 'Of course, Cressie – with you.'

She shook her head. 'Then you haven't. That's not love, Adam, I'm sorry to say. Don't waste any more time on me, do you hear? Go and find a girl who sets off fireworks for you and who you do the same for. The rest of it is a waste of time. I've just discovered that for myself.'

The bewilderment in Adam's eyes began to clear and indignation took its place. 'Here, are you saying—'

She put a hand on his arm to stop him, her white glove stark against his black dinner suit. 'I'm sorry if I've hurt your feelings but there's no point in prolonging it. Go and find that firework girl. She might be here right now, looking for you.' She passed him her glass of champagne and said, 'I'm going now. Goodbye, Adam.' She smiled at him, full of a sudden fondness for him. 'And merry Christmas.'

The taxi delivered her back to the Kensington house and she let herself into the dimly lit hall. On the table lay a letter with the handwriting she knew so well now. Gasping, she snatched it up and slipped off her spike heels so that she could run up the stairs. Throwing herself down on the bed, she read it eagerly.

My darling
I'm sorry it's taken me so long to write to you. My heart and mind have been full of nothing but you, but I couldn't bear to scrawl off some nothing. I needed to write something that would reflect what you mean to me. I miss you more than I can say. With every moment that passes, my love for you grows deeper and my hunger for your presence more intolerable. But I can bear it because now I know you feel something of the same for me. Before that, I was dying of it. Now I'm growing stronger every day. Catherine has noticed, of course – how could she not? But she is delighted that her pills are working so well.

She has spoken to me of you. She's concerned that we haven't heard from you and that you're somehow displeased with us. She wants to write to you again, but I've told her to wait until after Christmas before she does any more.

She sees the sense in that. As it is, she's busy with our own arrangements. We'll spend Christmas here, as we always do, and Catherine will turn the studio into the most Christmassy thing you ever saw: she collects ivy from the common, and holly and branches of pine from wherever she can find them, and makes the place into the most splendid bower. Our tree is decorated on Christmas Eve and we'll go to Mass at the church. A kind patron of ours sends a hamper each year and we open it with all the excitement of the Cratchit family receiving their largesse, promising ourselves that some year we'll be able to afford these luxuries and more.

I usually take great pleasure in it. But I can't this year. It's all such hollow frippery when the love of my heart is away from me. It means nothing without you.

I do not know how to destroy the life I have but I only know that I must. I fear for you and for us, but when the chance – the only chance – for happiness comes our way, we cannot let it go, can we?

I don't know when I can see you, darling Cressida, except for every moment in my mind's eye, of course, and in your portrait – a delightful little instrument of torture that's turned out to be!

Wait for me. Think of me. Dream of me. I'm thinking and dreaming of you.

I'll write soon. Merry Christmas, my love.

Your Ralph xxx

She read it over and over and slept with it in her hand.

'Cressie, you look so much brighter. Has something happened?'

Her mother was gazing over at her. Lately Cressie had taken to reading aloud from a novel to amuse her in the afternoons when the nurse went off for her break. Cressie looked up from the page, startled. She flushed. 'Oh. Do I?'

Her mother smiled, lightening the wanness of her skin for a moment. 'Yes, you do, my darling. Bright and happy, and distracted and dreamy, and all the other things that being in love do to you.'

Cressie opened her mouth to deny it, and then couldn't. She smiled instead, a big broad smile bursting out of her. She longed to share her happiness. 'Yes,' she said joyfully. 'I am in love.'

'Ah.' Her mother's eyes brightened. 'Who is he? Someone you met at the school?'

'No . . . no . . .' She felt her happiness die down a little as she considered what she could tell her mother. Knowing that it was Ralph and that he was married would only make her miserable and unhappy. 'He's a friend.'

'Can you tell me about him?'

Cressie leaned forward and grasped her mother's hand with hers. 'Oh Mama, I long to tell you but I can't . . . not yet.'

'It's a secret?' Mama smiled again. 'All right. As

long as you promise to tell me everything when you can.'

'I will, I will.' She burned to talk about Ralph, to extol him, rhapsodise about him, sing his praises for hours. She couldn't resist. 'He's very handsome, Mama. So tall and with such beautiful eyes. And his nose, it's perfect! His hands are so amazing, a true artist's hands, with long fingers. I'm sure he plays the piano—'

Mama broke in. 'Is he an artist?'

Cressie stopped short, discomfited by the direct question. 'Well . . . yes.'

'Oh dear.' Mama looked suddenly unhappy. 'Is it your portraitist?'

Cressie flushed at once, knowing she looked guilty. 'Yes,' she said, smiling despite herself.

Mama laughed. 'Oh, my darling, how wonderful that you feel this way! I'm so glad. It's marvellous, isn't it? But . . .' Her smile faded. 'You know that Papa won't feel the same at all.' She looked meaningfully at Cressie.

'I know,' Cressie replied in a low voice, her pleasure suddenly gone. 'He'll hate it.'

'My darling, he'll forbid it. We both know that.'

They stared at each other in silent understanding of Papa.

'What can I do?' Cressie asked desperately. 'Why does he want to ruin any chance of happiness I have?'

'He doesn't understand you, or anyone who wants to live in a way that's different from what he knows. He thinks he's doing what's best for you.'

'I can't live according to his demands! I won't!' Cressie declared.

'Of course not, it's impossible. It's taken me a lifetime of trying and I've never yet pleased him,' Mama said wistfully. She was lost in thought for a moment and then said, 'I'll do what I can for you, but it won't achieve much. If your love affair is ever to go anywhere, you must be careful.'

'I will,' Cressie promised.

Mama smiled at her. 'You're braver than I am.'

'That's not true,' Cressie protested. 'I've never known anyone braver. To live with Papa for so long and not hate him . . .'

'Hate is a terrible thing, Cressie,' her mother replied. 'I've always tried not to let it poison the life I have. Your father is worthy of love and I've given him all I can. That was my story. When you're ready to tell yours, I want to hear it.' Her mother smiled again. 'Now, shall we have a little more of the book?'

The sweet torment of Ralph's letter was that Cressie could read it over and over, but she couldn't write back, only wait for him to contact her again. Christmas passed, her brothers came home, grown plump and respectable in their City jobs, and her mother even managed to descend for Christmas Day, thinner and more wan-looking than ever. The new tonic did not appear to be having much effect but she was determinedly cheerful with her family around her.

At least there was a little sparkle and activity on Christmas Day: the walk to church, the festive lunch, the traditional jigsaw puzzle in the afternoon while her father read aloud to them from Dickens. Boxing Day dawned chill and grey and she felt bleak.

What now? This is agony.

She passed the time the only way she could think of: by opening her paint box and her little sketch pad and trying to draw Ralph. Her effects were amateurish and laughable when she thought of his skill, but it comforted her a little to spend time conjuring up his face in her imagination.

The card arrived the next day, a plain postcard in an envelope. She opened it with trembling fingers.

> Catherine is spending tomorrow with Mrs Bathurst. Meet me at the bandstand in Kensington Palace Gardens at 10 a.m.
>
> Rx

She was there the next day at a quarter to ten, wrapped up against the cold weather in her black astrakhan coat with the high fur collar, and in her fur-lined boots, a silk scarf around her hair. The bandstand stood near the Round Pond, slender white pillars supporting its ornate oriental-styled roof, but the gate in the iron railings that surrounded it was firmly locked, so she stood by it, looking about for Ralph, wondering which side he would approach from. She gazed over at the palace, its dark red brick stark against the grey park with its bare trees, then south towards Kensington Road, not busy at all on this early winter morning with the holiday feeling still in the air, and finally at the round roof of the Albert Hall rising in the distance.

A train from Blackheath to Victoria. A bus from the station up to Sloane Square and down Sloane Street to Knightsbridge. From there, along the park to the Albert Hall stop. Surely that's the way he'll come.

She leaned against the chilly railings, watching the people pass by, only interested in one figure.

Then her heart leapt. There he was, coming, as she'd thought, from the south, striding towards her, his hands deep in the pockets of his greatcoat, a grey almost military-looking cap on his head. He was smiling as he reached her, his eyes bright with happiness, his arms thrown wide for her to run inside them and let him enfold her in his embrace. She sought his lips, their coldness giving way to the delicious warm of his mouth.

'I've missed you,' he said with a groan when at last they pulled away from each other.

'Oh, I've missed you too,' she said. She felt complete again, enveloped in bliss by his nearness.

'You're freezing.' He touched her cheek softly with his fingertip.

'So are you.' She couldn't stop staring at him, absorbing every aspect of his face, each feature a fresh delight. He took her hands in his, clasping them tightly.

'I'd forgotten how beautiful you are,' he

murmured. 'My picture doesn't do you justice. I've been looking at it all the time and it's a sad and sorry substitute for you.'

'Of course.' She smiled. 'Because it can't do this.' She kissed him again, dropping small touches on his lips and cheeks, inhaling his scent that made her think of old sandalwood and lemons.

'Oh Cressida. Christmas was an ordeal. Nothing brought me joy. I only thought of you.'

'It was the same for me.' She pressed her forehead against his chest, then looked up, searching out his grey eyes. 'Ralph, what are we going to do?'

He bit his lips. 'I don't know. But . . .'

She was anxious at once. 'But what?'

'Not here. You're cold. Let's go somewhere warm. Somewhere no one will see us.'

They held hands and walked together north-wards, finding a small, steamy cafe near Queensway, a working man's place where Cressida was sure they wouldn't be known. Two big mugs of tea were put in front of them by a waitress who eyed them suspiciously.

'You shouldn't be here,' Ralph said a little forlornly, looking at the table with its chipped yellow Formica top. 'I want to take you to the best places there are.'

'Don't you understand?' Cressie put her hand on his, trying to convey all the earnestness she felt in her gaze. 'That doesn't matter. None of it matters if you're not there. I've been in some of the grandest houses in London lately, and I hated it – because you weren't there. As long as we're together, I can live any life. Any life anywhere.'

'That makes me very happy. I just wish I could give you everything you deserve.' He smiled at her, but his eyes were sad.

'What is it, Ralph? Is it Catherine? Has she guessed?'

He shut his eyes and a look of pain crossed his face.

'Ralph?' Anxiety rushed through her. 'What is it?'

He opened his eyes and said slowly, 'She hasn't guessed. At least, I don't think she has.'

'Then—'

'There is something very wrong between us – between Catherine and me, I mean. I can't explain, so please don't ask me to. All I can say is that the way I'm living right now . . . I believe it's killing me.'

She gasped. 'What?'

Ralph nodded. 'I know. It sounds ridiculous. Dramatic. But I'm not well, Cressie. I'm getting sicker.'

Icy fear gripped her, spreading through her veins and making her fingertips tingle unpleasantly. 'Your . . . heart?'

'I don't know. Perhaps.' He looked hopeless suddenly. 'I don't know what it is. I only know I have to get away from Catherine. She's . . .' He stumbled over his words, as though not knowing quite how to say what he meant. 'She would do something reckless to keep things as they are.'

Cressie stared at him, bewildered. 'But she loves

you. I've seen that since I first met you. Are you saying that she would hurt you?'

'She might not want to,' he said. 'But she might not be able to help herself if she felt that our life together was threatened.'

'But surely she would hurt *me*,' Cressie said. 'I'm the one causing the trouble, after all. I'm the problem. Without me, things would be as they were before.'

Ralph looked sadder than ever. 'You don't understand, my darling. Things could never carry on as they were. I told you, our love isn't what you think. Catherine knows it. She doesn't want to accept it.

'But why did you get married then? You must have loved her once!'

An agonised expression crossed his face. 'Please don't ask me that. I can't explain, not now. One day perhaps.' He took her hand again, his knuckles whitening as he held it in an iron grip. His eyes became intense, the gold in them flickering as he gazed at her. 'All I know is that I have to get away, and soon. Today Mrs Bathurst came to my rescue. There may not be another opportunity.'

'What do you mean?' Her heart began to pound again. 'Get away?'

'I have to leave. I think it might be the only way.'

'Where will you go? To your uncle?'

Ralph laughed shortly. 'No. That would be no escape. Besides, he tolerates me but that's about it. He'd welcome me like a dose of salts.'

Cressie's mind raced. The answer came to her,

clear as day in her mind. 'We'll go away together,' she said breathlessly.

'What?' He laughed lightly. 'I don't think your father would approve of that. Run away with me? He'd cast you off for something like that.'

She thought of her father's anger if he had the faintest inkling of what she was thinking, and imagined his rage if she actually went. She saw him storming around the house, bellowing and threatening the whole household, throwing things and smashing ornaments in his fury. 'I don't care about that,' she replied firmly. *Let him throw his tantrums, like a giant baby. I've had enough of living my life to please him.* 'Besides, there's no need for him to know that we're together. We have a house, a family house in Cumbria. It's empty and has been for ages. Someone looks after it for us when we're not there. There's no way that Catherine would know where you are, if that's what you're worried about. We could go there. Together.' As she spoke it aloud, the plan became more and more obvious and simple. She spoke rapidly to convince him. 'I'll tell my father I'm going to give up the idea of teaching entirely, and that I need to recover from the term I spent at Fleming. He'll probably be so glad I've given up the idea of it, he won't ask too many questions. But we'll go together.' She had a fleeting picture of her mother, left alone with Papa, but thought quickly, *We won't stay away for long. Just long enough to get everything clear. Mama told me to be brave, and this is brave.*

Ralph's eyes were growing bright. 'Perhaps it could work, perhaps it really could . . .'

'But it means destroying your life with Catherine. Are you ready for that?'

'I can't tolerate it another minute,' he declared, and she could see the fervour in his eyes. 'I have to leave. It will kill me to stay, do you understand?'

She nodded. 'I understand.' A great happiness swelled inside her. Was it really possible that she and Ralph would be able to be together, undisturbed by the outside world? She felt almost faint with pleasure at the thought. Her mind became focused on it – it must happen at all costs.

'The trains go from Euston station,' she said. 'I can telegraph ahead and the house will be ready for us. We could go tonight.'

'Tonight?' Ralph blinked and laughed almost disbelievingly. 'Yes, we could.'

She was eager, bursting with energy now. 'You go back to Blackheath and pack a bag. We'll meet at Euston in time for the early evening train. It's three hours or so to Carlisle. We'll find someone there to drive us to Howelland. We'll arrive late but I don't suppose that matters.' She felt her cheeks redden as she suddenly realised the implication: she and Ralph would be alone. They would spend the night together. The first of many.

Ralph was still absorbing the idea, as though trying to think of reasons why it was impossible and being unable to find one. His expression began to change: hope glowed in his eyes, and his whole demeanour altered, as though some burden was being lifted from him. 'It's really possible,' he muttered. 'She would never guess, surely . . . even if she learned that you'd gone away, how would she know where?'

'Hardly anyone knows of this place,' she replied. 'There's no way she could find out where we were, I'm sure of it.' *I'm wicked*, she thought as excitement bubbled through her. *I should send Ralph back to his wife, not lure him away.* But then she remembered how he had said he would leave in any case. It was obvious he considered his marriage over. *I'll learn more when we're alone together.* Her heart thrilled at the idea of being with him, hours and hours of blissful togetherness, with no one at all to interrupt them.

He gazed at her, the happiness growing in his eyes, mirroring what she felt. 'Yes,' he said, his tone intense. 'We can do it. But we must do as you say: go tonight. If we don't go at once, we'll never be able to, I'm sure of it. Are you really prepared to do this, Cressida? You'll be ruined if we're found out.'

She laughed. 'Ruined! This isn't the nineteenth century! I want to do it. We will do it. Shall we?'

He said simply, 'Yes.'

CHAPTER 19

'Wow. It's great. It really is.' Tom turned to Emily, excitement in his eyes. 'I love it.'

They'd gone looking for the old cottage the next morning after breakfast and had found it in a clearing of the small thicket of woodland on the edge of Emily's property, just as James had said. It was a ramshackle, neglected place, nowhere near as habitable as James had implied. The roof was heavily mossed, with slates askew or missing entirely, a couple of window panes were broken and the rest were filthy, and inside it felt damp and extremely cold. Leaves and rubbish covered the floor, some old furniture was gradually falling to pieces, and the kitchen wasn't much more than an old sink and a single tap. But it definitely had potential.

They had to locate the fuse box and switch on the electricity supply, and then the dusty light bulbs flared into life. The tap ran with fresh cold water and there was a working lavatory out the back. Upstairs, the two bedrooms were empty, with damp patches under the leaking roof and mess from birds and mice on the floor.

'Do you honestly like it?' Emily frowned as she looked about. 'It needs a lot of work.'

'A bit of a clean,' Tom said easily. 'I can do that, no problem.'

'The roof needs mending.'

Tom wrinkled his nose. When things were right, they were right as far as he was concerned, and nothing was going to get in the way. 'It's fine. I'm sure I can patch it up.'

'Roofs need professionals, I think.' Emily watched the children kicking the leaves in the bedroom. The place seemed generally sound, that was true. 'Would you live here?' she asked.

Tom put his hands on his hips and looked around the room, his eyes shining. 'It would be great to have the option. I could stop paying rent to Shelley and come here when I need some quiet space to work. The light's good but if we get the roof fixed we could also put a skylight in – that would make it even better. I wouldn't be here all the time, I'd have to be able to stay in London too . . . but . . . maybe I could camp with a friend.' He looked at her meaningfully. 'I really like this place.'

'Okay,' Emily said, glad to see him so happy. The talk they'd had the previous evening had unnerved her. She'd had no idea of the side of Tom's life that took him all over the world in search of psychedelic experiences from strange concoctions. But now he seemed perfectly normal and it was possible to forget it all. This morning he'd played with the children and helped her get breakfast, and everything had felt comfortable and familiar. Just the same as ever. She told herself there was nothing to worry about.

On the way back from Keeper's Cottage, Emily said, 'Why don't I get a builder to come and take a look at the place? If the repairs don't cost too much, I could pay for them and then the cottage can be yours for as long as you need it.'

Tom gave her a sideways look. He was carrying Joe on his back, bouncing him until the boy giggled uncontrollably. 'As long as I need it? I thought you were going to give it to me.'

She was silent. She felt as though, in a strange way, it wasn't hers to give. It was part of the whole, a part of December House. Was she really able to peel a bit off and give it away? 'Let's get the quote and see how it goes,' she said at last. 'I do want to make it up to you if you feel it's unfair that I got this place. We'll work out something that means we're both happy.'

'Okay,' Tom said, but he stared at the ground, frowning for a while. Emily had the distinct impression that he was only agreeing in order to buy time to strengthen his case in some way but she had no idea how.

That afternoon, while Joe was napping and Carrie was in front of her favourite cartoons, they went upstairs to the attic.

'Here it is,' Emily said, opening the door to the apple room. It looked a lot less spooky in the daylight. The apples were no longer grey but they looked old. Some were yellowing and wrinkled with mushy brown spots. 'James Pendleton told me there was an odd-job man who did work for Catherine Few. Maybe he put them up here and forgot to tell anyone. I don't think they'll be suitable for eating after all. Look, most of them are beyond it now.'

'Too much light in here, I should think,' Tom said. 'Whoever put them in here probably didn't expect to leave them so long. It would be dark and cold up here in the autumn and winter but it's getting too warm now. We'll chuck them out, shall we?'

'It seems a waste,' Emily said sadly. Something about the expectation with which the apples had been put here, and the reality that they would never be used, seemed terribly sad. Another intimation of mortality.

'You could turn them into cider,' Tom offered, stepping over them. 'Is this the crate you mentioned?'

Emily nodded. 'It was here when I came up.'

'Well, let's take a look then.' He put the hammer he'd brought with him under the crate's lid and with a few tries, he levered the lid off, wood splintering around the nails as it came free. 'Here we go. Let's see what's inside.' Putting the hammer down, he lifted out the straw covering the contents and peered in. 'Oh! Wow! Paintings.'

Emily bent over to look inside as well. Sure enough there was a small stack of unframed canvases in the crate. She lifted out the top one, looking at it curiously. It was a winter scene, well executed, showing the frozen snowbound landscape.

'She liked snow, didn't she?' remarked Tom, staring at it hard.

'Yes.' Emily tilted her head to one side and looked as well.

'It's very good,' Tom said, frowning. 'It takes skill to evoke snow like that. Look at the snowdrifts and the way she's given weight and form to them even though they're white on white. It's very skilful.'

Emily gazed hard. She could almost feel the chill coming off the canvas, the burn of the ice and the smoky frost on top of the drifts. There was something familiar about the scene but she couldn't quite identify what. 'Do you think it's of somewhere around here?'

'Most likely. She only stayed around here, didn't she? But the snow has a blanketing effect so it's hard to tell.' Tom stared at the painting, evidently fascinated. 'What are the others like?'

Emily peered in the crate. 'Very similar from what I can see. Snow scenes mostly.'

'Hmm.' Tom looked at her. 'Do you mind if I take this one? I really like it.'

'Of course not. It's beautiful. I might take one down myself for my room.' She took out the canvas on the top of the pile and regarded it. It was another evocation of the landscape covered in snow but painted from a slightly different perspective. 'This is nice.'

'Yeah, it is.' Tom frowned at it quizzically. 'I wonder why she painted the same thing over and over.'

Emily shrugged. 'Come on, we'd better go back down. And incidentally, how do you go about making cider?'

Tom went back to London on the Sunday afternoon train, the children waving him off on the platform. Emily watched him go with mixed feelings. It had been lovely to have company and the children had adored having their uncle with them.

Perhaps they're missing a male presence.

Carrie had stopped talking about Daddy almost entirely. She had started asking instead when James was coming to see them.

'James?' Emily had said surprised.

'Is he your boyfriend?' Carrie asked, playing with brightly coloured Duplo farm pieces. She'd carefully placed a sheep in a trough.

'Boyfriend?' Emily laughed, the word sounded so strange in Carrie's mouth.

Carrie fixed her with a solemn gaze and nodded. 'He stayed for a sleepover, didn't he? So he must be your boyfriend. Will he be our new daddy now that old daddy won't wake up?'

'Oh darling.' Emily swept her into her arms and pressed her lips into Carrie's sweet-scented hair. 'What makes you think that? James hasn't had a sleepover here.'

'He came for breakfast,' Carrie said, as if her

logic were irrefutable. 'You only have breakfast after you've been asleep somewhere.'

'He was outside, mending the fence for us. I just asked him in, that's all.'

'Oh.' Carrie took this in. 'So he's not your boyfriend?'

'No, sweet thing. He's just our friend. A kind and helpful friend who looks after us. Daddy will always be your daddy.' She clasped Carrie tightly, her heart swelling with love and sadness. She had no idea what went through the children's minds, how they processed all the things that were happening. The tantrums and the bewildered misery at their father's absence seemed to be tailing off – did that mean they were forgetting Will? That was sad in itself, for them and for him. She sighed heavily, taking comfort in Carrie's warm body.

'Will I ever see Daddy again?' Carrie asked in a small voice.

'Yes, darling, of course you will,' Emily said as stoutly as she could. 'We hope every day that he'll get better.'

When she said it to Carrie, she almost believed it too.

James recommended a builder who came during the week and had a good look at the cottage.

'It all depends what you want to do,' he said, as they stood outside after a thorough inspection. They both stared at the old place. 'How fancy do you want to go? You could make a nice little home there.'

'Simple, I think, for now,' Emily said, aware that

the bill for anything more could be quite substantial. 'Just the roof mending, a kitchen and bathroom putting in. It needs to be sound and habitable really.'

'You can do that for less than ten thousand,' the builder said. 'Depending on your specs, of course. But I'd say fifteen to be on the safe side – you're bound to run into unforeseeables.'

'How quickly could you do it?'

The builder shrugged. 'It's coming up to my busy time,' he said, 'but I reckon if you decide to go ahead quickly, I could get a mate of mine in and we could do it all in about three weeks. I've got a gap in a fortnight if you want to take it. Mr Pendleton's used me if you want a recommendation.'

'I know. He gave me your number.' Emily stared at the little cottage. Could she afford to spend some of her precious resources on getting the place sorted for Tom? And then give it to him? Surely it would reduce the value of December House if she gave away the cottage like that, it was so close to the main house. It could lead to all sorts of complications. 'Thanks, Mr Wilson. I'll ring you tonight with my decision.'

That night she lay in bed, thinking hard about the ramifications of giving away Keeper's Cottage. As she ran it all through her mind, she stared at Catherine Few's snowscape, now hanging on the wall just across from her bed. Her eyes searched it while she thought of other things and, as she stared, the whiteness of the picture gradually began to absorb her until she felt as though she was almost in the painting herself, standing on a crisp, chill layer of freshly fallen snow, feeling the wind biting her cheeks as it skimmed the drifts and whipped up smoky white clouds.

I'm not going to give Tom ownership of the cottage, she decided, her ideas at last resolving. *He can have free and full use of it – rent free – for as long as I live here. And I'll get it fixed up and maintain it for him, pay the bills and so on. But I can't separate it from the house. I feel it wouldn't be right.*

She felt sure he would be disappointed, resentful even. *But I'm sharing it. I can't do more than that. Not at the moment.*

As that thought at last settled everything she'd been thinking since that afternoon, another moment of clarity came upon her.

That scene in the picture . . . it's the view from the back of the house out towards the hills. I'm sure of it. I didn't notice at first – it's facing slightly to the left from the house so the perspective is a bit different to what I'm used to.

As she squinted at it, she realised that there was something else she'd been staring at without realising. *What is that object there in the snow? It's something I don't recognise.* But the painting was too far away for her to examine closely and she was too cosy to get out of bed.

She yawned sleepily. *I'll look in the morning.* Then she reached over and turned out the light.

CHAPTER 20

The house was not quite in darkness when they arrived. A lantern glowed in the window of the front hall, a welcoming golden light in the black of the night.

'Ursula remembered!' Cressie said joyfully. She turned to Ralph excitedly. 'She always used to do that when we arrived for the holidays. It meant we were really here.'

'Who's Ursula?' Ralph asked, paying the cab driver, who had left their bags by the door and was now ready to return to Carlisle. 'Thank you very much. Goodnight.'

The cab driver mumbled his thanks, touched his cap and got into his rackety car. It popped and spluttered and then pulled slowly out of the drive, its headlights making yellow tunnels through the blackness.

'She looks after the house for us. She lives in Keeper's Cottage just nearby.'

'Will she be here?' Ralph said warily.

'I should think so. She always used to wait in for us. But don't worry, she won't say a word.'

'Are you sure?' Ralph frowned. His face glimmered

pale in the darkness. 'Maybe I should wait here until she's gone.'

'No, really. Ursula is the soul of discretion, I promise.' Cressie smiled at him and took his hand. It was the first time they had touched for the whole journey. Meeting him at Euston had felt so strange – simultaneously dangerous and rather mundane. He was waiting at the agreed place, gripping a leather holdall in one hand and a large artist's box in the other. As soon as he saw her, his face lit up with pleasure and she hurried to him, but when they got close to one another, an awkwardness came over them. The reality of the bags they held and the way they indicated the intimacy they would soon share embarrassed Cressie, at the same time as her insides thrilled to the very same knowledge.

'Did Catherine see you?' Cressie asked, as they headed towards their platform.

Ralph shook his head. 'She wasn't there. She'll come home and find I'm gone.' His eyes hardened. 'I dread to think of the scene there'll be.'

Cressie was stabbed by a shaft of remorse. Catherine had always been kind to her. It was true that her instincts had never quite accepted the kindness: she had felt from the beginning that motive lay beneath every act of hospitality, and she had sensed that coded communication and warnings were just below the surface of everything Catherine said. 'Don't you feel rotten?' Cressie had said almost timidly. 'To leave her like this?'

The suddenness of what they were about to do frightened her. Ever since that morning she had been seized by excitement and a sense of purpose and adventure. At last, her dream of being with Ralph was going to come true – they were going to fly into the night like Porphyro and Madeline in Keats's 'The Eve of Saint Agnes', young lovers escaping together in the face of everyone's wrath. Love made everything all right, it excused anything. When two people had to be together, they were powerless in the face of it. And yet . . . She imagined Catherine coming into the studio and realising, slowly at first, that Ralph had gone. Perhaps it would be when she saw that his paints were gone. She would frown, look around for them, see that the pot of brushes had been emptied and then, suspicion growing in her mind, she would rush to their bedroom and fling open the wardrobe door. The missing clothes, the holdall gone . . . she would know for sure then. And what would she do? Shriek? Throw things? Rip down curtains and send the marble bust rolling in the hearth? Or would she sit down, implacable and furious, to begin plotting how to find Ralph? Surely she would think of Cressie. Surely that would be her very first thought . . .

Ralph looked at her, his eyes burning with emotion. 'I don't feel rotten to leave her,' he said. 'I have to get away from her. One day, you'll understand.' He was suddenly almost pleading. 'But not yet. I can't . . . don't ask me yet.'

*   *   *

Cressie knocked on the door and then pushed it open. 'Ursula? Are you there?'

She stepped inside. The house was not as cold and dank as she had feared it might be. A fire glowed in the huge fireplace in the hall, and she could feel a warmth coming from the back of the house. The next moment, the door to the passage opened and Ursula stepped out.

'Miss Cressida, hello,' she said. 'I'm glad to see you've arrived safely. I got your telegram; the boy brought it in the afternoon. I've done what I can in the time, but it's not as much as I would have liked.'

'Ursula, hello.' Cressie rushed up to her and kissed the other woman's cheek, seizing her hand. Ursula was dear to them all; she had looked after the family summer after summer, and kept the house in their absence. It had been so long since Cressie had seen her. 'I've missed you,' she said firmly. 'And I'm sure the house will be absolutely splendid.'

Ursula smiled happily. 'It's a pleasure to see you too, miss. It's been a long time.' Her gaze slid over Cressie's shoulder to where Ralph stood in the doorway. 'I made up two rooms, as you said. I wasn't sure if it was one of the boys coming with you or not.'

'Ursula.' Cressie gripped the other woman's hands with hers. They were roughened by hard work. Ursula must be in her forties now, and she'd brought up a young daughter alone since she'd been widowed years ago. It must have been quite a task, Cressie thought. No wonder she was lined and furrowed with it. 'We have always been close, haven't we?'

The other woman nodded, looking apprehensive.

Cressie went on. 'Well, now I need to ask you something very important. I want you to keep a secret. It's a very great thing to ask, I know that, but . . . Ralph and I are hiding here. It's very important that no one knows he is here with me. As far as everyone is concerned, I'm here on my own. Will you keep that secret for us? Please?'

'Oh miss . . .' Ursula's mouth had fallen open as understanding dawned on her. Her eyes took on a sad look. 'Oh miss . . .'

Cressie tightened her grip. 'Please don't look like that, Ursula. I know how it must seem, but it's not what you think. It's not as cheap and tawdry as it must look to you. I can't explain everything now but I will and then you'll understand why we're here, and why it's a secret.'

Ursula thought for a moment and then said in a determined tone, 'You've always had a fine character, miss, and I think the world of you, you know that. If you say it's to be a secret, then a secret it shall be.'

'Your loyalty to my parents won't be tested, I promise,' Cressie said, relieved. 'They won't ever ask you about this, I guarantee it.'

Ralph shifted behind them, evidently uncomfortable.

Ursula leaned into Cressie and said quietly, 'And will there be a trip across the border soon, miss?'

318

Cressie blinked at her. 'What do you mean?'

The other woman whispered. 'To Gretna Green.'

'Oh!' Cressie coloured. 'Not yet. No . . . now
. . . shall we take our bags upstairs?'

Ursula left them alone, after she had taken Cressie
up to the bedrooms she had prepared, fires in the
grate already warming them, and then showed her
to the morning room where a supper had been
laid out.

'Just cold things, as time was so short. I thought
you wouldn't mind eating here tonight rather than
make up the dining room.'

'Exactly right,' Cressie said. 'Thank you. Now,
you must get home, Ursula. No doubt Maggie is
waiting for you.'

'She's a sensible girl, now she's twelve,' Ursula
said, putting on her coat. 'She helps me a great
deal. I'll bring her up tomorrow to say hello.'

'No need to come early,' Cressie said, colouring.
'We can get our own breakfasts.'

'Very well,' Ursula said, not meeting her eye. 'I
shall see you around lunchtime, miss. Goodnight.'

'Goodnight, Ursula. And thank you.' Cressie
watched Ursula head out into the night, a torch
with her to light the way back to Keeper's Cottage.

'That was awkward,' Ralph said in a low voice.
He was standing in the hall, his hands in his
pockets, staring into the glowing embers of the
fire there. 'I wish we could have avoided it.'

'She would have to know,' Cressie said. 'She'll

often be here. But she's fond of me, she won't tell anyone. It will be best to have her on our side just in case.' She went over to him and gazed up into his face, her stomach twisting pleasurably at the sight of his fine features and the intense grey eyes she loved so much. 'And we're here. Everything's working out just as we hoped.'

A smile half twisted his mouth and he took her hand, raising it gently to his lips. Then he said softly, 'I'm being ungrateful. I'm here, with you, and that is a miracle. I just want to keep our world containing only us, do you see? I don't want anyone else intruding on it.'

'They won't,' she breathed, her pulse racing suddenly. 'I promise they won't.'

'Other people won't understand. They'll judge us. They'll judge me, when they don't know anything about it.'

'That's why we won't let anyone else near us.'

'Oh Cressida.' He pulled her close to him, and she felt the delicious warmth of his body against hers. Her insides felt like molten gold as she looked up at his lips. She had thought of them over and over since that morning – was that really today? It seemed a lifetime ago – when they had kissed her so deliciously. All day she had hungered for them, longing for the time when they would be hers again. He bent down and pressed his mouth to hers, and the next moment they were both possessed by a wild yearning. The kiss grew fiercer and all she knew was that it mustn't stop. But he pulled away.

'Cressida, you do want this, don't you?' he asked, breathless. His fingers dug into her arms where he held her.

'Yes,' she said fervently. 'It's all I want.'

'I don't know if we can go back from here.'

'I don't want to go back. I'm never going back.' She gazed up at him, feeling that all her passion and desire was burning in her own eyes. 'Don't you understand, Ralph? We've made our decision by coming here. It's done now.'

'Yes.' He smiled at her, a sudden joy transforming his face. 'It is. It's done.' He bent to kiss her again.

Cressida woke, her head against Ralph's smooth, warm chest, coming to consciousness gently and deliciously. Remembering where she was, and that she was with Ralph, sent a rush of pleasure through her – a first-day-of-the-holidays feeling magnified by the heady memory of the night before.

Ursula had made up beds in different rooms, so they were squashed together in one, in a small box room with a view out over the garden. Ralph had taken the wall side and his back was pressed against it, one arm around Cressie as he slept deeply, his mouth open just a little as he breathed slowly.

Cressie didn't move so as not to wake him, despite her tingling urge to wriggle and stretch with happiness. So now, at last, she was not burdened with that tiresome virginity. She had learned, finally, the secret of what happened between men and women, and it was exactly what she had hoped it would be. When Adam had failed to ignite a spark in her, she'd feared that perhaps there was no joy in sex, or none that she could feel, but Ralph had put pay to that idea. She'd never felt so alive, as he'd slowly undressed her by the light of the candle on the tiny chest of drawers, marvelling over her beauty as he did so. Every touch of his fingers had brought a shivering response. The sensation of his breath on her skin had driven her almost wild. The feel of his warm skin under her fingertips and pressed against her body had left her speechless with wonder that she could feel so much and so intensely. The drag of his fingernail over her breast had made her cry out – it had been almost too much to bear. When at last he had made love to her, she'd expected pain and awkwardness but it had been the most natural and beautiful thing in the world. Nothing stopped their union; they simply melted into one another as though that was how it was always meant to be. She had never wanted it to end, but it had been impossible not to get caught up in that vortex of feeling, to feel the urgency of his excitement and be pushed forward upon it, and when it finished, at last, they collapsed together to a whole new sweetness that she'd never known awaited her: the aftermath of love.

I want to do it again. Now. She sighed with contentment in the grey light of the morning. It was cold outside their blankets, she could tell. The fire in the minuscule grate had become a small heap of grey ashes. *Brrr. This is the first time I've been in December House in December.*

The New Year was almost upon them, she realised with another thrill. It felt so grown up to be away from home, hidden away. She had left a letter for her father explaining that she was going to stay with her friends, the Ropers, for a while. He would be pleased, she knew, and would not wonder where she was for at least a week. Then she would telephone and make more excuses and after that she would see what was best to do. She agonised about what to tell her mother but in the end, just as she was creeping in to tell her not to worry, the nurse had barred her way with the sternly whispered injunction not to wake Mama as she was sleeping.

We have a week at least. I'll probably be home in a fortnight. Until then, it's just us. And I want to enjoy every second.

In deference to Ursula's feelings, they were dressed and respectable by the time she came at lunchtime, and the other bed had been mussed and clumsily remade so that appearances might be kept up.

But, Cressie thought, Ursula was bound to guess what was happening by the dreamy happiness that must surely show in her face and by the way she and Ralph moved towards each other constantly, as though unable to bear being apart for more than a few moments. Ursula came up to the house with her daughter, Maggie, a quiet girl with the same dark red hair that her mother had, only falling in long ripples around her shoulders. She seemed struck by Cressie and watched her all the time.

'Thank you for coming up, Ursula,' Cressie said, smiling. She was smiling at everything and everybody. Before they'd got up, she and Ralph had made love again and it had been even more intense and spectacular than the night before. Being able to see his face clearly as he moved was almost too much. The excitement had been wild and intense and she'd been glad no one could hear the cries she'd been unable to suppress. Surely no one else had ever found this extraordinary bliss in their physical connection; this had to be unique to the love she and Ralph felt for one another. Only that could explain this overwhelming pleasure. *It's our secret*, she thought happily. *How lucky we are.*

'You're welcome, miss. I'll stay the afternoon and clean and make your dinner. Will that suit you?' Ursula wore a white apron and cleared away their lunch things briskly.

'Very well.' Cressie smiled at Ralph, thinking that already he looked healthier. Surely that was a touch of pink she could see in his complexion . . . he'd been white as marble the day before.

'Thank you, Ursula,' Ralph said. 'You're very kind.'

Ursula stopped for a moment, then darted him a look from under her lashes and said, 'You're welcome too, sir, of course.'

Cressie saw it with dismay. *Oh, she doesn't like him! She thinks he's my seducer. I can't bear it.*

She followed Ursula into the kitchen, where Maggie sat on the floor in front of the range, feeding it with logs, dropping them in by her fingertips as close to the range as she dared.

'Ursula,' she said in a confiding tone. 'You know what you said last night – about a trip to the border?'

'Yes, miss.' Ursula gave her a questioning look and then glanced at Maggie, but the girl did not appear to be listening.

'Well . . . perhaps a trip there might be happening sooner rather than later.'

A look of relief crossed Ursula's face and she smiled broadly. 'Well, I am glad about that, I must say. I don't like to think of you being here without proper prospects, if you understand me. I didn't want to be a party to it. I expected you to arrive with one of your brothers so it was a shock when you had a young man with you. I know times are changing but I can't helping thinking it's not decent. But if you're engaged . . . well . . .'

'We are,' Cressie said firmly. It was a lie she told easily and without guilt. Protecting Ralph from censure was more important than strict truth. He was right: the world was going to judge them while knowing nothing of their circumstances. 'He's wonderful, Ursula. Really.'

'I'm sure he is, miss,' the other woman said, more relaxed now. 'He's certainly good-looking, I'll give him that. He's got a heartbreaker's looks.'

'Don't worry, he won't break my heart,' Cressie said confidently. 'I'm very happy, can't you tell?'

She gazed out of the window over the grey and brown winter landscape. 'And it's so beautiful here. I never knew how lovely it is in winter. So bare and majestic.'

'But hard,' Ursula remarked. 'Don't forget that. It's hard here too. It's not a soft life at all. No one comes here expecting that.'

They soon fell into an easy rhythm. They moved into the main bedroom and its larger, more comfortable bed, where they would wake late, make love, and lie lazily together telling each other a hundred different things about their lives – except that, by tacit consent, they did not speak of Catherine or of Ralph's life with her at all. Then they would make breakfast and after that, Ralph would want to paint. He had paper and a roll of canvas in his bag and together they dismantled the bed in the second largest bedroom and turned it into Ralph's studio.

'We'll send to Carlisle for an easel and whatever else you need,' Cressie said, and she wrote the letter that very day, giving it to Maggie to take to the end of the lane and put in the postbox.

Ursula and Maggie came at lunchtime, and even though she must have noticed while tidying up that Cressie and Ralph had moved into the main bedroom, she said nothing about it. They stayed until there was a meal ready for the evening, and then trudged off into the darkness when there was nothing more to be done.

'Isn't she marvellous?' Cressie demanded, cuddling into Ralph in front of the fire in the sitting room. 'She brings everything we need. We can stay here as long as we want.'

'She is,' Ralph said, dropping a kiss on her nose. 'But can we really stay? What about your parents? Won't they wonder where you've got to?'

'I'll find a telephone – perhaps up at that farmhouse – and ring Papa. I'll tell him I've gone on to Nina's house. Honestly, he won't mind.' She rubbed her cheek on the soft wool of his jumper. 'He's longing for me to be social and see people so I can meet a suitable husband. He'll want me gone as long as possible, and he'll believe me too.'

She suddenly felt bad as she said it. She might be abusing her father's trust, and soon the bills for food and other things would arrive for him to pay, but it was her mother who came into her mind. Was she wondering where Cressie was, perhaps even suspecting that she was not simply away with friends? December House belonged to her mother, not her father, and it had been her grandmother's before that. How would Mama feel if she knew what Cressie was doing, right here, in the bed she used to sleep in? Cressie felt hot and flustered with embarrassment at the thought. *She'd probably cheer*, she told herself. But that wasn't really why she felt guilty. *I've left her alone with him. She's too weak to stand up to him and he's bound to make her miserable. I should go back. Be with her. I will. But not yet.*

She obstinately closed her mind to everything beyond the here and now. She didn't know how long she and Ralph had together in this wonderful cocoon of bliss but she wasn't going to spoil what time they did have by worrying.

The easel arrived in only a few days, a van puttering up to the house to deliver it along with canvases, stretchers and all the other paraphernalia Ralph needed. Then he began to paint again.

In the bedroom that had now been requisitioned as a studio, the rug had been rolled up and the curtains taken down. A small sofa was brought up from the study and placed against the wall furthest from the light. Here Cressie sat, reading aloud to Ralph or talking to him as he painted. Sometimes she felt an odd jolt, as though she were not herself at all, but Catherine, curled up on the sofa in the Blackheath studio, tearing up fabric for painting rags and carefully directing the painting work. Once, when she spoke, she almost heard Catherine's lilting cadence coming out of her own mouth, and it felt very odd. She almost had to fight to get her own voice back. She watched Ralph's brushstrokes, and the way he loaded paint on his brush and mixed it on his palette to get the shade he wanted.

'You need more Prussian Blue,' she said one day, watching him. 'If you're making the colour for the sky.'

His brush stopped for a moment, then he looked up at her and smiled. 'Thank you.' He picked up a touch of Prussian Blue on his brush and added it to the mix.

I've become his eyes, she thought happily. *I knew we'd be complete together.*

One day she picked up some paper and began to sketch as well.

'Let me see,' Ralph said, interested. He regarded her drawing carefully and seriously. She had sketched the room: the easel and the fireplace and the view out of the window beyond, all done in quick strokes of the pencil. 'It's not bad.'

'I'll never be a portraitist,' she said quickly. 'I'm nowhere near as talented as you.'

He stared at it for a while longer and then said, 'I can teach you how to use oils. If you like.'

'Yes please. I would like that.' She smiled over at him, her heart bursting with happiness. Everything at last had a purpose and that was for her and Ralph to be together.

She refused to think of a time when it might have to come to an end.

CHAPTER 21

'Emily! How lovely you could come! Get down, Kipper.'

James pushed away the panting springer spaniel who'd come to greet Emily with a friendly bark and wet tongue, and stood back to welcome her in. He was smart in a dark jacket and a tie, and she was glad she'd dug out one of her few remaining posh dresses and changed into her heels before knocking on the door.

'Thanks for asking me,' she said, smiling as she stepped into the hall. 'And for finding me a babysitter. Heidi seems very nice.'

'She's a good girl. I've known her since she was a baby. Hard to believe she's going away to university next year. Makes me feel bloody ancient. Now, come along. You must meet Mum before we all get started.'

'That would be lovely.' It was, in fact, the only thing she was looking forward to about tonight. James had been so happy to be able to introduce her to neighbours but it was Mrs Pendleton she really wanted to meet.

She followed James through the hall, and along

a corridor that led off to the side of the house. Emily looked about as they went. It was the sort of place that had clearly been lived in by the same family for years with little done to it – shabby but comfortable, full of furniture and pictures, with nothing matching, a hotchpotch of periods, styles and tastes.

'We arranged the house a while back so that Mum has her own bit. She likes her privacy.' James stopped in front of a firmly shut door and knocked. 'Mum!'

'Come in,' called a voice from behind. 'It's open.'

'She often locks it,' James remarked as he opened the door. 'Don't know why she seems so keen to keep me out.' He grinned at her. 'I ought to ask her.'

They went into a small hall. Emily noticed at once that this part of the house was very different from the rest: tidy and carefully decorated, with a sense of calm and order. A lamp glowed on a mahogany side table, and a large porcelain stand held umbrellas and walking sticks. A row of gentle watercolour landscapes hung on the ivory-painted wall.

'I'm in here,' came the voice again, and James led the way into a cosy sitting room furnished with comfortable armchairs. In one, by a woodburner with a glowing belly, sat an elderly woman, her grey hair short and neat, her blue eyes bright behind a pair of gold-framed spectacles. Her skin sunk into hollows beneath her cheeks and was well lined, but she had a vigorous air about her, and she stood up as James and Emily came in, smoothing down her floral skirt.

'Evening, Mum. I've brought Emily Conway as promised.'

Emily stepped forward. 'Hello, Mrs Pendleton. How do you do?'

The elderly lady put out her hand for Emily to shake, and smiled. 'Hello. I've heard a great deal about you from James. How are you finding life at December House?'

'Very nice, thank you. We're pretty well settled now.'

'It's lovely to have a young family there. The place will be much livelier now, I suppose. Old Mrs Few wasn't seen much towards the end. She had someone in to look after her when she got ill, and then she left for good to go to a home, and died not long after. So the house has been empty for quite some time.' She smiled at Emily again. 'I wasn't expecting to be her executor, but I was glad to hear she'd left the house to someone who had a connection with it. I'd imagined it would be sold and the money donated to the charity she nominated. That's what happened to all her possessions.' She gestured to Emily to sit down and took her own seat again. 'James, what about a gin and tonic for Mrs Conway and one for me?'

'Good idea,' James said, heading out.

'Please, call me Emily.' She sat down on the edge of the sofa. It was covered in a slippery floral chintz, similar to Mrs Pendleton's skirt material. 'I don't know how much of a connection I can boast of, to be honest. I'd never even been to this part of the world before we moved here.'

'But James tells me you're a Fellbridge.'

'That's right. But I had no idea that my family once owned December House. My father never mentioned it.'

Mrs Pendleton nodded. 'Oh yes, they did, I'm quite sure of it, although everything I know about that period came from my mother-in-law. She lived here at the time the Fellbridges owned the place. It was their holiday home, I believe, but they stopped coming up for whole summers in the fifties and the house was virtually empty for years. They sold up to the Fews in the early sixties.' She frowned, her brow crinkling. 'I remember my mother-in-law telling me that your aunt Cressida came for a while and that it was the last time a Fellbridge was here. Not long after that, the house was sold and the Fews arrived. They were very reclusive, I've heard. Mrs Few refused all invitations and was almost never seen. I arrived here in the late sixties, after my marriage, and my mother-in-law went into a home herself. It was only then that I got to know Mrs Few, and her husband. She emerged little by little. But only in a very vague sense – they still kept themselves to themselves. He died not that long afterwards, poor young man. At least, he seemed young to me at the time. He had some kind of early onset dementia,

I think. I saw Mrs Few every now and then, but she didn't appear to need much company. Content by herself, you know.'

James came back with the gins and handed one to Emily. 'Giving Emily all the gossip, are you, Mum?'

'It's fascinating,' Emily said, the long glass cold in her fingers. 'But did Mrs Few ever mention the Fellbridge family, or why she wanted to return the house to us?'

Mrs Pendleton shook her head. 'Not a word. We didn't talk of intimate matters. We didn't have that kind of relationship.' She frowned. 'But I do remember one thing. I was surprised when I learned that she had left the house to your family because I did get the distinct impression that she was afraid of the Fellbridges in some way. I don't know why exactly, as I can't remember her mentioning them at all, but I suppose she must have for me to have had that strong sense – that she was afraid that one day they would come back.'

'How odd,' Emily said, interested. 'That seems rather contradictory.'

'Doesn't it?' Mrs Pendleton smiled. 'That's the limit of my knowledge, I'm afraid. Now. James says you have two very charming children. Do tell me all about them.'

Later, Emily wished she could be back in the cosy sitting room, sipping gin and tonic with Mrs Pendleton rather than in the middle of James's dinner party.

It's not his fault, she thought. *He's done all this for me. It's so nice of him. But . . . I can't help wishing that he hadn't.*

The other guests were three couples who all appeared to know each other quite well, and while they were friendly enough, they didn't pay much attention to Emily, instead shouting at each other in great guffawing tones as though they were putting on some kind of show for her entertainment.

James was absent most of the time, in the kitchen cooking supper. He appeared, red-faced and wearing an apron, to call them through to the dining room with the air of someone who had achieved something he never thought possible. Emily followed them all through, and on the table were two steaming casseroles full of something rich and meaty, along with dishes full of mashed potato and a cheerful mix of carrots and sweetcorn.

'It's not cordon bleu,' James said apologetically as they all sat down. 'But it should taste okay. And there's stacks of wine. So dig in.'

'Looks lovely, darling,' drawled one of the women – Emily hoped it was Harriet, otherwise she'd forgotten her name.

Once they had passed everything round and all the plates were loaded up with food, the man next to Emily – *Andy? Or is it Simon?* – turned to her and said, 'So, still wearing your ring, are you?'

'Sorry?' She looked at him, confused.

He nodded at her hand. 'Your wedding ring. You're still wearing it.'

'Yes,' she said.

'So were you the left or the leaver?'

The woman on his other side – *now, I'm sure she's Georgina* – said, 'God's sake, Si, you do sound callous! Excuse him, Emily, he's basically a rhinoceros.'

Simon ignored his neighbour and said, 'You're divorced, right?'

Emily blinked and said, 'Er . . . no.'

'Whoops!' he said, grinning. 'I thought you must be a sexy single brought in for James's amusement. He's quite the gay divorcé, aren't you, Jim?'

'What? What's that?' James looked over from where he'd been listening hard to one of the other women while eating stew very fast.

'Just saying that you're on the market!' Simon laughed again. 'I thought Emily must be in the same boat. But apparently she's still married! Where is he then? Does he let you out to play on your own? Bit foolish of him, if you ask me.'

Emily saw James's face turn brick red and he opened his mouth to say something so she said quickly, 'He's in London. We are separated. But not divorced.'

'Ah.' Simon nodded. 'I thought it must be something like that. Here's my advice. Do what James did when he and Jojo split. See a mediator, not a lawyer, and work out all the terms yourself. Lawyers tell you to go for as much as possible, everyone gets greedy, then angry, and all perspective is lost. Mediators help everyone stay reasonable. Jojo could have taken half the farm if she'd been the sort but she understood how that would have shafted James, so they came to quite an amicable agreement, didn't you, Jim?'

James looked even more embarrassed. 'Well, I—'

'Simon!' The woman James had been talking to looked mortified. She was evidently Simon's wife. 'That's Jim's private business.'

'Sorry!' Simon said amiably, not looking in the least apologetic. He glanced at Emily's glass and reached for the wine bottle. 'You need a top-up, Emily. Better get you a bit tipsy if Jim's going to stand a chance. You're far too toothsome for a bloke like him.'

James winced and looked away, while Simon's wife turned her eyes up to the ceiling and said, 'I knew he shouldn't have had that third G&T before dinner.'

'I'm not pissed, if that's what you mean,' Simon said. He looked at Emily again, squinting at her curiously. 'I say . . . what's that bloody great scar running down your face? Did you walk into a door after a few too many beers or something?'

Emily felt the blood rush to her cheeks. She should have been ready for something like this, but she wasn't. At the mirror earlier, doing her make-up, she'd tried to use concealer to cover up the dark red line running down her face but the make-up hadn't made much impact on it. She'd told herself that it was still too early for the scar to have begun to fade – that sort of thing took months, even though she was using a special oil on it every evening – and she'd worn her hair down so that she could keep the side of her face covered if she wanted to. But she'd forgotten it and tucked her hair behind her ear. The great red jagged line must have been very visible to her neighbour.

'Simon!' his wife said, agonised. She looked over at Emily. 'I'm sorry. He's awful! So rude . . .'

James said in a steely voice, 'Simon, that's enough, mate. Emily's my guest. I can't have you talk to her like that.'

Simon looked surprised at the reaction. 'All right, all right,' he said mildly. 'Sorry, Emily. Didn't mean to upset you. It doesn't spoil your looks, if that's what you think I'm saying. I just wondered how you'd done it.'

'That's the point, Simon,' James said before Emily could reply. 'You don't know how it happened. You could cause Emily pain by raking up something you're completely ignorant of.'

'Fair point,' Simon said, nodding. 'I see that. None of my business.'

'It's all right, really,' Emily said. She smiled at James, who was gazing at her now, a look of apology in his eyes. 'I don't mind talking about it.' She'd been intending to keep quiet on her circumstances, but it seemed better to say what needed saying. 'I was in a bad car accident. My husband is in a coma in a London hospital and they don't know if he'll ever wake up. The children and I have moved up here to recover.'

Simon gaped at her, horror growing in his eyes. 'I say, I'm a bloody idiot. Georgie's right, I'm a rhinoceros, blundering in like that. I'm most terribly sorry. God, that's awful.'

The whole table was silent now, sympathetic eyes turned to her. It was obvious that no one knew what to say to her revelation.

'It's fine,' she said. She smiled encouragingly at James. 'I don't mind talking about it. Really.'

James smiled back, making an expression of contrition at the same time.

'Don't be silly, we wouldn't be so rude,' Simon's wife said. 'We're all very sorry to hear about the accident, it sounds beyond awful. I hope your husband makes a full recovery too.' She paused and said in a different tone, 'Now, Emily. Tell me, have you found a school for your children yet?'

'Not yet. But Carrie's only four,' Emily said, grateful for the subject change.

'You'll need to get her name down soon,' she said. 'I think the applications close next month. And you'll probably want to find a nursery too, if you want some childcare out of term time.'

They were soon discussing the local provision and whether Emily would like the name of a good child-minder, which led to some descriptions of local characters, including one childminder who was rarely seen without a cigarette dangling from her lips and who handed out packets of crisps and bottles of cola to keep her charges quiet. Emily warmed to them all a little more as the evening progressed. Out of sympathy for her, they toned down their raucousness, but she sensed that the evening was just getting started; the wine was flowing hard and voices were getting louder again. By eleven, there was a general air of drunkenness.

'I say,' Harriet said in a slurred voice, 'shall we get some music on? I feel like a bit of a boogie!'

I think that's my cue to leave. Emily got up. 'I'm afraid I must get home,' she said. 'The babysitter needs to be back before eleven thirty and I have to drive her.'

They tried to persuade her to stay but she was firm and made her farewells. After a round of goodbye kisses, some sloppier than others, and some muttered words of sympathy, she followed James out to get her coat.

'I'm so sorry about earlier,' James said, as he led her to the door. 'Simon's a bloody clumsy fool. He was abominably rude.'

'It's not your fault,' she said, smiling at him comfortingly. 'Besides, people are going to be curious. I know my scar is hard to miss.'

'I hadn't seen it at all,' he said gallantly. 'I've only ever noticed how pretty and glamorous you are.'

'You're very kind,' she said, touched by his slightly awkward compliment.

'I mean it,' he said. He looked down at her, suddenly more boyish than ever in the half-light from the hall behind him. 'You're lovely. Your scar doesn't change anything about you.'

She heard the sincerity in his voice and was

warmed by it. 'Thank you, that means a lot. And thanks for a very nice evening.' She leaned in to kiss his cheek, tilting her face upwards to him. He went to do the same, and they both turned to the same side, so that their lips touched briefly before they shifted quickly and ended up with a clumsy brushing of cheeks to mouths.

'Sorry,' James said, embarrassed again. 'I'm quite the klutz tonight.'

'Goodnight, James. See you soon,' she said and turned to head for her car, hoping that he hadn't noticed how much the strange little half-kiss they'd shared had affected her. Her lips were tingling where they'd touched his. In that instant when their mouths had met, she'd been almost over-whelmed by his nearness and by the powerful sense of his strength and masculinity. Her nostrils had filled with his scent: a musky sweetness of male skin mixed with aftershave. To her astonish-ment, her whole body had responded with a strong rush of something she hadn't felt for months.

What is it?

Her fingers were trembling as she fumbled for the car key in her bag. She already knew.

But I don't fancy James! He's not my type at all!

James was a bluff country squire, the kind of person who was the butt of jokes in films. He wore cords and checked shirts and drove a Land Rover. He had pink cheeks and hair that stood straight up on end, like a fluffy chick's. A sex god he was not. And yet . . .

Oh my goodness. Her skin was tingling hard as though she had received a bolt of electricity through it. It felt like everything in her had been dormant, and now a great alarm had rung, waking her up suddenly and completely. She felt jittery as she drove the car slowly out of the driveway and onto the lane.

But . . . James? She recalled the touch of his mouth on hers and felt the same burning shiver course through her. *It can't be him. It's just because he's a man. Because it's been so long since I've had a man kiss me or touch me.*

Her eyes suddenly filled with tears and she blinked them away, trying to damp down the sudden flood of sadness that rushed through her.

That's what this is about. Loneliness. She bit her lip and tried to laugh. *As long as I don't get carried away with the idea that this is anything to do with James. Whatever happens, I mustn't do that.*

CHAPTER 22

It was the boy on the bicycle who shattered the peace of Cressida and Ralph's idyll. He brought up a telegram from the post office, working his way up the hill on his bike, arriving puffed but exhilarated from the effort.

'Here you are, miss,' he said to Cressie, who was at the kitchen door with logs for the range when he came pelting round to the back of the house.

She dropped a log and took it, staring at the envelope. It could only be from home. She had gone up to the Pendleton place a few days before and rung her father. She told him airily that she and her friend Nina had decamped for a while to December House. 'For some walking,' she told him. 'And rest. We're both bushed. It's like a tonic up here. I'm enjoying it tremendously.'

'Good,' her father had said. 'Take your time and get well rested while you can.'

Now there was a telegram.

She tore it open.

**Come home as soon as you can stop
mother gravely ill stop time of the
essence Papa**

She read it over and over as the contents began
to sink in. Ralph came into the kitchen.

'Have you been log gathering?' he said. 'You
look quite the woodcutter's daughter, all covered
in shards of wood and bits of bark. I shall
have to paint you like that. Shall I put some
coffee on?'

She looked up at him, stricken. 'I've had a telegram. My mother has taken a bad turn. My father
wants me to go home immediately.'

Ralph went to her quickly and hugged her. 'I'm
sorry, darling. What awful news.'

Cressie looked back at the telegram with shaking
fingers. 'I can get the lunchtime train, if we hurry.
As soon as Maggie comes, we'll send her up to
the farmhouse to ask them to ring for a taxi. Oh
Ralph.' Her eyes filled with tears.

He hugged her again. 'I know. You must be so
worried. We can only hope for the best. Shall I
come with you?'

'No . . . no. You can't. Where would you go? You
couldn't come home with me. Stay here. I hope
it's one of the bad spells she sometimes has and
I'll be back in a few days.'

'All right.' He glanced at the clock. 'We won't
wait for Maggie. I'll go up to the house myself
and ask for that taxi.'

'No, don't do that. I don't want them to know we're here together. Maggie won't be long.'

He frowned and then said reluctantly, 'All right. I want to help, that's all. And I hate to think of you so far away.' He kissed her head. 'I'll miss you terribly.'

'I'll miss you too.' The thought of being away from him was agony. She buried her face in his chest, desperate to be close to him. When the taxi arrived and she climbed in, and the driver tucked her bag next to him on the front seat, she felt as though she were leaving her heart behind as Ralph stood on the lawn, wrapped up in his coat, waving at her.

'Come back as soon as you can!' he called after her.

'I will, I will!' She waved frantically out of the back window, unable to tear her eyes away from him until he finally vanished from sight behind the hedgerows.

The train journey was even more miserable than the ones she remembered from the end of their family holidays. She was leaving behind the man she loved in panic at the state of her mother's health, the other person she loved most in the world. The telegram said so little, but her father would hardly send for her unless it were serious. Mama had taken many bad turns before now, but she had always pulled through. It chilled her that the summons had come like this. It could only mean that the situation was grave this time.

Oh Mama, she thought, staring out at the bleak wintery landscape flying past the window. What if death finally came to claim her this time? The thought made her chilly with fear and despair. What would happen to the family without Mama? Even though she had lain so ill upstairs, seemingly ineffectual, she'd actually anchored them together. Without her, they would have all fled their father. Her sweetness and love had kept Harry and Gus returning. It had kept Cressida at home, trying to comfort and care for her, and provide a buffer against her father's bullying ways. If she was no longer there, would they all ricochet off into their own separate worlds?

I can't bear to lose Mama. But as long as my world contains Ralph, I will survive.

It was late when the cab finally pulled up in front of the Kensington house. Ellen answered the door before she had time to knock – they had been looking out for her. Her father came out of the drawing room, his expression anxious, to greet her with a hug.

'I'm so glad you've come,' he said. 'The boys are here too.'

Cressie handed her things to Ellen and went in. Her brothers were sitting by the fire, Harry white-faced and tense as he stared into the flames and Gus nervously twisting his fingers. They looked glad to see her and said their hellos in tones of relief, as if someone had at last arrived who could tell them what to do and how to act.

Cressida turned to her father, sombre in his dark suit, his white hair uncharacteristically mussed about as though he'd been clutching at his head in despair. 'How is she?'

'The doctor is with her now. But he has been most grave about Mama's health. I'm afraid he's begun to talk in terms of hours rather than days.'

Cressie gasped and seized the back of the sofa for support. 'Hours! No!'

Her father nodded. He seemed bent over, weakened. 'Yes, I'm afraid so. She's sickened considerably. An infection in her lungs, apparently, and she lacks the strength to fight it.' An agonised look crossed his face and she saw that his fingers were shaking.

She felt fury suddenly surge through her, and wanted to shake him and shout, *It's all very well to be sad now, when it's too late! It's all very well to be weak and frightened when she's almost gone. What about when she was here with us?* But she said nothing, just dropped her eyes and tried to absorb the terrible news.

Her mother was upstairs and dying. She might die tonight. She might be living her last few earthly hours and then she would be gone forever. Cressie's heart hurt at the thought. *No,* she said to herself desperately. *No, no.* But she knew that nothing would stop the inexorable move towards her mother leaving them.

They sat down and waited for the doctor to descend, talking quietly as though they might disturb the patient with loud voices. Ellen brought tea but no one drank. The house was full of a grim foreboding, and a louring solemnity.

At last Ellen knocked on the door again and said, 'The doctor would like you all to come up one by one, Miss Cressida first.'

Cressie looked at the others with frightened eyes, then stood up. 'Very well,' she said as bravely as she could. She longed to see her mother and yet she was also afraid that now, so close to death, she would be different. Unrecognisable. Perhaps Cressie would walk into the bedroom and discover that her mother was already gone. She didn't know what she would do if it was a stranger lying there, dying in her mother's bed.

She went up the stairs slowly. The doctor was just coming out, looking at the pocket watch he wore on the end of a chain.

'Ah, good, she wants you,' he said with small smile when he saw Cressie walking along the corridor. 'Go in. She's waiting.'

Cressie pushed open the door and saw the room inside, lit by lamps and almost cosy except for the sour smell of medicine and carbolic. A nurse was moving around quietly by the window, arranging bottles of medicine. The bed, lavishly made up in soft white linen, held her mother, most certainly the same person, except for the thinness of her face and the look of absence that was already creeping over her. She opened her eyes as Cressie came near.

'My Cressie? Is that you?' Her voice was creaky, as though it had not been used for a while.

'Yes, Mama. I'm here.' She went forward awkwardly, her eyes blurring with tears.

Her mother smiled. 'Good. Come close. I can't see you, my darling.'

Cressie sobbed, unable to stop herself. She took the thin hand her mother held out to her.

'Now, don't cry,' said her mother in the same frail voice. 'I don't want to see my girl sad. I want to see you smile. Can you try to smile for me? I always loved your smile.'

Cressie tried to smile through her tears, attempting to pull up the corners of her wobbling mouth.

'Now, that's better.' Her mother breathed slowly and deeply as though gathering the strength to speak again. At last she said, 'My dearest Cressie, I've always wanted the best for you. I'd hoped to see you settled before I left you. But I'm so happy about what you told me. That you're in love. You went away so suddenly . . .'

'I'm sorry, Mama! I shouldn't have left you,' she said in a broken voice. She stroked the hand and kissed it. 'I'm so sorry.'

'Now, now, don't be sorry. But tell me, were you with him? Your lover?'

Cressie nodded.

'Good. And he loves you?'

She nodded again and said, 'Yes. He does.'

Her mother sighed, a small smile on her lips. 'I'm glad. I don't want to leave you without knowing you're loved.' She breathed with an effort, closing her eyes for a moment, and then said, 'Is he a good man?'

'Very good. Kind. Gentle.'

'Oh Cressie. I'm so happy. Thank you.'

Cressie bit her lip to stop the sobs that wanted to be free.

The cool, thin hand moved slightly in hers and her mother spoke again with an effort. 'I know you'll find your path. I want you to be free. Don't let them keep you here, will you? They'll want to. Papa will need you. He'll try and make you stay but you're not made to be imprisoned like I was.'

'I'll try,' she whispered.

'You'll have this burden too – the knowledge that we women have to be stronger than men are, all through our lives. It feels unjust sometimes. But as long as you are loved, cherished and honoured . . . You must get back what you deserve and need. Promise you'll never forget that.'

Cressie nodded, the world swimming in front of her tear-filled eyes, unable to speak. *I am cherished. I am loved.* 'I promise.'

Her mother looked up at her and smiled weakly. 'I think you need a little ballast against the world. You'll face challenges the boys will never know. That's why I want to leave December House to you.'

Cressie stared, surprised. 'To me?'

Mama nodded. 'Only to you. Your brothers will be well provided for, and I want the house to be your haven and your possession. You always loved it best anyway. This way, you can keep it always.'

'Thank you, Mama,' she whispered, deeply touched. The house had felt like hers over the last couple of weeks as she and Ralph had settled in. To know that it now would be her own, even at this dreadful cost, was a small comfort. 'I promise to look after it.'

'Kiss me, darling.'

Cressie leaned over and took her frail mother in her arms, feeling her bones through the paper-thin skin, and began to sob in earnest. She kissed her mother's cheek and held her tightly. 'Don't leave us, Mama,' she begged.

'My darling, I would do anything to stay with you. But I don't think I can. And at least there will be no pain.' The soft voice diminished to a whisper. 'I'm looking forward to being free of it.'

Cressie wept bitterly and only let go of her mother's hand when the nurse gently freed it.

They all took their turn in the sick room. Afterwards, as though she were finally released from her duty, Mama sank into unconsciousness. At three in the morning, when Harry had fallen asleep on the sofa and Cressie was almost asleep herself, the nurse came down to summon them all.

Wide awake now, Cressie went up the stairs behind her father, followed by her brothers. In the sickroom, there was the rattling sound of the last breaths a person would take. Her mother was as white as the linen she lay on, her skin stretched thin over her face. They stood around her bed and looked at her. Papa took her hand, his expression shocked.

'Priscilla,' he said in a stricken voice.

Mama did not respond. The ghastly breathing became silent, started again and quietened again. Gradually the gaps between the breaths grew longer. At last, there was no breath at all. Her body relaxed. All pain left her face. Death had released her.

Cressie turned to Harry, who stood beside her, and threw her arms around him, crying, knowing that she had lost something precious and irreplaceable.

'She is in heaven now,' her father said solemnly. 'And earthly woes cannot touch her. We should be happy, children, because she won't suffer any more.'

Cressie wrote to Ralph to tell him she would stay in London until after the funeral. Then she would return to December House, which had now become hers. Ralph wrote back, sending all his love and comforting her in her sorrow. He missed her desperately but she must not hurry back on his account. He was painting and being looked after by Ursula. He would be fine until she was able to get back to him. She should stay with her family for as long as she needed to.

I long to get back. There's nothing here for me now.

She clutched his letter to her as though she might be able to absorb something of his essence through it, but it was a miserable replacement for him. Every bit of her body yearned for him. He had awoken her and now she could not put her desires back to sleep. The grief and loss she felt only seemed to intensify them.

The funeral took place less than a week later. The arrangements had been in place for a long while and the service went exactly as Mama had planned. The rawness of Cressie's sorrow seemed to have passed a little and she was able to feel some gladness that her mother had finally reached the end of a long and painful journey. Her father appeared broken by his loss and leaned on her throughout the day. She stood at his side when they welcomed the mourners into the house for the wake and stayed close by at all times. She knew he was going to resist her leaving but every day that passed away from Ralph was more difficult than the day before. Over the week, he wrote every day, posting a letter in the afternoon that she received the next day by second post. They were long letters, illustrated with pen-and-ink sketches of what he had seen that day that conjured up the house for her: its thick stone walls, the flagged floors, the deep fireplaces and the beamed ceilings. She saw the bleak January garden, bare and lifeless, and the hills rising darkly beyond, their peaks lost in the lowering grey sky. Her body ached for him with a physical hunger and she dreamed of their bed, soft, warm and delicious, rich with kisses and caresses. Her own lonely bed was comfortless without him. When she wept for her mother, she wanted only his arms around her.

Two more days perhaps, and I can go . . . Papa will have to let me. Besides, December House is mine now. He can't keep me here any more.

But Papa showed every sign that he expected Cressida to remain at home, take Mama's place and tend to his every need.

Cressie turned the corner into the street where the Fellbridge house stood, grand and imposing in a row of similarly grand and imposing houses. She had been on an errand for Ralph, buying some new brushes he'd asked for in his last letter, and she held the bag in one hand, her umbrella in the other, protection from the icy drizzle that fell miserably over the city. London, she thought, was particularly grim in this relentless drenching mist of rain.

As she neared the house, she saw the front door open and a figure step out of the house. It was a woman, in a long blue mackintosh, a shapeless thing. She was pulling a woollen hat over her hair as she stood for an instant on the steps and glanced up the road, but not in Cressie's direction. A moment later, she went down the front steps and began hurrying away towards the other end of the street.

Cressie froze at the sight, clenching the umbrella handle as hard as she could, her breath coming in short fast pants.

Catherine!

It was certainly her; there was no mistaking the short dark curls, or the way she held herself.

But what was she doing at my house?

Cressie waited, breathless and shaking, until the figure had disappeared around the corner, and then she dashed along the wet pavement up to the front door and let herself in. Dropping her umbrella on the mat, she pulled off her coat, calling, 'Papa? Are you here?'

'Here,' came a voice from the drawing room.

Cressie hurried in and came to a dead stop as she saw her father standing in front of the fireplace, staring up at the mantel. There, propped in front of the mirror, was the portrait of her. She gasped to see it. It seemed to come from another lifetime, that luminous image of her sitting in the Blackheath studio, the light falling upon her from the arched window. She remembered the view of the church, the shaggy garden with its tribe of birds, the ragged shrubbery. The portrait had caught her exactly but in a moment of unusual perfection: her hair glistening with reddish lights (she remembered Catherine's tender touch as she'd lifted strands of hair into position), her skin dewy, her eyes deep and thoughtful. The pearls around her neck glimmered, and the white shirt flattered her, giving her a buccaneering edge that countered the feminine softness of her face. She remembered that the shirt contained a body that was partly hers, and partly Catherine's. But there was something in the

355

portrait she hadn't seen before. Her right hand now held what looked like a silk scarf, in that bright, vibrant blue she had seen so often.

She heard Catherine's voice in her mind: *That's my blue. My special colour. I mix it for him and he puts it into every painting.*

There it was now, a blue scarf in her hand that was most certainly not there before. And as she gazed at it in horror, she noticed that it was speckled with dark red spots that looked like flecks of blood.

'It's very fine,' her father said, turning to her with a smile, the first she'd seen since Mama died. 'Few was right, the boy is talented. I like it enormously; he's caught you just as I see you. What do you think?'

'Very good.' Her voice was light and airy as she fought for breath. 'Yes. I'm glad it's finished at last.'

'No frame yet,' her father said. 'The young lady said she would send me some recommendations for framers. But she thought I would like to have the portrait now. And of course, she wanted me to settle the bill. I was happy to. I like the painting immensely. Perhaps you would like to find a framer, Cressida. I know you're talking about going back to Cumbria, but surely a few more days—'

She interrupted. 'Papa, the young woman . . . Mrs Few. Did she ask after me?'

'Of course. She expressed her condolences for our loss – she'd read about it in *The Times* apparently – and said that she quite understood why you hadn't been in touch with them lately.'

'Did she . . .' Cressie's hands were shaking. 'Did she ask where I am? How she might see me?'

'Yes,' her father said. 'But I told her that you weren't likely to be here for much longer as you intended to continue your holiday in order to recover from recent events.'

Recent events . . . as though losing Mama is like a dose of flu.

'But' – she tried to hide the desperation in her voice – 'did you tell her where I'm going?'

Her father frowned, hooking his thumbs in his waistcoat pocket. 'Do you know, I can't remember. She did say how much she loved the Cumbrian scenery, so perhaps I did. Did we mention the house? I can't say I quite recall. What does it matter? Perhaps she wishes to write to you there, a letter of sympathy or some such.'

She wanted to howl with frustration and make him remember. *I have to know what she knows! But if I can't . . .* 'Papa, I have to leave today, I'm awfully sorry. I must get back.'

'Today?' Her father look startled. 'What on earth is the rush, Cressida? Leave today to get back to that empty place in the middle of nowhere? I simply do not understand.'

'Please, Papa, I feel the strain of losing Mama, everything that happened last year . . . I need the peace and calm to recover, just as you said. You know that.' She tried to damp down the urgency in her voice but with every second that passed, the greater her need to get back to Ralph became.

Catherine knew, she was sure of it. It was a question of what she did with the knowledge. And Ralph and Cressie had to be together to face her, there was no doubt about it.

Her father sighed. 'Very well. I can't keep you here forever, I know that. But I insist that you stay for lunch. The Gladwells are coming and I need you here. Perhaps you could go tomorrow.'

'Today,' Cressie said simply. 'After lunch if I must. But I'll leave today.'

He stared at her. She had never used such a commanding tone with him and she could see the surprise in his eyes. *You'd better get used to it. You won't be able to bully me any more.* She turned on her heel and went out. She must pack, prepare to leave. She would send a telegram to Ralph and warn him that Catherine could know where they were and to be ready.

As she turned to dash up the stairs, her eye was caught by a white envelope propped up on the hall table. It had her name on it in block capitals, but there was no stamp. It had been hand delivered. Ellen must have seen it on the mat and picked it up. Cressie went over to it, tore it open and pulled out the sheet inside. It was written in simple capital letters but each one was deeply impressed in the paper, almost piercing it.

I WILL NOT LET YOU KILL HIM

CHAPTER 23

The night of the dinner party at James's house, Emily had a powerful dream but not the nightmare she'd been dreading. Instead, she was back in James's house, alone with him in a bedroom, and they were, without any awkwardness, lying together on the bed, clothed, and their bodies entwined, their hands tightly clasped. They were talking quietly in a state of perfect friendship and yet she knew that very soon he would kiss her, and the thought filled her with intense pleasure. His scent filled her nostrils again, the sweet woody smell of maleness, and she found it deeply comforting and pleasurable. She didn't feel passionate desire but a closeness that came from the ability to be completely herself with him. He accepted her as she was, and in her dream, she knew with certainty that he loved her.

She woke before anything physical happened, but nevertheless, the dream left her agitated, constantly blushing hard at the memory, and gripped by a wistful yearning to feel in real life that deep contentment, and to experience the pleasurable prelude to a promised joy that she had felt in the dream.

Oh God, she thought, as she stood in front of the mirror, seeing her cheeks flush red again at the thought of it. *I don't fancy James. This is very embarrassing. I must put it out of my mind and forget about it.*

But the memory of the warmth and pleasure of being close to James stayed with her all morning. When his car roared up in front of the house later that day, she instantly recalled the whole thing in a vivid rush and as he got out, she was appalled to find herself feeling trembly and awkward. She could hardly meet his gaze.

'How are things?' he asked cheerfully as he strode up to her and dropped a kiss on her cheek. 'I hope you've recovered from last night.'

'I hope *you* have,' she returned. 'It looked as though it was going to be a late one.'

'It was. Three a.m. before they finally got on their way. You should see the empties outside the back door.' He made a face. 'Felt a trifle vinegary this morning, I can tell you. Now, I was just sorting through a drawer and I thought Joe might like these.' He uncurled his hand to show three small battered Matchbox cars in his hand. 'Seventies memorabilia. I think they were mine. Would he like them, do you think?'

'He'd love them,' Emily said. She was suddenly possessed by a powerful urge to step forward and bury her face in James's soft wool jumper and inhale.

That scent – picked up during their awkward kiss and then again in her dream – seemed to awaken a strong response in her, but quite what it was, she couldn't tell. *I don't fancy him!* she scolded herself. And to remind herself of the fact, she stared hard at his pink cheeks and friendly blue eyes. He was so far from Will's eagle-ish handsomeness and hard, gym-taut body. He wasn't her type at all, apart from the height.

'Everything all right?' he asked, aware that she was staring at him.

'Oh yes. Fine. Sorry. Thanks for the cars, it's very thoughtful of you. Would you like a cup of tea or something? The children are watching telly, then we're going for a walk after I've pegged out the washing.'

'No, I'd better not. I'm behind after a late start anyway.' James smiled at her, a shy look coming over his face. 'Thanks again for coming last night. It was lovely to have you there. You should come again.'

'Yes. That would be very nice,' she replied. It hadn't been too bad, she thought. After that rocky start.

'I hope you didn't hate my friends too much. They're all right really, when you get to know them.'

'Of course I didn't hate them.' She was relieved to feel the urge to press herself up against James diminishing. *Stupid dream. The sooner I can forget about it, the better.*

A thought occurred to him. 'Did Wilson come by to see you?'

'Yes. He sent a quote, it was pretty reasonable. I've asked him to start on the cottage as soon as he can. My brother's going to use it once it's finished. Mr Wilson said it won't take long.'

'Your brother?' James nodded, smiling. 'That'll be nice for you. I worry that you're on your own so much.'

'You really don't need to. I'm fine.'

'I know. You're very self-reliant, I've guessed that.' He grinned at her. 'Right, I'd better be on my way. Bye, Emily. See you soon.' A moment later, the car was disappearing out of the driveway and she went back inside to check on the children.

Tom called while they were finishing up lunch. 'Hi, Em. How's things?'

'All right,' she said, scooping up a forkful of pasta and getting it into Joe's mouth before he could look away. 'You?'

'I've just been looking at that picture I took away with me – you know, that one of the snow.'

'Yes, of course I know it. I worked out it was the view of the back garden. It looks different because of the angle.'

'That's what I realised too. But the thing that's strange is that there's something poking out of the snow on my picture – something that must be quite tall as it comes out of the drift. I can't remember anything like that in your garden. Is there something out there?'

Emily stared out through the window to the garden. 'Just trees, I think.'

'It's not a tree.'

'Well, I don't think so then. But it's hard to see clearly from here. I'll have a look afterwards and let you know.'

When they went for their walk, Emily headed for the direction shown in the painting in her room. She'd gone up after Tom's call and examined it carefully in the daylight, holding it by the window, and she could see that there was something poking out of the snow under a large drift and the spiky top of a bare tree. *Of course. I noticed it myself. But what is it?* She had squinted at it but could make out only a grey smear that could have been anything. As they set out, she oriented herself so that she was facing the same view as in the painting, with the mountain in her vision exactly as represented on the canvas. She saw that the position of one of the large drifts exactly followed the line of the old stone wall that lined the boundary of the garden. Beyond it was the paddock and that marked the far boundary of the land belonging to December House.

As Emily strolled in the direction of the wall, the children running off and circling back to show her odd-shaped twigs or interesting stones that they'd discovered, she worked out that if she were right, then there ought to be something – whatever that grey smear might be – in the space between the edge of the property and the tree on the edge of the orchard, which was the only tree that could possibly be in the painting. But there was nothing at all that she could make out.

If whatever it is emerged above the snowline, it must surely be fairly tall. And there's absolutely nothing there.

She wasn't mistaken, she was sure of it. Perhaps something had been removed in the intervening years. There was no reason why it mattered really, but her curiosity was piqued.

'That's strange,' Tom said when she called him back. 'So it's in your painting too? Go up to the attic and see if it's in the other pictures as well. I'll keep trying to work out what it is.'

'Okay. I will.' She made a mental note to go and take a look in the crate as soon as she could.

Mr Wilson had a cancellation and he and his team were able to start earlier than expected, which meant Emily spent some long evenings in front of websites, working out costings for a kitchen and a bathroom, and getting everything ordered so that it was on site for when the builders needed it.

She emailed Tom:

Great news! They're going to start right away on Keeper's Cottage and Mr Wilson says it will take around three weeks. I'll keep you up to speed on progress but I'm sure it won't take much

longer than that. Apparently it's very straightforward (but there's bound to be at least one hitch). I'll send pics as they go along.

Tom wrote back:

Fantastic! Can't wait to get in there. Shall we discuss the ownership issue? I think we'll need to get a lawyer involved if we're going to get title deeds, etc. drawn up. I don't know much about it – I'll talk to someone and see what I can find out.

Her heart sank when she read that. He was determined to get possession of the cottage. She'd known he would be. It had been naive to think that Tom, who was remarkably stubborn when he set his mind to something, would just forget about it. Owning Keeper's Cottage seemed to mean something important to him and she worried how he would react when he learned what she meant to do.

She didn't reply directly to his email, just sent some pictures of the builders putting up their scaffolding, but she knew she couldn't avoid him forever. He sent her persistent messages about getting a legal agreement of the transfer of ownership of Keeper's Cottage drawn up.

I should call him and discuss it, she thought wanly, but she chickened out and instead wrote an email saying that she'd thought it over very carefully and had decided that it was best for Keeper's Cottage to remain part of December House. She would maintain it and he could treat it as his own for as long as he wanted. Perhaps, if she ever sold the house, they could work out a way for Tom to share some of the proceeds to make up for it. She hoped he understood and sent her love.

She was filled with apprehension as she pressed 'send' and checked her email every few hours afterwards, waiting for a response. But nothing came.

The work on the cottage kept her busy over the next couple of weeks but she didn't mind. It was a pleasure to walk over there with the children, with the sun warming them and the countryside bursting into life around them, and see what the builders were up to. There were always new problems to sort out – lights that didn't fit, faulty goods, a space that was too small or too large, a rotten beam that needed replacing, plaster that was blown – but everything was resolved eventually, after much standing around and staring and drinking mugs of tea, with Emily phoning merchandisers or tile suppliers or heading home to fire up the internet and send off emails. Gradually the little place was becoming brighter and cosier, with a sound roof, a small but efficient bathroom, and a kitchen installed with a decent cooker. Radiators had gone up too, and a wood-burning stove with a round pot belly was sitting snugly in the small sitting room fireplace.

James came along to check on progress and was very admiring. 'You're doing a wonderful job,' he said as he looked around the new kitchen.

'Well, it's Mr Wilson really,' Emily said modestly but she was proud of what she'd achieved. She'd never been so hands-on with any building work before and she'd enjoyed it much more than she'd expected, despite the frustrations and niggles.

'You should do this full-time,' James said, nodding as he looked about. 'It's very nice indeed. So when does your brother move in?'

'I . . . I'm not sure,' she said haltingly. It was now nearly two weeks since she'd heard from Tom and she was beginning to worry that she'd caused a rift between them. Sometimes she considered ringing him up and telling him he could have the damn place if it was going to cause so much trouble between them, but something always stopped her. She had a very strong sense that she couldn't give the cottage away, even if she'd wanted to. And the truth was, she didn't want to and she didn't really understand why.

It was a relief when at last an email arrived.

Hey Em
Sorry not to write before. I've been working flat out finishing a project, hardly had a minute to myself. I understand what you're saying about the cottage. I'm planning to come up and take a look so I can see what furniture,

etc. I might need. Maybe we can talk about it then.

I'll let you know when I'm on my way but I hope to be there pretty soon.

Love

Tom

P.S. did you look at the other paintings?

She released her held breath, and smiled with relief. It was going to be all right. Tom was still her familiar, loveable brother, a kind and reasonable man who would try and see her side of things. She relaxed, realising that she'd been retaining a nasty anxiety for a while now. Tom's email had put her mind at rest. She tapped out a reply immediately.

Come whenever you like! We're here (of course) and would love to see you. I've put a bit of furniture in the cottage already so you can use it right away. Mr Wilson is just doing snags now. It's liveable as soon as you're ready.

E xxx

P.S. I'll go and look at the paintings now.

But she kept forgetting and didn't go up to the attic at all.

* * *

The dream about James and her strange reaction to it seemed nothing more than a slightly embarrassing private joke. Emily saw him quite frequently and she always monitored her reaction to him just in case. As he climbed out of the Land Rover and headed her way, sometimes with a bunch of flowers from the garden, a cake baked by his mother or some old toys for the children, she would test how she reacted at the sight of him and was relieved to find that it was quite normal.

But it isn't the sight of him that's the problem.

If he stood too close to her, that odd feeling would creep over her: a deep yearning to press herself against him and soak in the strength and comfort he could offer her, and to revel in that scent of his.

What does he wear? she wondered. She caught elusive hints of it when he was near and she found that it would send a tremble along her skin and set off a strange dizziness in her brain. Thoughts about what his aftershave might be started to preoccupy her, and she found herself imagining how she might sneak into his bathroom and look in his cupboards, and planning a trip to a department store in Carlisle so that she could sniff the sample bottles in the perfume section. She imagined spraying a pillow with it so that she could sleep with it in her nostrils. Then she would catch herself up and laugh. *I'll just ask him,* she told herself. *One of these days.* But it was quite a personal question and she found she never could.

Maybe I can ask Harriet or Georgie, she thought. The invitations to coffee and lunch had followed after the dinner party and she'd decided to take them up as soon as the cottage was finished. It was time to start making some new friends.

It was only when a letter arrived from Diana that she realised with a shock that she hadn't thought about Will for days, if not weeks. This place was so gloriously untouched by any memories of him, and she felt so free since the nightmares had stopped, that she had been able to close him off almost completely, as though his role in her life was finished, and he was relegated to a closed box of memories.

Dear Emily

I'm sorry not to have heard anything from you recently. You sent that nice card with your address and the children's pictures and there has been nothing since then. You have not even rung to find out how Will is doing. If you are interested, he continues as he was, with little change. The doctors are still monitoring him and I remain convinced that he will wake eventually, no matter what they say to the contrary.

I can't pretend to be anything but appalled by your coldness towards your husband. You have your reasons, but Emily, where is your Christian charity? How can you act so callously towards the father of your children,

370

and the man you swore to love through richer, through poorer, in sickness and in health?

I refuse to beg, Emily, but I hope you will find it in your heart to reunite a man who has made foolish mistakes with the children he loves. It is his hour of need. I have always esteemed you and thought highly of your character. I hope so much that I will not have to revise that opinion.

I too would like to see the children. Please contact me and perhaps we can discuss a time for you to visit.

With my best wishes
Diana

Emily kept the letter with her and read it over several times, each time with a rush of horror and outrage. She had almost succeeded in blotting out and forgetting the frightful image of Will in his hospital bed, but Diana had brought it all flooding back; brought back the guilt and fear and sense of desperate terror.

What should I do? she wondered, the letter burning in her pocket as she read the children their bedtime stories, pulled the curtains shut against the still light sky, and kissed them goodnight. *Do I take them back to London?*

The thought made her feel suffocated.

Should I see Will again? I know I should but . . .

She wouldn't think about it now. She'd talk it over with Tom and see what he thought.

When there was a knock at the door at mid-morning the day after Diana's letter arrived, Emily half thought it might be Tom, arriving after taking the first train on an impulse. She was expecting him any day now that the cottage was finished.

She pulled open the door ready to greet him, but it wasn't Tom on the doorstep. Instead, she found herself staring into a pair of cheerful bright blue eyes set in a tanned face under a mop of dark brown hair. It was a man who looked in his late twenties, stocky and brown-limbed, dressed in a T-shirt, shorts and sandals, a small backpack hanging over one arm. In the drive beyond Emily could see a motorbike parked with a helmet dangling off the handlebars. She hadn't heard him pull up outside but then the washing machine had been on its spin cycle, so maybe that was why.

'Hello?' she said.

'Oh, hi there.' He grinned, revealing white teeth. 'I'm looking for Cressida Fellbridge.'

She gaped at him, startled, not knowing what to say.

'Do you know her?' he asked in a friendly tone. There was a sing-song upward twang to his voice. *It's an Australian accent.*

'Well . . . yes . . . I suppose so, in a way. I'm her niece. Emily Conway,' she said, puzzled.

The man's face cleared and he smiled broadly. 'Hey, that's great! Something's gone right, that's fantastic! I've been looking for you.'

'Really? But why?' Emily realised she was

372

clutching on to the door handle so hard, her knuckles were turning white.

'Ah, sorry. You don't have a clue who I am or why I'm here.' He stuck out a broad brown hand. 'I've come on a bit of a mystery tour but I'm harmless, I promise. It's a pleasure to meet you, Emily Conway. My name is Cameron. Cameron Baxter. How are ya?'

CHAPTER 24

Lunch with the Gladwells was torture for Cressie. Her mind was racing and her insides churning with fear, apprehension and a desire to be on her way. She was clumsy, knocking over a glass of water and dropping things, and so distracted that her father could hardly hide his annoyance with her.

The Gladwells were polite and sympathetic – the family was in mourning, after all – and said they quite understood when Cressie, unable to bear it another minute, got to her feet and said she was very sorry but she must leave them.

'Forgive me, Papa,' she murmured to him as she kissed him and he grunted stiffly. Then she hurried from the room to get her things, calling to Ellen to get a taxi to take her to Euston.

'Did my telegram go?' she asked as she stood in the doorway pulling on her gloves. The taxi waited at the kerb, the engine purring softly.

'Yes, miss. Have a good journey, miss.' The maid bobbed to her.

'I will, thank you.' She ran down the steps to

the taxi and as they set off for the station, she felt a small scrap of calm return.

The journey was difficult. She couldn't concentrate on anything, not the paper she had bought at the station or the book she had packed. Only sketching in the little pad she had bought at the artists' supplies shop that morning could bring her any peace. Even so, her mind ranged wide as she drew, playing with scenarios and possibilities.

Perhaps Papa didn't mention December House. How would she find us in the whole of Cumbria? Would she bother to look for us anyway? She has the money from my portrait, perhaps more if she sells Ralph's pictures. Maybe she'll just leave us alone.

But she knew that was impossible. There was the note in her pocket, after all. *I will not let you kill him.* What on earth could that mean? As if Cressie could possibly hurt Ralph. He was ill, that was certain; Catherine had told her all about it. But he had not suffered from the arrhythmia at all since they'd been together, and if it came back, then Cressie intended to take him to a good doctor. Homemade remedies were all very well, but surely a proper medicine would be more effective.

But that was envisaging a life beyond Catherine, and she knew in her heart, with horrible foreboding, that Catherine would not permit it.

I've always known that. She's told me over and over

again, in hundreds of tiny ways, that Ralph is hers. And he is. She's his wife.

She slumped back in her seat, almost beaten at the thought that everyone respectable in society would be on Catherine's side. She had morality and the law to back up her claim.

And yet . . .

She saw again the blue silk scarf in her painted hand with its ominous flecks of blood. She saw the look on Ralph's face – the agonised dread – when they had spoken of his relationship with his wife. He had said that it would kill him to stay with Catherine but that she might do something reckless to prevent him from leaving.

The fear began to rise in her again.

I know exactly how it is. Catherine knows where Ralph is. She knows I'm not there. She is on her way, just ahead of me, hurrying to reach him first so that she can take him away from me.

Everything was now crystal clear in her mind. The pencil dropped from her hand onto the pad.

I have to stop her. Ralph is in danger.

Carlisle was in chilly darkness when she at last stood on the platform. Everyone seemed to have gone home for the night and she felt desperately alone. Ralph was so close now – just a few miles away – but how could she reach him? Outside the station, there was nothing at all. No traffic and no taxis. The only light came from a telephone box at the side of the road. She went to it.

Inside, the phone books were tatty and torn but she found the number she needed, and then fumbled in her purse for some change. When the telephone at the other end was answered, she pressed the button and her money went clattering into the phone's black belly.

'Hello? Mrs Pendleton? It's Cressida Fellbridge here. I wonder if I could possibly ask a great favour. I'm at the station in Carlisle and I need to get to the house. There are no taxis here. Would you kindly be able to arrange one for me? I don't know the name of the taxi company. Thank you . . . thank you very much . . . The lights are on at the house? Yes, that's right. Some friends of mine are staying there. Mr and Mrs Few. I'm joining them there this evening but stupidly forgot to book a taxi . . . Thank you again. Goodnight.'

She hung up the telephone. All she could do now was wait.

Despite what Mrs Pendleton had said, the house was virtually in darkness when she arrived, with only the faint hint of light beyond the rooms at the front. As the taxi pulled up outside, she was filled with a sense of awful foreboding. Was Catherine here already? Where was Ralph? She had telegraphed her train time; surely he would be looking out for her, expecting her?

She didn't want the driver to go but didn't know how to ask him to stay. Once he had driven away she was left in the bitterly cold night, facing the house and desperately afraid. Where was Ralph? She longed to see him. She had sent him the telegram:

Coming on 2.30 train stop Catherine may know and be on her way

Had that been enough? And what could he have done anyway?

Gathering all her courage, she went up to the front door and pressed it open. It was not locked. *So he didn't lock her out.* A horrible shiver spread over her skin. Catherine could be inside right now.

She went into the dark hall, putting her case down on the flagstone floor. The fire was dead and the lantern unlit. Had Ralph heard the taxi arrive and leave? She was about to call out when she decided, suddenly, not to draw attention to herself. It was possible that the taxi hadn't been heard. Perhaps no one knew that she had arrived at all. If so, there was no point in giving away the element of surprise. Pushing open the door of the passage, which squeaked a little as it moved, she stepped forward as quietly as she could. There was a light on in the kitchen at the end, but no sound came from there. She went back into the hall and went up a few of the stairs. The first landing was in darkness but she could see a dim light beyond. Slowly and carefully, with as little noise as possible, she continued upwards, tread by tread, holding her breath. As she turned from the first landing to the next shorter flight to the second floor, she heard a noise from the bedroom she and Ralph shared.

Instantly she halted, her heart pounding, and listened as hard as she could. It was a sound that turned her blood icy cold with fear. She could hear a woman's voice, talking musically and then crooning softly. It was muffled behind the closed bedroom door. Cressie stepped forward inch by inch, trying to keep each step as silent as she could, listening hard for the voice to become clearer. Adrenalin surged through her and she felt sick and shaky. *Perhaps it's Ursula*, she told herself, hoping to stay calm. *Ralph feels unwell. He's asked her to nurse him.*

But as she approached little by little, she knew with a horrible certainty that she was listening to Catherine's voice, still muffled but a little easier to make out as she got closer.

'Now, now, you've been very sick, but don't worry, we're going to make you better. You're going to be all better, I promise.' Cheerful humming followed, and the noise of someone bustling about the room. 'You'll sleep very well now. And in the morning we can decide what's best to do. When you're better.'

In answer, there was a groan.

Ralph! Cressie's skin prickled almost painfully at the sound of his voice. He was there, with her. She had him in her control somehow. *I have to help him, I have to stop her from doing whatever it is she's doing . . . But how?*

She looked about for a weapon of some kind, and noticed a warming pan that had been hung on the wall as a quaint decoration. She went over on tiptoe and lifted it very carefully off the hook on the wall. It was heavy and the brass pan seemed dense enough. It would make a good weapon if she had to use it. Gripping the wooden handle tightly, she turned back towards the bedroom door. The crooning had started up again, sounding like a ghastly sort of lullaby.

She's mad. The thought came clearly into Cressie's mind. *Whatever has happened has sent her out of her mind.*

Then she tripped on the stringy edge of the landing mat and stumbled forward, the warming pan banging hard on the floor with a resounding dong. She gasped in horror and glanced up at the door of the bedroom. There was a moment of silence, then footsteps and the door swung open. Catherine stood there, her face hard and her eyes blazing. She barred the way, her small, stocky body standing determinedly in the doorway, but Cressie could see Ralph beyond in the bed. He looked pale and ill, his eyes feverish as though he wasn't quite aware of what was happening.

'You!' Catherine spat. Her lip curled in distaste. 'So you came back, did you? I suppose your daddy told you how helpful he'd been. I hoped the old fool would forget it in the excitement of receiving your portrait. But you dragged it out of him, did you?'

Ralph turned his head to look at her. It seemed

to cost him a great effort. His expression was a mixture of pleasure and agony at seeing her. 'Cressie,' he said through dry lips.

Catherine whirled round to face him. 'Don't be so stupid. You can't possibly be glad to see her. She's spoiled everything! It was supposed to be different from this. She would give us what we needed, not destroy everything.' She went over to him and sat on the edge of the bed, taking his hand in hers and rubbing it. 'We can get it all back. It will still be all right.'

'What are you doing here?' demanded Cressie. Her fright was making her braver now. She sensed that they were about to do battle and she knew that she must win. There could be no other outcome. 'You have to leave at once.'

Catherine turned to stare at her, her eyes a dark, flinty grey. 'Don't worry, we'll leave first thing in the morning. Ralph needs to recover his strength. Then he's coming with me.'

'No.' Cressie lifted her chin defiantly. 'He stays here with me.'

Catherine looked down at the warming pan still tight in Cressie's grip, and laughed. 'And you plan to make me obey, do you? Just give in to what you want? I suppose it's what you've known all your life.' She gave her a scornful look. 'You're very stupid. Don't you understand that you'll do irreparable harm if you refuse to allow me to care for Ralph? I won't allow it. I simply won't allow it.'

'Cressie . . .' Ralph spoke in the same weak voice.

'I'm so sorry. I had no idea she was coming. At the door . . . she came in. She seemed so reasonable and we had tea but she must have drugged it with something. I can hardly see . . .'

'What nonsense,' Catherine said briskly. 'You see how ill you are? You can't remember that I arrived just in time to save you from another attack. You were so awfully ill – it was lucky I had brought all my medicine with me.'

Cressie looked in the direction of Catherine's glance and saw on the chest of drawers a collection of bottles and potions, a hypodermic syringe, cotton wool and other medical paraphernalia.

Catherine was looking down tenderly at Ralph. 'I had to give you an injection, didn't I, darling? To make you better.' She turned steely eyes on Cressie again. 'I know your plan. You want to take him away from me. You want to destroy everything we've built up together. But I won't let you.' Her eyes flickered menacingly. 'I'll kill you before I let that happen.'

Cressie tightened her grip on the warming pan. *She means it. She's dangerous. Oh my God, she's mad.*

Ralph closed his eyes and breathed deeply. He seemed to be summoning his strength. He looked at Catherine again and said, 'But you know that's not true. You're killing me. You're killing me right now. Whatever you injected into my arm . . . I can feel it creeping through my veins, freezing me.'

'No, no,' she said gently. 'Making you better!'

'Not making me better. Killing me.' He swallowed

and said, 'We need to tell the truth, Catherine. Can't you see? It's over now.'

This seemed to trigger something in Catherine. She began to tremble and jumped up, her eyes wild. 'No! No, why are you saying that, Ralph? Why would you say something so awful? You're everything to me! I've devoted my life to protecting your talent, to nurturing you, to making the world recognise that you are a genius! Of course I'm not killing you!'

'You may not mean to,' Ralph said in the same low voice, 'but you are. I wasn't born colour-blind but I've lost more and more of my ability to see colour and everything you've done to make me better has made me worse.'

'You need me!' she cried in a quavering voice. 'I'm your eyes!'

'You made yourself my eyes because you caused the need in the first place. Whatever you brew for me – your tablets, your medicines – they are destroying the talent you claim you want to protect. And they make me more dependent on you.'

She stared at him, her face working oddly as she took this in. Then she laughed. 'Ridiculous! I would never harm you, not for the world! Why are you saying this, Ralph?' A look of hurt and bewilderment crossed her face. 'I don't understand.'

He looked at her sadly. 'Oh Catherine, I don't believe you do. I've only just begun to understand it myself. But that's why we have to tell the truth now. Don't you see?'

'No.' Her fury was back. Her lips hardened, her lip lifted in snarl. 'I don't see! I want you to come home, for everything to go back to how it was.'

'It can't,' Ralph said simply. He shifted his head so that he could see Cressie. His grey-gold eyes softened. 'Cressie . . . I love you. I want to marry you.'

Catherine gasped and stared over at Cressie, hate in her eyes. 'You can't marry her!' she cried wildly. 'You're married to me!'

Cressie was speechless. He had said it, in front of Catherine. At the same as she was filled with fear at how the other woman would take this, she felt a rush of exhilaration and joy. *He loves me!* But fear followed hard on its heels. What had Catherine done to Ralph? Was it possible that he was dying? *Oh God, please, no . . .*

'Catherine . . .' He had fixed her with a look that seemed to speak volumes to her. She covered her ears with her fists and began to moan. 'Catherine, it has to stop now. We aren't married.'

Cressie gasped. 'You're not married?'

Catherine's face had screwed up in an expression of pain. She began to rock back and forward.

Ralph looked at her sorrowfully, his eyes tormented. 'Catherine isn't my wife. She's my sister.'

'Your sister?' Cressie felt stunned, dazed as though she had been hit hard. 'Your sister?' she repeated stupidly. 'But . . . why . . .'

Ralph looked tired and sicker than ever. 'Please

forgive me, Cressie. It was a stupid lie. Catherine came up with it when we saw the flat for rent. It was so perfect for us, you see, the studio was exactly right. The light was wonderful, the view, the garden . . . we wanted it so badly. But the advertisement said only single professional men or married couples need apply. We wanted the flat. It didn't seem such an awful lie to tell.'

Catherine had taken her hands from her ears and had frozen, listening to the story with an appalled attention as though this was the first time she had heard it.

Ralph went on, 'I thought no one else need hear it but the landlord. But the lie spread. We were stupid. We didn't realise how people talk. We never thought they'd be interested in it. But the neighbours thought we were married, so did the shopkeepers. Catherine bought a ring and put it on. She began to tell people we were married as if she really believed it were true. I always thought when we move away, we'll go back to the truth. But the lie became so powerful and Catherine kept feeding it, as though she wished that we really could be married.' He looked pleadingly at Cressie. 'There was nothing between us but the bond of siblings.'

'Why didn't you tell me?' Cressie asked.

'I should have. But even speaking it aloud would have been to admit that I colluded in it. I suppose that I knew she needed me. I cared too much for her to destroy her fantasy until it was too difficult to destroy. It had entwined us both.'

'Oh Ralph,' Cressie whispered, trying to take it in. He was free. That thought was flying around her mind like a brightly coloured kite. He wasn't married and never had been. He was hers entirely and completely.

Catherine spoke again, her voice soft now, high and tender. 'You only had me. I'm all the family you have. There was only me to look after you, to make you the great artist you were born to be. You couldn't do it without me.' She cast a contemptuous look at Cressie. 'Do you think that someone like *her* will ever give you the devotion I've given you? Only I can be your helper, see colours for you. Only I can treat your illness.'

'But . . .' Ralph's voice was quiet but it cut like a knife through the room. 'There never was any illness, was there?'

She frowned. 'Of course there was.'

'No. I was quite well when you began to diagnose me with weakness, anaemia and all the rest of it. And once I began to take your medicine . . . that's when it all changed. I can see it now. I wish I had seen it then.'

'I've never hurt you!' Catherine said, her eyes frightened. 'I would never do such a thing.'

'But you did hurt me,' Ralph said. 'Can't you see it? You've been killing me.'

'I wish you would stop saying that!' she shouted, fury crossing her face. 'Killing you! I would never do it!'

'Catherine.' Ralph's eyes searched her face with

something like pity in them. 'I've had to time to think, time to work it all out. I saw you once, back at home. You were mixing your potions and medicines on my old palettes. That's what you used, didn't you?'

'Yes. But I cleaned them, of course.'

'Not well enough. You must have picked up flakes of my paint and mixed them into the tablets or injected them into me.'

Catherine stared at him in horror, unable to speak.

'That's why I'm ill so often. The fatigue, the nausea, the things that you like to call my heart problem. My hearing is failing along with my eyes. That's why there's no colour to me. I'm as white as the white lead paint you've been feeding me. You've already killed me.'

Cressie gasped. Catherine's hand went to her throat and clutched it. 'What?' she cried out wildly.

'Yes, it's true,' Ralph said. 'You know it is.' He gave a wan smile. 'We always knew that white lead is deadly, didn't we? That's why I never let you touch it. I'm dying of it. Can't you see?' Cressie stared in horror but Ralph's eyes were fixed on his sister. 'That's why you have to let me go.'

The expression on Catherine's face was awful to witness. There was a moment of horrified stillness, and then she ran out of the room, pushing past Cressie and across the landing into the studio. She slammed the door shut and there was the sound of heavy scraping.

'What's she doing?' Cressie asked, bewildered, looking across at the shut door. 'It sounds like she's barricading herself in with the sofa.' She turned to look at Ralph, who sighed heavily. He looked utterly drained, as though the effort of talking had removed the last of his strength. She dropped the warming pan and rushed over to him. 'Oh Ralph.' She hugged him, dropping kisses on his face.

'Cressie.' He smiled at her. His hands clasped hers. 'I'm so happy to see you.'

'You'll feel better tomorrow,' Cressie said, 'when whatever she's given you has gone out of your system.' She gazed at him anxiously. 'But my darling, is it true what you said, about the lead paint?'

Ralph looked at her, his eyes sad. 'I fear so. I've wondered for a while if I'd somehow been poisoned by it but I was so careful. I had no idea how I might be ingesting it. Then I thought of how much better I've felt since I've been here and that's when I remembered seeing Catherine making her remedies on my palette.'

Cressie tried to stifle her fear. 'We'll get you the best doctors,' she said fervently. 'The best treatments. We'll make you better.'

He smiled. 'Yes. I'm always better when you're here.'

'You're not really dying, are you? You only said that to frighten her, didn't you?'

'I'm not really dying. I'm sure I'll get better.' He

sighed, then smiled. 'We can be together properly now. I meant what I said.'

From behind the door of the studio there was no sound. Cressie went to the bedroom door and locked it, then returned to the bed and curled up next to Ralph.

'We'll have to wait it out,' she said. She had so many questions for him but she knew he was too drained to answer them. 'Do you think she'll go in the morning?'

'I hope so,' he said sadly. 'I hope that at last she knows that the lies are over with. I didn't want to hurt her but in the end I knew I wouldn't survive if I didn't.'

She kissed his cool cheek. He was, she thought, as white as he had said: like white lead paint, the same colour that had made her own portrait luminous with life and yet was, at the same time, deadly. The atmosphere outside the house felt suddenly heavy.

'I think the snow is coming,' she whispered.

She curled against him and they fell asleep, the house filled with an eerie silence.

PART III

CHAPTER 25

Once the children had been given their lunch and Joe put down for his afternoon nap, Emily could begin to concentrate properly on what Cameron Baxter had to say to her.

'This is very, very odd,' she said, picking at Carrie's half-finished ham sandwich. She'd made Cameron his own sandwich and he'd eaten that and was finishing up their cherry tomatoes and carrot sticks with hummus too. 'So let me get this straight. You're on the trail of my aunt Cressida.'

'That's right. Because of my dad.'

Emily nodded. She'd taken in that part of the story. Cameron's father had been at school in London in the early sixties before his family had emigrated to Australia and he had been taught there by Cressida.

'Okay. I didn't know she was a teacher – but then I don't know much about her at all,' Emily said. 'So he met her in London, you say? Not in Australia?'

'Oh no, absolutely not,' Cameron said firmly. 'It was definitely London. My dad was born in the

393

East End, you see. Post-war London, pretty grim, not many opportunities for kids like him. But your aunt was this incredible influence on him – gave him private lessons and everything. And when she heard he was going to Australia, she even gave him a box of books as a going-away present. Man, he really treasured those books! He's still got them on his shelves.'

'Is that why he wants to track her down after all these years?' Emily asked.

'Yeah. Well, I told him I was coming on a trip to England and he asked me if I would try and find her. He's always wondered what happened to her, and when he attempted to find out himself, he drew a blank. He gave me the address of this place but when I looked it up online, there wasn't a Fellbridge registered here. I guessed it must have been sold or something.'

'It was, but it was sold ages ago. About fifty years ago. There hasn't been a Fellbridge here since then.' Emily frowned, puzzled. 'Besides, I'm surprised that your father didn't meet up with Cressida in Australia.'

Cameron laughed. He had a merry face and his teeth looked very white against his tan. 'Yeah, well, Australia's quite a long way to go for a reunion.'

'No . . . I mean, why didn't you track her down there? She's lived in Australia for years.'

A look of surprise crossed Cameron's face. 'What?'

'Yes.' Emily nodded. 'She went out there in the

sixties herself. Maybe your father gave her the idea. She's lived there ever since. Of course, she might be dead by now. For some reason, she lost contact with the family. I must try and get in touch with my uncle Harry and ask him about her.' Thoughts of her mysterious aunt had been floating into her consciousness more and more. As Emily connected ever more strongly to the countryside and the house, she had begun to wonder more about her family and what had brought her to this beautiful place.

'Nah.' Cameron popped another cherry tomato in his mouth and shook his head firmly. 'Definitely not.'

'What?'

'She wasn't in Australia. No way. Because Dad wrote to her here. She gave him the address and he wrote to her for years. And she replied.'

'What?' Emily frowned again. 'That's impossible. Are you saying that she wrote letters from here all through the sixties?'

'Yep. You got it.'

'But she couldn't have. She sold the house to Catherine and Ralph Few in the early sixties. I think the legal papers said 1963. I've got them somewhere, in the batch of stuff the lawyers gave me. So she couldn't have written to your dad from here, because by then she'd left.'

Cameron fixed her with a firm blue look. 'Well, we're going to have to part ways there, because I know she did live here. I saw the letters myself.

Dated right up to the end of the decade and posted from here. There's definitely no mistake.'

Cameron stayed into the afternoon and they talked over the mystery the entire time, trying to work out how their differing versions of what had happened to Cressida Fellbridge could be reconciled.

'I'm not sure how we would find out what we want to know,' Emily said, as they were out walking with the children, the fresh spring air buffeting them as they went. 'I suppose online searches are the way to go.'

'Doesn't anyone in your family know?' Cameron asked. 'Surely you know what happened to your own aunt?'

Emily gave him a bashful look. 'I'm afraid we aren't a very close family. My father never talked much about his sister. I just got the impression that there had been some kind of separation. My parents are dead, so I can't ask them now. The only one's who's left is my uncle Harry but he's in Spain. I last saw him at my parents' funeral. That was a long time ago, just before I met Will, my husband. Harry still sends me a cheque for ten pounds every Christmas and I send him a card too, but we don't talk.'

'Families, eh?' Cameron said with a grin. 'Overrated, so they say. Why don't you give this uncle of yours a ring and see what he says? He might know something.'

'That's a good idea,' Emily said, cheered. 'You're right. I'll do that. What about you? Are you heading off now?'

'I didn't fancy going anywhere today after the time it took to get here,' Cameron said, 'so I booked into the local pub for the night. Thought I'd just see how it goes. I'm footloose at the moment, going where I feel like. It's my last few days before I fly back to Oz.'

'Why don't you stay for dinner tonight?' Emily offered. 'And you can be there when I call Uncle Harry.'

'Great idea, and very kind of you too,' Cameron said, grinning. 'Dad'll be pleased to know that I've come close to finding your aunt. He's always had a sentimental attachment to her. Always wondered what happened to her.' Cameron winked. 'Personally I think he had a little crush on her.'

'I'm sure we'll find out,' Emily said. Privately she suspected that Catherine Few had written the letters to Cameron's father, not wanting to let a young boy down. What other explanation could there be? But they would find out what Harry had to say first.

After the children were in bed, Emily dug out her address book and settled down with the phone. Cameron sat across from her on the sofa in the sitting room, munching on a packet of the children's crisps. 'These taste like sawdust,' he said, making a face. He examined the packet. 'Organic,

397

all natural, salt and sugar free. That explains it.'
Watching Emily flick through the pages of her
address book, he said, 'How exactly did you get
this house then?'

Emily told him quickly about Catherine Few and
the bequest.

'Cressida's dead then,' Cameron said flatly, and
then looked apologetic, adding quickly, 'Sorry.
Didn't mean for it to come out like that, I know
she's your aunt. But she must be dead otherwise
this Catherine person would have returned the
house to your aunt, right?'

'Or she just assumed Cressida was dead.'

'She knew enough to know about you. So why
not say in her will, "I return this house to Cressida
or, if she's dead, then to her niece Emily". But
she didn't do that. There's no assumption that
Cressida's alive, so I reckon she knew Cressida
was dead.'

'How would she know that?' Emily asked,
puzzled. 'Not even her family know.'

Cameron nodded at the phone in Emily's hand.
'So call your uncle. Let's see what he has to say.'

It was strange tapping in the number from the
old entry in her address book and waiting for it
to ring. When she heard the beep at the other end
to indicate it was ringing, it struck her how easy
it was to phone someone and how, really, there
was no excuse not to do so. It was dreadful that
she had never contacted her uncle in all this time.
She thought of Diana too, and the way she told

herself that she was too busy to ring her, when the truth was that—

'Hello, Harold Fellbridge speaking.' The voice was elderly but crisp and with the patrician tones of a well-brought-up Englishman. It sounded very like her father's and Emily was surprised by the rush of affection that surged through her.

'Uncle Harry? It's Emily. How are you?' She smiled down the phone, imagining his surprise.

'Well, well! Emily. How lovely to hear from you. How on earth are you?'

'I'm . . . fine . . .' It seemed too much to launch into the story of what had happened lately, especially with Cameron there, so instead she said, 'Guess where I'm calling you from . . . December House!'

There was such a long pause that she wondered if he'd gone and then he spoke, his voice cracked with emotion. 'December House . . . our old place in Cumbria? But Emily, how . . . what are you doing there? Have you rented it or something?'

'No. I live here now. I was left it by a lady called Catherine Few. She said she was sold the house by Aunt Cressida in the sixties.'

There was another pause while he absorbed this, then he spoke again. 'That's right.' Harry's voice came heavy down the line. 'I remember it very well. It wasn't long after our mother died. It was all very sudden. Cressida had been away at the house and one day she pitched up and told us she was leaving England and going to live in Australia.'

'Just like that? With no warning?'

'That's right. She was quite a stubborn character in her way, and very keen on women's rights and what have you. It didn't sit well with our father. He was rather an old autocrat, it must be said. He wanted nothing more than to make her stay and keep house for him after our mother died. Cressie wasn't going to have that. I sympathised with her. He bullied her almost as badly as he did our poor mother. I couldn't blame her, though I was naturally sad to see her go. We got some letters from her at the start of it all, telling us about life in Australia. And then . . . well, we lost touch with her. No address for her. The last contact we had was when the old man died and we sent notice of her inheritance through the lawyers. She claimed that, I believe.'

Emily frowned as she listened. 'I see . . . So Cressida told you that she'd sold the house to Catherine Few and that she was going off to Australia. Just like that. And then you never saw her again.'

'That's about the size of it, Emily. It was very sad. Much later, when your poor parents died, I tried to track Cressida down in Australia. I should have done it years before. I had no luck at all. There was a record of her arrival, and after that, nothing at all. I simply couldn't find her. No house purchases, no medical records, no nothing. I managed to find the law firm that had handled her inheritance and the office said the records showed she had come into his office with her proofs of identity – a birth certificate and a passport – in order to claim it and that she had had a bank account for the money to be paid into but there was no more than that.'

'So you never found her?' Emily said quietly.

'No. I supposed that she must have married and changed her name. We have no hope of finding her – if she's still alive.' He sighed heavily. 'Well, well. So you're in December House. How things do come around in a curious way. Tell me, what's the old place like? Are the Pendletons still in the farmhouse?'

She talked to him for a while, conscious of Cameron sitting impatiently opposite her, and then promised to be in touch again soon. 'You must visit us,' she said, thinking how much she would like that.

'That sounds a splendid idea. Listen, I've had a thought. I'm going to send you something. A surprise. You'll know when it arrives that it's from me. I don't know how long the Spanish post will take. But you'll know it when you see it.'

When Cameron heard what Emily had learned, he sighed. 'Well, that's not much help.'

'It is a bit. Because it places Cressida in Australia about a year after she sold this house. So she can't have been answering the letters your father sent – not from here, anyway.'

Cameron frowned. 'Yeah, I see that. But it still confuses me. Because those letters look bona, they really do.' He stared over at her, a serious expression on his face. 'When I left home, I thought I was going to meet some sweet old lady with a few memories of my dad. But I'm really puzzled now. This is a mystery and I don't like unanswered questions.'

Emily smiled at him. 'Nor do I.'

Cameron said, 'When I get back, I'll work at it from my end. I must be able to find out a bit more about Cressida if she was ever actually in Australia. We can keep in touch. Meanwhile, you find out about this Catherine Few woman.'

'My theory is that she's the one who answered the letters from your father, pretending to be Cressida,' Emily said with an apologetic look. 'It's probably something as mundane as that.'

Cameron thought for a moment and then shook his head. 'Nah. I don't know why but I don't believe that. Sorry, but there is definitely more to all this than that.'

After Cameron left, Emily went upstairs and lay in bed with a book but she couldn't read with her thoughts in a whirl. These two women – Catherine Few and Cressida Fellbridge – were intimately tied up in her own world, much more than she'd ever realised. Her aunt had only ever been a shadowy figure to her before now, a woman whose name she knew but whose existence meant nothing at all. Now she had a sense of Cressida as a real person, a girl who'd been bullied, who needed her freedom so much she was prepared to go to the other side of the world to find it.

A bit like me coming here. Getting away from my old life. She thought about Uncle Harry and seeing him at her parents' funeral. Everything had been so terrible then. So uncertain, so miserable. Tom had started smoking weed then, and had drunk too much for a while. But she'd been lucky; she'd met Will, a man who seemed to be the answer to all the insecurities of life. He'd known what he wanted and how to get it. He'd offered Emily love and security, as long as she did things his way. *I can't think about that.* The bitter taste of her guilt came to her mouth and she pushed the picture of Will right out of her head, and stared at Catherine Few's snow painting instead.

What was Cressida escaping? What would make a young woman suddenly go, all alone, to Australia and lose all touch with her family? It's a very strange thing to do.

Her imagination lost itself in the snowy landscape again as she thought it over.

Cameron is right. Catherine must have known that Cressida is dead, or she would have mentioned her in the will. So . . . were they in touch? Did they stay friends somehow? Maybe there are clues here in the house.

She sat up suddenly, putting her book on the bed beside her, and gazed about at her bedroom, trying to imagine Cressida here. She saw a young woman alone in the house. Perhaps too alone . . . perhaps driven mad by solitude and cold and deciding, suddenly, to leave for a new life in a warmer world.

It's a sort of answer, I suppose.

She tried to picture Catherine Few – what would she look like? Emily imagined a tall, slim woman with fine features. An artist with a noble look to her face, opening letters from a small boy in Australia and deciding to answer them. It was an odd thing to do, there was no doubt about it. And yet . . .

How else could the letters have been answered, if Cressida wasn't here and Catherine Few was?

Emily suddenly remembered the crate of pictures in the attic and her promise to Tom. On impulse, she got out of bed, put on her slippers and grabbed her torch. *No time like the present . . .*

Upstairs, the apples were still there. She must remember to take them downstairs. Making cider would never happen; she would chuck them out and keep the best ones for crumbles. The crate was still sitting in its place, the lid left on the top. Tom hadn't bothered to nail it back down. She put the lid on the floor. There were probably eight or so canvases stacked beneath. She lifted out a few and placed them in a manageable pile. Then, tucking her torch under her arm, she picked them up and took them downstairs to her room. There, she laid the canvases on her bed and looked at them.

She liked her snow.

Each one was set in a land blanketed in white,

and each contained the same view, although from different angles. One looked back at the house, another caught just the side of it, but they all had a view of the mountain beyond and the garden. Emily had the distinct impression that they were not painted in the same year, though she couldn't say why. Every one had something emerging from the snow in exactly the same place, not far from the orchard, alongside the back wall.

Emily noticed that one of the paintings had a clearer image of whatever it was than the others. She pulled it up off the bed and held it under the lamp, squinting at it.

Well, how odd. It's . . . an angel. A stone angel. You can just see it emerging from the snow. It must be a garden ornament of some kind. But there's nothing there now – I would have noticed an angel in the garden, I'm sure of it. I'll double-check tomorrow, though, just in case.

Now that she'd identified it, she saw that all the pictures held the same thing, covered in snow and sometimes barely visible but most definitely there. A stone angel with a pair of stone wings and a bowed head, emerging from the blanket of snow.

How strange. And somehow . . . how sad.

CHAPTER 26

Cameron inspected the paintings, which Emily had laid out in a row along the windowsill in the morning room. He'd come up early from the pub after breakfast.

'Bloody hell, these are bleak,' he said, then cast a look at the children eating their toast. 'Sorry, but they are.' He shivered. 'It's cold enough now – I had to wear my fleece to bed last night. It must be pretty awful in the winter.'

'I just thought you might like to see them. You were very interested in Catherine Few yesterday. This is all I have of her. Her other things were sold.'

'What, everything?' asked Cameron.

'Only two things were left. This dresser' – she gestured to it – 'and the easel upstairs.'

Cameron looked at the dresser with interest. 'Well, this looks promising.'

'It was completely empty, I checked it. And it's just got my bits and pieces in it now. Amazing how quickly it filled up with junk.' There was a knock at the back door. 'Hold on, I'll get that.'

James stood on the step, a box in his arms. He smiled at Emily as she opened the door. 'Hello there! I've got some things for the children. I found some old jigsaw puzzles and a brilliant wooden train set that I thought Joe will love.'

'That's so kind of you, James, do come in.' She stepped back to let him in and he came into the warm kitchen.

'I've got plenty more bits and pieces, you know, and they're just mouldering away in the . . . oh.' James stopped abruptly mid-sentence as he caught a glimpse of Cameron in the morning room. When he turned to Emily, she saw that his cheeks were stained red.

'I'm terribly sorry,' he said gruffly. 'I didn't realise you had a visitor.'

She saw his awkwardness at once. 'Oh, this is Cameron Baxter. He's from Australia. Cameron, this is my neighbour, James.'

'Hi there, mate,' Cameron said with a friendly smile.

'Hello.' James looked stiff, and didn't smile in return. He looked at the row of pictures on the windowsill. 'Artist, are you?'

'Nah, these aren't mine. They're by the woman who lived in this place before.'

'Mrs Few,' James said, his voice sounding very English and disapproving.

Emily glanced at him. *Oh no, he's jealous! He must think I've picked Cameron up.* 'Cameron came on the trail of my aunt,' she said quickly. 'It's an interesting story. In fact, I must talk to your mother again and tell her what we've found out.'

'Yes.' James stood staring at Cameron, his eyes hostile.

Cameron picked up on the atmosphere. 'Well, Emily,' he said easily, 'I think I'll be getting on my way. I think we've come to the end of the line for now. Let's keep in touch, all right? I'm heading home the day after tomorrow. I'll see what I can find out when I get back.'

'All right. Thanks for calling in, it's been really intriguing. I hope you have a terrific trip back to Perth.'

When Cameron had gone, James said, 'So he's just some random bloke who turned up, is he?'

'Yes,' she said calmly. His jealousy was amusing and rather sweet.

'It just makes me worried, that's all,' he said darkly. 'Thinking of you here, all alone, at the mercy of whoever might happen along.'

'I'm perfectly all right, you know that. Now let's have a cup of tea and we can get this railway set up.' She went through to the kitchen, glancing out into the garden as she went. A thought struck her. 'James, did you ever see a stone angel in the garden?'

'What?' he called through the doorway. He was showing Joe the trains from the box.

'A stone angel over by the wall, near the orchard. Did you ever see one?'

'No, I didn't,' James called back. 'Very glad about it too. It sounds gruesome. More suitable for a graveyard than a garden if you ask me. Creepy things, angels.'

Emily stared out across the garden, so different in its spring raiment from the bleak snowscape of Catherine's picture. 'Yes,' she said, with a sudden shiver. 'Maybe you're right.'

Tom didn't come by train in the end. He drove up in his van, bringing a lot of stuff with him for the cottage. He seemed in a high mood when he arrived, full of excitement, his eyes sparkling. He greeted Emily with a big kiss and a hug, which was a relief.

'Hey, it's amazing!' he said as they went into the brightly refurbished interior. 'Your pictures were great, but the real thing . . .' He sighed happily. 'It's perfect. What more can I say?'

They spent a happy afternoon unpacking and setting the cottage to rights, Carrie and Joe rushing about trying to help but adding to the chaos. It was still bare by the time they'd finished, but it was comfortable.

'It has everything I need,' he said. 'Except . . . food. I completely forgot about that.'

'Don't be silly, come to us for supper tonight and then you can make a trip to the supermarket tomorrow for a big shop.' Emily smiled at him. She was glad to see him so happy.

'Great idea. Thanks.'

'Oh,' Emily said, 'and here's a house-warming present I got for you.'

Tom said, 'You didn't need to do that, Em, after all you've done here.'

'It's only little.' She handed over a small package and watched as he opened it.

'A torch!' he said, as he pulled it free of the wrapping. 'Now, that's something I didn't think of.'

'It's not just for power cuts,' she said. 'If you're going to be walking back from our place to the cottage, you'll need a good strong light. It's pitch black out there. Honestly, it's a bit of a shock to the system after London.'

'Ah, thanks, sis.' He hugged her again. 'Very thoughtful.'

'You're welcome. Listen, I'll take the kids back and give them their supper. You have a bit of chill time in the new place, and come over when you're ready. It's stew for dinner, so no hurry to get to me.'

The evenings were getting ever longer as the spring ripened towards summer. The walk back from the cottage was beautiful in the hazy light, the birds singing in the woodland, the undergrowth full of life and lushness. She watched the children, Joe stumping along in his boots looking for any patches of mud he could jump in, and Carrie with a long stick, singing to herself as she brushed it through the brambles. There was such utter calm and peace.

I'm so glad this house came to me. We're safe here. She thought of Catherine Few, living here after the death of her husband and into her old age, until she came to contemplate her own death and what should happen to December House after-wards. *Thank you, Catherine, for giving it to me. I think perhaps you saved my life.*

The nightmares had gone. Her serenity, shattered in the accident along with her leg, had returned. *It's like it was before that terrible night.* But in her heart, she knew that things had been turning bad before the accident. She just hadn't wanted to think about it. Her life with Will had seemed too complete, too stable, too outwardly perfect, for her to start admitting the truth. If she'd done that, she might have had to begin destroying it herself.

Will did that for me. He brought the whole thing crashing down so that I could start again. In a way, perhaps, he's done me a favour.

But he had paid a heavy price. He lay in hospital still, sleeping on and on in his limbo state.

He wanted to die, she thought. She could find so little feeling for him now that the fears were at last at rest. A kind of remote pity was the best she could do. *But I'm alive. What will happen to me? What will I do?*

Existence had been so day-to-day for months now that she hadn't tried to look to the future. At some point she would have to re-enter the world, think about working again, perhaps even contemplate a relationship. *I don't want that yet,* she thought firmly. Perhaps it wasn't only a conscious decision, though. Her body seemed to be telling her that it had its own needs and intended to wake her up to that fact – if her unlooked-for response to James's presence meant anything. She watched the children, their heads bright against the undergrowth. *They come first. I'll be alone for as long it takes to make sure they're all right.*

Tom came over for dinner, walking from the cottage as the evening became soft and balmy and tiny black shapes swooped rapidly through the air.

'Bats,' Emily said, as one flicked soundlessly past. 'They live in the barn, I think.'

Tom held out a bottle of wine. 'I forgot food but I remembered the booze. Here you go.'

'Thanks. Come in. The children won't go to sleep till you say goodnight to them, so you'd better go up.'

She was just serving up the dinner as Tom came into the morning room after his goodnight duties were completed. They sat down and ate, talking over the practicalities of the cottage.

'How long are you staying?' Emily asked, chasing up the last of the stew on her plate.

Tom shrugged. 'Not sure. I've got some work to do but I brought everything I need with me. I'm going to use that second bedroom as a work room. There's no rush for me to go back.'

'That's great. The children will love having you near.'

'I might need to pop up here to use the internet. Will that be all right?'

'Of course. Whenever you like. I'll give you a key so you can come in when you want.'

'Did you look at those paintings? I meant to ask you earlier.'

'Yes, I did. The thing in the snow . . . it's an angel, a stone angel, always in the same place and always covered in snow.'

'Really?' Tom looked bemused. 'How weird. I take it there's nothing there now?'

'Nope. And James from up the road says there's never been anything there at all.'

'That's really strange. I'll take a look at the paintings tomorrow and maybe scout around a bit.' He looked down at his plate, toying with the remains of his mashed potato. He frowned and when he looked up at Emily, his eyes were grave. 'I was kind of pissed off with you about the cottage – not giving it to me outright, I mean.'

Her heart sank. They'd been getting on so well. Was it all just a prelude to a row of some sort? 'Oh.'

'Yeah. I felt like there was a selfishness of spirit there that I didn't expect from you, Emily. We've always been close, you've always looked out for me. But I got the impression that you were going to keep all this for yourself, even though it only came to you through being related to Aunt Cressida, just like me.'

She stared at him, not knowing what to say. How did she explain to him the powerful urge she had to protect her children and provide for them? 'It's . . .' She bit her lip. 'You see, Will was our breadwinner, the man who brought in the money. Lots of it. Suddenly he wasn't just not there, he'd taken everything we had and left us exposed and naked. I was terrified. Then . . . when this place came . . . well . . .'

'Yeah, I can see that, of course.' Tom leaned back in his chair, still serious. 'I totally get that. But that's almost my point in a way. Will.' He fixed Emily with a piercing stare. 'I think he's infected you with his spirit.'

She blinked at him. 'What do you mean?' she said cautiously. They were entering that territory again – that way of thinking that Tom had adopted slowly but surely over the last few months.

'I'm going to say some things you might find hard to hear,' Tom said, 'but I know them to be true, so I want you to hear me out. The truth is that you've changed. There's a hardness about you now, a selfishness that isn't really part of your character. And I believe there's a reason for it.'

'Yes?' She felt a pang of hurt but told herself not to respond. *Better to hear him out and see where this is leading.*

'That reason is Will.' He stared at her as if assessing the impact of his words upon her. When she said nothing, he went on. 'I believe that Will is part of the dark forces in this world. He manifests all their characteristics. He works in finance; he's materialistic and status-conscious; he's greedy and grasping and would sacrifice just about everything in pursuit of money.'

Emily stifled a small gasp, struck by the word *sacrifice*. Tom was right about that – Will had been willing to sacrifice so much for the sake of his pride. Did that mean Tom was right about other things too? He'd always been perceptive and attuned to others. Maybe he really did have some kind of deeper understanding of what was going on in the world.

'That places him in a very dark part of the spectrum,' Tom went on. 'I'd go so far as to say that he's probably possessed by evil.'

Emily blinked at him in surprise. 'Really?'

Tom laughed sardonically. 'I know it sounds crazy. You're probably thinking I am crazy.' He leaned forward suddenly and fixed her with a penetrating gaze. 'But I'm not. I always sensed Will's aura was an unpleasant one: red and prickly and full of anger and malevolence. I worried for you when you married him but I could see why you fell for him. It was just after Mum and Dad's accident and you needed someone like him to put the world to rights. Perhaps you couldn't see that other side of him. For a while I wondered if you would be the making of him but it hasn't happened that way. Instead, his evil has overpowered your goodness and begun to turn it into its own creation. That's what evil wants: to destroy good and create more creatures in its own mould until the whole world is divided into masters who rule in luxury, and slaves who have to obey them – the universe run on satanic lines.'

415

Emily felt a chill tingle her skin. This was strong stuff. It sounded utterly crazy and yet for some reason it affected her.

Tom spoke quietly but in a tone of utter conviction. 'You've been infected, Emily. You've got an evil spirit inside you. Will put it there. But don't worry. I can help you get it out.'

Emily lay awake after Tom had gone, staring into the darkness, troubled. Tom was not only utterly convinced by what he was saying, he was extremely convincing in turn. He'd spent the rest of the evening telling Emily about his encounters with evil in the world and how he'd come to the knowledge that certain forces were out to destroy him.

'I always knew that Will had a hatred for me,' he'd said. 'I could read it in his face. Do you know he actually recoiled from me when I came too close to him? I noticed in the last year or so that he could hardly bear to be near me. I knew what it was: the spirit that possessed him hated me coming too close. He knows that I've got the power to recognise and destroy him.'

It's like The Exorcist, Emily had thought. *Is it real?* Her scepticism told her that it was not but she'd always respected Tom's opinions and valued his intuition. Where would she draw a line? 'So what's happened to Will's spirit now? He's in a coma. Is the spirit in one too?'

Tom had sighed heavily. 'That I don't know. I'm

going to seek guidance on that. Perhaps the spirit is free once Will's unconscious, or perhaps it remains trapped in his body. I need to do some research on that.'

Another ayahuasca ceremony? Emily wondered as she lay in the darkness. *Are they legal in this country?* She felt a stirring of fear, the first she had felt since she came to December House. She'd looked forward to Tom coming to the cottage, but that was because she still thought of him as the old Tom. *The normal Tom.* Had that Tom really vanished forever and been replaced by this new, rather spooky version with his talk of possession and spirits and evil? With his confidence in his own power as someone who had secret knowledge and possessed the power to confront demons?

Or maybe he's ill. The cannabis he smokes – they say it's much stronger now than it used to be. Maybe he's got some kind of mental issues from using too much of it.

She would do some research herself, she resolved. Then she felt a kind of black amusement at the mental picture. Tom would be researching how to deal with evil spirits inside a comatose person, while she'd be researching cannabis-induced psychosis.

But Tom's my brother. I have to look out for him. I just wish I was more qualified to do it, that's all.

The next day, the red post office van came roaring up the drive. The postmen always drove like

417

maniacs, Emily thought. What was it that made them all so reckless?

'Postman Pat!' shouted Carrie when they saw the van.

'I think Pat's a slightly safer driver, actually,' Emily murmured as the postman went to the back of the van and pulled out a long, flat parcel.

'Here you are,' he said, propping it on the ground by the front door and holding out a pad. 'Sign here.'

'Thanks.' She scribbled her signature and looked at the parcel as the postman strode back to the van and headed off. It was a cardboard box, well sealed with tape and with lots of 'Fragile' stickers on it.

'How mysterious,' she said as she tried to lift it. 'It's much lighter than it looks.' She laid it on the hall table, which it almost filled. 'Let's get the scissors.'

It took a while to slice through all the masking tape and then to cut away the cardboard. Inside, the contents were wrapped in thick layers of bubble plastic, bound with more tape. She cut it all away, catching a flash of gold as she did.

'Birthday present!' cried Joe, jumping up and down. Carrie was wrapping herself in the discarded bubble wrap, turning it into a dress.

'I don't think so. My birthday's not for a month,' she said. Under the bubble wrap, there was a soft cloth covering. She tugged that away and revealed at last a painting, large and framed in an ornate gilt frame. 'Oh my goodness, it's a portrait. And what a beautiful one!'

The painting showed a young woman gazing out of the picture in a three-quarters profile, her brown eyes serious. She was beautiful, her dark hair shining with lustrous colour, her fine eyebrows arched, her mouth in calm repose. She wore a white shirt and a string of pearls around her neck and in her hand she held a bright blue silk scarf.

The children lost interest, more keen on playing with the detritus, but Emily stared at it, transfixed. *She's lovely.*

Just then Carrie held something up that she'd found on the floor. 'Look, a letter!'

Emily took it. 'Ah, the explanation.' She opened it. Inside was a handwritten note on thick ivory paper.

Dearest Emily

Such a pleasure to talk to you the other night. I'm so happy to think of you and your family in December House. I'm happy, too, to send you this because I think that December House is where it belongs. It's a portrait of your Aunt Cressida, painted not long before she left for Australia. It captures her very well. It is by an artist called Ralph Few, the person to whom she insisted on selling the house. I inherited it from my father and it's right that it returns to the house.

Don't leave it too long before you call me

again, it was a delight to hear your voice. Shall we try and bring some togetherness to this fractured family of ours?

    With love

      Uncle Harry

'Aunt Cressida!' she exclaimed, and looked at it again. She had never before seen a picture of her aunt, she realised. She touched her own brown hair. *Do we look alike?* she wondered. *I hope so – she was so pretty. But what a wonderful painting. So Ralph Few painted it – Catherine's husband. He was obviously very talented.*

She picked it up and looked at it again, seeing the brushstrokes and the use of the paint close up so that the painting ceased being a portrait and became a collection of colours and lines. She pulled away and it resolved into a woman again.

'I'll put it in the sitting room over the fireplace,' she said out loud. 'I think that's the perfect place.' Then she smiled at the portrait. 'Welcome home, Aunt Cressida. You're back in December House.'

CHAPTER 27

Emily was at her computer early, with the chorus of birds already loud in the garden. Now that the days were lengthening, she was waking early and sneaking downstairs for tea and a quiet read of the news websites before the children woke up.

The sound of an incoming Skype call made her jump and she quickly accepted it. A moment later, Cameron Baxter's face came into view on her screen. When he saw her, he smiled broadly and waved. 'Hi, Emily! Greetings from Perth!'

'Hi, Cameron.' She smiled back. She could see her face in a small box in the corner of the screen but she tried not to be distracted by it. 'How are you? How was the trip back?'

'Yeah, good, thanks. Nice to be back in the warm. So, any developments at your end on the where-abouts of your aunt?'

Emily shook her head. 'No. But my uncle sent me a picture.' She picked up the laptop and walked it through to the sitting room, where the portrait hung over the fireplace. She angled the camera so Cameron could see it.

He whistled lightly. 'What a looker! No wonder my dad couldn't get her out of his mind.'

'Did you tell him what we found out?'

'Or didn't find out, more to the point. Yeah, I explained it to him. He was puzzled. But the thing is, Dad's not well. That was partly why I wanted to find your aunt: it would make him really happy. He's thinking it over but he was sure that it was your aunt writing to him from England all through the sixties.'

'So we're back where we started.' She took the computer over to the sofa and sat down. Cameron's face looked rather washed out over the internet connection and the electric light behind him was harsh. *It must be evening over there.*

'Kind of.' Cameron smiled at her. 'I did some detective work of my own and I've discovered that a Cressida Fellbridge was registered as arriving here in 1963. So I have to concede to you that, yes, she arrived. But I think she must have gone back. After her money came through. She went back to England.'

'And lived here with Catherine Few?' asked Emily, frowning. 'I think someone might have noticed.'

'Would they? Maybe the two women did live in your house together. You said Catherine Few was reclusive, right? Maybe that's because there were two of them and they didn't want to be seen at the same time by anyone.'

'But her husband Ralph was here too,' Emily pointed out. 'Until he died.'

Cameron grinned. 'Lucky guy! A nice little *ménage a trois*, maybe.'

'Ha ha.' She thought for a moment. 'I don't know. I'm just not sure about that. He painted that picture, by the way, the one of Cressida.'

'Did he? I thought the wife was the painter.'

'They both were.'

'Well, if you ask me, he fancied your aunt something rotten. He's made her into a stunner.'

'Or he did that for the money. It's hardly a warts-and-all job. I'm sure she looked a bit less glamorous in real life.'

'Hmm. Well, listen, I'm gonna keep looking. I'm gonna look at the letters your aunt – or whoever – sent to my dad as well. There might be something in them. He's going to look them out for me.'

'That's good,' Emily said, intrigued. 'I'd love to see them myself.'

'I'll get some copies, if he'll let me. Well, that's all the news from Oz right now. I'll buzz you again if I find out anything more, okay?'

'Okay, Cameron. Bye. And thanks!'

Tom didn't come after lunch as he usually did. They had fallen into a pattern – he would work during the morning, then come up to use the internet and do his emails. He'd hang around for a while, playing with the children, and then head off again in the evening to do more work until he slept.

Emily kept looking out for him, wanting to tell him about Cameron's call that day. But although he was interested in the mystery of Aunt Cressida's whereabouts, it didn't seem to have the same fascination for him. Even the portrait of Cressida had failed to pique his curiosity very much. He'd stared at it for a while and said, 'A bit chocolate-box for my tastes.' Then he'd looked at her and said, 'How much money is this guy's work going for these days? Do you think it's worth much? Because I think we should consider it a joint possession, don't you?'

She'd agreed. It must seem unfair, the way things kept coming her way from the family. It was only right to share it.

When Tom didn't appear, she wondered if he was on the trail of the stone angel in the paintings again. As soon as he'd realised that the same statue was in every painting, he had become quite interested in looking for it. It certainly wasn't in the garden and he'd not yet found it in a shed or ditch. He hadn't stopped searching for it, though. Emily gave up waiting for him and got the children into their sturdy shoes. 'Come on,' she said, 'we're going for a walk to Uncle Tom's cottage!'

They were both delighted, and the walk through the garden, over to the woods and on to the cottage was a pleasant one. The door was unlocked and she opened it, saying, 'Hello! Tom? Are you there?'

The downstairs was empty and looked different from when she had last seen it. It was messy, with rubbish and art materials scattered everywhere. Empty plates and mugs had been abandoned on every surface, and the ashtray on the table was overflowing. There was a strong fug of cannabis in the air.

'Oh lord,' Emily said, looking around. Her spirits sank. This wasn't what she had hoped to see. She'd imagined a neatly kept home alive with the spirit of industry, but maybe that wasn't how Tom accessed his creativity. What did she know about it, after all? She went over to the table and saw that Tom's laptop was there, with a webpage open. She peered at it and saw that it was about the scientific breakdown of the ingredients of something. *A drug? Is he going to try and make something? And where is he?* Emily turned to the children and said, 'Carrie, will you play with Joe outside, darling? Don't wander off. I'll be out again in a moment.'

She went quickly upstairs. The door to the second bedroom was open and she glanced inside. It had a work table and shelves now, and there was stuff everywhere: paper mostly, but also scattered pens, books, old posters and newspapers. Every surface was covered, and another ashtray spilled ash onto the table. Emily went to the other door and pushed it open a little. Tom was on the bed, sleeping soundly, his long deep breaths resonating around the room.

He seemed more than just asleep, almost as though he'd passed out. But perhaps that was her imagination.

He probably had a late night, she told herself. *He's an adult. He can live how he likes. It's not for me to say.*

Nevertheless, she felt gloomy as she descended the stairs, and she was glad to get outside again to the fresh air after the fug of the cottage. It seemed as though Tom was doing a lot of smoking.

I must look up the effects of cannabis. I'll do it when I get back home.

When they reached the house, though, it was just in time to see James's Land Rover pulling to a halt outside. He jumped out and waved as he saw them approaching across the garden.

'Hello, Conways!' he called. 'I hope you don't mind a quick visit.'

'Of course not,' Emily said, swinging Joe up into her arms so that she could carry him swiftly over the grass. 'Are you stopping by for tea?'

'Just quickly,' James said. 'I've got Mum in the car and remembered you said you'd like to speak to her again. We were just passing and I thought . . . well . . .'

'Oh,' Emily said, trying not to sound flustered. 'How nice. I'm not sure what state the house is in.'

'Don't worry about that,' James said, going round to the passenger door. 'We don't mind.'

People always say that but it's me who minds, Emily thought, hoping she hadn't left everything in too much of a mess. She went round the car to greet Mrs Pendleton.

The old lady looked at her with sympathetic eyes as James helped her down. 'I told him drop-in visits aren't always welcome but he wouldn't have it.'

'It's fine, really. Lovely to see you. Please come in.'

She led them down the passage to the morning room and James and his mother sat at the table while she made the tea.

'The house is looking charming,' said Mrs Pendleton, glancing about approvingly. 'So very nice to see a young family in here again. A place like this needs to be kept alive. It's the only way old houses mean anything. They're quite useless when they're empty.'

'Thank you,' Emily said, collecting cups from the dresser. 'We love it here. It's a quiet life at the moment, but that seems to suit us.'

'Yes. James told me a little of what you've been through,' Mrs Pendleton said, with a sympathetic look. 'And he said you've got some more questions for me.'

'Well . . . I had a visitor from Australia and he said that he thought Cressida Fellbridge had lived here much longer than we'd assumed, because she wrote letters to his father. From here, apparently. And we wondered . . .' She laughed. It sounded very fanciful to say the idea aloud. 'We wondered if there was any way that Catherine Few and Cressida Fellbridge could have lived here at the same time.'

Mrs Pendleton looked startled. 'Oh no. I don't think so. I saw Mrs Few often enough to know her well. I never saw anyone else, only her husband. He was getting a little confused towards the end, though. He didn't appear to know her name at times, poor man. So sad when she clearly adored him. I don't think there was ever anyone else here, and I'm certain we would have known if there was a Fellbridge here. I told you how I had the impression that Mrs Few didn't want to see any of the old family in any case.'

'That's right,' Emily said, frowning. 'I'd forgotten that.' She put the cups on the tea tray. 'Shall we go through to the sitting room? It'll be much more comfortable in there.'

They stood up and James led the way through the door at the far end of the morning room that led into the sitting room. Emily followed, stopping to put the teapot on the tray. When she got into the sitting room, Mrs Pendleton was standing in front of the fireplace, quite transfixed by the portrait.

'I meant to tell you,' Emily said, seeing her there, 'that my uncle sent this over to me. Isn't it lovely? It was painted by Ralph Few, as it happens. It's my aunt Cressida, the woman who sold the house to the Fews.'

Mrs Pendleton turned to look at her, amazement in her eyes. 'Oh no, my dear, it's not your aunt, I'm afraid. Most certainly not.'

Emily gasped. 'What do you mean?' she stuttered. 'Of course it is.'

'No, no. I'm quite certain.' Mrs Pendleton turned

to look back at the portrait. 'She looks younger and more glamorous than she did when I knew her, but there's no mistake. I saw her quite often, and this, my dear, is Catherine Few.'

CHAPTER 28

'I bloody hope this is worth it.' Cameron's face looked bleary on the screen and his hair stood up on end where he had mussed it with his hand.

'It is, it is,' Emily said excitedly. She was so glad he'd answered, knowing it was the early hours of the morning in Australia. But Cameron evidently kept his computer in his room. 'You'll never guess what . . . I showed the portrait of my aunt to Mrs Pendleton and she says that it is definitely Catherine Few.'

'What?' Cameron looked bewildered.

'Yes! I know! She knew Catherine for years, she can't be mistaken. But it was sent from my uncle Harry and he should know what his sister looked like, right?'

'Right.' Cameron screwed up his face. 'God, I can't follow this. I'm still asleep. What are you saying?'

'That Catherine Few and Cressida Fellbridge were the *same* person!' Emily could hardly contain her excitement. It all made sense, a strange, crazy sense. 'She never went to Australia! She stayed here!'

'Hold on.' Cameron yawned and then said, 'But she did come to Australia, remember? I found the evidence. And she appeared at the lawyer's office with her ID when she claimed her inheritance, according to your uncle.'

'Oh yes.' Emily's excitement died down a little and then she said, 'So she went and then came back, like you suggested.'

'Maybe that's it. It's certainly the only answer.' Cameron grinned at her. 'But good work, Emily. I'm impressed. It's a huge piece of the jigsaw you've just fitted there. Looks like we've got a case of an identity mix-up. We just have to work out exactly how it all happened, that's all. But hey, no problem! We'll do it. I'm gonna get my hands on those letters as well and take a look. I'm going over to Dad's today.' He gazed into the camera. 'There's just one thing. There was an actual Catherine Few, right? So what happened to her?'

Emily shrugged. 'I don't know. I just assumed Catherine Few was a made-up person and that Cressida called herself that for her own reasons – to escape her family and live with Ralph Few.'

'Ah. So it was love all along. Yeah . . . that makes sense. But see what you can find out about Catherine Few before she married Ralph, okay? And we'll reconvene later.'

It was hard for Emily to find the time to do the research she longed to devote herself to when she had to look after the children. There was still no sign of Tom and no message from him. He was probably still sleeping off whatever had knocked him out so comprehensively.

In the end, desperate for some time to herself, she parked the children in front of one of their favourite films and closed the study curtains against the glorious day outside.

Bad mother. But just this once . . . I have to get some free time.

At the table, she bent over her computer, following search terms and directions to web pages as she trailed Catherine Few back through the years. She had tried this before, when she'd first learned of her bequest, but she hadn't applied the kind of rigour she now did.

I have to think laterally. I can't just stop when I seem to hit a dead end.

The search term 'Catherine Few' brought up so little. So she tried again, typing in 'Ralph Few' instead. This was a richer source of exploration and she soon found herself on a trail that delivered tiny snippets of information, leading her from web page to web page, some useless or incomprehensible, others giving her just a little piece more. Eventually she found a download of an old sales catalogue that included works by Ralph Few. There was an artist's biography too; just a few lines but it included his birth and death dates, and where he had been born. *That will help.* She scrolled through the pages of the catalogue until she found some of Ralph's pictures. They were beautiful – vibrant and striking. Most were of men but there were a few of women too. Emily stopped suddenly and gasped. She was looking at a portrait of a girl in a dark overcoat against a stormy sky, with dark hair, grey eyes and a determined chin. It was titled 'Catherine'.

Catherine!

Was it a coincidence? A different Catherine altogether?

Emily stared at the picture on her screen, her heart pounding. *No, it must be the real Catherine – and she's nothing like the picture on my wall in the sitting room.*

Her eye was caught by a small explanation under the picture's title. It read: 'This is believed to be a portrait of the artist's sister.'

Emily read it over two or three times. *His sister? But that's impossible . . . isn't it? She was his wife. Or . . .*

Her mind began to whir. She stopped looking at the screen and gazed unseeingly into the garden as the possibilities began to flood into her mind. After a while she stood up and said, 'That's it! That's it! I've got it, I'm sure I have.' She sat down and began to write an email as fast as she could.

Cameron, I've got it. They swapped identities. It wasn't Cressida who arrived in Australia – it was Catherine! It's the only answer. I'm sure of it. Call me when you can and we can discuss it.

She pressed 'send' and sat back, triumphant. She had solved the mystery. But what an amazing story it was. If she was right, then the Catherine Few who had lived here all these years was not Catherine at all but her aunt Cressida. Emily got up and went through to the sitting room, where the portrait hung over the fireplace. She gazed up at it as though trying to read the truth in those lucid brown eyes.

So Cressida, is that what you and Ralph did? You took on his sister's identity and pretended to be his wife? But why? Did your family disapprove of him so much? Why couldn't you have simply married him as he was and become Cressida Few? And why send Catherine to Australia disguised as you?

She stared at the pink, slightly parted lips, as though they might suddenly move and begin to tell her the truth. Emily felt obscurely frustrated. The mystery was only half resolved. She might now know that Cressida had taken on Catherine's identity but she had no idea of why. A thought crossed her mind and she hurried back to her computer, to the open web page. Then she picked up the telephone to make a call.

'Yes, you're quite right,' the man's voice on the other end of the telephone said in a rather quavering tone. 'I did compile the catalogue for the sale that included Ralph Few's work. Goodness me, that was a long time ago.'

'That's wonderful news. I don't know if you'll be able to help me as it was so long ago, but one of the portraits was titled "Catherine" and you had it down as the artist's sister, rather than his wife. Why was that?'

The man sounded surprised. 'It was because his wife told me that the portrait was of the sister. She brought the paintings to us to sell, you see. The artist was dead by then. She was also Catherine Few, but the portrait was most certainly not of her. She told me that it was an early work done of his sister but that she was now dead. I remember it quite distinctly because his wife was such a striking woman. And her air of sadness struck me at the time. Yes, Catherine Few. I never forgot her. The work sold well too.' The old man on the other end of the line sighed. Then said, 'I'm sorry, will you excuse me? Someone has come into the shop. Give me your number and I'll call you back as soon as I can.'

'Of course.' Emily recited her telephone number. 'I'll wait to hear from you.'

When the old man had rung off, she sat back in her chair thinking hard. *I refuse to believe that it's a coincidence that his sister was called Catherine and that's the name Cressida took on. Because it was certainly Cressida who sold those paintings. I've never been more sure of anything.* Another thought struck her. *But Cressida must have become an artist herself. She must have painted those landscapes, the ones with all the snow.*

Emily stood up, eager to look again at all the paintings. If they were really by her aunt, then they had a deeper, more emotional significance for her.

She went to go to the door when the telephone rang. Stopping, she scooped it up to answer it. 'Hello?'

She'd expected the quavery tones of the art dealer so she was surprised when it was a woman's voice on the other end.

'Emily?'

It was a voice she knew and yet it was hard to place it at first. It was so full of emotion, so suffused with a bubbling joy, that it was quite unfamiliar.

'Yes?'

'Emily, it's Diana. I had to ring you at once. You have to know. It's Will! He's . . . Oh Emily! He's woken up! He's come out of his coma! Isn't it marvellous news?'

When Tom arrived an hour later, he found all the doors locked. He pounded at the back door.

'Emily, are you there? Open up.'

Emily heard it from some place within her dazed brain. She was sitting at the kitchen table, a blanket around her shoulders to stop the shivering. She got up and went to the back door, checking first that it was Tom, then unbolted it.

'Tom,' she said in a dull voice.

'Christ, Em, what is it?' There was concern all over his face. 'What the hell's happened? Where are the kids?'

'In the study, watching telly.' She looked in the direction of the passage. 'They're fine but I need to get them their supper soon. They've been in there most of the afternoon.'

'Okay, I'll do that.' He led her back to the table. 'But what's happened?' He looked down at the table, a worried expression on his face. He picked up the kitchen knife that was lying there. 'And what's this doing here, for goodness' sake?'

'Tom . . .' she whispered and began to shake again. 'It's Will.'

'Will?'

She nodded, her eyes wide. 'Diana called. He's out of his coma. He's woken up.' The fear began to possess her, a vile sickness, everything she had felt in her nightmares. She saw Will's eyes flicking open, green and malevolent. She saw him twisting and getting out of his hospital bed with one thought on his mind. To find her. To kill her. To take the children. She began to sob. 'What am I going to do?'

Tom wrapped her in his arms. 'Hey, don't be scared. I'm here. I'll look after you.'

She sobbed wildly for a few minutes, managing to pant out words into his chest. 'I . . . I got away . . . we're safe here . . . and now . . . everything I've done, all I've built without him . . . he's going to come and tear it down and . . . destroy us!'

'Hey, Emily, why are you so frightened?' Tom pulled away, and gazed at her searchingly. 'What is it? This is more than Will waking up. You're fucking terrified! You've got a bloody knife! What did he do, Emily?' Tom's voice took on a commanding tone. 'Tell me what he did.'

'He . . . He . . .' Even now the words were so hard to say. She had told no one. No one knew. But she had to explain what happened if she was going to protect the children. 'He ran the car off the road on purpose,' she said, and at once she felt a shuddering relief that the words were out. 'He wanted to kill us both. It was an attempt at murder-suicide because of what he'd done, the way he'd ruined us.'

An appalled look crossed Tom's face. 'Christ! He did that?'

She nodded. 'I haven't been able to say it before now because . . . I just couldn't. It's too terrible.'

Tom's expression hardened and his blue eyes turned icy. 'It's evil. It's sheer bloody evil.' He got up and began to pace about, his face serious. 'This is much more serious than I ever understood. It's in deeper than I suspected.'

She was shaking again. Was Tom going to respond in his strange new way? Was he going to start talking about demons again? *I don't need that*, she wanted to shout. *I need help – real help in the real world!*

'What did Diana say?' demanded Tom, turning to face her.

'Not much really. She said he's woken up and they're making arrangements to move him out of the intensive care unit. She said he was doing well, really well.' Nausea swirled around her stomach again. 'I don't know what that means. I couldn't take it all in. She wants me to go down, take the children to see him.' She gazed up at Tom, agonised. 'I don't know how I can! I thought I'd never have to see him again, or face him after what he did. I've put him out of my mind, I've started to get better. Oh Tom!' She began to heave soundless, heavy sobs of sheer terror. 'He's going to come here and take it all away!' Her voice stuttered into silence and tears poured down her cheeks.

'We'll stop him, don't worry,' Tom said firmly. 'Listen, you'll be fine. Don't worry about your knife and locking the doors. He won't be coming here any time soon, I promise. And I'm right nearby. You can always reach me if you need me. I had no idea what he'd done. I have to get some advice on this. Listen, I'm going back to the cottage, okay? I want to make some calls. I'll be back later to check on you. Now, calm down and look after the children. Just be completely normal. We're going to be fine, I promise.'

She nodded, trying to keep calm. She knew rationally that there was no way a man who had just woken from a coma of some months was going to jump in a car and drive up here, but that did nothing to damp down the horrible fear pounding in her chest. 'Are you going to leave me alone?' she asked in a small voice.

'Just for a while. You'll be all right, I promise.'

Tom turned to stare her in the face. 'I'm doing what's best for you, you need to believe that. We have to sort this out once and for all.'

It took all her strength to cook a simple supper for the children and act as normally as she could around them. They didn't seem to notice anything as she put their pasta in front of them, helped them eat, gave them fruit and yoghurt and then wiped them up and took them upstairs. After a while, behaving normally began to calm her. She could almost believe that things were just the same as they ever were as they all cuddled up on Emily's bed for stories. She read them more than usual, not wanting to lose the comfort of their small, warm bodies, and she finished on *Peter Rabbit* before she took them into their rooms and tucked them up for the night. She went in to Carrie last, kneeling down by the little bed to kiss her and stroke her head and talk about their day.

'Goodnight, darling,' she whispered as she got up to leave.

'Mummy, Mummy . . .' Carrie looked up at her with solemn eyes. 'I have to tell you something.' She reached out a hand to Emily and pulled her back down to her level.

'What is it?' She turned her head so that Carrie could whisper into her ear.

'Mummy . . .' – the voice came soft and sweet – 'stay away from Mr McGregor's garden. It's *dangerous*. Do you promise?'

A wave of sadness and fear crashed over her. Her eyes stung with tears. 'Yes, darling. I promise,' she whispered. 'Goodnight.'

Downstairs she paced about, unable to settle. She poured a glass of wine but it tasted bitter, and she didn't take more than a sip. She couldn't even think of eating. All she could do was move around the house, checking the doors and the windows were closed and locked. Her emotions veered between fear – she jumped violently at the slightest sound – and anger. This house had been her safe place, her refuge, the sanctuary that had been given to her when Will had destroyed everything. Here, the nightmares had gone away, and now they were back. She knew with certainty that they would infect her sleep again, and even if they didn't, she was living a waking nightmare now that she knew Will had woken up.

She stopped in front of the portrait in the sitting room, looking up at the sweet, unchanging face. *What do I do, Cressida? Did you ever know fear like this when you lived here? Or should I call you Catherine?* The world seemed suddenly more confusing than ever, with its shifting characters. One moment, the woman in the painting was Cressida Fellbridge, then she became Catherine Few. She was a wife, then a sister and then a wife again. She was in December House and in Australia at the same time. Will had been, to all intents and purposes, dead but now he was alive again, resurrected for some

441

awful reason, and she was afraid now. Even Tom, once her rock, had begun to change into someone she didn't know, someone who had visions, communed with spirits, spoke to the dead, and believed that evil had to be cast out.

I need something I can trust, something I can rely on.

She stared at the portrait for another moment, and then went to the phone.

James arrived ten minutes after she called him and one look at her face was enough. He enfolded her in his arms, hugging her closely to him, and she found herself in the position she had, very strangely, longed to be in. She was pressed to his warm, firm body, her nose buried in his jumper, engulfed by that sweet yet masculine scent, with the tang of woodsmoke, the faint aroma of citrus and a kind of honeyed musk. The whole thing acted like a sedative on her, and she felt the panic leaving her body almost as though it was expelled with her breath.

'Emily, what is it? What's wrong?' he said gently. 'You sounded very upset on the phone. I'm worried about you.'

She pressed her cheek to him, her arms around him now, inhaling. *I could get addicted to this*, she thought hazily.

'Emily?' He pulled away from her and looked down, concern in his blue eyes. 'What is it? Something's wrong.'

She nodded. 'Come through.' They went to the sitting room and sat down on the sofa together. When he was sitting near her, a worried frown creasing his forehead, he said, 'So?'

'I've had a phone call,' she said. 'My husband's woken up from his coma.'

James took this in. 'But that's good news. You must be pleased.' He looked at the expression on Emily's face. 'Aren't you?'

She gazed down at the cushion she'd pulled onto her knees. 'No,' she whispered. 'I don't want him to get better. I wish he was dead.' She glanced up to see his reaction to this awful, inhuman state-ment. *He'll hate me now. Despise me. He'll get up and leave.*

James gazed at her without saying anything. His expression did not become outraged or disgusted, as she'd feared it might. 'I see,' he said after a while.

'I know it sounds a terrible thing for a wife to say but' – she swallowed – 'he did something very bad. He caused the car accident we were in on purpose, to kill us both. Because he'd taken all our money and gambled it away. He didn't succeed – we both survived. But . . .' She looked at him, and then turned her eyes away, biting her lip.

'No wonder you felt that then,' he said in a steady voice. 'Who could blame you? I don't think anyone would feel any differently. He did a wicked and cowardly thing. It takes a while to recover from someone treating you like that, if you ever do. I

443

think you've been very brave, Emily. You've sorted out your life and brought your children here and started again. It takes courage and resolution to make that happen.'

'But . . .' She closed her eyes. 'It wasn't like that. You see, he'd changed before that. For months beforehand, I knew there was something wrong, and I did nothing about it. He became so frightening; he wasn't the Will I'd married at all. Or maybe he'd been like that all along and I'd never seen it. But he got worse, whatever it was. He was angry all the time, obsessed with work; I couldn't do anything right; the children couldn't do anything right either . . . and I thought that if I was just a good enough wife, then I could fix it. I tried to be better and better but the harder I tried, the angrier he got, and the more I seemed to fail. He found fault with everything. He started . . .' She gulped and stopped herself. She couldn't quite tell everything. 'I didn't want anyone to know that we weren't the perfect family any more, and that Will was losing it. I couldn't admit to myself that everything was going wrong and that I'd have to start taking everything apart.' She was trembling again. 'So you see, the crash was my fault too. I didn't tell anyone or do anything until it was too late and he tried to kill us. And after that, I couldn't bear to say it, or speak it aloud, because everyone would know what I'd done. And they'd know what he was. They'd think we were both monsters. Maybe . . . maybe they'd even take the children away.'

James look appalled. He reached over and took her hand. 'Emily, you can't blame yourself! It sounds like Will was having some kind of breakdown; you can't be responsible for that.'

She ran a hand through her hair and over her forehead in despair. 'But I was responsible for myself and for the children. I risked all of it, I risked their futures!'

'You can't think like that.'

She went on, hardly hearing him. 'All I knew after the accident was that he'd wanted to kill me. I had to get away. I had to get as far away from him as I could.' A sob began to shake in her chest again. 'But now I don't know if it's far enough!'

'Emily, this is terrible.' James looked aghast. 'I had no idea you felt like this. I hate to think what you've suffered all alone. No wonder you're in shock.' There was a pause and then he said firmly, 'You shouldn't be on your own tonight. Is your brother about?'

'He's busy. I . . . I don't want to be on my own.'

'I'll stay,' he declared. 'You've got a spare room, haven't you?'

She nodded.

'Good. I'll make it up and stay here with you tonight. All right?'

Relief washed through her. 'Thank you.' She felt that she should be strong enough to face the night alone but it was too much for her. She needed another presence to stop the terror from overwhelming her.

'That's all right.' He smiled at her.

'James . . . can I ask one more thing?'

'Of course.'

'I know it sounds strange . . . but . . . would you hug me again? Just for a while?'

'Of course I would.' He held out his arms. 'I've been thinking that you look like you need a hug.'

'I do,' she said, feeling shakier than ever. She moved across the sofa into his embrace. At once, she felt calmer. Through his jumper she could hear the soft thud of his heart and feel the rise and fall of his chest. 'Thank you, James.'

'You're welcome,' he said, his voice rumbling through his chest and tickling her ear. Something in her felt as though it was melting, and she was filled with the feeling she had experienced in her dream: a serene anticipation of joy soon to come and a sense of complete acceptance. She stayed there, warm in his arms, until she fell asleep.

CHAPTER 29

Emily woke in her bed and then remembered with a rush of embarrassment that James had eventually woken her and helped her upstairs to her room. She hoped he had found the linen for the spare room.

But no nightmares, she thought with a feeling almost of triumph. *I slept all through without any.*

She went downstairs to find James already in the kitchen making a pot of coffee. 'Good morning,' he said brightly. 'How are you?'

'Fine.' She smiled sheepishly. In the fresh light of day, her fears seemed a little foolish. 'Thanks for staying over, James. I feel a bit embarrassed about it now.'

'Don't be silly. You had a shock. You needed to recover. Don't worry at all.' He went over to the sink to fill the kettle. 'I'm glad I could help.'

'Will your mother be worried about you?' she asked.

He stopped, turned and looked at her seriously. 'Emily, I'm a grown man. My mother doesn't worry about me. She might live in the same house but we're not exactly cheek by jowl.'

A stain of embarrassment crept over her cheek. 'Of course not,' she said. The way he had said 'grown man' made a shiver go through her, and her pulse began to race. *Oh no. Not while he's here!* The more uncomfortable she became, the stronger the feeling inside her grew. She was trembling lightly, not with fear this time, her skin hot and tingling, a strange ache in her belly and groin. The knowledge of it was making her blush harder.

'Emily?' he said, his voice low.

She released a shaky breath, staring at the flag-stoned floor. *What's wrong with me? I can't stop this!* James took a step towards her and a rush of something hot flared up inside her, like the range when the logs caught. It made her gasp. He put the kettle down on the counter and said again, 'Emily.'

She couldn't look up, but could only stare at the floor, feeling as though she were burning up, filled with an intense longing and unable to do anything about it. Then James was closer to her than ever. *He knows. He must see it* . . . Part of her was mortified and the other desperate for him.

He reached out a hand and touched her arm. At last she raised her eyes to him, and saw in his that same serious, intense look that had started all the trouble. He could read everything in her face and in the way she was shaking, she was sure of it.

He was close to her now, his body heat radiating out and inflaming her even further. Every proof of his solid, living maleness was turning her to jelly. There was nothing to do to stop it. *I'm power-less.* She relaxed suddenly. *It's going to happen. I want it to.* She tipped her face upwards as he put his arms around her, pulling her into his embrace, and then his mouth was on hers. His lips opened and she tasted him – *he tastes as delicious as he smells* – and then they were kissing hard and passionately, as though they'd both hungered for it for an age. Emily was utterly lost in the feeling, a dark velvety sensation that resonated inside her. She had not been kissed like this for a very long time, and she felt like a leaf unfurling in the sunshine after a long, dark winter.

The door in the passage banged, sending them both apart, breathless and staring at each other in surprise at what had just happened. The kitchen door opened a moment later, and Carrie stood there in her nightie, trailing her teddy after her.

'Mummy,' she said in her lilting voice, tinged with a tone of accusation. 'You forgot us and Joe can't get out of his cot!'

'Oh, I'm so sorry, sweetheart. I'll come up right now.' She glanced over at James, a shy look, and said, 'I'm sorry . . . I—'

'Oh no,' he said quickly, his cheeks pink. 'I'm sorry. That is . . .' He turned away and picked up the kettle. 'I'll just make that coffee.'

'Yes,' she said faintly, and followed Carrie out of the kitchen.

* * *

449

Breakfast was somewhat awkward. Both she and James were almost too shy to look at one another and so they focused all their attention on the children, who seemed very pleased to have so much hearty adult input into their breakfasts.

When it was over, Emily said, 'I must get the children dressed.'

James got up at once. 'Yes, I should be on my way. Are you sure everything's all right now? You're okay on your own?'

'Yes, absolutely.' The terror she had felt yesterday now seemed overblown and a little ridiculous.

'Would you like me to come back tonight?' he asked.

Embarrassment flooded through her again. After what had just happened in the kitchen, if she said yes, it would surely sound like an invitation and, tempting as it was, she wasn't sure it was the right thing to do. And if she said no . . . 'Oh,' she said. 'Um . . . I'm not sure.'

'No. Of course.' The same idea seemed to have occurred to James, and he looked just as embarrassed at having offered himself. 'Don't decide now. I mean . . . just, whatever you like. Call me if you need me.' He headed for the door, picking up his coat as he went. 'I must be getting on. Goodbye, kids. See you soon.'

She watched him go, half relieved, half wistful. *That kiss* . . . Her lips still tingled where he'd pressed his mouth on hers and she could feel the scratch of stubble on her cheek and chin. *Don't think about it, Emily!* she reproved herself. *As if you don't have enough to worry about. Today I need to decide what to do about Will.*

Before she could clear the breakfast table, her laptop chirruped the little tune that told her there was an incoming Skype call. She lifted the lid and accepted the call, slipping into a chair as she did. A moment later, Cameron appeared on the screen.

'What's up?' he called down the line, when he saw her. 'How ya doin', Emily?'

'Are Australians always so cheerful?' she said, smiling.

'Pretty much,' he replied, grinning back. 'And always when we're winning at the cricket. So, any developments your end?'

She told him quickly what she'd discovered the day before. 'So, if the art dealer is right, there was a Catherine but she was Ralph's sister. Cressida said she had died.'

'But your email sounded spot on – that it was Catherine who went to Australia in Cressida's place. I mean, that makes perfect sense, right?'

'Yes. We still don't know why, of course, but it does explain how Cressida could be in two places at once.' She was glad to be able to focus on the mystery of Catherine Few again, as though she could erase the things that had happened since she last spoke to Cameron. She remembered what he had said the day before. 'Did you find those letters?'

'I did. There were only six of them. They were mostly very boring, the usual teacher-talking-to-pupil thing – lots of description of the countryside, yapping on about books and poets and reminding my dad to work hard and all of that. But there was something a bit strange.'

'Yes?' Emily cocked her head to listen more intently.

'In one of them, she asked Dad to do her a favour. She asked him to go to an address in his town and give a message to the lady there. And the message was "Miss Fellbridge wants to know if you've received the money."' Cameron paused to let this sink in.

'That is strange,' Emily agreed. 'So, what did your dad do?'

'Well, I talked to him. He drifts in and out a bit these days but he seemed to remember when I reminded him. He told me that he went after school on his bike one day. The house was over the other side of town, quite a nice side of town too. He knocked on the door and asked if he could speak to the lady there. It was a young woman who answered the door – hardly more than a girl really. And Dad said he saw the name on the mailbox. It was Kemp.'

'Kemp,' echoed Emily. It meant nothing to her. 'And what happened?'

Cameron went on. 'Dad said that the girl told him to give her the message, so he told it to her and she said, "Tell her yes, and thank you very much." He thinks she might have said more, but he can't remember it. He just recalls that the answer was yes, they had the money. So Dad went home, wrote it down and sent the letter back to England. There was only one more letter after that, and it didn't mention any more messages or anything like that.'

'The correspondence ended there?' asked Emily.

Cameron laughed. 'Yeah. Dad said he grew up that summer. Fell in love with a girl and started writing to her instead. That was the end of that.'

Emily stared at his face on the screen. 'But what does it all mean? Who was the girl he took the message to?'

'Search me.'

'Does your father remember the address?'

'Vaguely.'

'Well, we have a name and an area. Do you think you can chase it up a bit?'

'Sure thing, that's exactly what I intend to do,' he said. 'Just keeping you in the loop as I go along.'

'It's great progress,' Emily said encouragingly.

'I'll keep on it,' Cameron said. 'Signing off for now! Bye, Emily.'

'Bye.'

She clicked to disconnect the call and sat back in her chair. *Cressida, what were you up to? And why?*

In the afternoon, the familiar sense of fear began to crawl over her skin again.

I have to face this, Emily thought, sitting down with the phone. *James thinks I'm brave. I should be braver. I'm really a coward.* She dialled the number of the hospital in London and waited until she was connected to the ward where Will had spent the last few months.

'I'm afraid he's not here any more,' the nurse on the ward said down the phone.

'Oh, okay. I was told he might be moved to another ward. Do you know where he's gone?'

'No – he's left the hospital. He's not here at all. I don't know where he is, I'm afraid. You could try the consultant's secretary in the morning.'

'No, that's fine, thank you,' Emily said, her mouth suddenly dry. 'Goodbye.' She put the phone down, the surge of sickness rising in her gut again. *He's well again. He's walking. He's dressed and in a car and on his way here.* Then she told herself firmly not to be so silly. She tried Diana's mobile and then her landline with no success.

Stay calm, she told herself. She wondered if she should call James again. Already she was thinking of the night with dread. But she knew exactly how it would look if she did. *I'll be asking him to kiss me again, maybe more . . .* Even if her body responded to the idea with pleasure, she knew that it would make life very complicated indeed.

Where's Tom? He'd said he would be back later to check on her and he'd never come. Still, if she thought about it, she was glad in a way that he hadn't come. James's presence was more reassuring.

I mustn't be scared. There's nothing to be scared of. I'm safe.

But the frightened feeling grew stronger as the day went on. By the children's suppertime, she was on edge and jumpy, feeling the same prickle at her neck whenever her back was to a window or a door for too long. The children were crotchety. They'd hardly been out for days now, and she was running low on supplies too. *Tomorrow we'll have to go shopping.* Tomorrow, no doubt, she would speak to Diana again, and she would learn the truth about Will's progress and his whereabouts.

Then I'll discuss with her the practicalities of getting a divorce.

It was the only option, she knew that now. She couldn't pretend that his life had anything to do with hers any longer, and she couldn't go through a farce of visiting him when the sight of him repelled her. He would have a right to see the children, she supposed, but she would get some advice on that. Diana would be the raging tigress but Emily was prepared to tell the whole truth if necessary. If she had to, she'd press charges on Will.

Will. Diana will have told him by now – about me selling the house and all his things, and taking the children up here.

She could imagine him now, his expression set into one she remembered well: the cold, implacable fury that would not be satisfied until she knew the full force of it. That was what she had not been able to tell James, barely admit even to herself, that just before the accident he had started to turn dangerous. He'd begun to push her hard against a wall or onto the bed in his anger. Sometimes there had been fists in her face and a spitting fury close up, filling her with fear. Occasionally it had turned into something strange: sex, hard and unpleasant, when he'd gripped her throat and entered her roughly, or had forced her to take him in her mouth hard, filling her throat as he pulled her head onto him, thrusting hard. Only his climax, always quick she'd been relieved to discover, had eased his fury.

That was over stupid things. When I dyed his tailor-made shirts pink. When I spent too much on those shoes. When I nicked the car against the lamp post.

Little things . . . so much anger over those little things. And then . . . She closed her eyes. How much anger would there be over what she had done now?

He'll come for me. Nothing will stop him. He'll kill me. He's tried before.

The fear came corkscrewing up from the pit of her belly. Would this come every night? How on earth would she ever be free of it?

'Oh God!' she said out loud. 'I can't stand it. I don't know how I'll stand it.'

The children were in bed. She had got through the bedtime routine, her need to keep calm in front of Carrie and Joe helping her to seem outwardly serene, but as the darkness came, the world seemed full of danger again. Half a dozen times she went to the phone to call James but then stopped herself. It seemed so weak and cowardly to call a man when she was afraid. She had to be able to cope alone.

Nevertheless, she couldn't stop herself going to the windows and doors and bolting them all. In the back of her mind, a small voice was saying over and over, 'Six hours to drive from London to here. What if he left at midday? He'd have to stop for petrol and food, so . . .' Her mind's eye followed Will in his car (the one that was destroyed in the crash so she knew it was impossible, but . . .) as he travelled through London, out onto the motorway and northwards. He was stopping for lunch in a motorway services, going to the loo, buying a chocolate bar in Smith's, back in the car again, roaring along the motorway. He was off the motorway and entering the beautiful starkness of the Cumbrian landscape. The afternoon was coming to an end as he zoomed along the winding roads. On the seat beside him was . . . She gasped. She saw the glitter of a knife. Then the cold dullness of a hammer. Then a gun, black and deadly. *He can't even fire a gun!* she told herself but that wasn't enough to stop the panic.

The car was approaching Howelland. He was minutes away now.

Oh my God, oh my God . . . She ran to the phone and picked it up in shaking hands.

He was turning into the lane, slowing down as he peered out of the window to see the house.

I'm calling James . . . She slammed the receiver down. 'No!' she exclaimed aloud. 'This is stupid. STUPID.' She called out to the house. 'I won't be afraid!'

There was a bang at the front door. She jumped violently, crying out. *It's him. Oh shit.* She walked along the passage, her heart pounding, feeling giddy with the horror. Will was outside the front door. He'd come and he'd found her. He was out there, like the Big Bad Wolf, and she was inside, one of the three little pigs he'd come to devour, only the walls between her and the snapping jaws. Or the slice of the blade across her throat, or the crash of a hammer on her skull, or the explosion of a bullet between her eyes . . .

The door knocker banged again and she cried out in terror. 'Who's there?' she called.

'Emily?'

A male voice. *Will?* It could be. It was hard to tell.

'Who is it?' she demanded, desperation soaking her voice.

'It's me. Tom.'

Tom. Relief saturated her and she let out a great breath. Going to the front door, she started to unlock it. 'Tom!' she called through the wood. 'Why didn't you say? You frightened me half to death.' At last the bolts were out of their homes and she pulled open the door. 'Thank goodness you're here, I've been getting myself seriously spooked.'

She looked him full in the face. His face was set like stone and his blue eyes glittered.

'Don't be frightened, Emily,' he said in a strange voice. 'We have to do this. You'll understand afterwards, I promise.'

CHAPTER 30

Emily backed away from him. 'What's wrong, Tom? You don't look right.'

'I'm fine,' Tom said. He had a backpack over his shoulder and he took it off as he came into the hall. 'I've brought some stuff with me.'

'What stuff? What for?' She eyed the backpack suspiciously. 'Are you all right? Have you been smoking?'

Tom stopped and gave her a look that was half pitying and half scornful. 'I'm sure you'd love to explain away what you don't understand by blaming the things I take. You don't see the world the way I do; sometimes it's hard for me to remember that. Most people don't share my perception but that doesn't surprise me. You and I have always been close, though – I expect you to think the way I do.' He smiled suddenly. 'Come through to the morning room. Let's sit down.'

'I've been wondering where you were,' she said, following as he went down the corridor.

'Oh,' he said vaguely. 'I've been travelling.'

'Travelling? Where to?'

'Here and there. There are places I can access that aren't exactly on this dimension.'

Her heart sank. 'Oh.'

In the morning room, he swung his backpack onto the table and started to unpack it. 'I've brought some things,' he said. 'We need to address this problem. It's time.'

'What problem?' she asked apprehensively. 'What are you talking about exactly?'

'Emily, I saw the fear in your eyes yesterday. You're terrified of Will – and that's because he's become your spirit master. To put it frankly, he's infected you with a demon who wants you dead. That's why you've hidden the angel, isn't it? I've guessed it all. You've taken the angel and destroyed it, at the bidding of your demon.'

He was talking in such a matter-of-fact way that it seemed impossible that he was saying such crazy things. But he was evidently completely serious and she was sure that dismissing what he was saying was not the right approach.

'But there isn't an angel,' she said as calmly as she could. 'James says there never was an angel.'

'There's only *your* word for that, isn't there? I've the proof in the paintings – it's there, over and over. Why would she paint something that wasn't there? And your demon couldn't stand the sight of it. And it wants you dead too.'

'A demon wants me dead?' she asked cautiously.

'Well, in fact, the demon wants *me* dead. But he

also intends to wound me. He'll undermine me by harming you.'

She stared at him. When had he gone so far along this road? It was as though he was vanishing into the distance, heading into a world where she couldn't follow. She didn't want to follow – it seemed like a world full of self-perpetuating mysteries, a place of dark menace and great threats based more in ancient myth than reality. She could see how it could attract those with strong imaginations and a pull towards the great epic fables of good and evil, the legends conjured up since humans could first express their wonder at the duality of the world and their fears of death and destruction. But once the lines between myth and reality began to blur, once the world was seen through that lens and a person began to act according to those precepts . . . She suddenly saw how ordinary, intelligent people were pulled into cults, persuaded to kill themselves because the world was about to end, or the aliens were coming, or the Rapture was about to begin. If the world were shifted just far enough on its axis, if mysteries of existence suddenly seemed to have reason and answers and a pattern and purpose . . . how comforting and reassuring would that be?

Tom's world had been shattered when their parents died in that one stupid moment, when a lorry smashed into their car. Emily herself was almost killed on the road. Was it random and pointless? Or was there a purpose behind it? An evil consciousness against which it was necessary to do battle? Better to be able to take up the sword – or the drug – and fight against a destructive force on the side of good than accept that stupid, sad and unnecessary things happened every day.

Is that it? Is it Tom's way of coping with all the shit?

'Here.' Tom pulled out a flask and put it on the table.

'What's that?' she asked, eyeing it.

'Something I've made. It's rough but I tried it myself and it was quite effective.' Tom stared at her. 'You need to start healing. You have to expel whatever it is inside you, and begin your journey.'

Apprehension began to curl in her stomach. 'Hold on, Tom, what do you mean?'

'Just what I say.' He gave her another of his half-pitying looks. 'You need to start on the journey. As soon as you can.'

She took a step away with a nervous laugh. 'I'm not taking anything, if that's what you mean. I have no desire to drink a potion you've concocted according to some stuff you've read on the internet. What's in it?'

'It's fine,' he said impatiently. 'Listen to yourself, Emily. It's not you talking. It's the evil living inside you. It doesn't want to be expelled!'

'Oh right, so the more I tell you I don't want to drink that stuff, the more convinced you'll be that I need to.'

He smiled. 'Will's demon is strong. Even the one

463

inside you is scared of it. Don't you want to be free?'

'You're frightening me, Tom. Please . . . please stop this.' She looked at him, hoping her fear didn't show in her eyes. 'I don't like it.'

'I bet you don't.' He suddenly reached into his backpack and pulled out a silver amulet in the shape of an Egyptian ankh studded with snaking symbols. He held it in front of her face and began to snarl at her in strange gibberish words.

'Tom, stop it!' She backed away but he took a step towards her, the amulet still pressed close to her face. 'Stop it!'

'Drink the potion,' he urged. He put the amulet down and snatched up his flask, pouring some of the thick dun-coloured liquid into the lid. It smelt vile. 'Drink it.' He pushed it towards her lips. 'Drink it, demon!' he shouted and tried to push it into her mouth.

She opened her mouth to protest, pushing at him with her palms. 'No, Tom!'

As she spoke, he tipped the cup forward and a slosh of the fluid hit her mouth. It burned her tongue and the taste was abhorrent. It filled her mouth and nostrils and she started to retch, trying to spit it out.

'You reject what you know will harm you!' shouted Tom. He gripped her hair at the back, pulling her head up, attempting to slosh more of the liquid in her mouth. 'You know that this powerful life force, this healing force, will expel you, demon!'

The stuff filled her mouth, but her body refused to accept it. Her gorge rose, she felt her throat constrict and heave, and she retched again. A rush of it hit the back of her throat as she struggled for breath and burned its way down her oesophagus. She heaved again and began to choke. Tom was still shouting at the demon inside her, and trying to throw more of the liquid into her mouth. She couldn't breathe.

I'm drowning, she thought in a part of her brain that wasn't gripped by panic. She tried to fight him off with her weak hands, but the liquid was flooding her from above, and her stomach was trying to expel everything from below. There was no room for breath. She could hear the noise in her own throat – a ghastly choking, bubbling sound, a rasp that started and stopped as she fought for oxygen.

'What are you saying, demon?' bellowed Tom. 'I know your tongue! I know your frightful language, you are afraid!'

Something huge and dark was possessing her brain. A pressure was building up in her skull that she felt sure would resolve soon in the great darkness sucking her into it. And once that happened, she knew that she would never come back.

I'll go to oblivion. To Will's world. The place he lived in for all those months. Maybe beyond it to the place no one returns from.

The pain in her throat and mouth was overpowering. Perhaps the darkness would be welcome relief.

Then the word came to her. The word that had been her first thought when death last came near to her and when life returned.

Children.

She saw them asleep in their beds, blissfully unaware of the struggle going on below them. A struggle she could see now was quite clearly between madness and sanity.

Children.

I can't leave them.

She wasn't going to let this happen. She had survived one attempt to tear her from them and she would survive this one too.

I didn't fight to lose it all now.

Emily summoned all her strength, every last bit that was remaining now that the great blackness was encroaching on her brain, and with it, she kicked up with her knee, hard as she could, hitting Tom's groin with all the power she could summon.

He howled and fell back. Her head was free and she tipped it forwards so that she could choke out the liquid in her mouth and throat, and then gasp for breath. She was retching and coughing but she knew there was no time to linger. Tom's face was transformed with pain and fury, but also with a kind of relish, as though he was enjoying the sensation of doing battle with the demon he imagined had possessed her. In another second he would lunge at her again and his strength would easily overpower her.

He isn't seeing me, she realised. *He's seeing the*

spirits that have been haunting his imagination. He wants to destroy them.

She reached out her hand and switched off the light, plunging the room into blackness. Her one advantage, she realised, was that she knew the house better than Tom did. The instant the darkness enveloped them, she ducked and stumbled towards the door to the passage, still gasping for breath and choking on the remains of the liquid in her throat. Tom heard her and followed her at once.

'You won't escape me,' he hissed. 'Emily, don't obey that spirit! Turn around and come back to me – it's your only hope!'

Misery engulfed her as she stumbled along the passage. *Oh Tom. Tom . . . what's happened to you?*

She reached the cupboard under the stairs and opened the door so that it blocked the passage and then stood pressed against the wall as Tom came along the hallway towards her. He was coming fast but uncertainly, one hand feeling his way against the wall.

'Emily?' he called. 'Emily, where are you?'

What state was he in now? she wondered. Did he still want to force that gunk down her throat or had he come to his senses?

'Where are you?' he crooned, and the hairs on her skin tingled and stood up. He was almost upon her now. She had only one chance to get it right.

She held her breath. He was next to her in the passage and he could sense her closeness but was disoriented by the darkness. Something told him to stop just before he hit the door and he stood beside her, breathing hard, his eyeballs glimmering in the darkness. She froze utterly, preparing herself. He knew suddenly that she was beside him and turned towards her.

'Found you!' he said and reached out a hand towards her, but she was too quick. She bent, dashed forward and pushed him in his middle with all her strength. Taken by surprise, he stumbled sideways with a yell and she pushed again so that he fell into the cupboard. He struck something inside as he fell and was quiet. She slammed the door, shutting him inside, and rammed home the bolt on the top of it.

Then she slumped against the door, sobbing. 'Tom . . . Oh Tom, are you all right? Oh my God. Tom . . . I'm sorry. I had to do it.'

CHAPTER 31

James called her when he saw the flashing lights of the ambulance in front of the house, the red cutting through the darkness of night.

'Emily?' he said, panic in his voice. 'Are you all right?'

'Yes,' she replied. The paramedics had Tom on a stretcher with a brace around his neck just in case of any damage and were securing him ready for the transition to the ambulance. 'It's Tom. He's been hurt. He has to go to hospital.'

She could hear the relief in his voice when he spoke, and guessed he'd been worried about her and the children. 'Oh no, poor Tom. Are you going with him?'

'I need to . . . but Carrie and Joe . . .'

'Don't worry, I'll come down right away. I'll bring Mum and she can sit with them until you get back. Then I'll drive you to the hospital.'

'I ought to go with Tom in the ambulance.'

'They'll probably want to leave sooner than that. Wait for me and we'll be there as soon as possible. Okay?'

'Okay,' she said, relieved that James was making

decisions for her. She was in a state of shock but the medics were concerned with Tom. His head had struck some old paint tins as he fell and he'd been knocked unconscious and had suffered a gash to his temple. He was coming round now but groaning with pain and talking incoherently. She told them he'd fallen in the dark.

When James arrived with his mother, the ambulance had only just left, and within a few minutes, Emily was next to him in the Land Rover's passenger seat.

'What happened?' James asked. 'Tell me everything from the beginning.'

So she went right back to the start, from the time she first noticed Tom's behaviour changing and the way he had begun to think and act towards her. As she related it, she realised how it must sound. It was obvious that Tom had developed some kind of mental illness, most likely exacerbated by his use of drugs. When she reached the events of that evening, it was clear from James's face that the problem was more than just a bit of New Age hocus pocus.

'For God's sake, Emily,' James said, his face pale. 'He could have killed you.'

'No, no, I'm sure . . .' She broke off, remembering the vivid feeling that she would soon lose consciousness and the helplessness she had felt. He hadn't realised what he was doing, she was sure of it. But like a child killing a duckling by squeezing it with affection, he could have harmed her in his desire to save his sister from the evil he perceived was damaging her.

'He needs help, you must see that,' James said gently. 'What he did isn't normal. It isn't right. You must tell the doctors everything that happened and ask their advice.'

'Will they put him away somewhere?' she asked, panicked.

'I don't know.' James watched the road with a serious expression. 'But they'll make sure he's not a danger to you or to himself. That's the most important thing.'

James stayed with her during the long hours in A & E. Tom was stitched up and seemed to be making a recovery, though he was concussed and very dazed, but Emily gave a full report of what had taken place to the duty doctor. She was then checked over and had a blood sample taken so that she could be tested by toxicology to make sure she hadn't ingested anything poisonous in the concoction Tom had given her. While they waited for the results, half asleep on slippery hospital chairs, they were visited by a second doctor, a police officer and a social worker so that Emily could tell the whole story again.

As dawn broke, a murky grey lightening to blue, the official decision was that Tom would remain in hospital for a psychiatric assessment and that he would, if necessary, be moved to a mental health unit.

'Sectioned?' Emily said fearfully. James held her hand tight.

'If that's best for Tom,' the social worker said

471

gently. 'I don't think he should be round you for a while, Emily. We all need to make sure he's better before that happens.'

'Is he –' she stumbled over the word, gazing at the social worker with fearful eyes – 'schizophrenic or something?'

'We can't tell. But his behaviour does warrant an intervention by the mental health crisis team.' She smiled. 'Don't worry, Emily. He'll be well looked after. Now, we'll need you to fill in some paperwork for us. You're the next of kin, is that right?'

Emily filled in all the necessary forms, her eyes swimming with tears as she noted down Tom's date of birth and address. *Is this really happening? I'm giving them permission to take Tom away and lock him up.*

But she only had to remember the terrifying moment when he'd bellowed at her demon and tipped whatever it was into her mouth and she knew she was doing the right thing.

The toxicology report came back clear. Whatever she had swallowed was either harmless or had been taken in such a small quantity that she'd suffered no ill effects. She was free to go.

The sun was up as James drove them back to December House.

'Your poor mother!' Emily said. 'She's been there all night! She must be in a terrible way. And' – she looked at her watch – 'the children will be waking up around now.'

James gave her a sideways look. 'She's a hardy soul, Emily. She was a farmer's wife for forty-five years; she's done the odd night shift, don't worry about that. And she had four children.'

'Four?' Emily blinked. She hadn't imagined James having brothers and sisters.

'Yes. Robert is a solicitor in Worcester. One of my sisters lives in the States; the other is a teacher in London. I'm the only farmer among them.' He smiled at her. 'So it's me and Mum for now.'

'Since your divorce,' she said.

'That's right.' He stared back at the road. 'Jojo and I split up two years ago. Quite amicable, as these things go. She didn't like life up here at all, and ended up running off with the bloke we hired to design Mum's extension. Fancy architect bloke called Elijah. Luckily he finished the job before he ran off with the missus.' He laughed a little, then shrugged. 'Ah well. It wasn't meant to be. I just got on with it really.'

She stared out of the window at the rolling hills. They seemed to calm her spirit. The summer was coming now and everything was vigorous and alive. The quiet grandeur of the landscape let her breathe, and took away the horrible suffocation she felt when she thought of her old life. Just then, her mobile rang.

'I've got reception,' she said brightly. 'That's lucky.' She took it out and saw Diana's name on the front. Panic at once quivered through her but, taking a deep breath, she answered it. 'Hello, Diana. Thanks for getting back to me. How's Will?'

When they reached home, Mrs Pendleton had the children up and dressed and breakfasted.

'Carrie has been most helpful,' she said. 'She's a smart little thing. Now, it's obvious you've had no sleep at all. I'm going to walk these young people up the hill to the house and they can have a play there. Then I'll give them lunch and we'll come back afterwards. You can get to bed for a while. How does that sound?'

'Thank you,' Emily said gratefully. 'That sounds wonderful. Will you be good for Mrs Pendleton, children?'

She gathered them up and kissed them as they nodded and chorused, 'Yes!'

'I'll see you up at the house, James,' his mother said. 'Come along, Carrie. Come along, Joe. We're going to look for beetles all the way back and we'll be there in no time.'

She marshalled the children out of the back door and the little group headed up the garden towards the gate so that they could cross the fields to the farmhouse further up.

Emily watched them go, unable to take her eyes off their stumping legs in their bright wellies and their fair heads flashing against the deep green of the grass. *I'm still here. I won't let anyone take me away from them.*

She turned and found that James was staring

at her in that earnest, intense way of his, the one that made her stomach burn and contract, and the blood rush to her face.

'Emily,' he said in a low voice, and the next minute they were in each other's arms, kissing furiously, unable to get enough of each other. It was frantic and fervent, as they kissed, stumbling from the kitchen to the passage and up the stairs, pulling off each other's clothes as they went. By the time they reached Emily's bedroom, a trail of discarded jumpers, shirts, shoes and jeans showed their path there. They fell onto her bed, absorbed only in one another and in their hunger for each other's mouth and their need for the touch of skin on skin, as their hands caressed and their bodies responded. Everything was heightened and intense, fatigue adding to the dreamlike situation.

I'm in bed with James in my underwear and he's wearing bright blue boxers and he's going to make love to me. And I'm loving every single second of it.

'Oh dear,' she said sleepily. 'When your mother said I ought to get to bed, I don't think this is what she meant.'

'Maybe she did,' James said, running his fingertip along her arm. 'She's a wily old girl. I think she probably guessed how much I fancy you.' He touched his lips to her shoulder. 'My goodness, you're beautiful, Emily.' He tucked her hair behind her ear and then softly kissed the scar that trailed from her forehead to her jaw. 'Every bit of you.'

He lay back and stared at the ceiling, a huge smile on his face. 'I think I must be the luckiest man in the world right now.'

Emily laughed. 'What I want to know, James, is how I didn't notice right away how incredibly sexy you are.' She nuzzled into him, picking up the deliciousness of his scent. 'Because you are.' She sighed happily, thinking of how very nice it had been to make to love to him. Her body felt wonderfully languorous after being thoroughly pleasured. *Pleasured*, she thought with a silent laugh. *But that's what it was, top to toe. Pleasure. Mmm.* She shivered lightly at the memory.

'I'm a slow burner,' he said with a laugh. He raised an eyebrow at her. 'We farmers are quite well versed in the ways of nature, you know. We've seen the mare covered by the stallion often enough to know what to do.'

'Yuk! Charming image.' She made a face at him. 'I do like that eyebrow business, though, you can do that again.'

He raised his eyebrow and waggled it playfully. 'Sexy?'

'It was . . . but now I'm not so sure.'

He rolled towards her and pulled her into his arms, enveloping her against his strong chest. He kissed her, then said again in the low voice she liked, 'Sexy?'

She sighed happily. 'Oh yes.' A thought occurred to her and she said, 'James, can I ask you something?'

'What is it?'

'What on earth is your aftershave? I'm dying to know.'

'Aftershave?' he echoed. 'Don't wear the stuff. Never have.'

'Wow,' she said in awe. 'So it's all natural. I can't buy it in a bottle.'

'What is?'

'Oh, nothing. Just put it this way – I'm going to have to stay close to the real thing.' She leaned over and kissed him again.

CHAPTER 32

Diana had arranged all of Will's care. He was awake, it was true, but his functions were limited. He was bed-bound still, and could apparently recognise Diana and say some simple words. Diana, it transpired, had kept Will on her private medical insurance and she was able to get him into a facility where he was being well cared for.

'How long he'll be there for, I can't say,' Diana had said. 'We're going to get him back on his feet eventually. Believe me, Emily. I've come this far and I don't intend to go back.'

Emily knew that Diana would devote whatever time and resources it took to get Will better. It would be her life's work now. Emily was glad her mother-in-law was able to do what she never could. Her fears seemed strange and rather ridiculous now that she knew Will was unable to walk or speak. Getting out of bed unaided would be beyond him, let alone threatening her, and she felt in her heart that this would be his life now. He would never be that man he was again.

I wanted him dead, and all along he was dead. That

Will, who hurt and threatened me and tried to kill me, is gone forever. I don't have to be afraid any more.

She could afford to be generous to the shell of Will that remained. He had punished himself more than she ever could. He should see the children again, and they should see him. They would be a part of one another's lives now, and although he would be a different sort of father from the one they remembered, she knew that they would soon accept him and the Will who'd existed before the accident would vanish entirely.

'We're going to go down to London,' she told James one evening. They were sitting eating their dinner on the paved area outside the morning room, watching the sun sinking down behind the hills. It was not quite warm enough for eating al fresco, but Emily was cosy in one of James's huge jumpers.

He looked at her seriously. 'Would you like me to come with you?'

She shook her head. 'No. Thank you, but I should face him alone.' She shrugged and took a sip of wine from her glass. 'It's odd but my fear of him dominated my life for months after the accident. My worst nightmare was that he would wake up. And now he has, and my fear has completely vanished.'

'The reality has replaced the nightmare,' James replied. 'And you can handle the reality.' He smiled at her. 'You've never shied away from that, have you?'

She smiled back. 'Maybe not. I suppose I've realised that you can't run away from danger; it can come and find you wherever you are. I never would have imagined that Tom could hurt me, but he very nearly did.'

'How is he?' James asked gently.

'Doing well. He's on medication and he's responding well. He's having sessions with a psychiatrist.' She bit her lip. 'They still don't think he should see me. Not yet. He's having trouble adjusting to the knowledge of what happened, and to the challenge to his view of the universe. That's what they told me anyway.'

James reached over and took her hand. 'He'll get better, Emily, I'm sure of it. Once those awful drugs are out of his system.'

'I hope so,' she said. 'I just want him back. The old Tom. He's all the family I've got, you see.' She heard the laptop on the table inside chirrup, and sat up, putting her glass down. 'Oh, it must be Cameron. I've not heard from him for days. I'd better go and talk to him.'

Inside at the table, she called up Cameron's smiling face. 'Hey, Emily!' he said cheerfully. 'How's life in sleepy old England?'

She thought back over what had happened recently, and said, 'Oh, much the same. All very dull. How are you?'

'Just call me Sherlock Baxter!' Cameron said with a grin. 'I've found the Kemps!'

'You have?' Excitement bubbled up inside her.

'Excellent work, Cameron. What have you found out?'

James came through from the garden and stood beside her, looking down over her shoulder at the screen.

Cameron said, 'Hello, you've got a friend there, have you? Oh, it's your mate, James!'

'Hi, Cameron,' James said, in a much friendlier tone than he'd used previously. 'How are things?'

'Yeah, good. So listen, Emily, it took a while because ladies have an unfortunate habit of marrying and changing their bloody names, but I tracked down that Kemp woman. She had got married, so it wasn't easy at all. But eventually I found the records we wanted. She got married in sixty-six to a bloke called Rogers. Once I'd made that link, we were laughing.'

'So, who is she?'

'Kemp,' James put in, suddenly. 'That rings a bell. My mother was talking just the other day, after she saw your picture, Emily, the one of Cressida. She said that there was a woman who used to look after this place called Ursula Kemp.'

Cameron's mouth fell open. 'Yeah, that's her. Ursula!' He frowned and pursed his lips. 'Have I just been working my arse off and all along you knew who Ursula Kemp was?'

Emily looked up at James. 'You knew her?'

'Knew of her,' James said, looking apologetic. 'Sorry. I wouldn't have said—'

'No, it's fine,' Emily said quickly. 'Cameron's

only kidding, aren't you, Cameron?' Thoughts began buzzing through her brain. 'Hold on . . . What are we saying here? Ursula Kemp lived around here and then turned up in Australia.'

'Yeah,' Cameron broke in. 'But that's the weird thing. There's no record of her arriving in Australia. Nothing at all. She's just . . . here. Then my dad visits her when she's still Kemp, then she gets married and becomes Mrs Rogers. Then she dies. About ten years ago.'

'Oh.' Emily's spirits sank for a moment, and then she said, 'But there has to be a link, right? She's from here, from Howelland, isn't that right, James? And she ends up in Australia and Cressida sends a message to her via your father. What was the message again, Cameron?'

'It was something like "Miss Fellbridge wants to know if you got the money" and the answer was "yes, thanks."'

'But it wasn't Ursula Kemp who it was delivered to,' Emily said thoughtfully. 'It was a girl, right?'

Cameron nodded. 'I think it must have been her daughter, Maggie Kemp.'

'And have you found her?'

Cameron looked pleased with himself. 'Yes, I have, actually. But you'll have to take over from here, Emily. Because she's in England. In London, to be more precise.'

Emily stared at him. 'London?'

'Yep. And I have an address too.' Cameron grinned. 'So I suggest you get down there and ask her a few questions, and maybe we can nail this thing.'

The care facility was bright, clean and modern. As much as possible had been done to minimise the presence of the medical equipment that each patient relied on, but it was still there. The nurse who led her down the long corridor told her that one wing was reserved for those in long-term vegetative states. 'They probably won't ever wake up,' she said, adding cheerfully, 'so it's lovely that your husband is one of the lucky ones!'

It didn't seem so lucky to be confined to this place, Emily thought as they walked behind the nurse. Carrie gripped tight to one of Emily's hands, her eyes wide. She knew that they were going to see Daddy but also that Daddy would not be like before. More than that, Emily couldn't say because she knew so little herself. She carried Joe, who had wrapped both small arms around her neck and was clinging to her.

'Here we are!' the nurse said, looking down at Carrie. 'Your daddy has a room all to himself.' She opened the door.

Emily stepped forward, her heart pounding. The last time she'd seen Will had been months ago, when he lay obscured by masks and tubes and all the rest of it. In her nightmares he'd been curiously untouched by the accident, the man she'd known from before. She looked at the bed that dominated the room. Beside it sat Diana, as neat and well turned out as ever, smiling happily to see the children, holding the hand of the man in the bed.

So there he is. That's Will.

The figure in the bed was shrunken, its muscles wasted away and its cheeks hollow. The hair, more grey than red now, was almost gone. But what shocked her was the dazed look in his eyes, and the way one shoulder twisted upwards and one side of his mouth drooped down slightly. His skull was marked by a large scar and an indentation where he'd been operated on. He was so different from the flashing-eyed maniac in her dreams that she was washed with pity for him.

'Will,' she said, stepping closer to the bed. Her heart was beating fast, and into her mind came a picture of December House. It stood, beautiful and welcoming, nestling in the hills, surrounded by gardens and the orchard and the fields. She and the children were there in the garden, playing together, the wind whipping up their hair. They turned and waved to someone walking up the path to the house. It was a man. He scooped Joe up in his arms and jiggled him in the air before putting him down. He gave Carrie a bright red apple and he turned to Emily with a kiss. She saw now that it was James. 'Oh Will,' she said, her heart breaking for him. He would never know that joy now. He'd never walk up the garden to the home that held his family and his heart. Her eyes filled with tears.

'Will,' Diana said loudly, leaning towards him. 'Who's here, Will? Who is it?'

The vacant eyes moved over to her and blinked slowly. He said in a strange blurry voice, 'Emily.'

'That's right!' Diana was delighted. She patted his hand. 'Yes, it's Emily. And look who's with her!'

Will looked at the children and a spark flickered in his eyes. He smiled slowly.

'It's Daddy,' Emily said to Carrie, who was clinging to her and eying the figure on the bed with trepidation. 'Go and say hello,' she urged.

Carrie stepped forward. 'Hello Daddy,' she said quietly.

'Carrie,' Will said, a wobbling emotion in his voice. 'Joe.'

'Oh, that's wonderful,' Diana said, her expression excited. 'Isn't that wonderful, Emily? He said their names! He knows them. He's come so far.' She smiled happily at the children. 'Come and see Granny,' she said to them, letting go of Will's hand and holding out her arms to them. 'I've missed you!'

'It was awful,' Emily said to Polly later that evening when she related the events of the day. 'He's just a shadow of what he was before.'

They sat in Polly's kitchen, the children all in bed, and steadily drank their way through a bottle of white wine.

'But he knew you all.' Polly shook her head. 'That's amazing. When you think of what he's been through. How long he was in that coma. The human body is an incredible thing.'

Emily nodded. 'Yes. But . . .' She didn't know

485

how to express the disconnection she felt from Will. She felt sorry for him in the way she would for a stranger. Except for that one flash of the life he might have had with them, she couldn't connect the man in the bed with the one she'd married and had children with. 'I have to divorce him,' she said frankly. 'I know I'll look like a villain, but I can't be his next of kin any more. That should be Diana. I'm going to see a lawyer tomorrow, if it's all right for you to take Carrie and Joe in the afternoon.'

'Of course it is. Mine are delighted that they're here, you know that.'

Emily smiled at her. 'Thanks. And you must come up and stay with us sometime.'

'We'd love to, when you've recovered from all the drama. I'm so sorry to hear about Tom,' Polly said earnestly. 'How is he?'

'All right, I think. It'll be a couple more weeks before I know any more.'

'Poor Tom. We're all hoping for the best.' Polly sipped her wine and then said teasingly, 'What I don't understand is how on earth you've found the time to get yourself a man as well! Honestly, Emily, is it the country air?'

Emily laughed. 'I suppose it is. A month in Cumbria and I couldn't stop myself!'

'Whatever it is, you're looking extremely good on it,' Polly replied. 'I'd better get up there pronto. I could do with a roll in the hay myself.'

CHAPTER 33

Emily walked the south London street until she came to the address on the printout in her hand. She didn't know this part of town, and it was obviously one of London's less prosperous areas. Among the large council estates, the betting shops, the twenty-four-hour grocery shops and the off-licences with the goods locked away behind padlocked windows, there were rows of small Victorian terraced houses, most in a state of despair but a few well kept. One of these was the house she was after. She knocked on the bright red front door and admired the window box on the bay sill.

The door opened at last. A woman with dyed dark red hair cut in a shaggy modern style and thick eye make-up stood just behind it. 'Yes?' she said suspiciously.

'I'm looking for Maggie Kemp,' Emily said politely. 'Or Rogers. I'm not quite sure which.'

The woman just stared at her, as if she didn't recognise either name. 'Why?'

'My name is Emily Conway and I'd like to speak to her about her mother, Ursula.'

There was a pause as the woman stared at her. 'What about her?' she asked finally.

'Just a question or two. Are you Maggie?'

There was a long pause as the woman gazed at Emily. She was in her early sixties, Emily guessed, and her skin was tanned and lined with the fine scrawl of sun damage.

'Yes, I'm Maggie,' the woman said finally, opening the door a little further. Emily could hear the Australian accent now. 'What's all this about? Why are you interested in my mother? She's been dead for a decade.'

'I know,' Emily said, trying to appear as friendly as possible. 'It's an odd story, I suppose. I inherited a house from my aunt, Cressida Fellbridge, and I'm trying to work out what happened to her. We thought she'd emigrated to Australia but it seems a great deal more complicated than that.'

Sudden amusement flickered in the other woman's eyes. 'You could put it like that.' She opened the door. 'You'd better come in.'

The interior of the house was neat and well kept. In the small front sitting room there was a desk with a computer on it and a printer underneath.

'I work from home,' Maggie remarked as they went in, as if to explain it. 'Do you want something? Tea?'

'No thanks, I'm fine.' Emily sat down gingerly on the sofa. It was difficult to assess exactly how welcome she was. Maggie sat down on the chair opposite, her expression now warmer.

'So,' she said, 'it's very interesting to meet you.

488

I always wondered when someone would start to ask questions. Your family must be a bloody odd one, if you don't mind me saying. Your aunt claims to be in Australia and no one so much as guesses that she wasn't there.'

'So we were right. She never went, did she?' Emily asked, excited to hear that their detective work had been successful.

Maggie nodded her head. 'That's right.'

'How much of the story do you know?' Emily said eagerly. 'Why didn't she go? What were you and your mother doing there instead?'

Maggie smiled. 'I'll tell you what I know. But first, I just want to say that we owe your aunt a huge debt of gratitude. My mother had always dreamed of getting away from England. Her life was hard and miserable here, and my future was pretty bleak too. Thanks to your aunt, we had a different life. My mum lived by golden sands and blue seas just like she'd always wanted. And she knew I'd have a decent life too. But your aunt also gave us money when times were tough. She never forgot us, even when we'd more or less lost touch with her.'

Emily smiled, delighted. 'That's wonderful. I don't know the whole story yet, but I'm so glad that there's something to celebrate. I've only just worked out that my aunt wasn't in Australia at all, and I'm still trying to find out what happened to her, and who was living at December House. I thought it was a woman called Catherine Few, but that doesn't appear to be the case. So I guessed that Catherine had gone to Australia, but that's not the case either if you and your mother were the ones who went.' Emily shook her head in bewilderment. 'But why? Where is Catherine? And how on earth did she manage to leave me her house if she never lived there?'

Maggie sat back in her chair and frowned. 'I'm not sure how much I can help, I'm afraid. I can only tell you what I know,' she said. 'About what happened to us. Mum never told me the whole story. But I was there for some of it. I was there when they first arrived.'

'Who? Catherine and Ralph?'

Maggie shook her head. 'No. It was her. Cressida Fellbridge. She arrived with the artist bloke.' She smiled to herself. 'He was good-looking, no doubt about that, and you could tell they were in love, it was written all over them. They seemed grown-up to me but they must have been young. In their twenties. My mother had looked after the house for the family for years, since my dad died, and in return we got to live in a little cottage on the edge of her land.'

'Keeper's Cottage?'

'That's right.' A faraway look came into Maggie's eyes. 'Poky little place but we loved it.'

'So Ralph Few and Cressida were at the cottage without Catherine.' Emily thought this over, then said, 'How long were they there?'

'Weeks, I think. They arrived in the depth of winter, I know that.'

'And then what happened?'

Maggie pursed her lips. 'The truth is, I don't know. I used to go up to the house to help Mum. One morning I got there and Miss Fellbridge was there, white as a ghost. She told Mum to send me away, so she chivvied me off to the cottage. But I stayed there, hanging around the garden, trying to see what was up. I couldn't make out anything. In the end, I gave up and went home. It was freezing, you see. I remember that cold.' She shivered. 'I couldn't cope with it now, not after the years of living in Australia. You never want your bones that cold again, if you can help it.'

'What did your mother tell you?'

'Nothing. But I knew something was up. She seemed in a state, though she wouldn't tell me what it was all about. All she said was that I wasn't to go up to the house until she said I could. I had to stay in the cottage. She made me promise. Two days she went up there without me. And then . . .' Maggie was lost for a moment in her memories. 'The snow came, the way it used to round there. The whole world buried in white. Oh, that wind! The chill. I never felt anything so bitter in my life. And once it came, there was no going anywhere. But I do remember that Miss Fellbridge came to us, through the snow. I don't know how she did it. And she stayed for hours in our little room downstairs, by the fire, talking to Mum. I sat on the stairs and listened as hard as I could, but they were too quiet for me to hear. The next day, my mother told me that we were leaving England for good, to live in

Australia. It was a shock for me. I knew it was something to do with Miss Fellbridge, but I didn't find out till years later what it was.'

Emily leaned forward, absorbed by the story. 'What was it?'

'She sent us there. My mum travelled there as Cressida Fellbridge. I was her niece, Miss Maggie Kemp, travelling with her aunt to Australia. And then, a while later, Mum went to a lawyer's office with the identification Miss Fellbridge had supplied, and accepted a sum of money on her behalf.'

'Some kind of payment?' Emily asked.

'Support, I suppose. Like I said, she never forgot us. Even years later, money would arrive for us somehow. Then, when my mum died, she wrote to me.'

Emily blinked. 'Do you have the letter?'

'Yes, I do, actually.' Maggie got up and went to her desk. 'I kept it as a memento, and because it was kind of intriguing.' She shuffled through some files and pulled out a piece of paper. 'Here it is.'

Emily took it, excited. A link to Cressida at last.

Dear Maggie

I was so sorry to hear that your mother had died. She was a wonderful friend to me, and always devoted to you. She helped me in my greatest hour of need, and I've never forgotten her kindness, strength and bravery. Many people would have quailed in the face of what we did together – I think I would have if she

492

hadn't been strong. Being able to help you enjoy a new life in Australia made me very happy. It was a small gesture of thanks to your mother for allowing me to have my own new life, living with the man I loved.

I send you all my sympathy and love. Bless you, Maggie.

CF

Emily stared at the paper. *CF. Cressida Fellbridge. Catherine Few. She couldn't bring herself to be one or the other in the end.*

'Does it mean anything to you?' Maggie said.

Emily shook her head. 'I don't know what she and your mother did.'

'Me neither.' Maggie smiled. 'They both took it to their graves, it seems. Maybe they robbed a bank.'

Emily laughed politely and then said, 'But there's something I don't understand about Cressida and Ralph being at the house. Where was Catherine Few? Did she arrive after you'd left?' Talking more to herself than Maggie, she said, 'But she couldn't have. Your mother took Cressida's identity with her. She must have had Catherine's ready to assume.'

'I don't know who this Catherine is that you're talking about. I never saw her at the house, only Miss Fellbridge and her bloke. My mother never mentioned her.' Maggie shrugged. 'Sorry. That's all I know.'

Emily sighed. She had some answers but not the one she really wanted. Why did Cressida send her housekeeper away with her identity? And what happened to Catherine?

Maggie fixed her with an intense look and said, 'There's one thing I will say. I was with my mother near her end and she said a few things that frightened me. I always knew she hid from me what happened in those days when I wasn't allowed to the house. It was hard to know what she was saying sometimes, but if you want to know the answer, then you should look in your garden.' She sat back again. 'That's all I'm saying. Look in that bloody garden.'

The children had one more afternoon with Will before they all headed back to December House.

Diana hugged Emily at the end of it. 'Thank you for coming and bringing the children,' she said, her eyes shining. 'It's made all the difference! Can you see how much better he looks?'

Emily had seen no difference at all but she nodded. She knew that Diana would cling on to the changes that only she could see. They would bring her hope.

The children were much more at ease with the new version of their daddy on the second day. His slow speech and twisted body didn't bother them and they were soon climbing on him, chattering away and almost enjoying the fact that busy, impatient Daddy now had all the time in the world for them.

'When will we see Daddy again?' Carrie asked, as the car made its slow progress out of the city.

'Soon,' Emily promised. 'Granny and I are

494

working out how we'll do it. But it won't be too long before we're back.'

She and Diana had also talked about the divorce and she'd been relieved at how easily Diana had accepted it. She had clearly come to terms with the fact and no longer wanted to berate Emily for her treachery. They talked about the legal advice Emily had received and how best to proceed. The financial aspect would not be controversial: Emily would keep what she had, and in return there would be no maintenance or help with the children.

'We can revisit that when Will's better and can work again. I'm sure his pride will mean he'll expect to support the children,' Diana said seriously.

Emily nodded, thinking that Diana's belief in this mythical recovery of Will's would make things easier in a way. *But then again, she was right about him waking up. Maybe she's right about him getting back to normal.*

But she didn't believe it. Will would never be the same again.

The return to December House lifted all their spirits, and the sight of James's battered Land Rover gave Emily a pleasant tingle of anticipation. James leapt out as they approached and was ready to greet her with a hug as soon as she got out.

'Are you all right?' he asked, kissing her cheek.

'Yes. It was fine,' she said.

'We saw our daddy! He lives in a bed now,' Carrie explained.

'So I understand,' James said. 'Isn't that lovely? Just like Charlie's grandparents in *Charlie and the Chocolate Factory*.'

Carrie thought about this and said, 'Yes. He has adventures in his bed because it can fly.'

'You have to tell me all about it,' replied James as he picked up Joe. 'Hello, old man. How was your trip to the smoke? Let's go inside and have a cup of tea and some apple juice. And my mother has sent you some rather special biscuits which she made herself.'

As they headed for the door, James scooping up most of the luggage with his spare hand, Emily looked around the garden at the front of the house.

Look in that bloody garden.

The words had played through her mind ever since her encounter with Maggie Kemp. Every time she thought of it, a nasty shiver prickled down her spine. *Why would anyone look in a garden except to find . . .* She didn't even want to think about it. Then suddenly an image floated through her mind: she saw a stone angel emerging from a blanket of snow, its head bowed in sorrow. She heard James's voice in her mind.

It sounds gruesome. More suitable for a graveyard than a garden if you ask me. Creepy things, angels.

She gasped, stopping as the others walked on. *Oh, Cressida. Is that what happened? Is that what your painting is trying to tell us? Oh no.*

PART IV

CHAPTER 34

The snow didn't come that night, but the threat of it lay over them, as heavy as a blanket. Cressie woke when she heard howling, confused at first, unable to understand what was going on. Then she remembered.

Catherine's here! She's shut herself in the studio. How on earth did I manage to fall asleep?

But they had, made drowsy by the warmth she and Ralph shared under the bedclothes and by the subsiding of the adrenalin that had rushed through them during the encounter with Catherine.

The howl was low at first, a kind of crooning sound, a night noise that might have been a fox if it had not been so near. It took a while until it sank far enough into Cressie's consciousness to wake her. When she realised that the sound must be coming from the studio, she slipped out of bed. She was still dressed. Letting herself out as quietly as she could, she crossed the landing towards the studio door and pressed herself up against it, listening. From behind it came that awful sound, like a crying without the tears, a long low wail of sorrow and despair.

Cressie listened, her heart beating faster. What would Catherine do now?

Her mind is unbalanced. It must be.

How could it not be? she wondered. What sister would try to take the place of a wife in her brother's life? What kind of desire for possession lay at the root of such behaviour? She had never sensed anything about their relationship that would cause her to question the truth of their situation. She had believed their story entirely. *But perhaps we often accept what we're told and don't see the clues in front of us.* In the light of what she now knew, when she recalled the days in the studio she thought she could see that the signs were there. But so slight and subtle that it had been almost impossible to pick up on them.

The sound of grief from behind the door made a mixture of pity and fear course through her. *It's hopeless for her. She can never have what she wants because what she wanted never existed.*

Perhaps she could forgive Catherine for her deception, of both herself and others. But what was impossible to forgive was that she had hurt Ralph. The slow poisoning of him. The medicines mixed up according to a hotchpotch of ideas and theories and fed into his beloved body. His face came into her mind: dead white, his eyes trying to focus, his strength ebbing away.

No. She's been killing him. She must never come near him again. She's dangerous. She had known the truth since the moment when she'd opened that one-line note in the hall of the Kensington house. That was what had propelled her up here on the frantic journey to reach Ralph before Catherine could harm him. She knew she was mad.

But had Ralph's words penetrated her fantasy world? Had they managed to rip away the veil of her delusions and show her the truth? And what would that knowledge do to her?

The howling behind the door seemed to answer that question. Catherine was in the throes of something but whether it was remorse or fury, Cressie could not tell.

She sank down to the floor and listened, clutching at her skirt with both hands as her breath came shakily. The noise was otherworldly and chilling. Someone possessed by emotion like that would be capable of anything.

We're alone together. Ralph is too ill to do anything. I have to be ready for whatever she might do.

The howling grew louder and higher, more like a woman's scream now. Then another noise accompanied it. Catherine was moving around. What was she doing? Footsteps moved over the wooden floorboards, going here and there as though she were circling the room inside. The screaming became broken by panting and gasps of exertion and Cressie could hear the tearing of canvas and objects hitting the floor and the walls.

She must be destroying the studio and everything in it!

Cressie stared wildly into space, trying to imagine what was happening behind the door. *What will she do when she's finished?* She would be worked into a state of destruction. Would she come out from behind the door and start on the rest of the house? Was she allowing herself to descend into a state of rage that would free her from her grief and perhaps enable her to do something terrible?

What can I do? How do I stop her?

Cressie got to her feet and hurried downstairs as quietly as she could. In the kitchen, she picked up a knife and hid it in her waistband, covering the handle with her cardigan. Then she raced back up the stairs, frightened that Catherine had taken this moment to emerge and find Ralph undefended. But there was a strange silence from behind the door, which was broken after a few moments by the sound of sobbing and muttered words that Cressie could not make out. The whirl of destruction seemed to be at an end and there was little more to hear apart from the soft crying. Cressie stood on the landing, poised in case she should hear the sofa being moved away from behind the door. Then, after a while, she sat down on the floor. She leaned against the wall and eventually, after what felt like hours, she began to doze. The house stayed silent.

Cressie woke with a start at the sound of a bang from downstairs, and then remembered that Ursula would have arrived first thing.

She jumped up, shaking sleep from her brain, and went to the studio door. From behind it came a curious noise that she could not identify, a strange sort of growl.

Cressie hurried downstairs to the kitchen, where Maggie was already at the range, feeding it with logs to start up the flames, while Ursula was getting breakfast ready.

'Ursula!' she cried as she went in. 'I'm so glad you're here, I need your help.' She cast a look over at the girl kneeling by the range, who looked up at her with mild curiosity in her chestnut-coloured eyes. 'Oh, Maggie, of course you're here too.' She stared at the girl, flummoxed, then turned to Ursula. 'I'm afraid we'll have to send Maggie home,' she said. 'It's really very important.'

Ursula looked at her questioningly and seemed to see in her face that Cressie was serious. 'Very well.' She turned to her daughter. 'You heard Miss Fellbridge, Maggie. You're to go straight home and don't dally. I'll be there later. You can get on with your schoolwork until I get back.' She said to Cressie, 'She hates school. Only goes when it suits her. Go on, Maggie, you heard me.'

'All right,' grumbled the girl. 'I'm going.' She got up and made her way slowly to the back door to put on her boots and coat.

'Go!' ordered her mother, and Maggie went out of the door, slamming it shut behind her.

Ursula turned back to Cressie. 'What's all this then, miss? Is there trouble?'

'Yes. I'm afraid there is. Please come with me.' As they went back up the passage and then the stairs, Cressie said, 'Mr Few's sister is here. She's not well at all – in her head, I mean. She's locked herself in the studio and gone berserk, and I'm worried that she's a danger to us all.'

'Mr Few's sister?' breathed Ursula, her expression concerned as she came up the stairs behind Cressie. 'But why?'

'Please understand that I can't explain. The main thing is that I think we have to get the door open. Mr Few is ill in bed and can't help us. I don't want to worry him. Will you help me?' She gazed at Ursula, her eyes pleading. 'Please!'

'Very well,' Ursula said, after a moment's hesitation. 'Let's see what we can do.'

At the door, they stopped to listen. The same awful sound was coming from behind it, a bubbling growl coming every few seconds.

'Miss, let's open this,' Ursula said urgently after a moment. She twisted the handle and tried to push the door but the sofa was jammed against it on the inside. 'Come along, we'll need both of us to get enough strength together to shift this door.'

The two of them pushed hard, pressing their shoulders to the wood and giving it all their effort. It took several tries before the door began to give, the sofa behind the door scraping across the floor.

'Come on now!' cried Ursula. 'We're nearly there! Nearly. Another good shove . . .'

Cressie gathered all she had and pressed against the

door, her teeth clenching with the effort. Then the sofa shifted a few feet over the boards and the door opened far enough that they could slip in.

'Oh miss!' Ursula said as they entered, turning to Cressie with frightened eyes. 'Oh miss!'

The studio was a shambles, the floor littered with everything that could possibly have been thrown on it. The walls were smeared with a filthy rainbow of colour in streaks and lines and daubs. The canvases were ripped and torn, some slashed and anointed with paint. Brushes lay scattered everywhere, along with palette knives, pencils and anything else Catherine could reach. A bottle of white spirit had been emptied into the mess and the stench was strong. In the middle of it all lay the prone body of Catherine.

Cressie rushed over. 'Catherine!' she cried. 'What have you done?'

Catherine's eyes were shut and her skin had a ghastly pallor. The awful bubbling growl came from her throat and now Cressie understood why. Around her lips and mouth was a horrible white mess, bubbling with spittle. In her hand was a large tube of white paint.

'What is it?' Ursula said, recoiling in horror at the sight. 'What's happened?'

Cressie was stunned, a sick horror climbing up from her belly. 'Oh Catherine,' she whispered. She turned to Ursula. 'She's eaten the paint! Look, she's sliced open the tube and she's eaten it! She's poisoned herself in the same way she poisoned

Ralph.' Panic ran through her. 'We must get a doctor, Ursula! You must go at once and get one.'

The other woman stood and stared down at Catherine with horrified eyes. She didn't move.

'Didn't you hear me, Ursula? You must fetch the doctor at once!'

Ursula moved her gaze to Cressie's. 'Oh miss, it's too late for the doctor. I can see that she's too far gone for that.'

'What do you mean?' Her panic grew. 'Oh no! We can't let her die! We must help her.' She dropped to her knees by Catherine and took her in her arms, trying to dig the paint out of her mouth with her fingers. There was so much of it; Catherine's throat seemed full of white gunk, paint mixed with the bile her body had thrown up to try and be rid of it. 'Catherine, you mustn't die . . .'

As she tried to free the other woman's mouth, Catherine's eyes opened. They were blank and unseeing and then they moved to Cressie's face and for a moment she thought she saw recognition there, but then the grey eyes rolled backwards, and closed. The bubbling growl turned into a choke. Catherine's chest convulsed and then she froze. The next instant, all breath left her and she relaxed heavily into Cressie's arms.

Shocked, Cressie held her, staring down at her. 'Catherine?' she said almost wonderingly.

'Oh, Miss Cressida,' Ursula said, kneeling down beside them. 'This is terrible. I'm afraid she's dead.'

'Dead?' Cressie looked back at Catherine's face. 'How is it possible? What shall we do?'

'We must tell someone, I suppose,' Ursula said. 'Perhaps you're right, the doctor must be called. He'll be able to certify it. He'll know what to do.' She got up.

'Wait.' Cressie looked up at her, suddenly thinking very fast. 'We can't tell anyone what's happened.'

'Why not?' Ursula frowned. 'We must.'

'But . . .' Cressie looked ahead into the future, at the inevitable scandal. She and Ralph would be parted, perhaps forever. A death at the house. The uncovering of everything that Catherine and Ralph had done, a terrible stain on his character and on his work. And Ralph himself – how would he not blame himself for what Catherine had done?

'This is awful,' Cressie said in a low voice, almost to herself. Catherine had had a brilliant revenge, she saw that. She had made it impossible for Cressie to be with Ralph in any normal way.

But . . . only we know about this. Only Ursula and I. Does the world have to know? After all, everyone believes that Catherine is Ralph's wife. What if . . . what if . . .

She looked down at the woman whose body lay in her arms, still warm. Was it possible? An awful fear mixed with a determination filled her. It was almost too much to think of and yet . . . She gazed up again at Ursula.

'This is a terrible accident,' she said intensely.

'If word of it gets out . . . everything here would come to an end. Please, Ursula. Let me think. Let me work something out. I don't want Ralph to know yet either. He's very ill. The shock of this could harm him very badly.'

There was a pause as Ursula took this in and then the older woman said, 'Do I understand, miss, that you're thinking of a course of action that doesn't involve the doctor coming at all?'

'I don't know!' Cressie burst out. It was all too much, too dreadful. She didn't know what to do; all she knew was that for now, it had to remain a secret until she could clear her mind enough to find an answer.

Ursula stepped towards her and put gentle hands on her shoulders. 'Put her down, miss,' she said. 'There's nothing more you can do for her now.'

Cressie lowered Catherine to the floor and laid her there softly. She stared at her, still unable to take in what had happened. 'I think she felt too guilty to go on,' she said at last. 'Knowing that she'd harmed Ralph. It's as though she wanted to take his place.'

'Miss . . .' Ursula coaxed her up gently. 'Please, Miss Cressida, go and wash your hands at once.'

Cressida looked down at her paint-smeared hands, thick rims of white under her nails. 'Yes,' she said almost dreamily. 'Yes, I must.'

The reality of the situation took a long time to sink in. Ralph lay upstairs asleep, still unaware of what had happened. Catherine's body remained in the paint-covered studio.

Downstairs, Cressie explained as much as she could to Ursula, who listened solemnly. As Cressie talked, she became more and more convinced that no one could know what had happened to Catherine.

'But they must,' Ursula pointed out. 'Even apart from the law, won't someone miss her?'

'But there's no family – an uncle who couldn't care less about them, that's all. And anyone else who knows them believes that Ralph and Catherine were married.' She gazed fervently at Ursula. 'I have to stay with him. I have to be a wife to him myself. But the scandal would destroy us, my father would force us apart, Ralph's career would be over. I can't let that happen to him. It would kill him, I'm sure of it.'

'So you're saying that no one will miss her,' Ursula said. 'That's a very sad thing. The poor lady.'

'I know. But there must be a way that will help us all. Nothing much will hurt Catherine now.'

Ursula looked shocked. 'Are you saying you'd deny the lady a good Christian burial?'

Cressie reached out and grasped Ursula's hand. 'It might be necessary, Ursula. Would you help me?' She stared into the other woman's eyes, half wondering where her own cold-blooded determination was coming from.

I'll do whatever is necessary to save Ralph and me, and keep us together.

'I don't know, miss, it seems very wrong.' Ursula looked distressed. 'I know it is wrong.'

'Wrong in a way . . . but we're not killing her. You heard me – I wanted a doctor for her, I wanted to help her! She's past all caring now, don't you see? But she could still hurt me, if what's happened here is revealed. I know it seems wrong, but really, it isn't. It's the best thing for us all. Honestly.'

Ursula stared at the table. Cressie wondered if she was wrestling with questions of faith – whether she believed it was wrong to deny a religious service to Catherine's body.

'Ursula,' she said. 'Please help me. You won't regret it.'

At last, Ursula raised her eyes to Cressie's. She took a deep breath. 'I'll help you, miss. You're a good person, and I loved your dear mother. I'll help you for her sake.'

Relief coursed through Cressie's body. 'Thank you.'

After a long pause, Ursula said, 'Do you intend to bury her?'

Cressie flinched at the words. They sounded so cold-blooded. They didn't reflect the truth of her situation, the great stakes she was playing for. But how could it be expressed? 'I think so,' she said. 'I think that's the only way.'

Gruesome images crossed her mind, of murderers melting bodies in baths of acid, or chopping them up with axes. *That's not me. I'm not like that. We'll respect her.*

'I see.' There was a pause while Ursula thought. 'It's cold, miss. The ground is hard. I take it it would be just you and me?'

Cressie nodded. Ralph would not know. He could not. She would tell him that she and Catherine had talked and that she saw sense and left, promising never to return.

Ursula said, 'What about Perkins's pit?'

Cressie stared at her. Perkins, the odd-job man, had dug a pit by the old fence, for what purpose no one really knew. He'd dug it and then left it, the soil in a mound beside it, where it had begun to sprout grass. It was still there. 'Of course. Perkins's pit is the answer.'

'Then we'd better start right away.'

They went out to inspect the pit in the freezing morning air. There was no one about. A shiver of horror went up Cressie's spine as she looked at the cold black mud where they would lay Catherine.

She'll rot in there alone.

It was an awful thought. Then she reproved herself. *She's dead. I didn't kill her. I just want to prevent her from harming us ever again.*

'That's where we'll put her,' Cressie said. She looked over at the pile of stony soil, frosted into hardness. 'That's what we'll cover her with.'

Ursula nodded. 'That'll be best.'

'Let's do it now.'

'Better to wait until later,' Ursula said. 'Just in case we're seen.'

511

'All right,' Cressie said reluctantly. She wanted it over now. The knowledge that Catherine still lay on the floor of the studio, waiting for her grave, was filling her mind with fear and horror. It was too much to bear, even with Ursula sharing the burden of the secret.

Once she's buried, I'll be free of it. Ralph and I can be together.

Cressie had the sudden thought that she would never be free now, but she pushed it away. There was work to do.

Later that day, she went to see Ralph, taking him some soup.

He'd been sleeping, his exhausted body conserving his strength to fight the illness inside him. He struggled to sit up and could only sip a few mouthfuls.

'Catherine?' he asked through dry lips. 'Where is she?'

'She left, my darling,' Cressie said in a soothing voice. 'She became very sensible. She understands what she's done to you and has agreed to leave us in peace. It's all going to be absolutely fine now.'

Ralph seemed to relax. 'Really?'

Cressie nodded. 'Yes. We're going to be happy. That's all that matters.'

When he was settled again, she left him to sleep.

They waited until dusk had come and then they wrapped Catherine in old sheets and carried her between them down the stairs and out into the garden. She was cold and very heavy, much more difficult to carry than Cressie had imagined. The work was terrible, and the noise of getting the body out of the studio and down the stairs very loud. Surely Ralph could hear them and would call out and ask what was happening. But he didn't say a word.

He's asleep still. He's very ill. Or, perhaps, he didn't want to know.

In the darkening garden, the chill was bitter.

'That snow is coming,' Ursula said. 'It'll be a good thing, I think. It will cover everything up.'

Cressie nodded. She felt sick and miserable, infected by all of the horror of the last day. 'Let's get her in,' she said, almost callously. *I want this to be over.*

They swung the body over the hole and released it. It tumbled into the pit, rolling over and coming free of some of the sheet as it did so. Cressie saw the thick dark hair and the pale pink tip of Catherine's ear. She gasped, sickness and horror at what she was doing rushing up to fill her whole body. *I'm going to be sick.* She felt a mad rush to leap in and shake Catherine awake, to apologise to her and to hand her over to the people who knew how to do these things properly. Then she quelled it, pushing one trembling hand to her mouth to keep her nausea in.

'Quick,' she mumbled when she could speak. 'Let's cover her.' And she swung the first shovelful of dirt into the grave, doing her best to land it on the hair and the ear so that she could forget who was there and what she was doing.

Ursula was right: the snow came that night. As it fell soundlessly, covering up all traces of the grave, Cressida couldn't sleep. She paced the house thinking and planning. She was a different person from the one who had arrived two nights ago. Her mind was infected with horror and her heart was harder than she'd ever known it.

I've come this far, she told herself. *I have to go on now. No one will ever understand what I've done. I'll end up in prison for murder if it's ever discovered.*

The reality of what she had done began to appal her.

What will we do? How can this ever be made right? I don't deserve to be happy ever again, not any more.

She walked restlessly, thinking over what could be done. Then it came to her.

It won't be Catherine who disappears. I'll let her live. She'll return through me, and I will take her place in oblivion.

As soon as she thought it, she knew that she had to do it. It was justice. It was the only thing to be done.

The next day, she set out through the snow to Keeper's Cottage. She knew exactly what she would say. She would offer Ursula and her daughter the chance of a new life in a land where they would have opportunities. All they had to do in return was to take her identity with them, land her in that new country and leave her there. Before they left, she would return to the studio in Blackheath and remove everything, taking all she needed to assume Catherine's identity. She would visit her father and brothers and explain to them that she had resolved to leave for Australia and that she had sold December House to the Fews.

After that, she was sure they would leave her be for long enough for the lies to be established.

The only person who knew the truth would be far, far away.

As she strode through the snow, her fingers numb with cold, she thought of Catherine, lying beneath the snow, unknown and unmourned.

I'll find some way to mark her resting place. I'll give her life and I'll also give her the grave she should have had. I don't know how, but somehow, I will.

The lights of Keeper's Cottage shone out over the white blanket. She puffed on through the snow, intent on reaching her destination.

EPILOGUE

Emily turned to look at the group following her up the hill. Carrie was at the head stumping up with purpose, her tongue out of her mouth as she concentrated on the climb. James was behind her, carrying Joe on his back, and they were both singing something, a nursery rhyme she thought. Behind them was Tom, walking slowly and carefully, his hands in his pockets. She watched him come, hoping he was enjoying the outing.

He'd only been back a week, staying with her and the children in the house. The doctors had assured her that he was no danger to them. In fact, his recovery had been rapid.

'It's quite unusual in these cases,' the consultant had said. 'We suspected a type of schizophrenia or psychosis but it seems to be something that's not quite either of those things. To be quite honest, Tom wants to get well very badly. He's taking his medication and he's a model patient.'

'I'd like him at home with us if that's possible,' Emily said. 'I don't like him shut up here.'

'We think that's a good solution.'

Tom had never spoken about the night he'd tried

516

to exorcise her but it seemed that he was the one who was now released from torment. He was weak and washed out, very subdued and often tired, but he seemed like his old self again. He was cheerful around the children and affectionate with her. She was hopeful that he would regain his vigour and complete his return to his former self.

Emily looked beyond the climbers to the garden. There was the place where the snow angel had sat in the paintings. In its place she'd put a stone sculpture that she'd found in a local shop. It was not an angel – that seemed too laden with meaning and too close to the source of some of Tom's troubles – but a beautiful abstract shape.

Of course, I don't know if there's anything under there and there's no point in disturbing things now. But just in case . . .

Confiding her theory to Cameron – that Catherine Few had died somehow and been buried by Ralph and Cressida – had convinced her not to tell anyone else.

'So Aunt Cressida was a killer!' he crowed happily when she filled him in on everything that had happened. 'Wow! I had no idea this search would turn up an actual corpse.'

'We don't know that she killed Catherine,' Emily pointed out defensively. 'We don't even know that she buried her. I mean, it was Maggie who implied that there's something in the garden. She must have heard that from her mother. Maybe it was Ursula who did it.'

'Er . . . wasn't Cressida the one painting spooky angels that marked the spot? They obviously did it together, maybe with that bloke's help as well.'

'Perhaps you're right. But that still doesn't mean they killed her.' Emily shook her head, seeing her little image in the corner of the screen do the same. 'I think it's out of character for them. Anyway, they both got punished. Cressida never saw her family again.'

'What are you saying, Emily? That going off to Australia is a punishment?' demanded Cameron in a jokily offended tone. 'I mean, I know it used to be, but those days were long gone. And Cressida got to while away her time painting pictures in Cumbria. Not all bad.' He shivered. 'Although thinking of how bloody freezing it is . . .'

'We can't know,' Emily said, smiling. 'We'll never know exactly what happened. But my theory is that Maggie knows something. I think Ursula told her exactly what happened here. Maybe one day she'll tell us the truth.'

'Yeah. Maybe. Until then, I guess that's case closed.'

She nodded at Cameron's friendly, open face, so far away but so immediate nonetheless. 'I guess so, for now.'

'But if Maggie ever spills the beans, you'll let me know, right?

'You bet. You'll be the first to know. I promise.'

★   ★   ★

518